This volume contains INU-YASHA PART 6 #3 through
INU-YASHA PART 6 #7 in their entirety.

STORY AND ART BY
RUMIKO TAKAHASHI

ENGLISH ADAPTATION BY
GERARD JONES

Translation/Mari Morimoto
Touch-Up Art & Lettering/Wayne Truman
Cover Design/Hidemi Sahara
Layout/Sean Lee
Managing Editor/Annette Roman

Editor/Julie Davis
V.P. of Editorial/Hyoe Narita
Publisher/Seiji Horibuchi
VP of Sales and Marketing/Rick Bauer

Printed in Canada

Published by Viz Communications, Inc.
P.O. Box 77010 • San Francisco, CA 94107
www.viz.com • www.j-pop.com • www.animerica-mag.com

10 9 8 7 6 5 4 3 2
First printing, May 2002
Second printing, January 2003

INU-YASHA GRAPHIC NOVELS TO DATE:

INU-YASHA VOL. 1
INU-YASHA VOL. 2
INU-YASHA VOL. 3
INU-YASHA VOL. 4
INU-YASHA VOL. 5
INU-YASHA VOL. 6
INU-YASHA VOL. 7
INU-YASHA VOL. 8
INU-YASHA VOL. 9
INU-YASHA VOL. 10
INU-YASHA VOL. 11
INU-YASHA VOL. 12

VIZ GRAPHIC NOVEL

INU-YASHA
A FEUDAL FAIRY TALE™

VOL. 11

STORY AND ART BY
RUMIKO TAKAHASHI

CONTENTS

c. 2

THE STORY THUS FAR

Long ago, in the "Warring States" era of Japan's Muromachi period (*Sengoku-jidai*, approximately 1467-1568 CE), a legendary doglike half-demon called "Inu-Yasha" attempted to steal the Shikon Jewel, or "Jewel of Four Souls," from a village, but was stopped by the enchanted arrow of the village priestess, Kikyo. Inu-Yasha fell into a deep sleep, pinned to a tree by Kikyo's arrow, while the mortally wounded Kikyo took the Shikon Jewel with her into the fires of her funeral pyre. Years passed.

Fast forward to the present day. Kagome, a Japanese high school girl, is pulled into a well one day by mysterious centipede monster, and finds herself transported into the past, only to come face to face with the trapped Inu-Yasha. She frees him, and Inu-Yasha easily defeats the centipede monster.

The residents of the village, now fifty years older, readily accept Kagome as the reincarnation of their deceased priestess Kikyo, a claim supported by the fact that the Shikon Jewel emerges from a cut on Kagome's body. Unfortunately, the jewel's rediscovery means that the village is soon under attack by a variety of demons in search of this treasure. Then, the jewel is accidentally shattered into many shards, each of which may have the fearsome power of the entire jewel.

Although Inu-Yasha says he hates Kagome because of her resemblance to Kikyo, the woman who "killed" him, he is forced to team up with her when Kaede, the village leader, binds him to Kagome with a powerful spell. Now the two grudging companions must fight to reclaim and reassemble the shattered shards of the Shikon Jewel before they fall into the wrong hands.

THIS VOLUME

After the conclusion of the battle with the false water god, both Miroku and Sango must face their greatest tests of character, as the hellhole in Miroku's hand threatens to destroy him and Sango is tempted by the return of her younger brother....

INU-YASHA
A half-human, half-demon hybrid son of a human mother and a demon father, Inu-Yasha resembles a human but has the claws of a demon, a thick mane of white hair, and ears rather like a dog's. The necklace he wears carries a powerful spell which allows Kagome to control him with a single word. Because of his human half, Inu-Yasha's powers are different from those of full-blooded monsters—a fact that the Shikon Jewel has the power to change.

KIKYO
A powerful priestess, Kikyo was charged with the awesome responsibility of protecting the Shikon Jewel from demons and humans who coveted its power. She died after firing the enchanted arrow that kept Inu-Yasha imprisoned for fifty years.

KAGOME
Working with Inu-Yasha to recover the shattered shards of the Shikon Jewel, Kagome routinely travels into Japan's past through an old, magical well on her family's property. All this time travel means she's stuck with living two separate lives in two separate centuries, and she's beginning to worry that she'll *never* be able to catch up to her schoolwork.

SHIPPÔ
A young fox-demon, orphaned by two other demons whose powers had been boosted by the Shikon Jewel, the mischievous Shippô enjoys goading Inu-Yasha and playing tricks with his shape-changing abilities.

NARAKU
An enigmatic demon, Naraku is the one responsible for both Miroku's curse and for turning Kikyo and Inu-Yasha against one another for reasons that are as yet unknown.

MIROKU
An easygoing Buddhist priest with questionable morals, Miroku is the carrier of a curse passed down from his grandfather. He is searching for the demon Naraku, who first inflicted the curse.

SANGO
A "demon Exterminator" from the village where the Shikon Jewel was first born, Sango lost her father and little brother to an ambush by a demon using a shard of the Jewel...a demon summoned by none other than the mysterious Naraku.

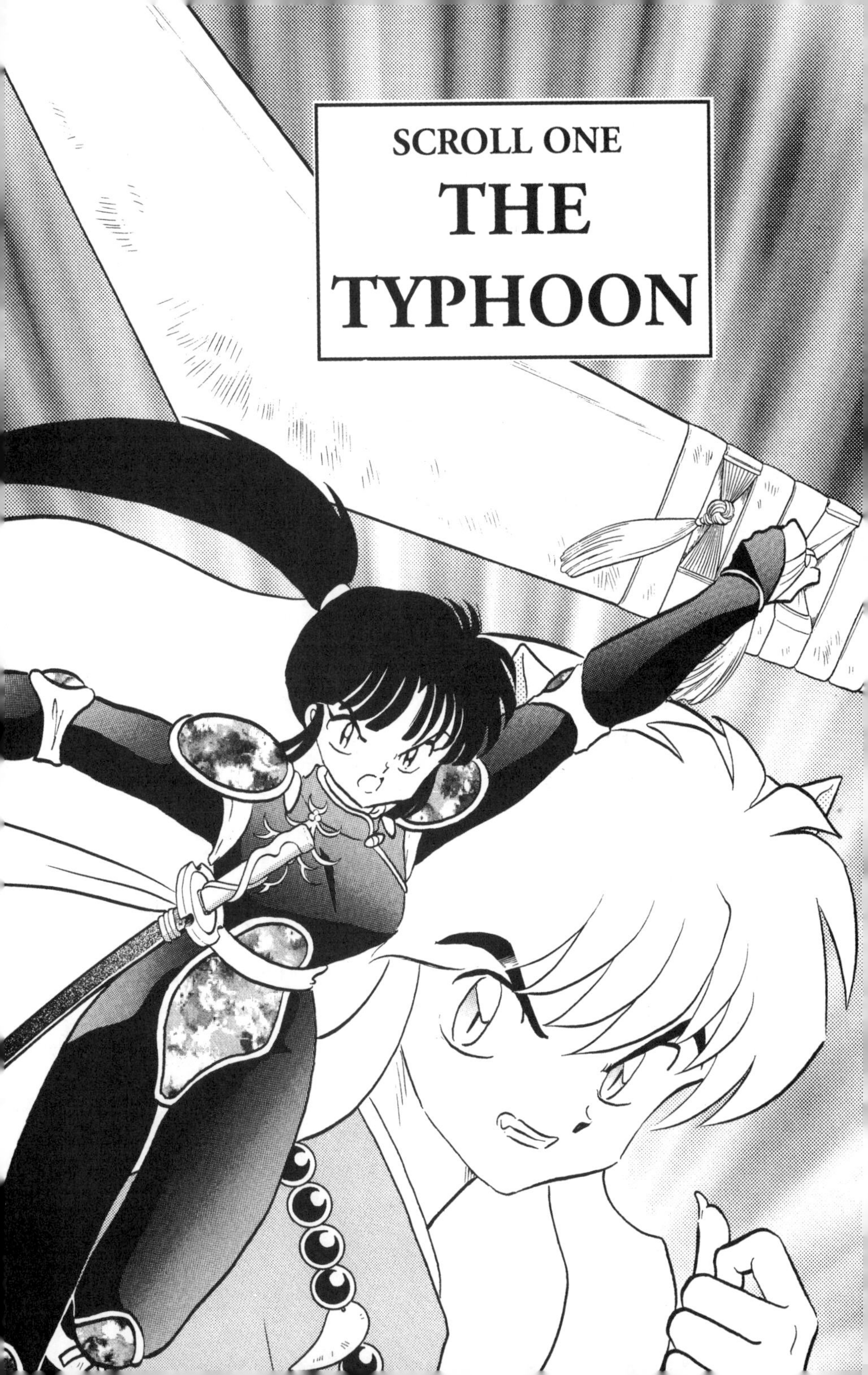
SCROLL ONE
THE TYPHOON

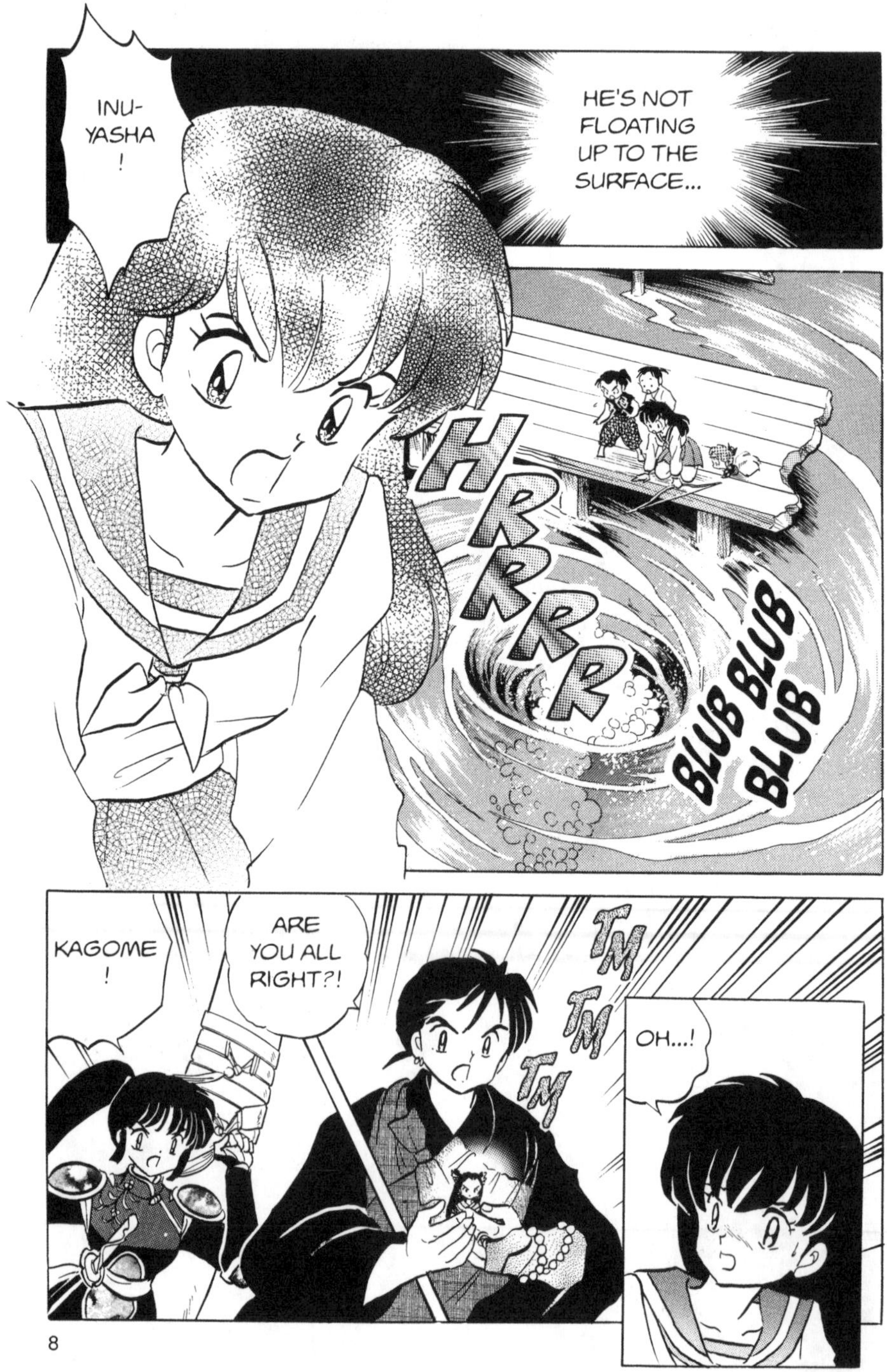
HE'S NOT FLOATING UP TO THE SURFACE...
HRRRRR
BLUB BLUB BLUB
INU-YASHA!
OH...!
TM TM TM
ARE YOU ALL RIGHT?!
KAGOME!

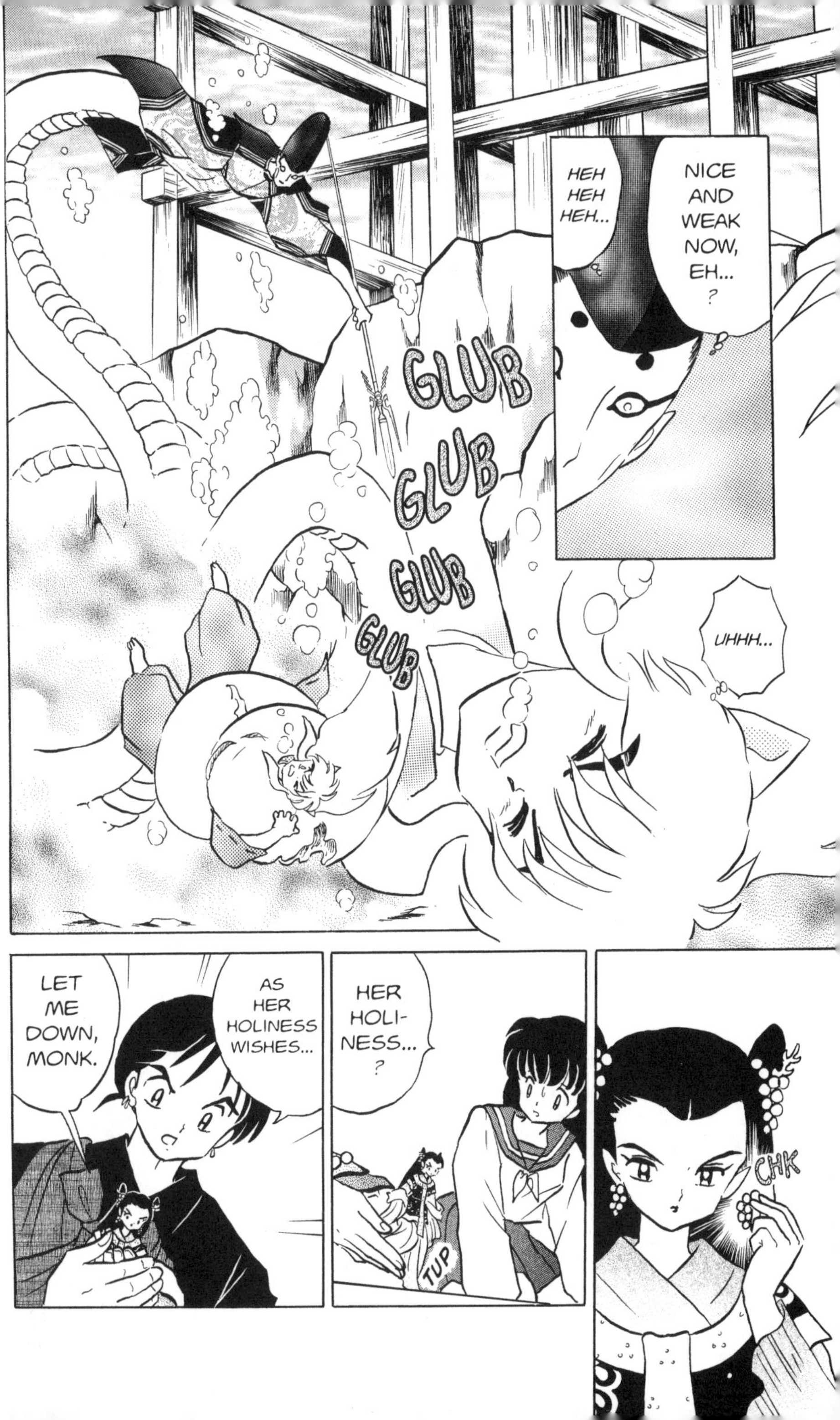
HEH HEH HEH...
NICE AND WEAK NOW, EH...?
GLUB
GLUB
GLUB
GLUB
UHHH...
LET ME DOWN, MONK.
AS HER HOLINESS WISHES...
HER HOLI-NESS...?
TUP
CHK

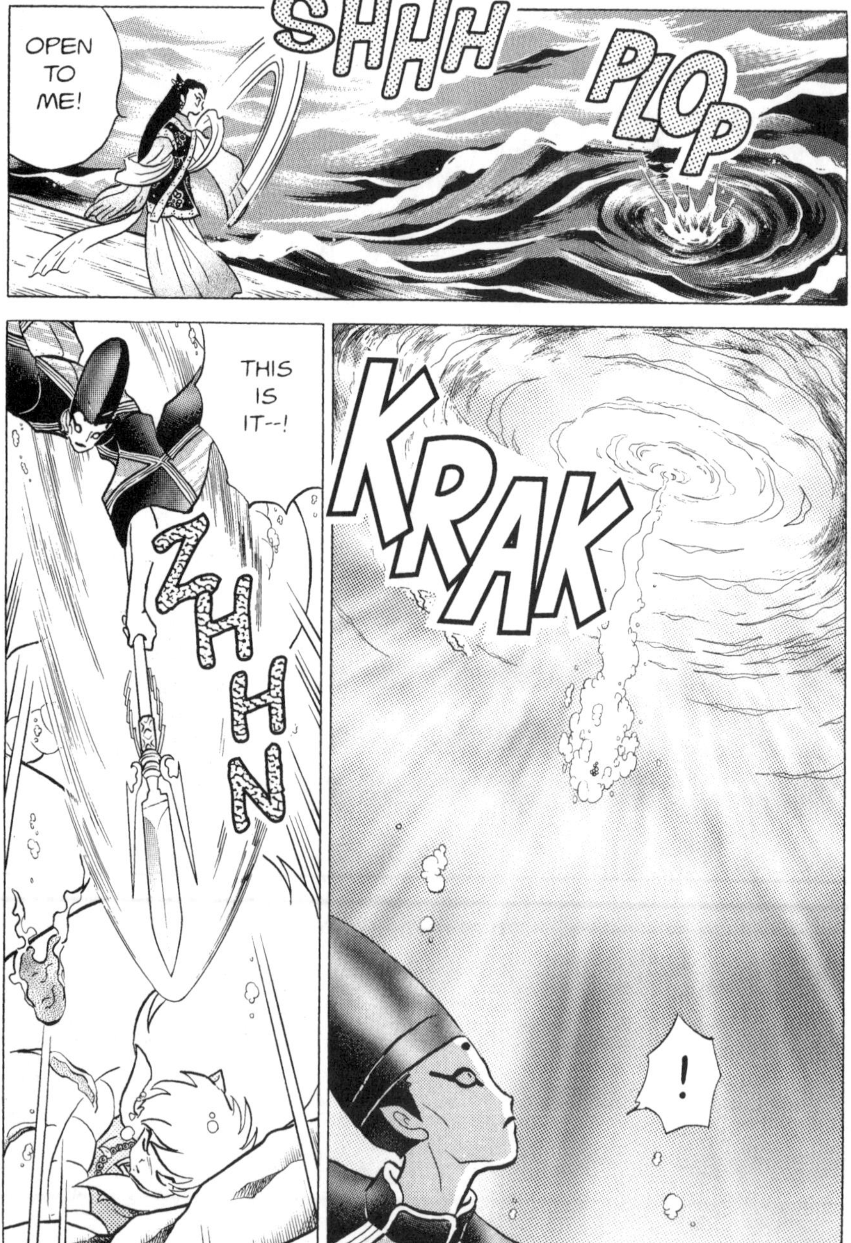

PLOP
SHHH
OPEN TO ME!
KRAK
!
THIS IS IT--!
ZHHN

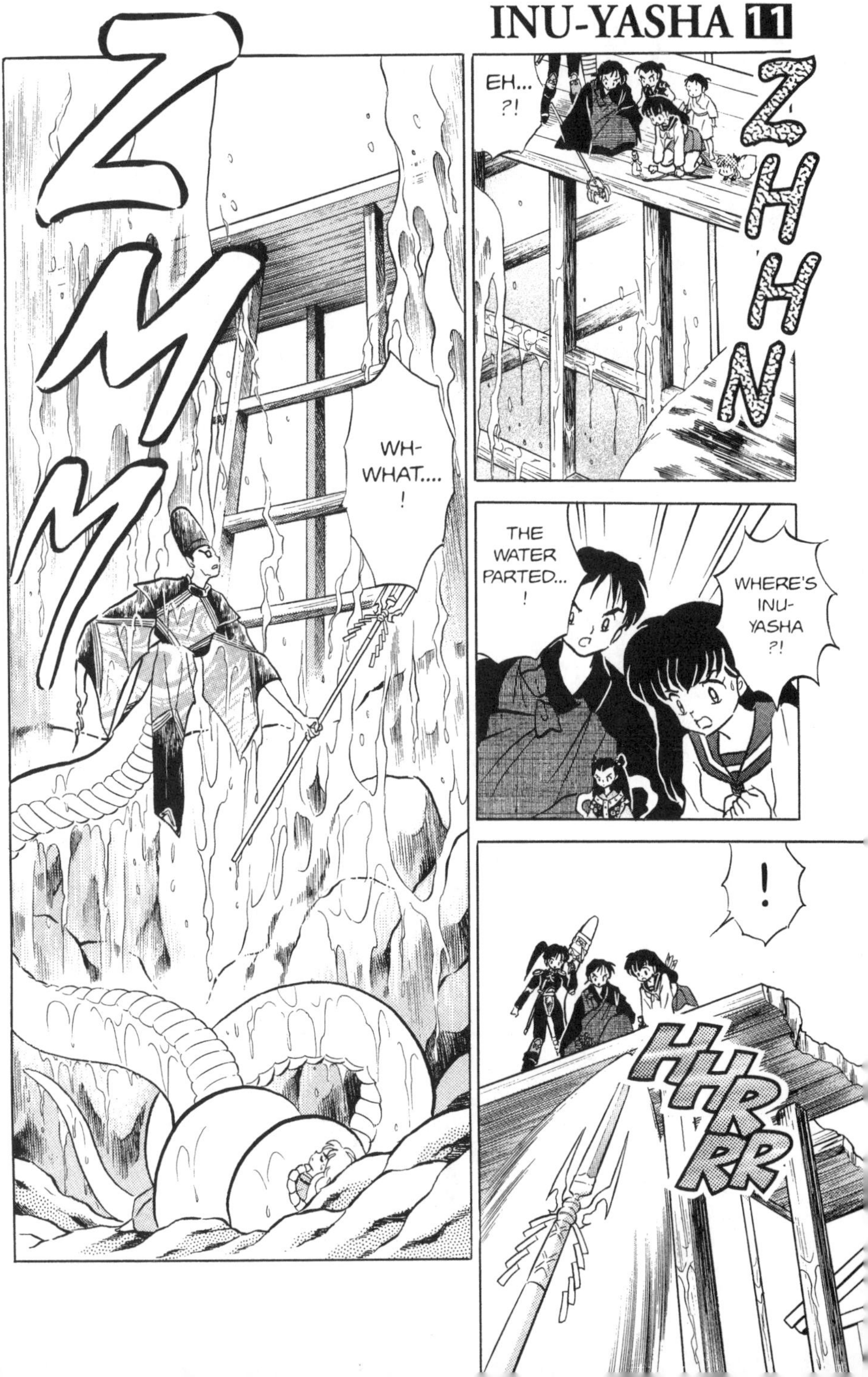
ZHHHN
EH... ?!
WHERE'S INU-YASHA ?!
THE WATER PARTED... !
!
HHRRR
ZMM
WH- WHAT.... !

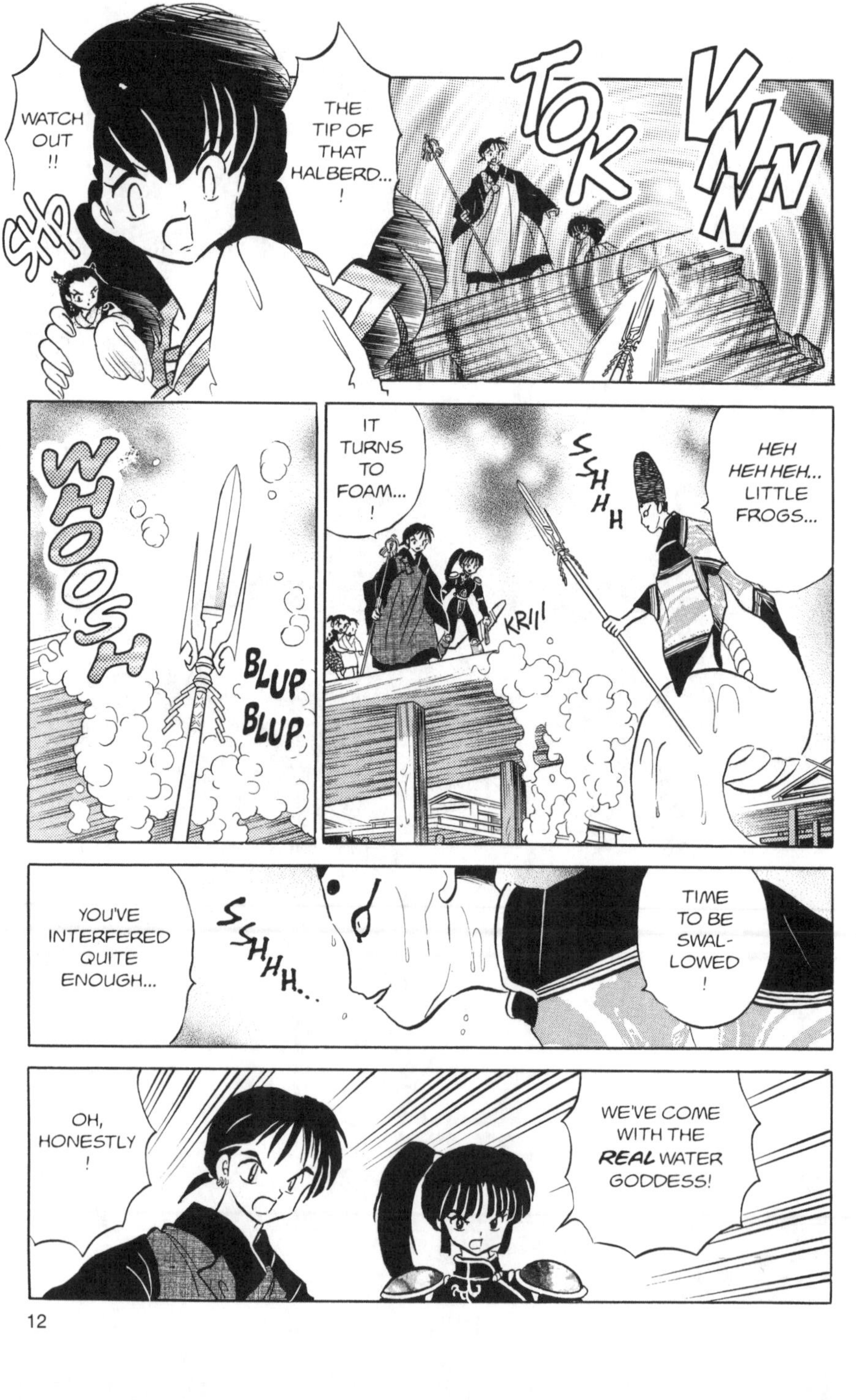
TOK
VNNN
THE TIP OF THAT HALBERD...!
WATCH OUT!!
SHP
HEH HEH HEH... LITTLE FROGS...
SSHHH
IT TURNS TO FOAM...!
KRIII
WHOOSH
BLUP BLUP
TIME TO BE SWAL-LOWED!
SSHHH...
YOU'VE INTERFERED QUITE ENOUGH...
WE'VE COME WITH THE **REAL** WATER GODDESS!
OH, HONESTLY!

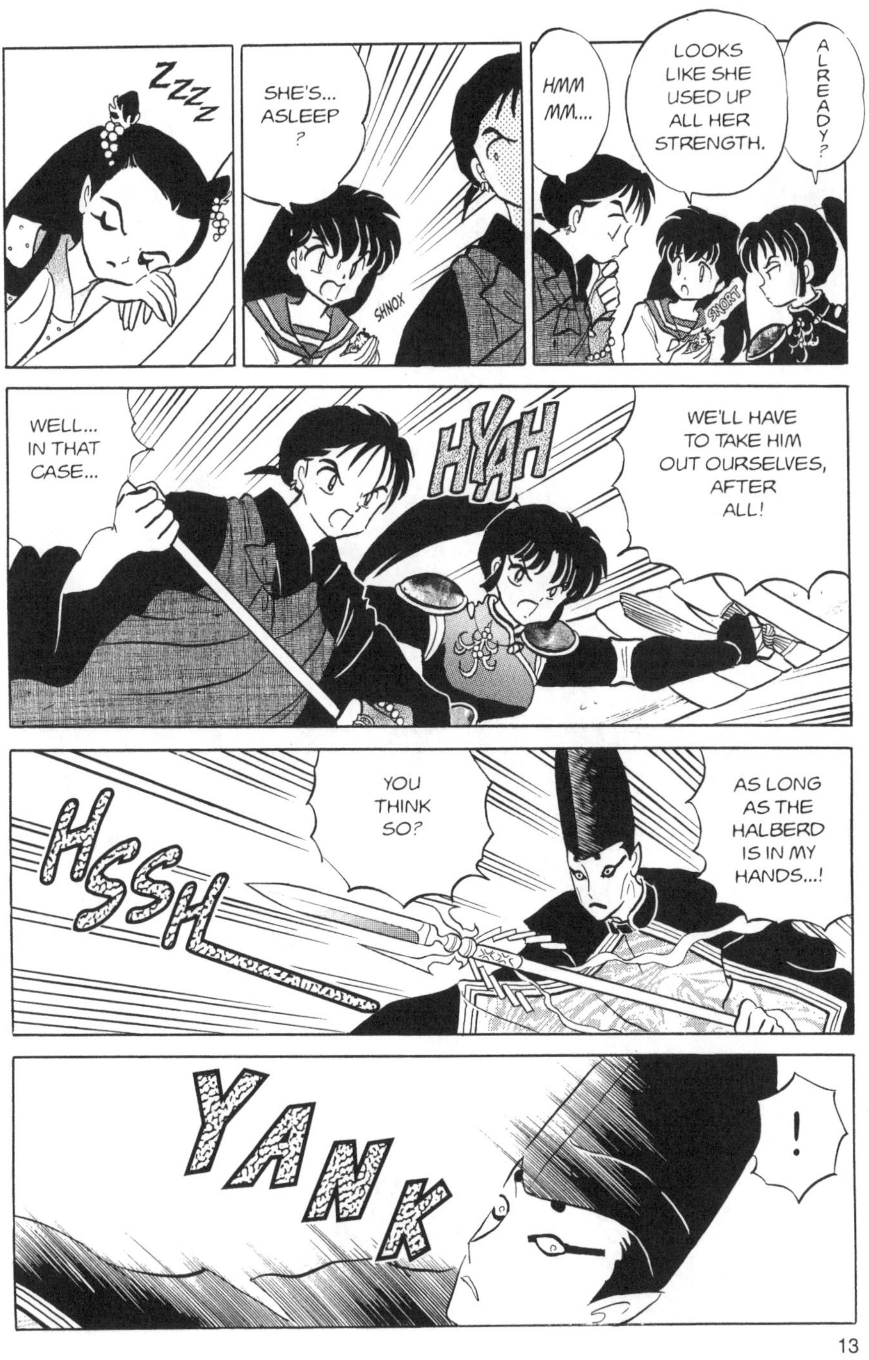
ZZZZ
SHE'S... ASLEEP?
SHNOX
HMM MM....
LOOKS LIKE SHE USED UP ALL HER STRENGTH.
ALREADY?
SNORT
WELL... IN THAT CASE...
HYAH
WE'LL HAVE TO TAKE HIM OUT OURSELVES, AFTER ALL!
HSSH
YOU THINK SO?
AS LONG AS THE HALBERD IS IN MY HANDS...!
YANK
!

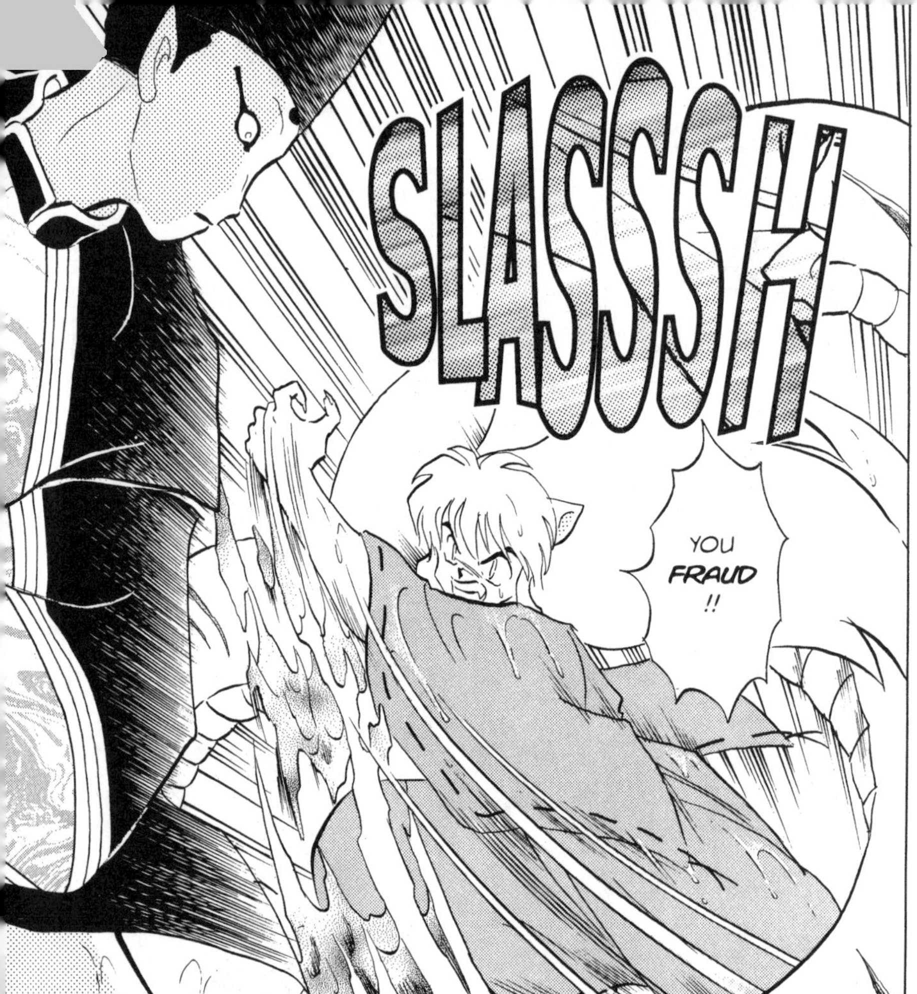
SLASSSH
YOU FRAUD !!
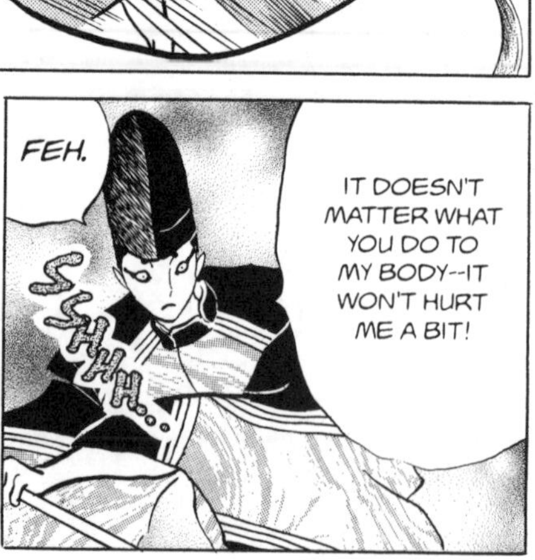
FEH.
IT DOESN'T MATTER WHAT YOU DO TO MY BODY--IT WON'T HURT ME A BIT!
SSHHH..
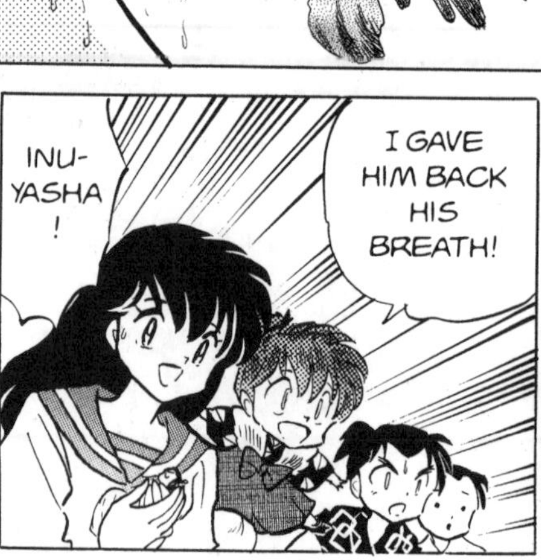
I GAVE HIM BACK HIS BREATH!
INU-YASHA !

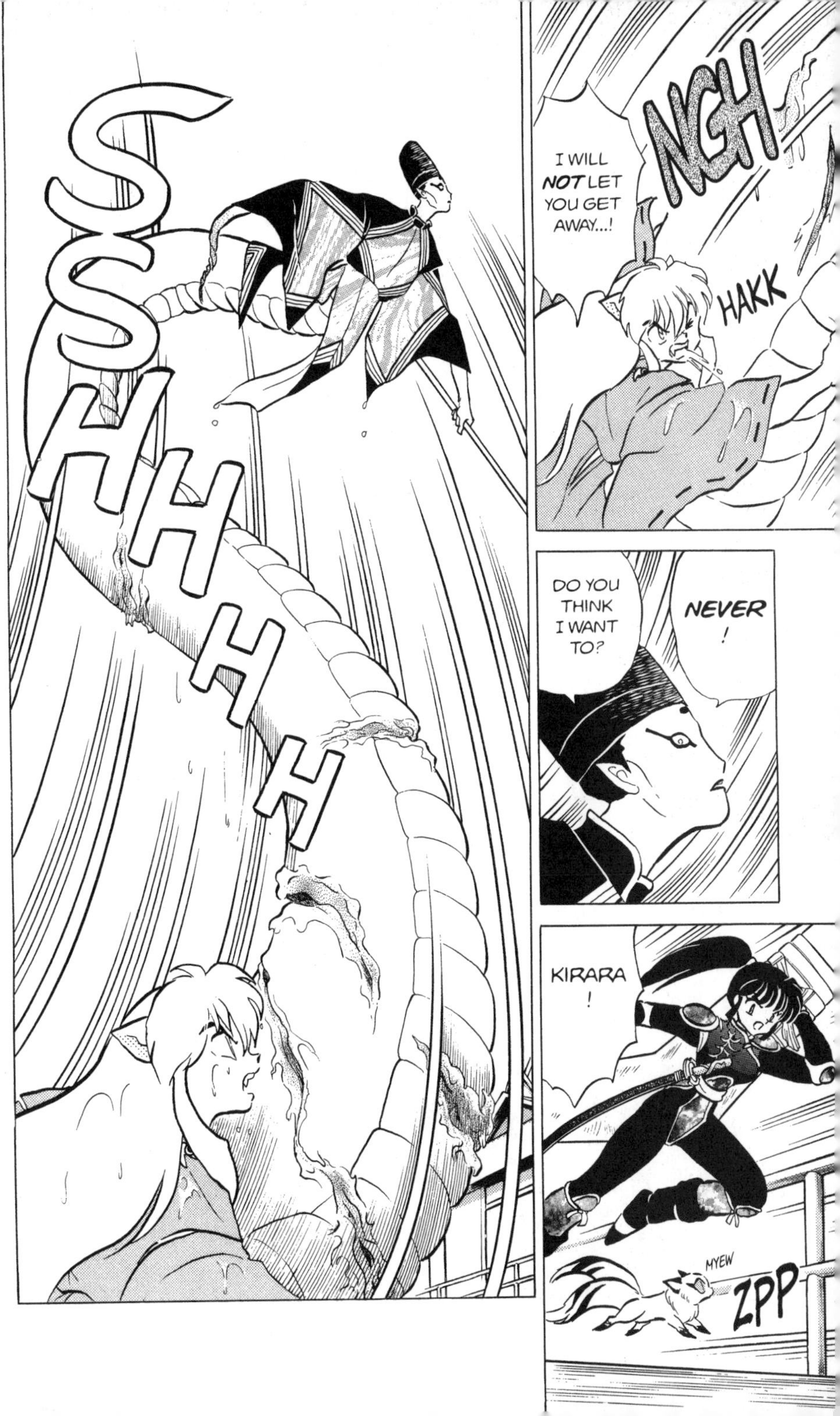
SSHHHHH
NGH
I WILL **NOT** LET YOU GET AWAY...!
HAKK
DO YOU THINK I WANT TO?
NEVER!
KIRARA!
MYEW
ZPP

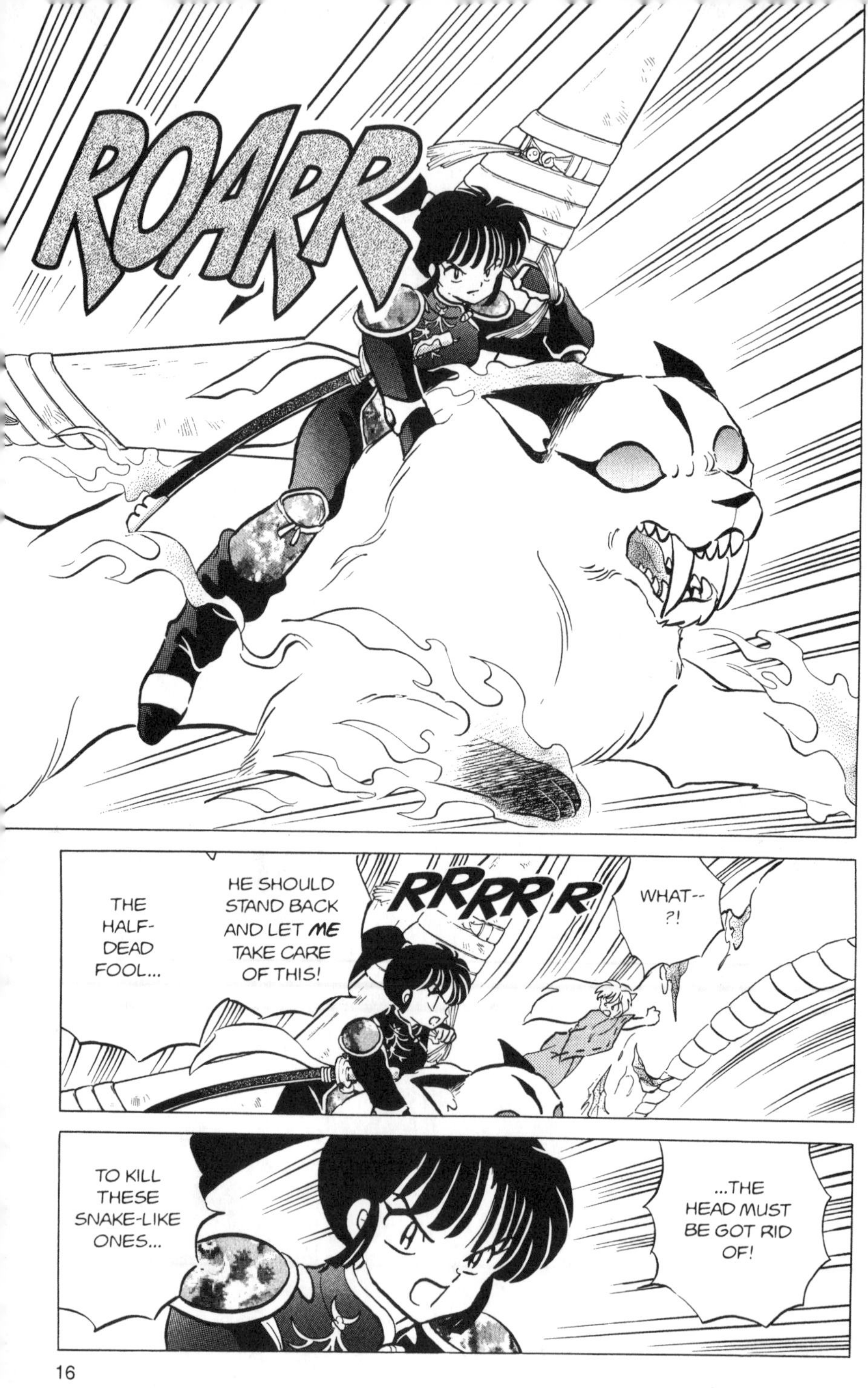
ROARR
THE HALF-DEAD FOOL...
HE SHOULD STAND BACK AND LET *ME* TAKE CARE OF THIS!
RRRRR
WHAT-- ?!
TO KILL THESE SNAKE-LIKE ONES...
...THE HEAD MUST BE GOT RID OF!

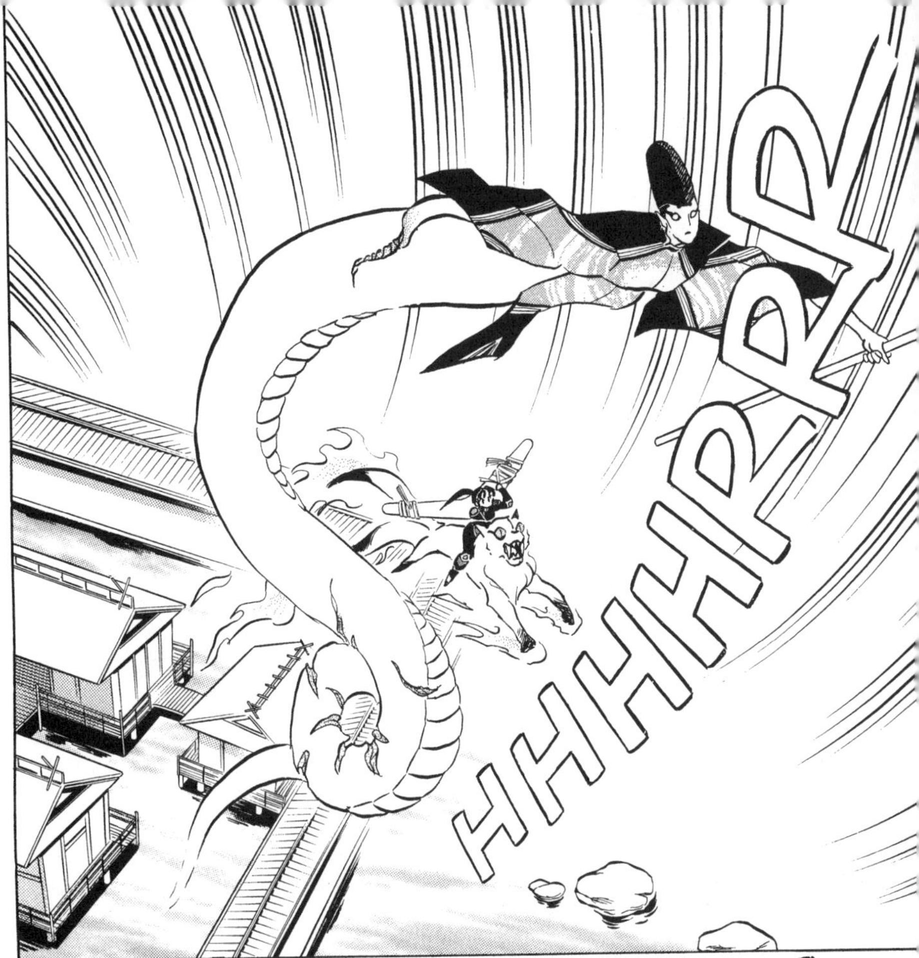
HHHHRR

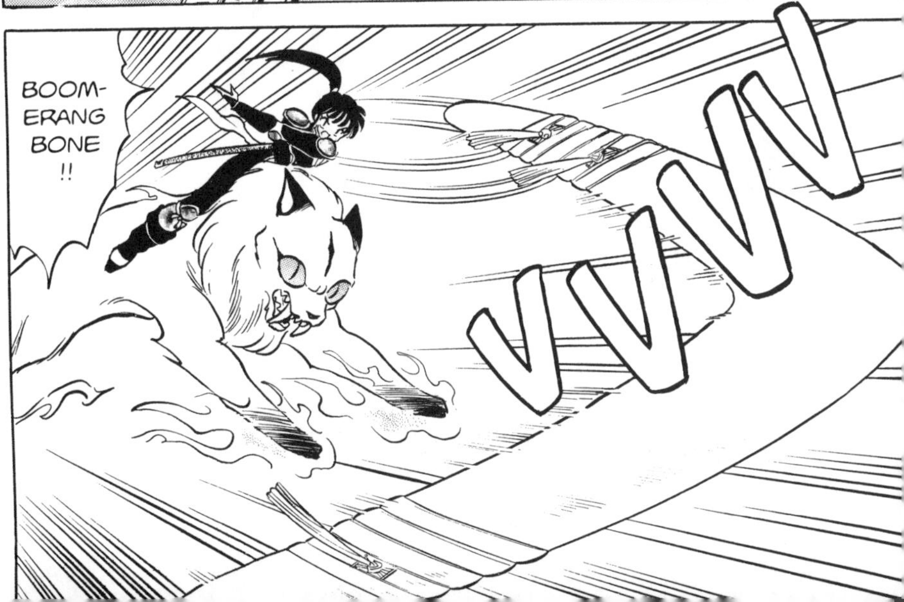
BOOM-
ERANG
BONE
!!
VVVVV

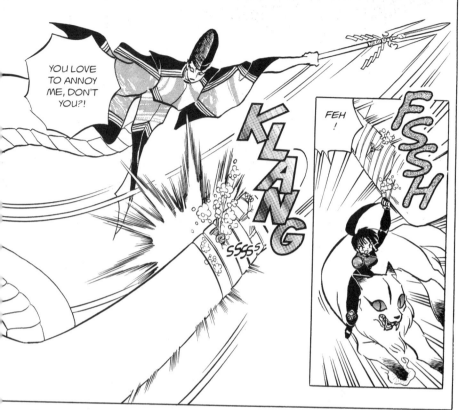

YOU LOVE TO ANNOY ME, DON'T YOU?!

KLANG

SSSSS

FEH!

FSSH

NOW... YOU MINNOWS WILL SEE THE TRUE POWER OF THE HOLY *AMAKOI HALBERD*.

ZHHM

KRI KRAK KRAK

RRRMM

SHFF

18

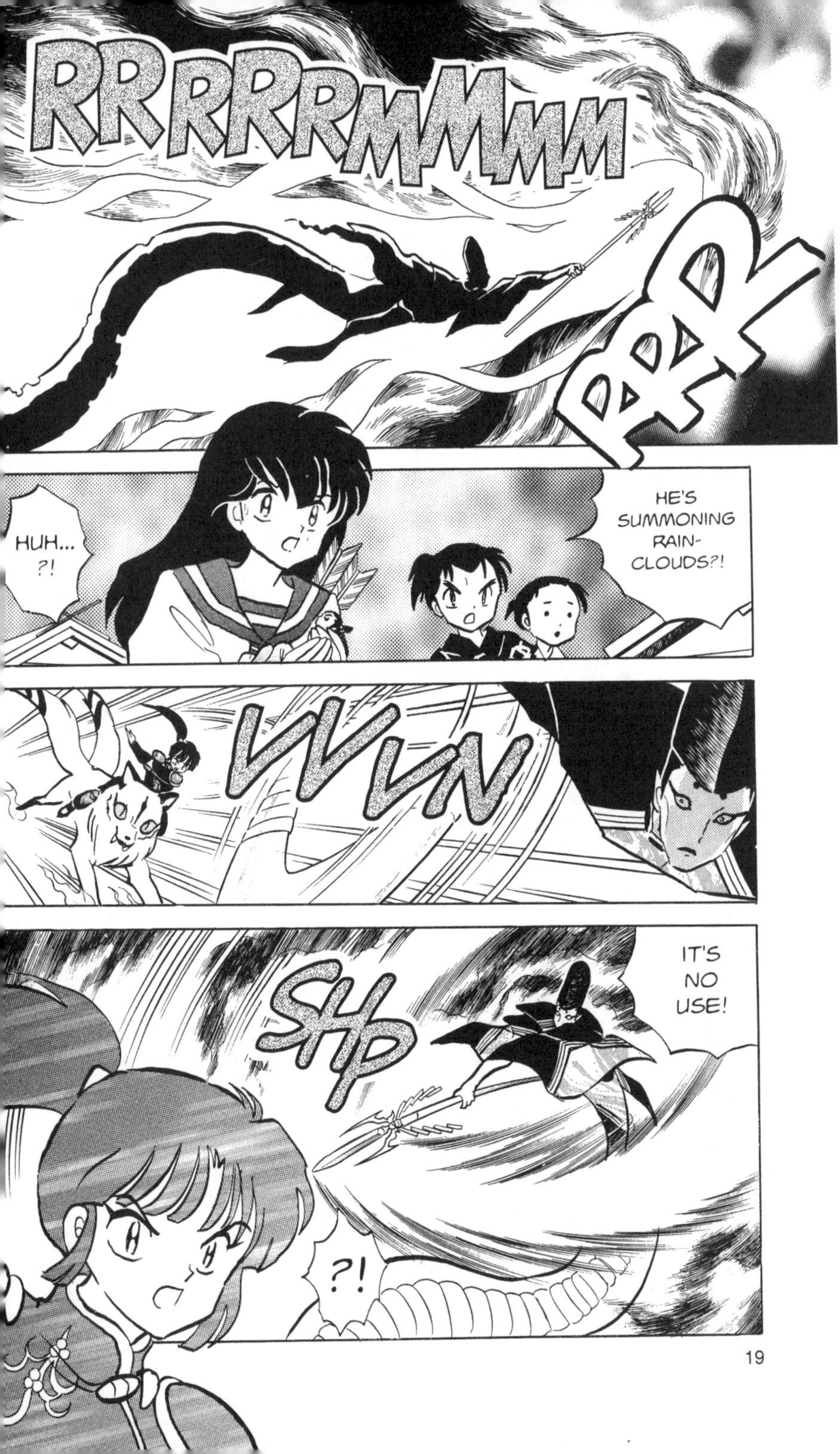
RRRRRMMMMM
PAPAP
HE'S SUMMONING RAIN-CLOUDS?!
HUH... ?!
VVVN
IT'S NO USE!
SHP
?!

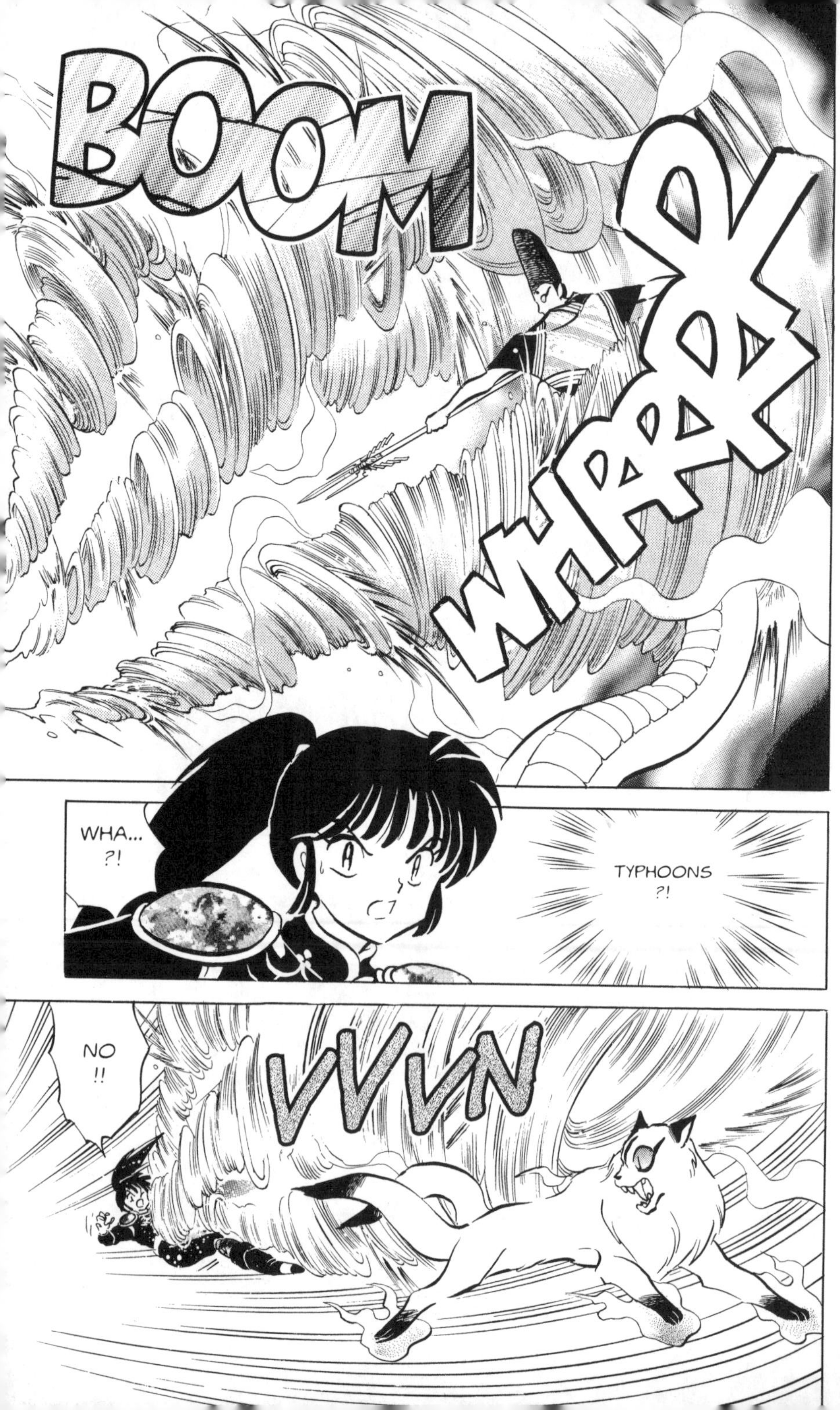
BOOM
WHRRR
WHA... ?!
TYPHOONS ?!
NO !!
VVVN

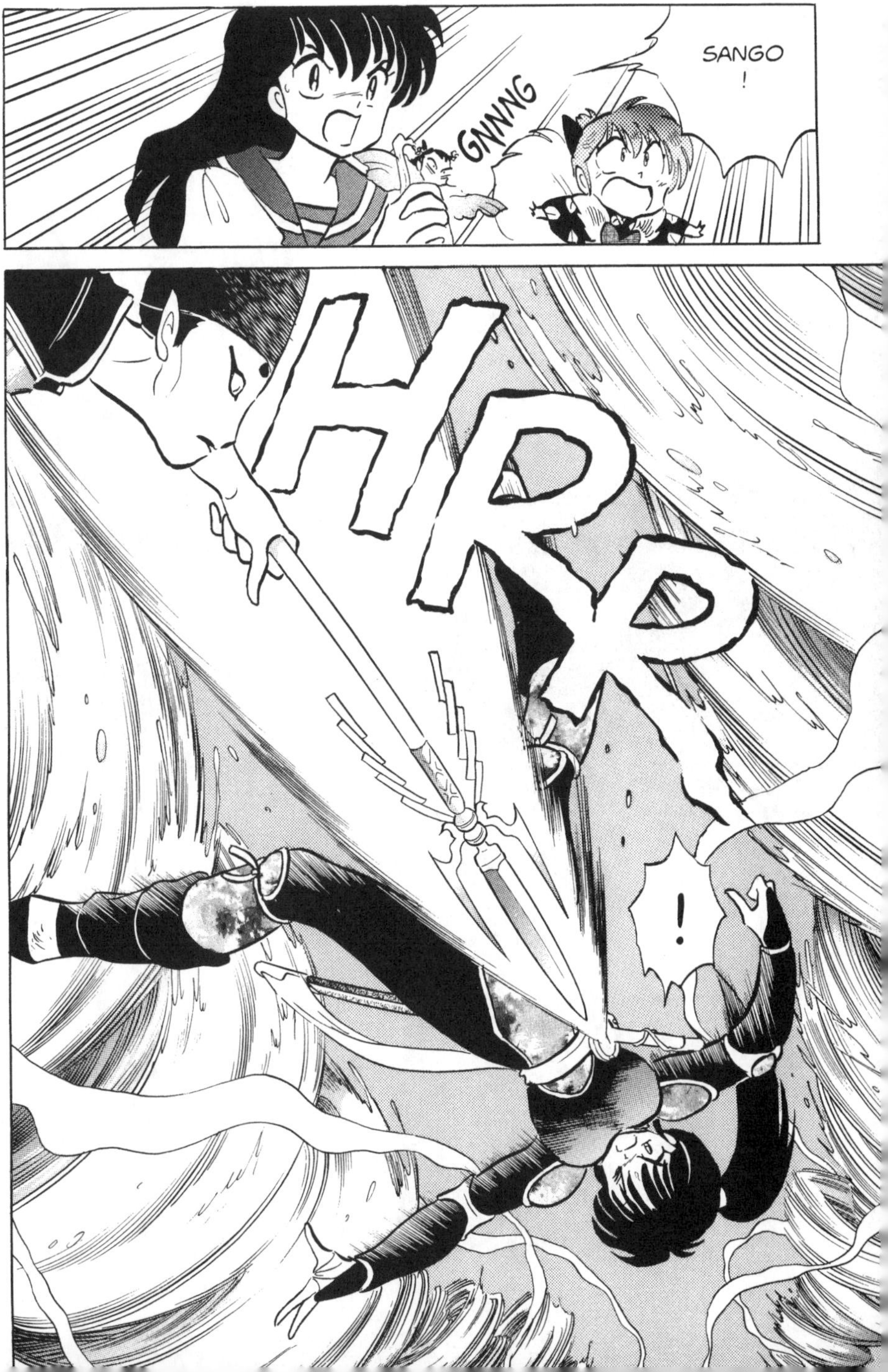
SANGO
!
GNNNG
HRR
!

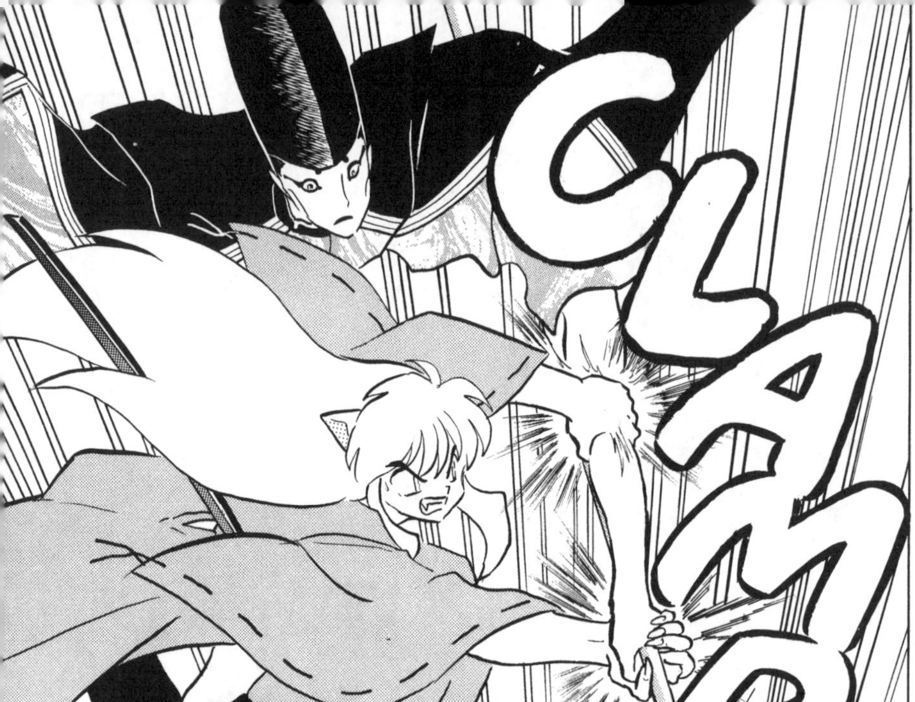
CLAMP
EH ?!

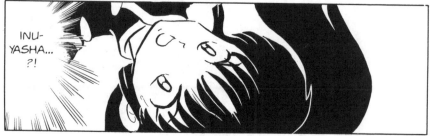

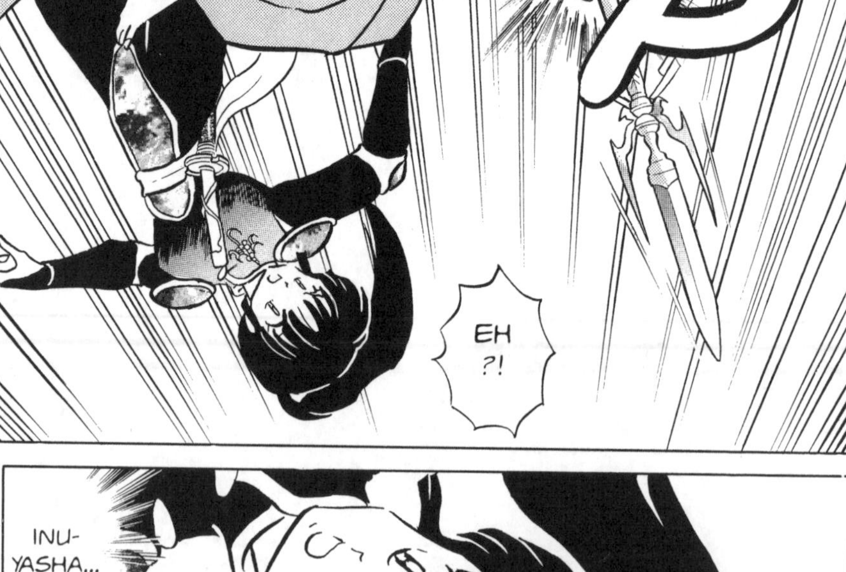
INU-YASHA... ?!

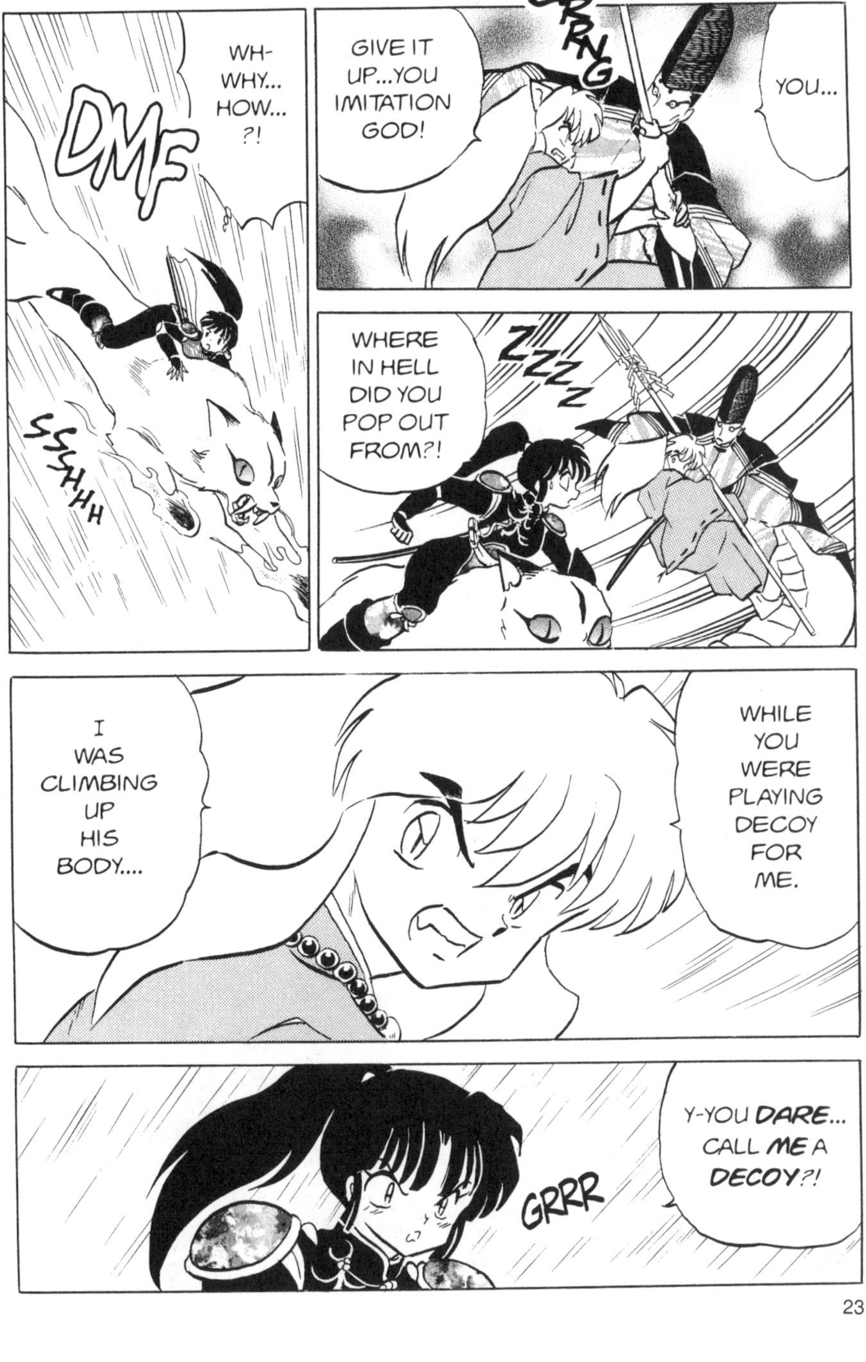
YOU...
GRRNG
GIVE IT UP...YOU IMITATION GOD!
ZZZZ
WHERE IN HELL DID YOU POP OUT FROM?!
WH- WHY... HOW... ?!
DMF
SSSHHH
WHILE YOU WERE PLAYING DECOY FOR ME.
I WAS CLIMBING UP HIS BODY....
Y-YOU **DARE**... CALL **ME** A **DECOY**?!
GRRR

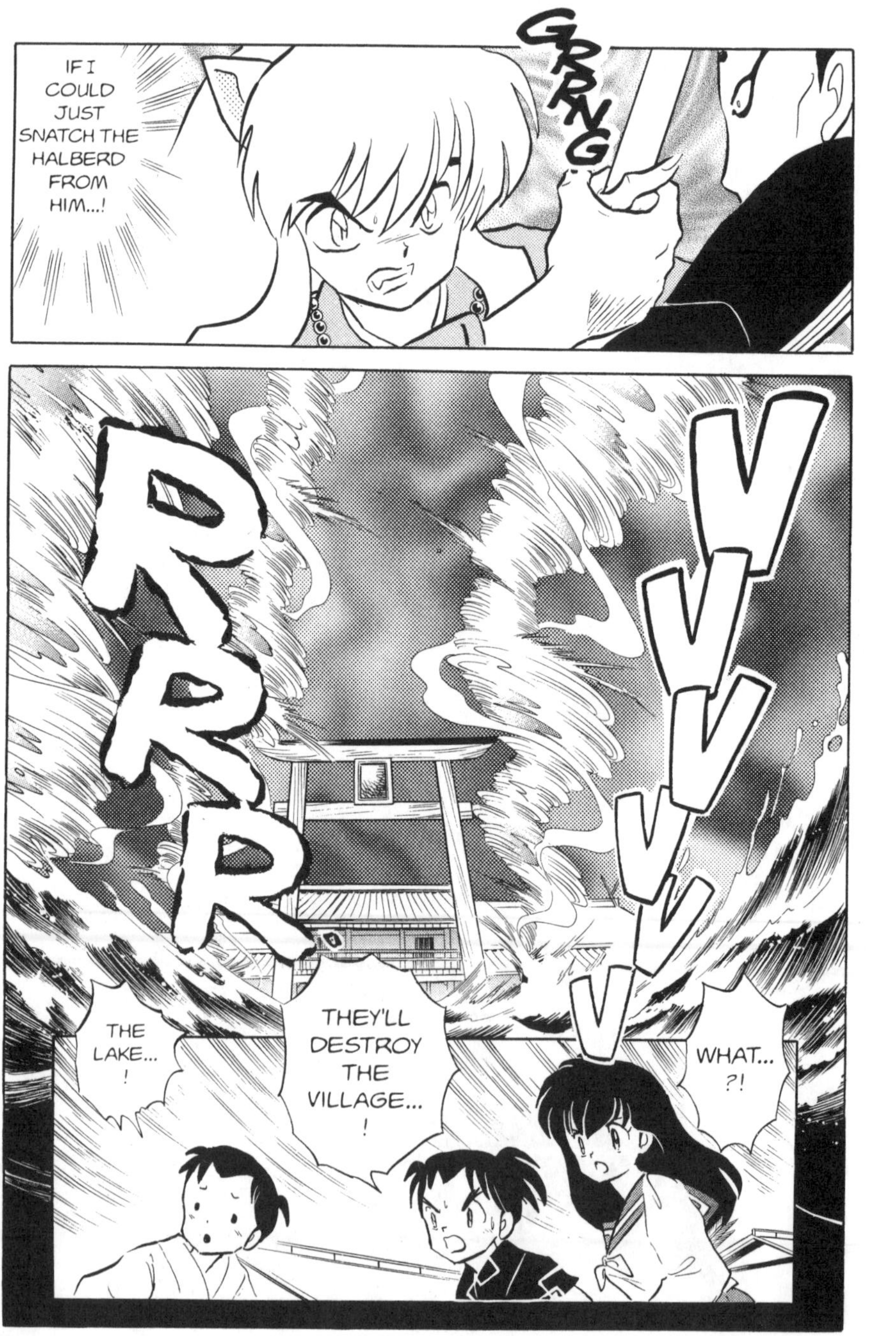
GRRNG
IF I COULD JUST SNATCH THE HALBERD FROM HIM...!
RRRR
VVVVVVVV
WHAT...?!
THEY'LL DESTROY THE VILLAGE...!
THE LAKE...!

SCROLL TWO

THE SLAYING OF THE SNAKE

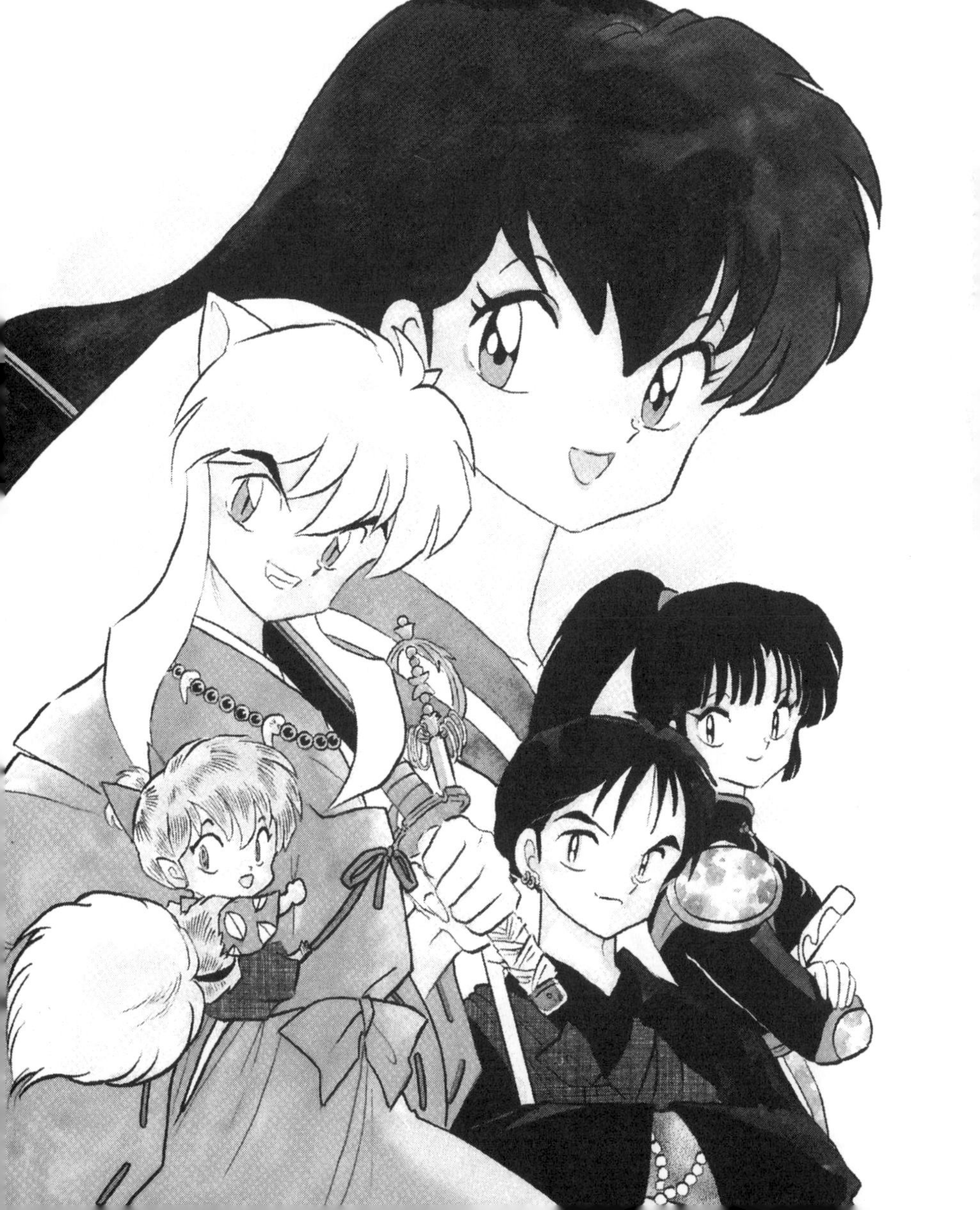

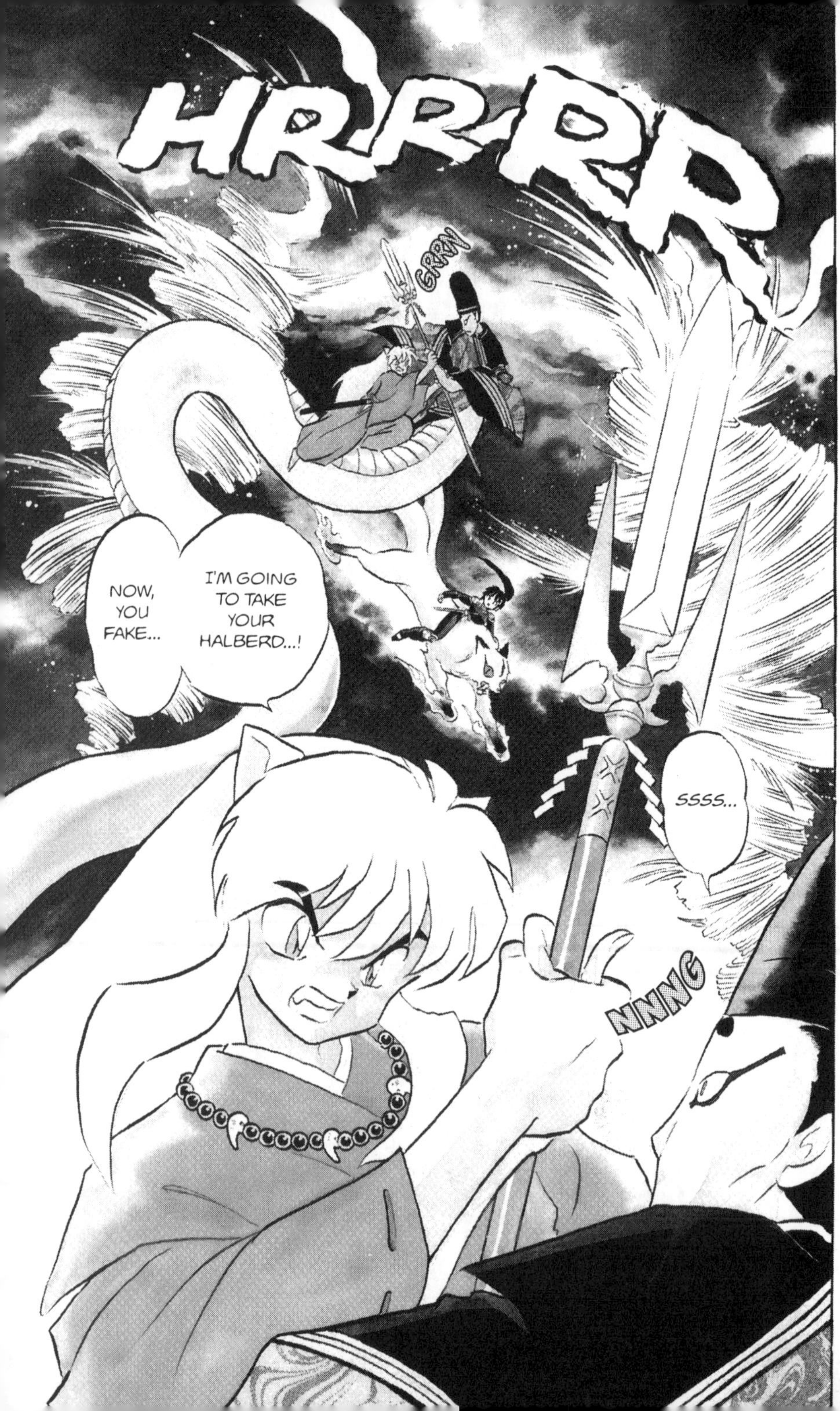
HRR-R-RR
GRRN
NOW, YOU FAKE...
I'M GOING TO TAKE YOUR HALBERD...!
SSSS...
NNNG

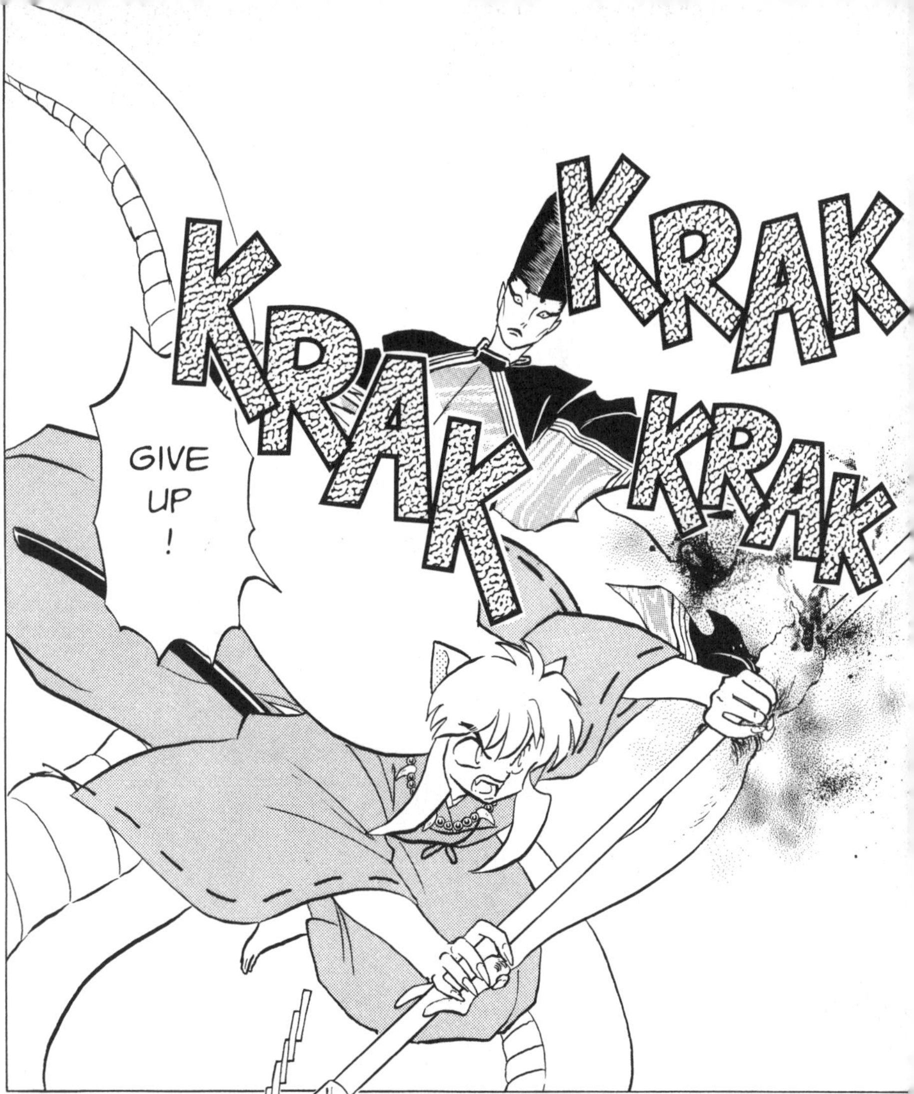
KRAK KRAK
GIVE UP!
KRAK KRAK

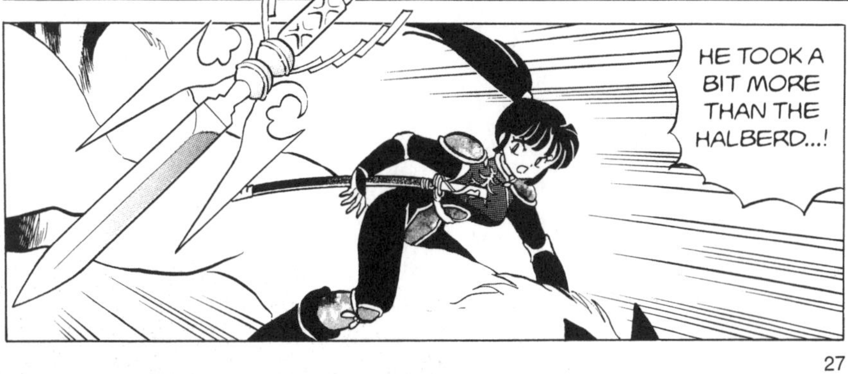
HE TOOK A BIT MORE THAN THE HALBERD...!

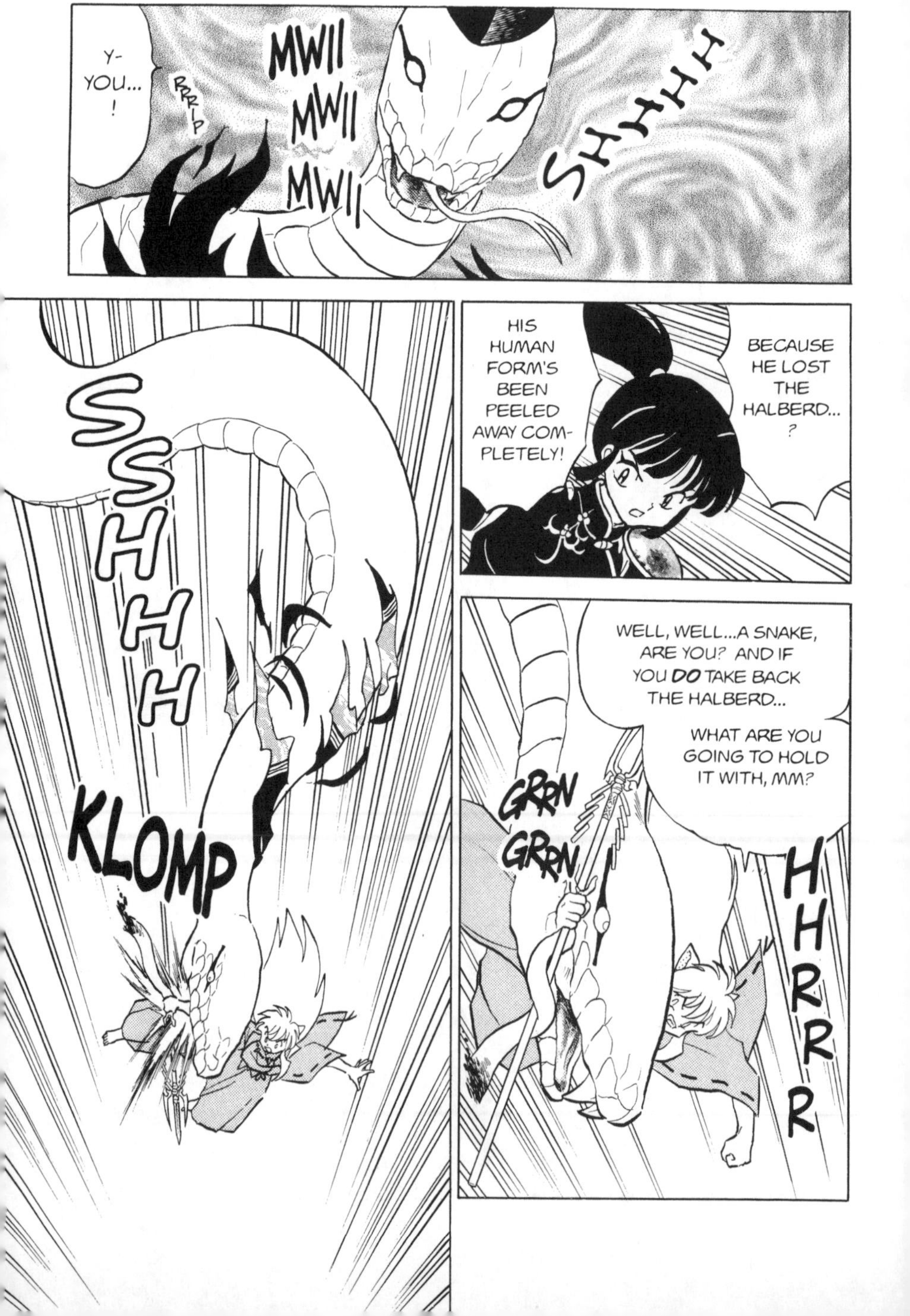
SHHHH
MWII MWII MWII
RRRIP
Y-YOU... !
HIS HUMAN FORM'S BEEN PEELED AWAY COMPLETELY!
BECAUSE HE LOST THE HALBERD... ?
WELL, WELL...A SNAKE, ARE YOU? AND IF YOU DO TAKE BACK THE HALBERD...
WHAT ARE YOU GOING TO HOLD IT WITH, MM?
GRRN GRRN
HHRRRR
SSHHHH
KLOMP

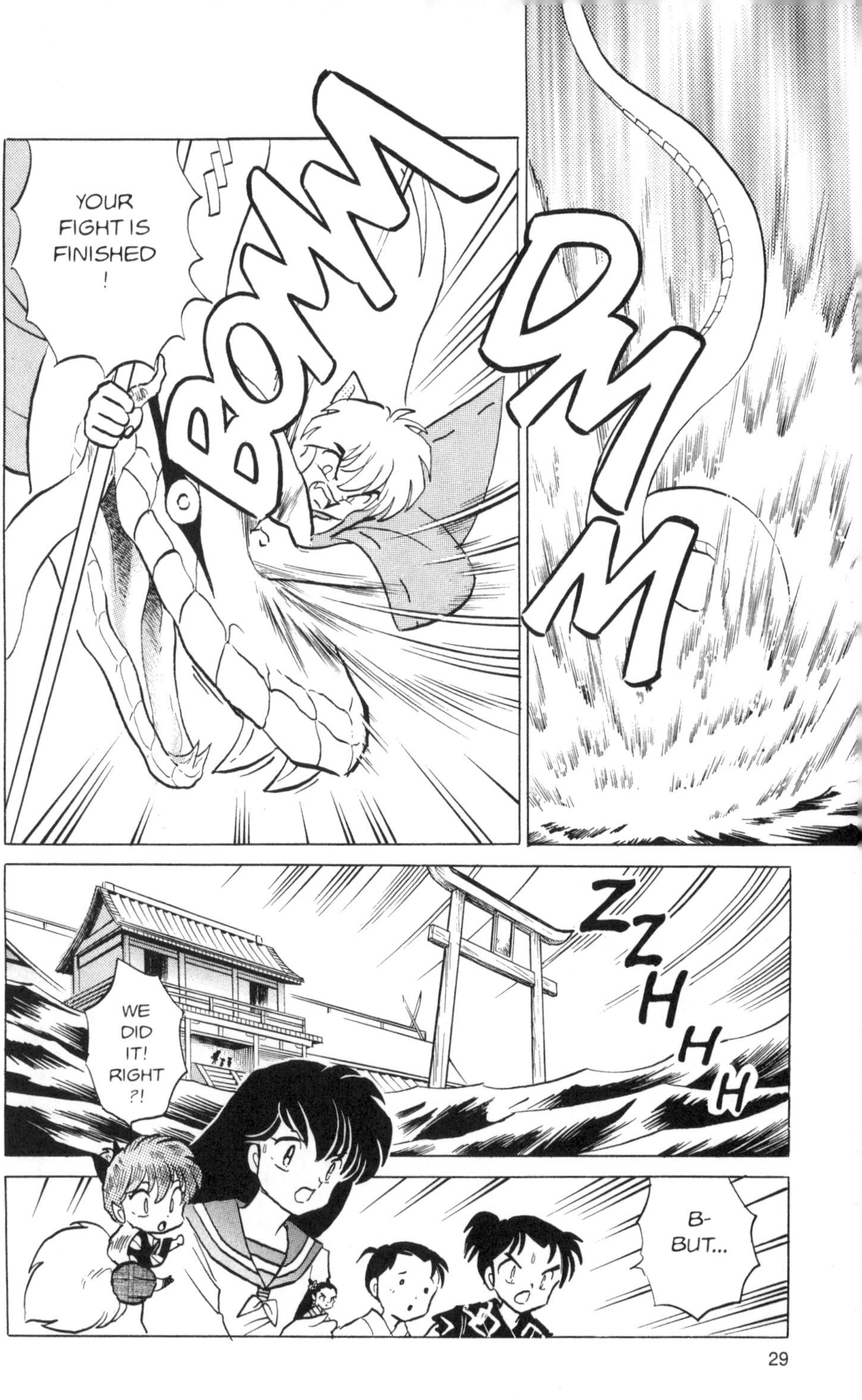
DMMM
YOUR FIGHT IS FINISHED!
BOMM
ZZHHHH
WE DID IT! RIGHT?!
B-BUT...

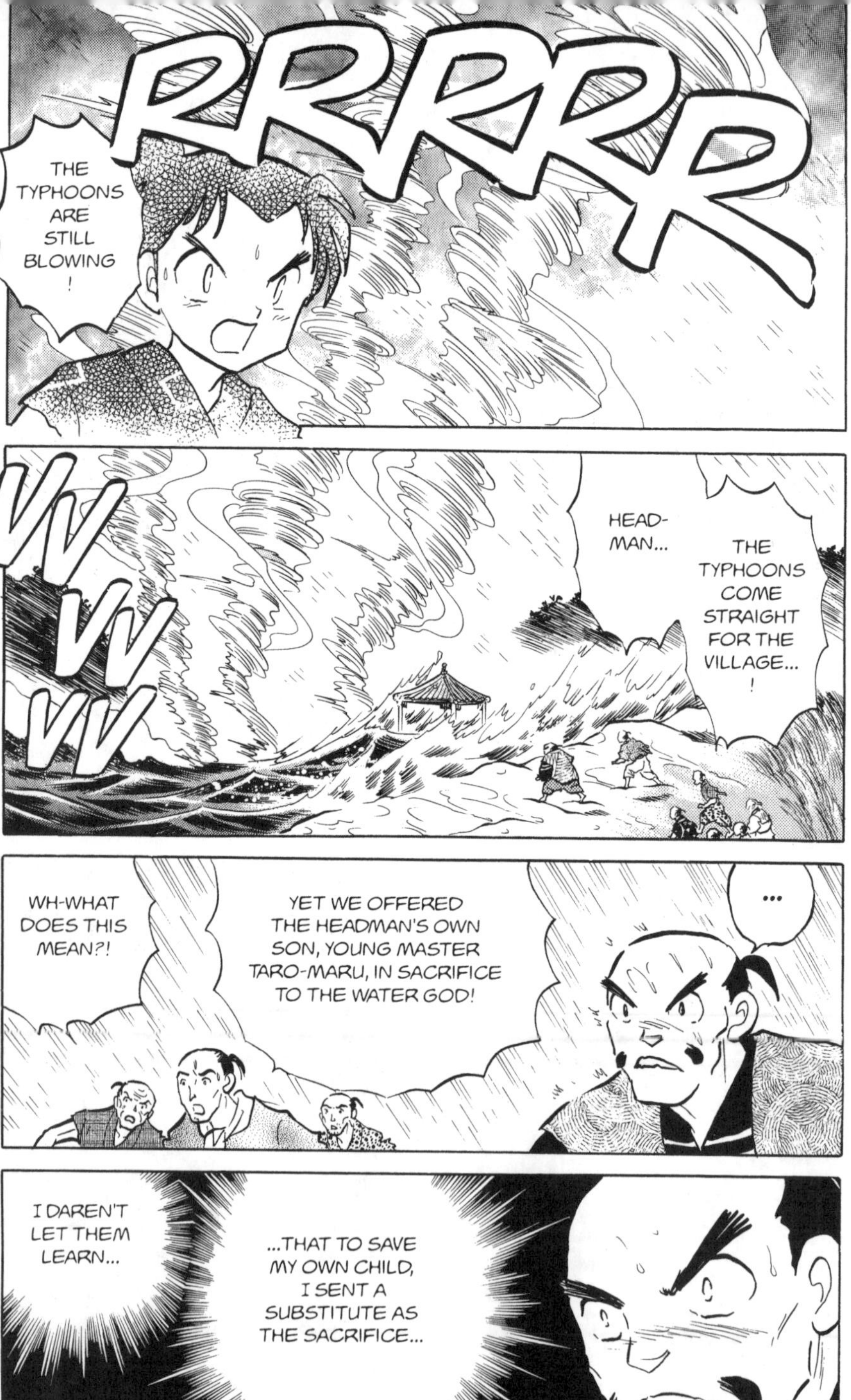
RRRRRR
THE TYPHOONS ARE STILL BLOWING!
VVVVVV
HEAD-MAN...
THE TYPHOONS COME STRAIGHT FOR THE VILLAGE...!
WH-WHAT DOES THIS MEAN?!
YET WE OFFERED THE HEADMAN'S OWN SON, YOUNG MASTER TARO-MARU, IN SACRIFICE TO THE WATER GOD!
...
I DAREN'T LET THEM LEARN...
...THAT TO SAVE MY OWN CHILD, I SENT A SUBSTITUTE AS THE SACRIFICE...

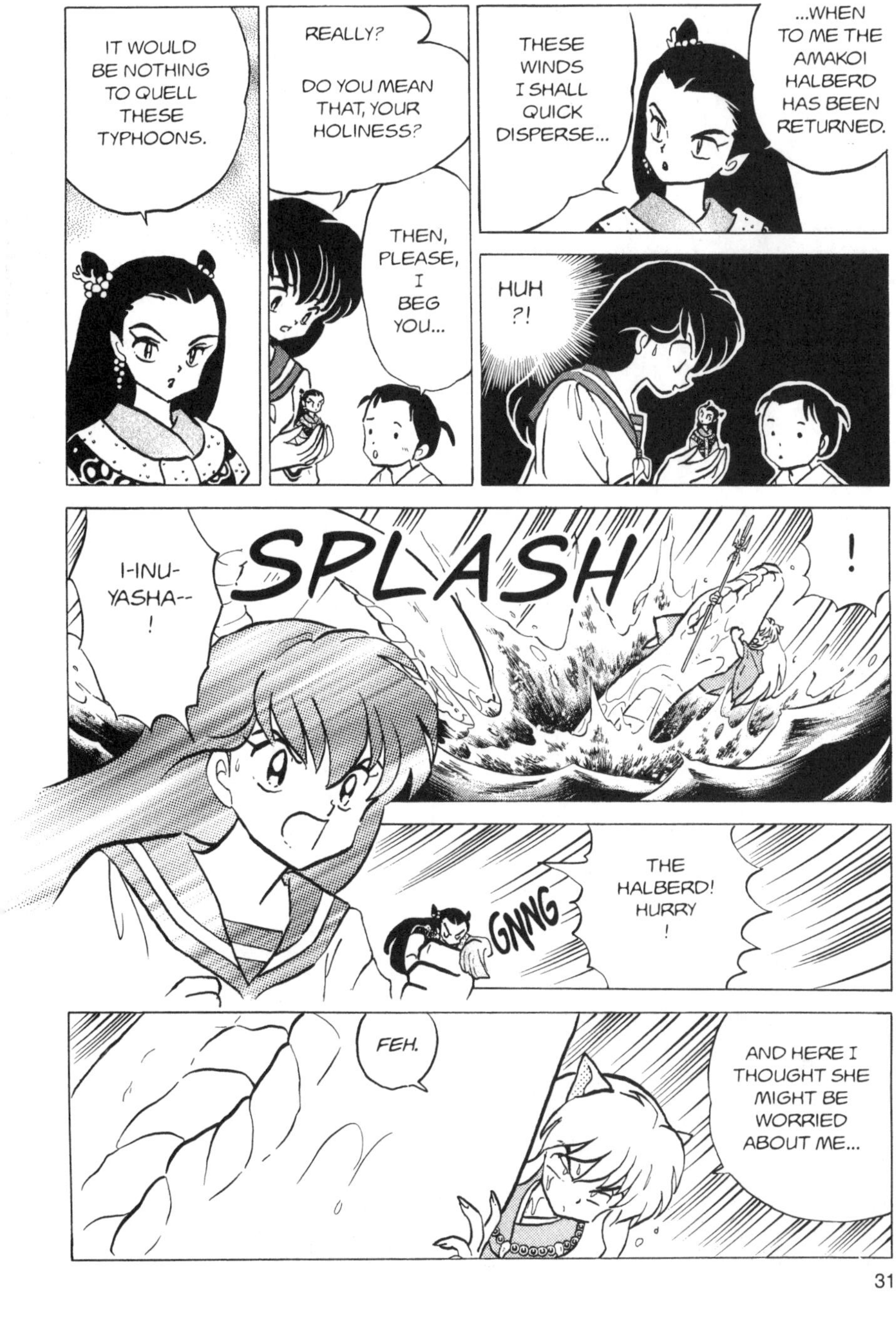
IT WOULD BE NOTHING TO QUELL THESE TYPHOONS.
REALLY? DO YOU MEAN THAT, YOUR HOLINESS?
THEN, PLEASE, I BEG YOU...
THESE WINDS I SHALL QUICK DISPERSE...
...WHEN TO ME THE AMAKOI HALBERD HAS BEEN RETURNED.
HUH ?!
SPLASH
!
I-INU-YASHA-- !
GNNG
THE HALBERD! HURRY !
FEH.
AND HERE I THOUGHT SHE MIGHT BE WORRIED ABOUT ME...

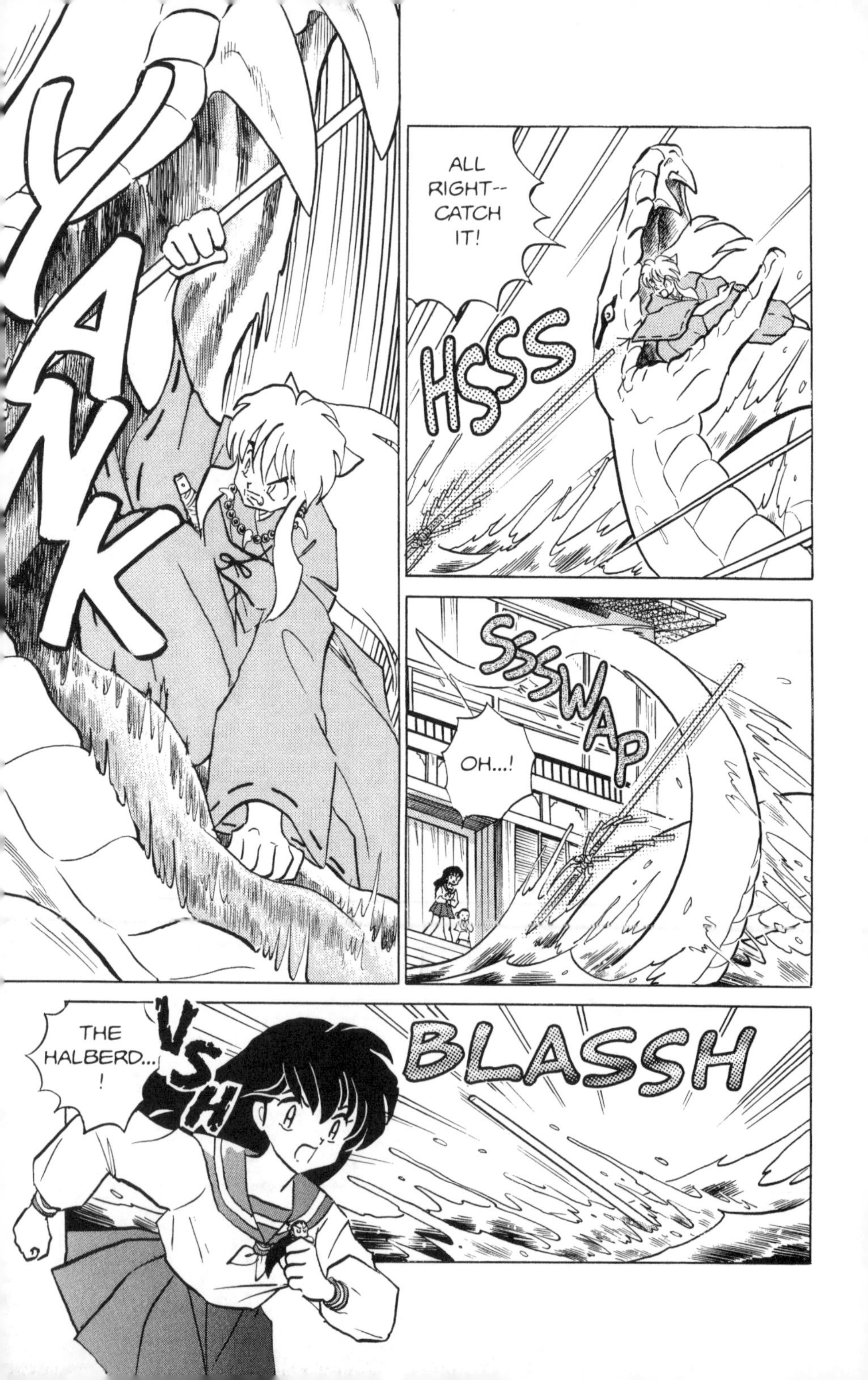
ALL RIGHT-- CATCH IT!
HSSS
SSSWAP
OH...!
YANK
BLASSH
THE HALBERD... !
VSH

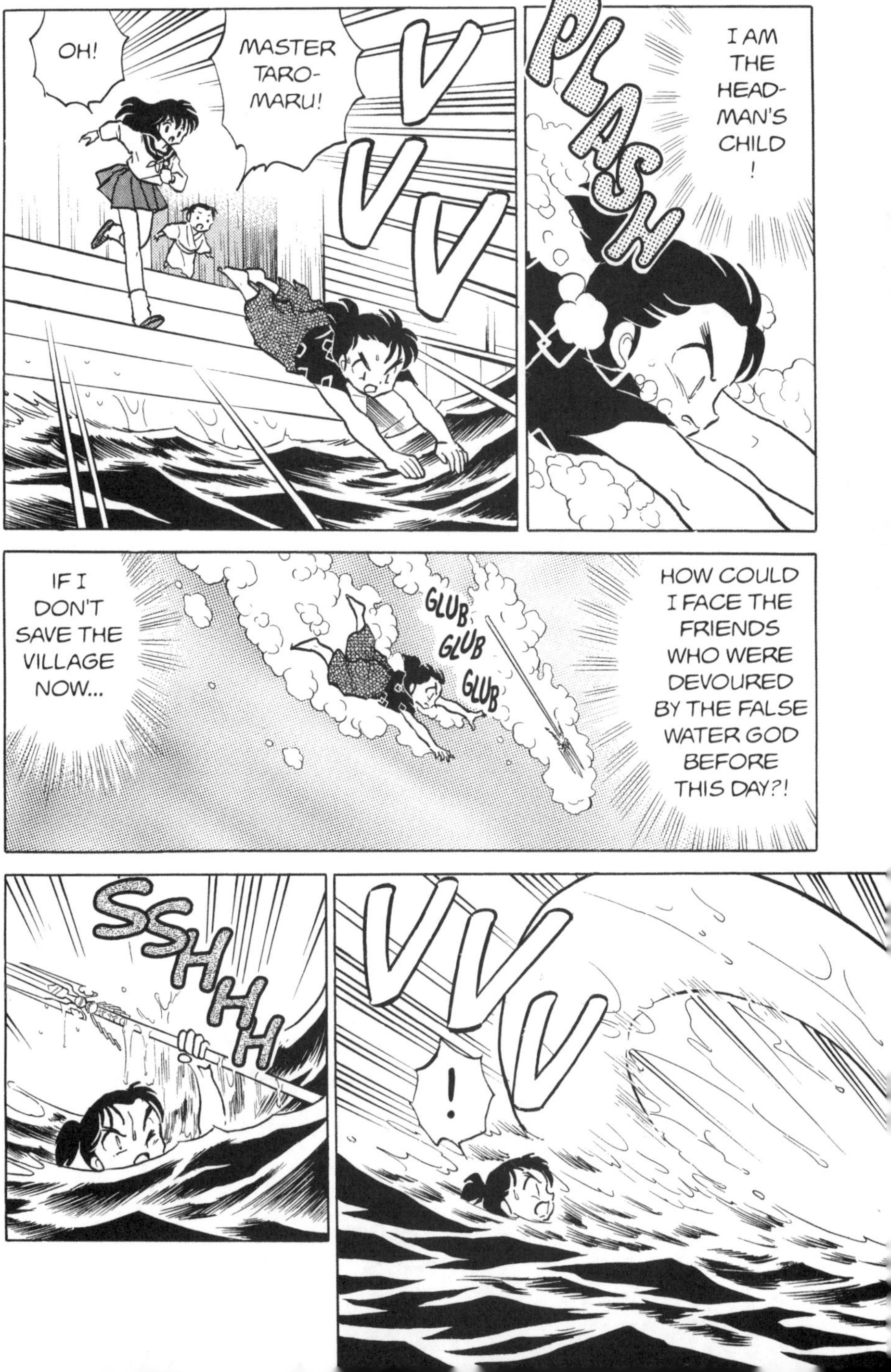
OH!
MASTER TARO-MARU!
VVV
PLASH
I AM THE HEAD-MAN'S CHILD!
IF I DON'T SAVE THE VILLAGE NOW...
GLUB GLUB GLUB
HOW COULD I FACE THE FRIENDS WHO WERE DEVOURED BY THE FALSE WATER GOD BEFORE THIS DAY?!
SSHHHH
VVVV
!

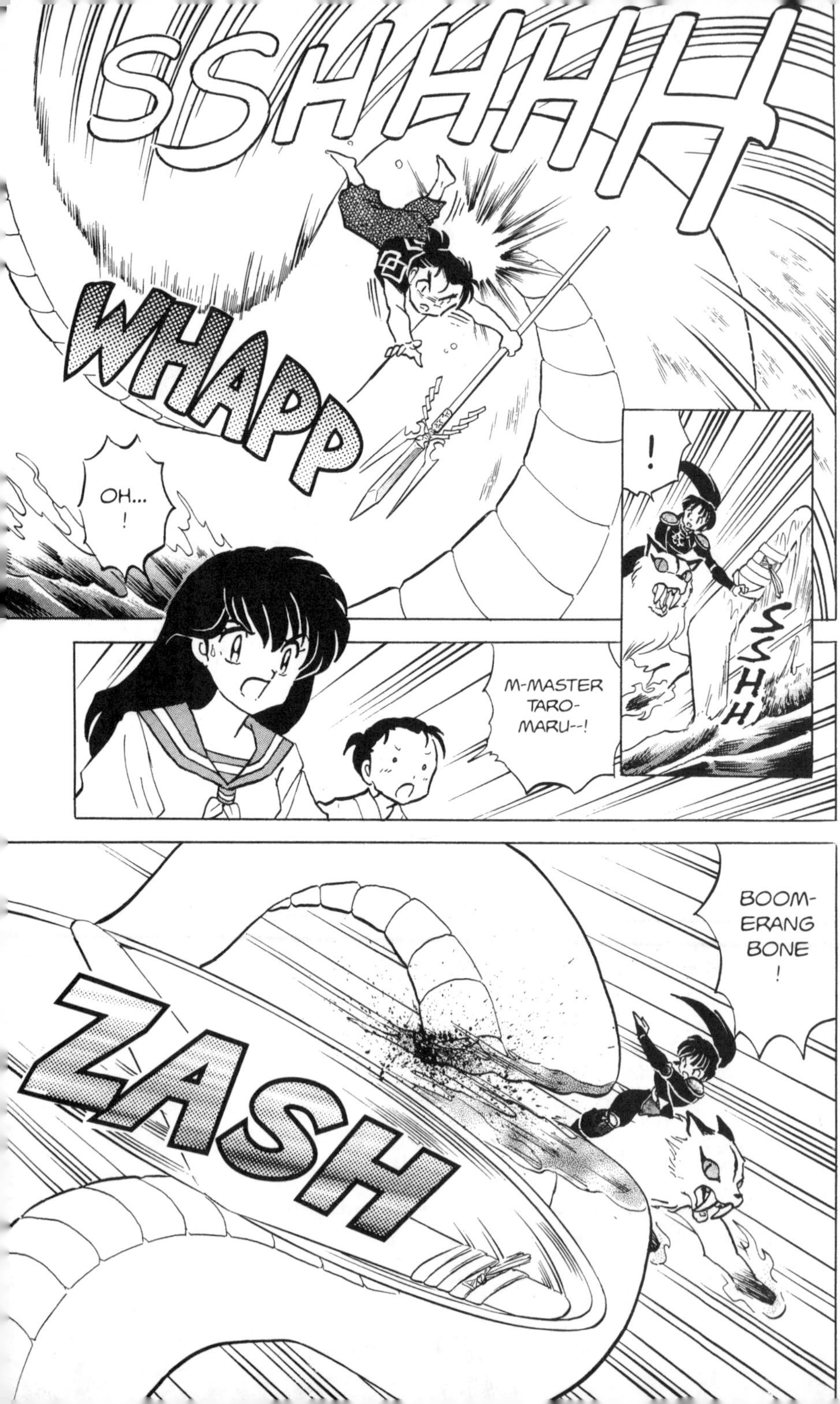
SSHHHHH
WHAPP
OH...!
!
SSHH
M-MASTER TARO-MARU--!
BOOM-ERANG BONE!
ZASH

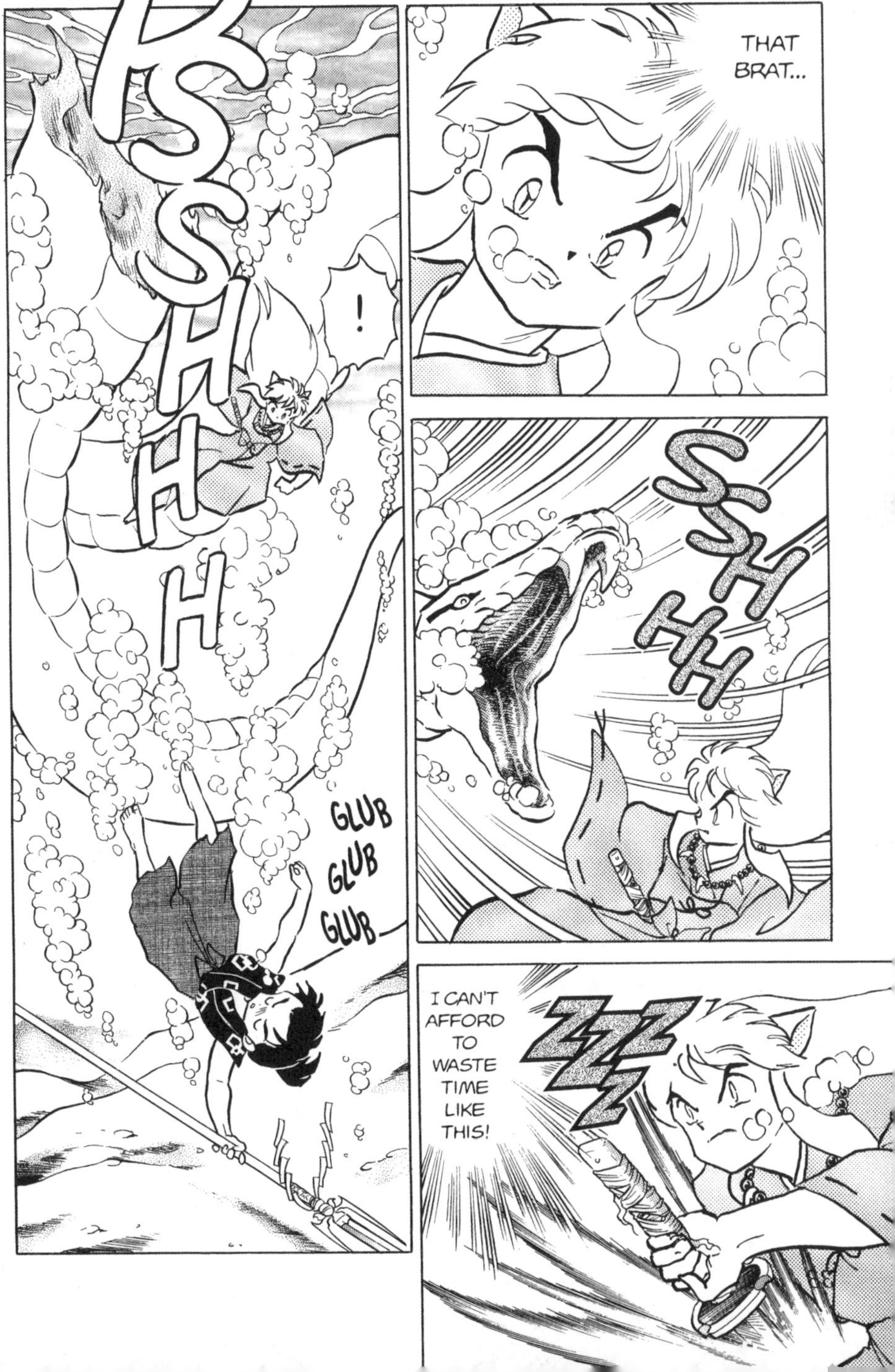
THAT BRAT...
SSHHHH
I CAN'T AFFORD TO WASTE TIME LIKE THIS!
ZZZ
PSSHHH
!
GLUB
GLUB
GLUB

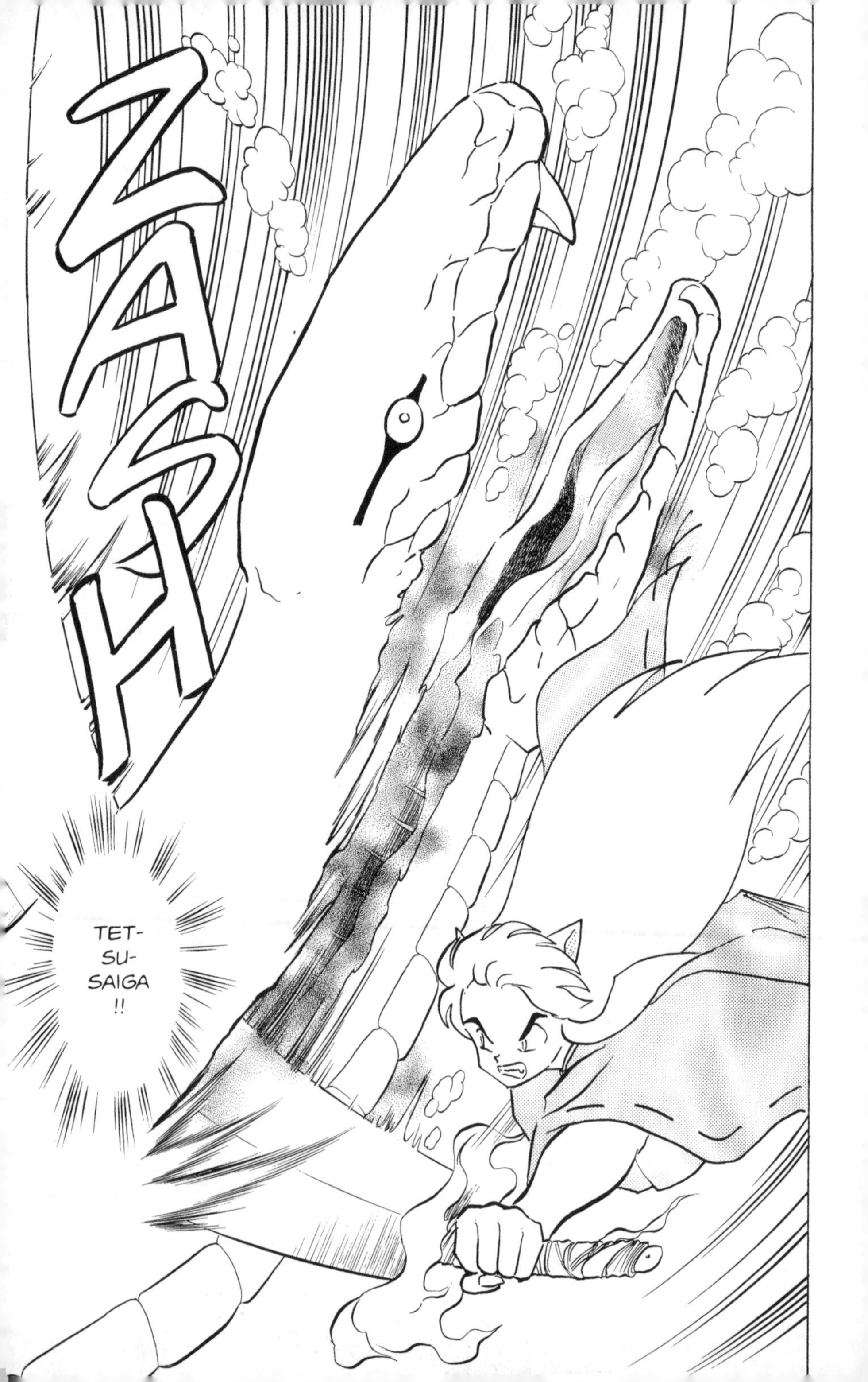
ZASH
TET-SU-SAIGA !!

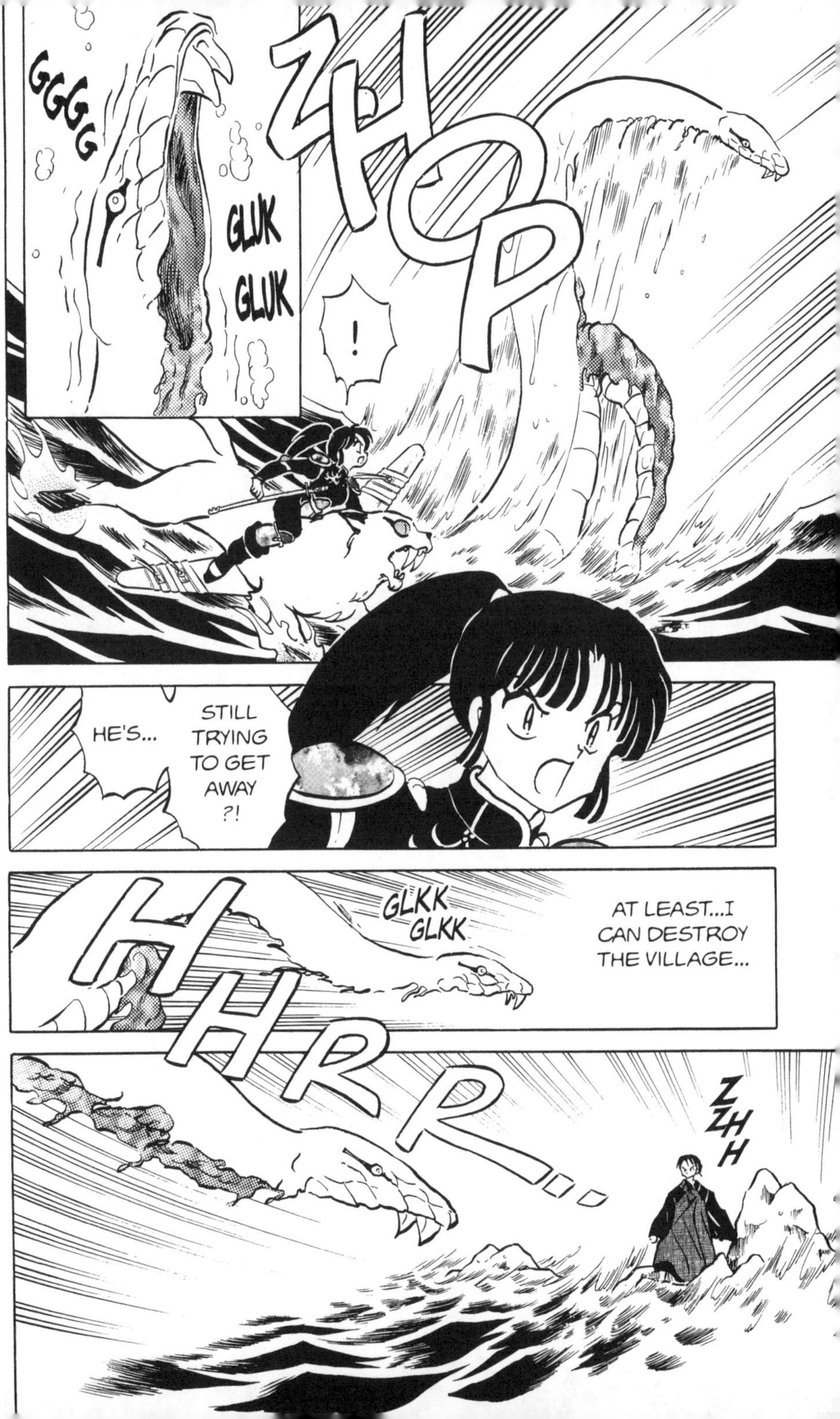
ZHOP
!
GGGG
GLUK GLUK
HE'S...
STILL TRYING TO GET AWAY ?!
AT LEAST...I CAN DESTROY THE VILLAGE...
GLKK GLKK
HHRR...
ZZHH

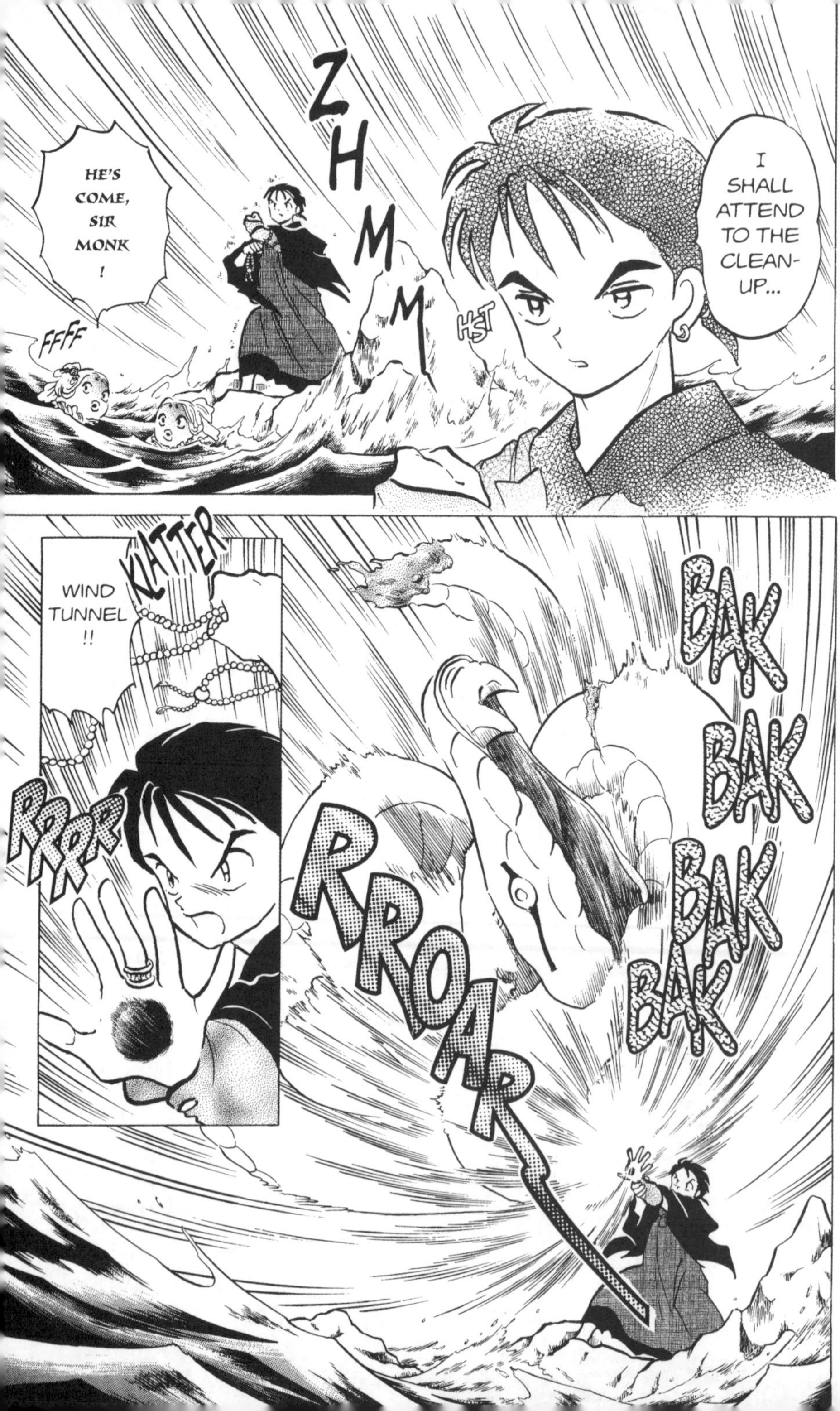
I SHALL ATTEND TO THE CLEAN-UP...
HST
ZHMMM
HE'S COME, SIR MONK!
FFFF
BAK BAK BAK BAK
RROAR
KLATTER
WIND TUNNEL!!
RRRRR

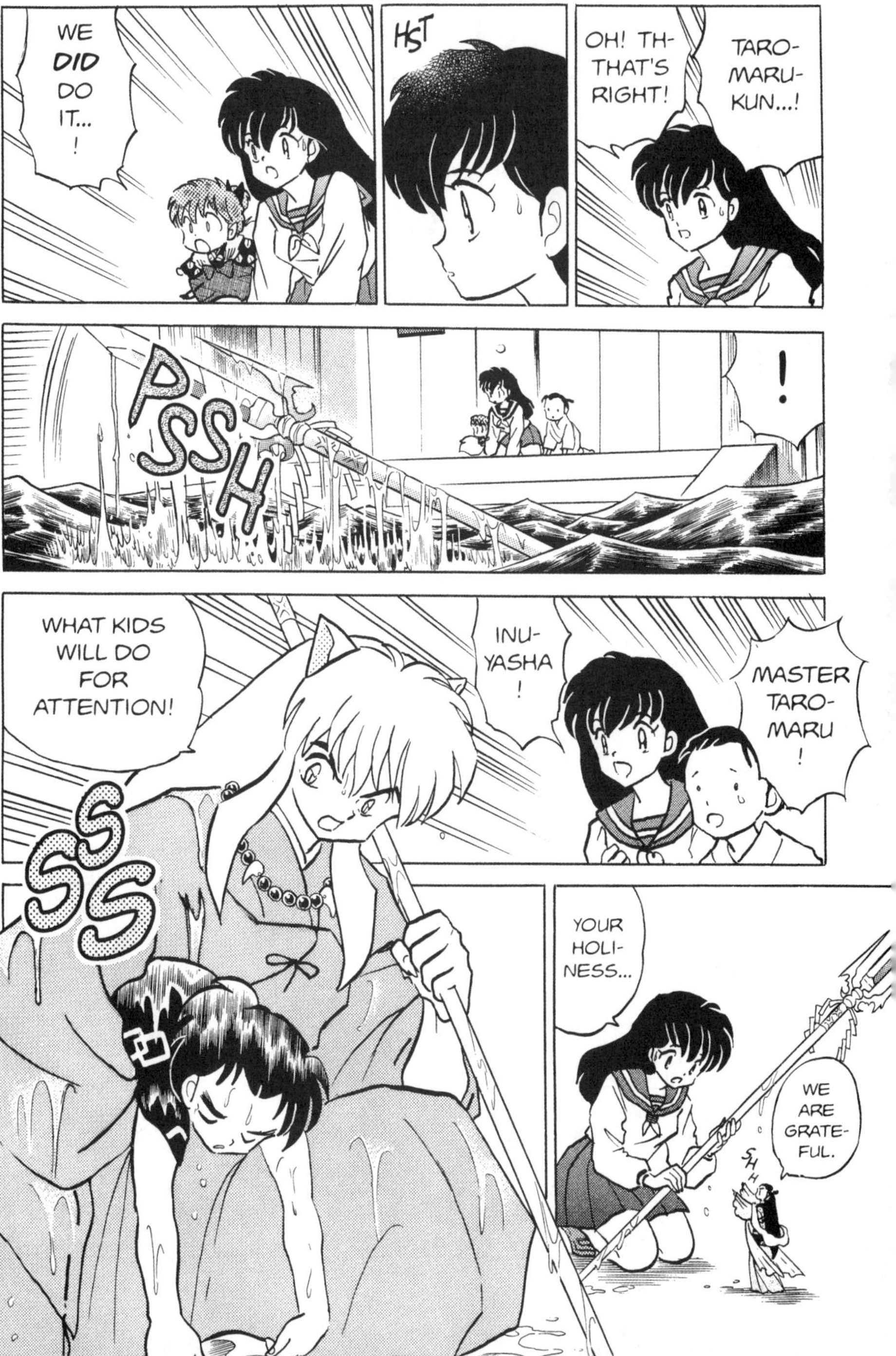
WE **DID** DO IT... !
HST
OH! TH- THAT'S RIGHT!
TARO- MARU- KUN...!
!
PSSH
WHAT KIDS WILL DO FOR ATTENTION!
INU- YASHA !
MASTER TARO- MARU !
SSSS
YOUR HOLI- NESS...
WE ARE GRATE- FUL.
SHH

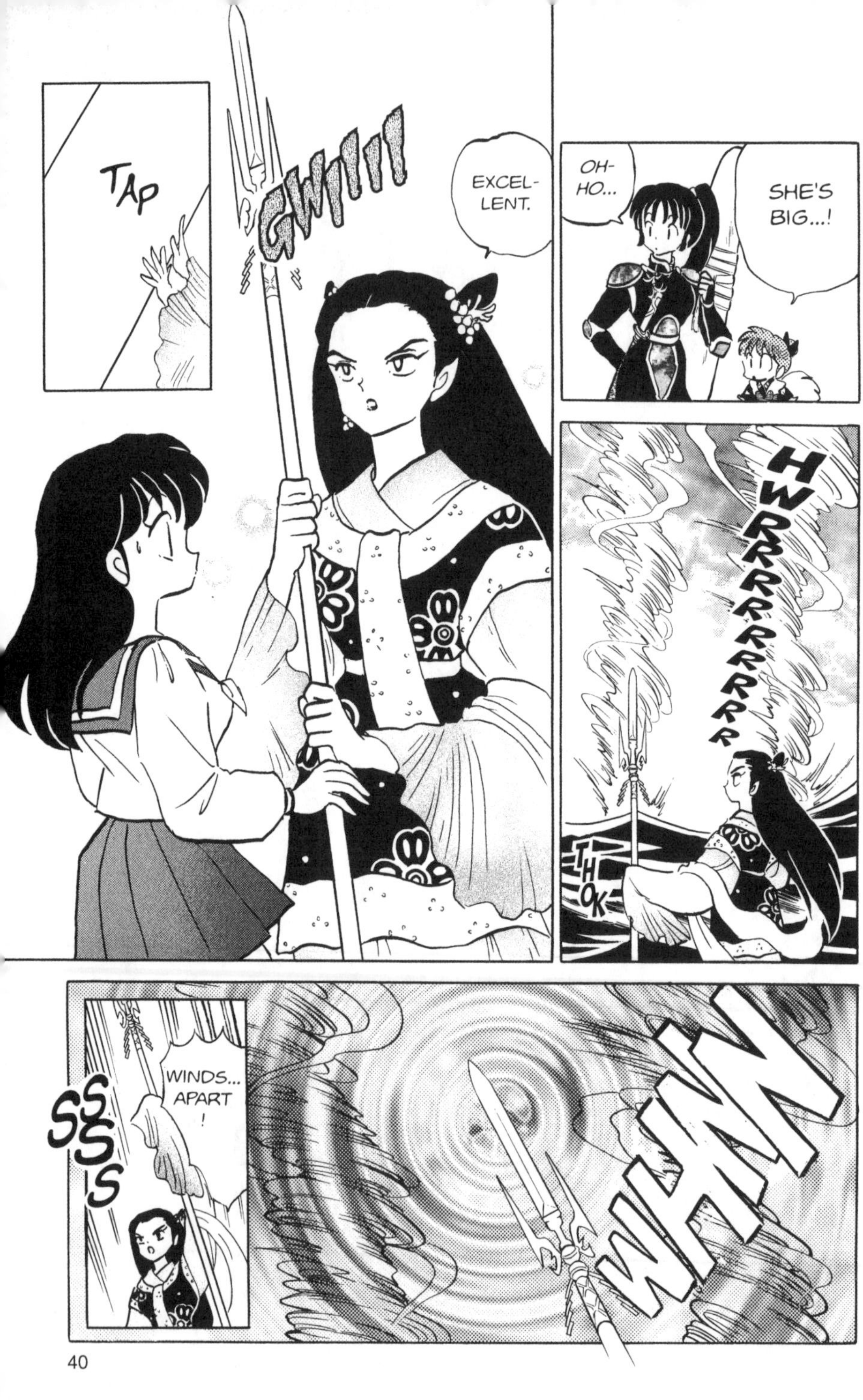

OH-HO...
SHE'S BIG...!
HWRRRRRRRRRR
THOK
EXCEL-LENT.
GWIIII
TAP
WHN
WINDS... APART!
SSSS

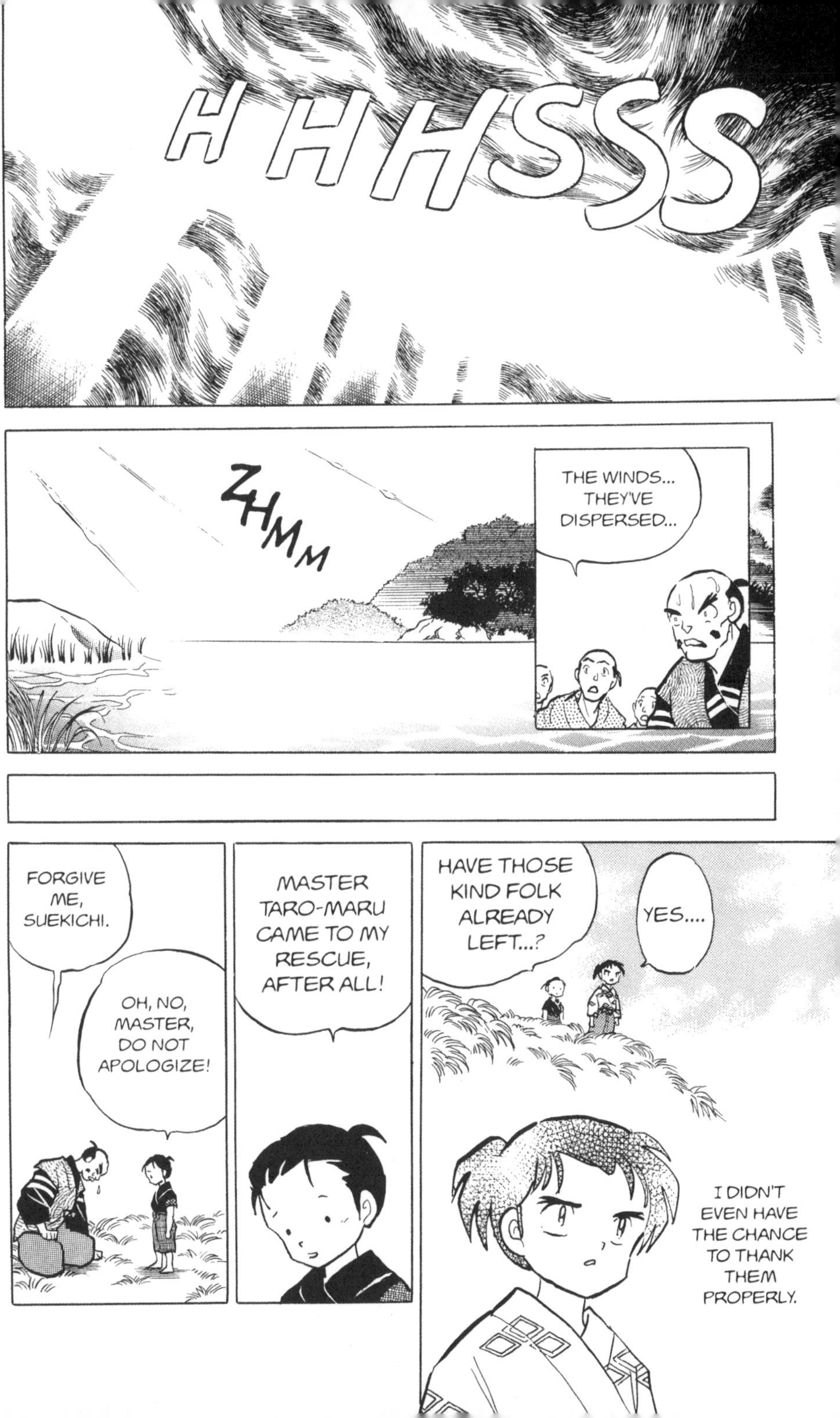
HHHSSS
THE WINDS... THEY'VE DISPERSED...
ZHMM
HAVE THOSE KIND FOLK ALREADY LEFT...?
YES....
I DIDN'T EVEN HAVE THE CHANCE TO THANK THEM PROPERLY.
MASTER TARO-MARU CAME TO MY RESCUE, AFTER ALL!
FORGIVE ME, SUEKICHI.
OH, NO, MASTER, DO NOT APOLOGIZE!

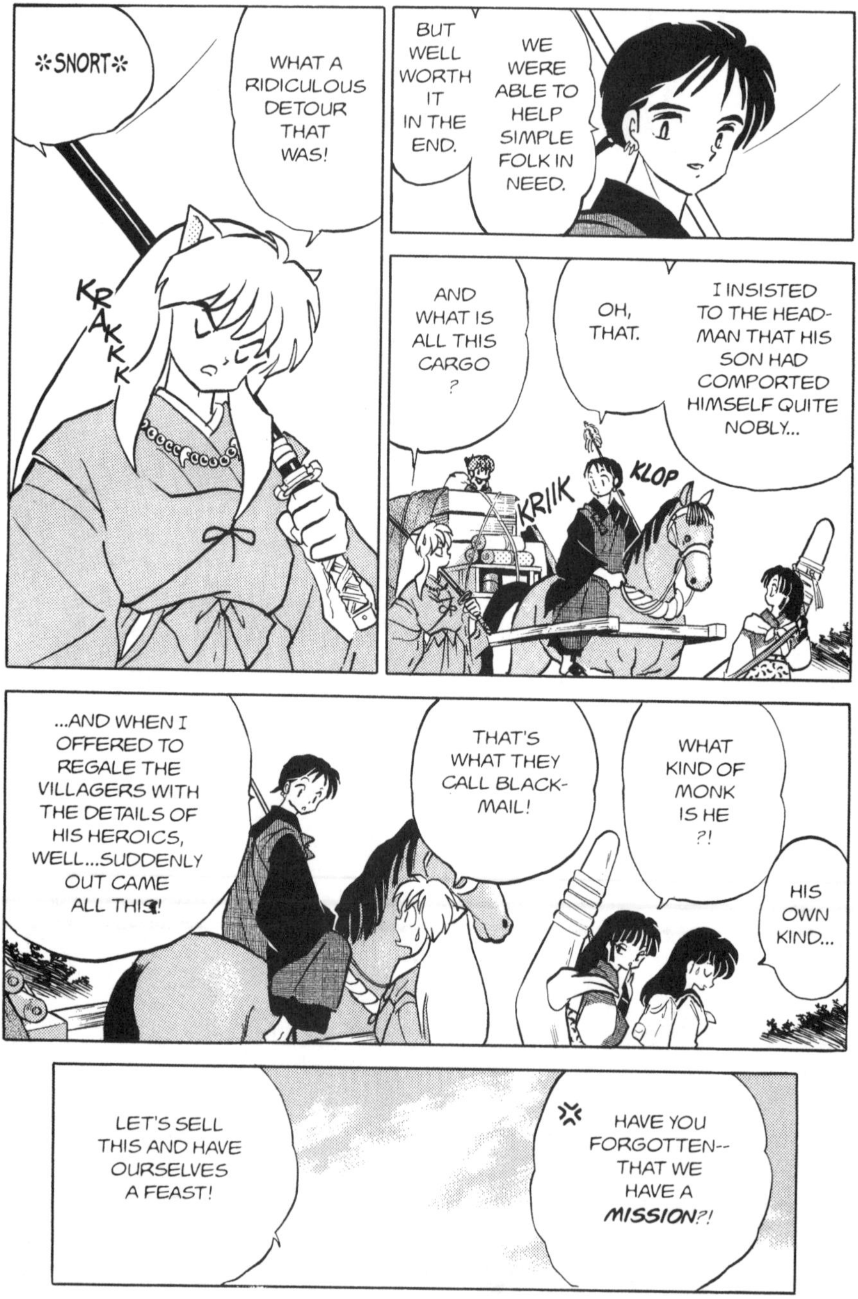

✲SNORT✲
WHAT A RIDICULOUS DETOUR THAT WAS!
KRAKKK
BUT WELL WORTH IT IN THE END.
WE WERE ABLE TO HELP SIMPLE FOLK IN NEED.
AND WHAT IS ALL THIS CARGO?
OH, THAT.
I INSISTED TO THE HEAD-MAN THAT HIS SON HAD COMPORTED HIMSELF QUITE NOBLY...
KRIIK
KLOP
...AND WHEN I OFFERED TO REGALE THE VILLAGERS WITH THE DETAILS OF HIS HEROICS, WELL...SUDDENLY OUT CAME ALL THIS!
THAT'S WHAT THEY CALL BLACK-MAIL!
WHAT KIND OF MONK IS HE?!
HIS OWN KIND...
LET'S SELL THIS AND HAVE OURSELVES A FEAST!
HAVE YOU FORGOTTEN-- THAT WE HAVE A MISSION?!

SCROLL THREE

THE WOUND AND THE WIND

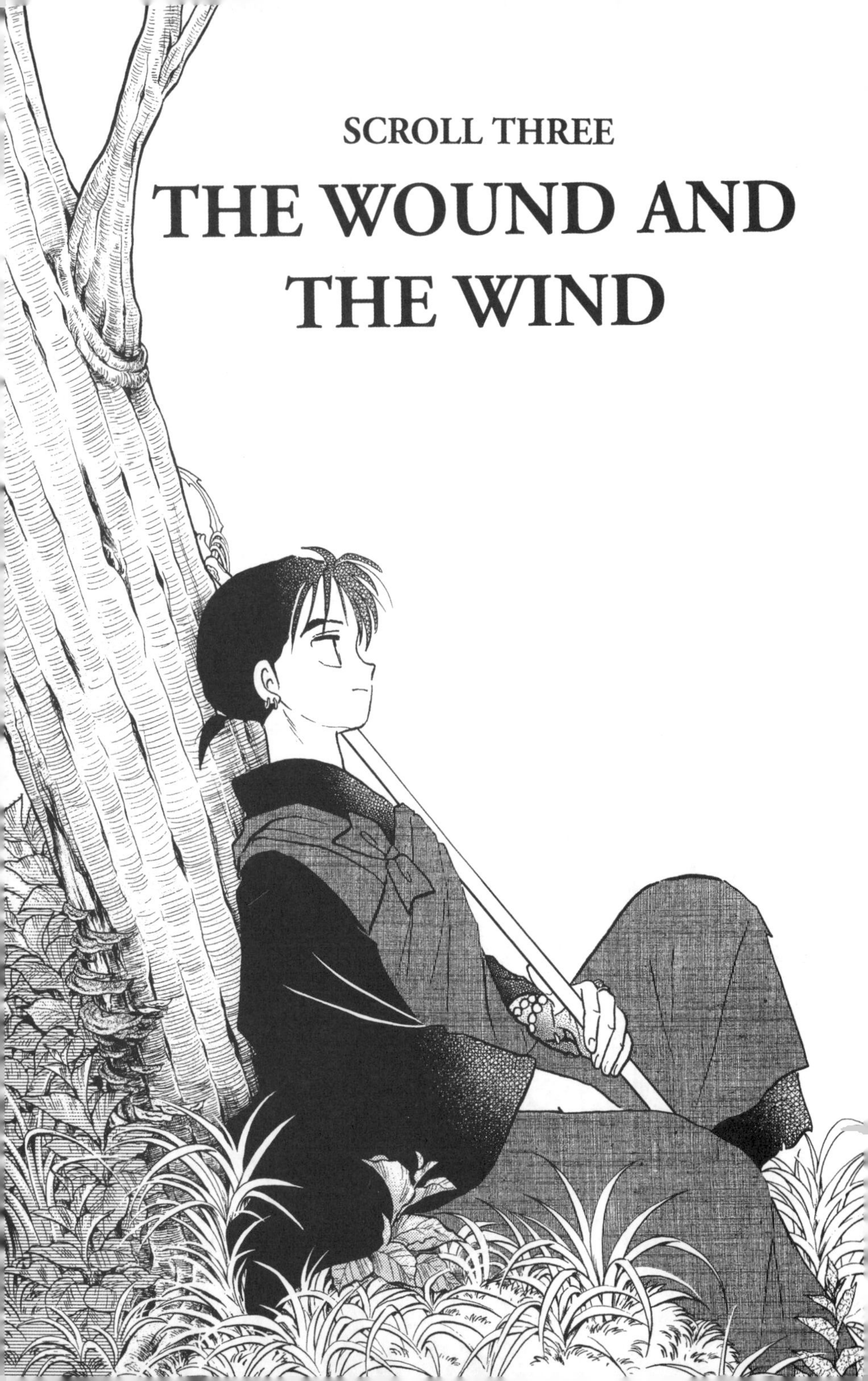

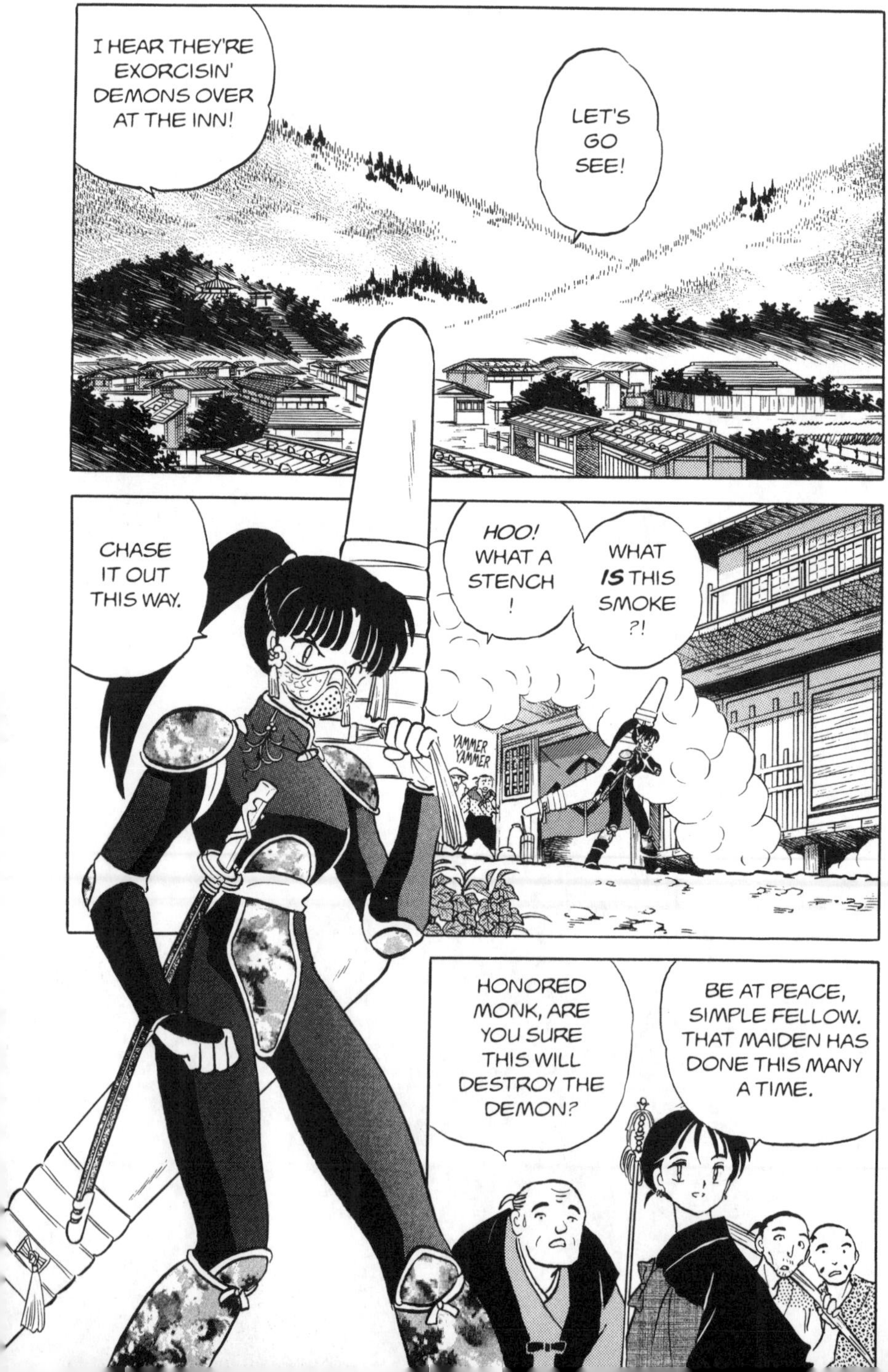
I HEAR THEY'RE EXORCISIN' DEMONS OVER AT THE INN!
LET'S GO SEE!
WHAT *IS* THIS SMOKE?!
HOO! WHAT A STENCH!
YAMMER YAMMER
CHASE IT OUT THIS WAY.
HONORED MONK, ARE YOU SURE THIS WILL DESTROY THE DEMON?
BE AT PEACE, SIMPLE FELLOW. THAT MAIDEN HAS DONE THIS MANY A TIME.

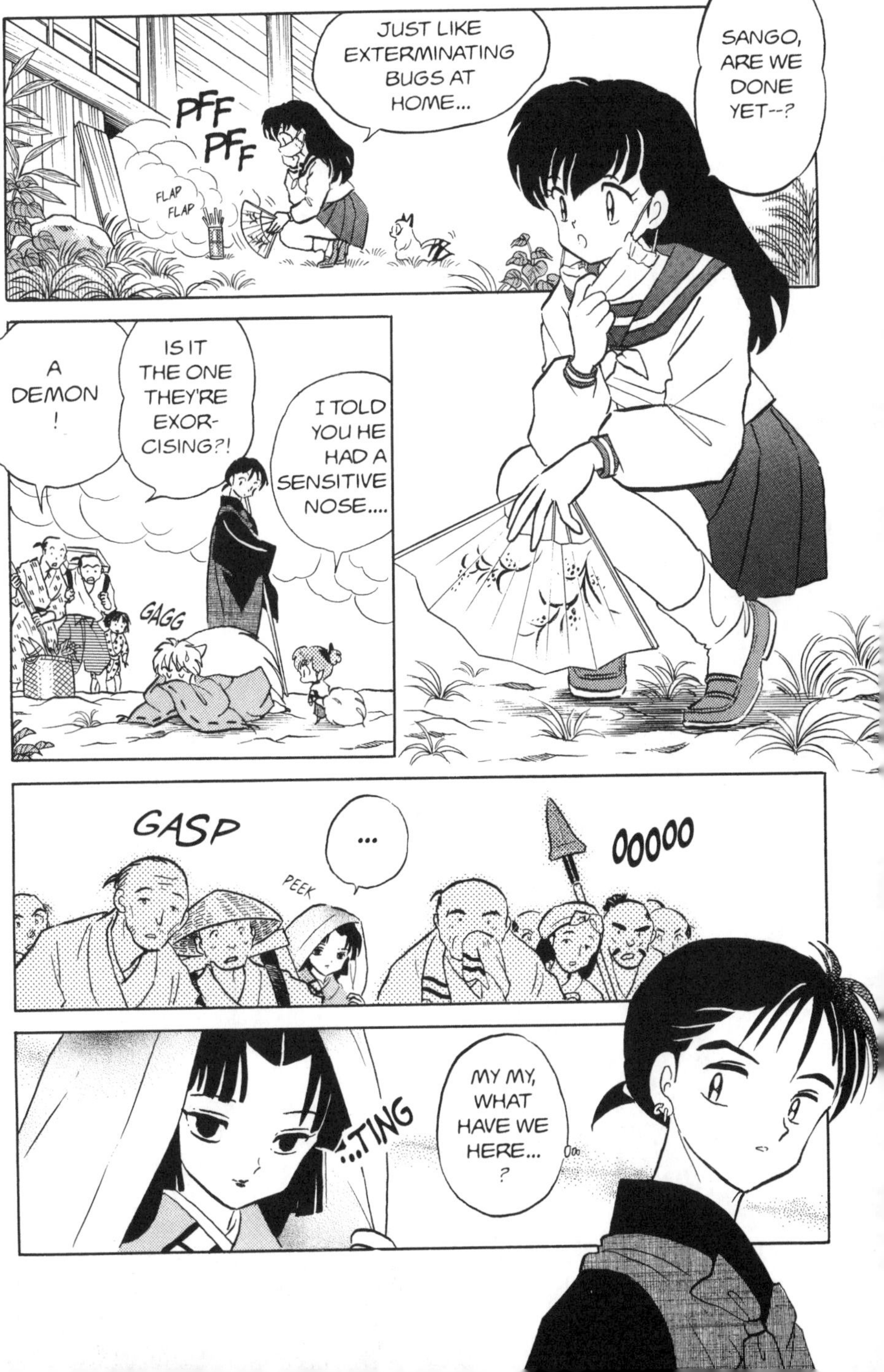
JUST LIKE EXTERMINATING BUGS AT HOME...
PFF PFF
FLAP FLAP
SANGO, ARE WE DONE YET--?
IS IT THE ONE THEY'RE EXOR-CISING?!
A DEMON!
I TOLD YOU HE HAD A SENSITIVE NOSE....
GAGG
OOOOO
...
PEEK
GASP
MY MY, WHAT HAVE WE HERE...?
...TING

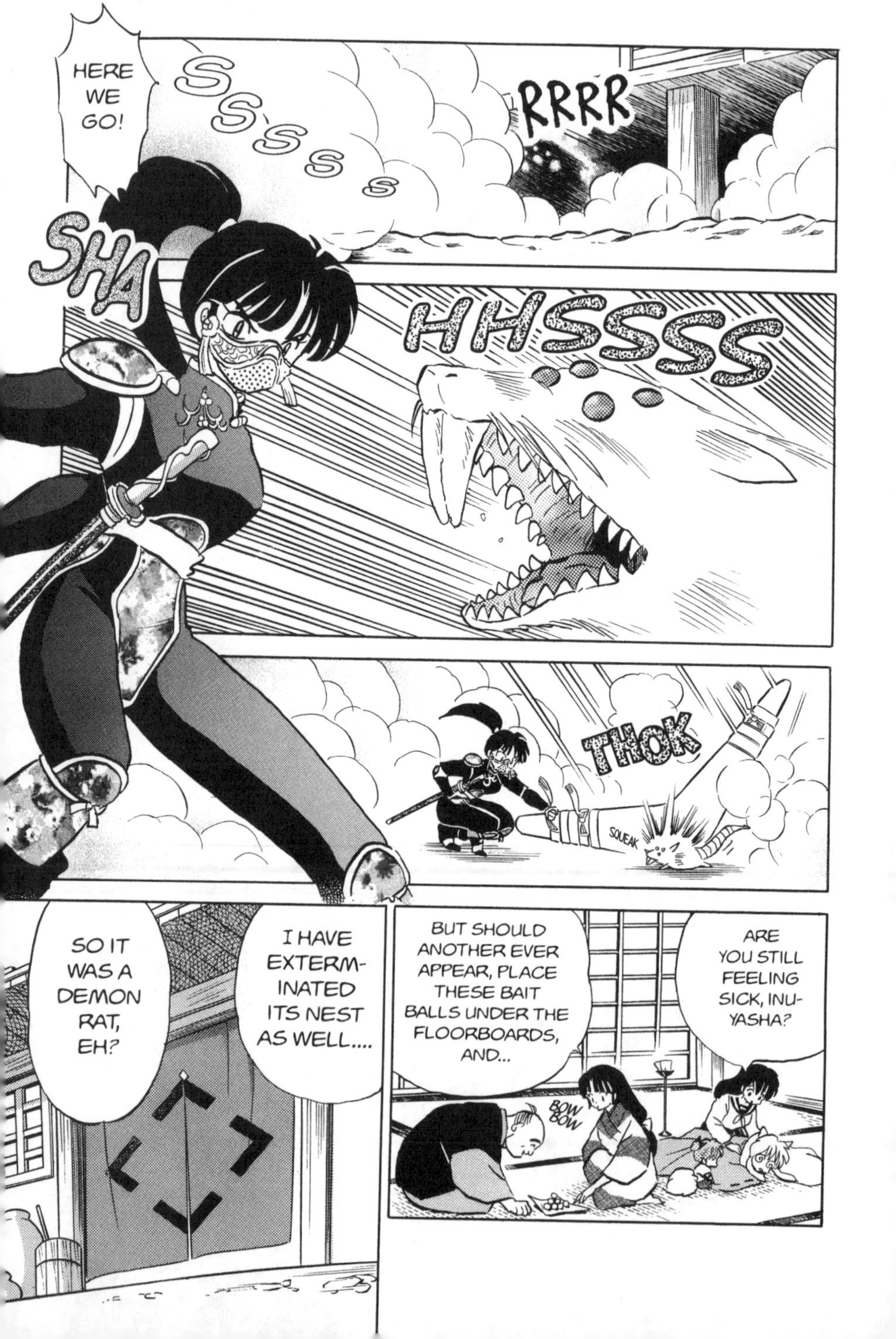
HERE WE GO!
SSSSS
RRRR
SHA
HHSSSSS
THOK
SQUEAK
SO IT WAS A DEMON RAT, EH?
I HAVE EXTERMINATED ITS NEST AS WELL....
BUT SHOULD ANOTHER EVER APPEAR, PLACE THESE BAIT BALLS UNDER THE FLOORBOARDS, AND...
BOW BOW
ARE YOU STILL FEELING SICK, INU-YASHA?

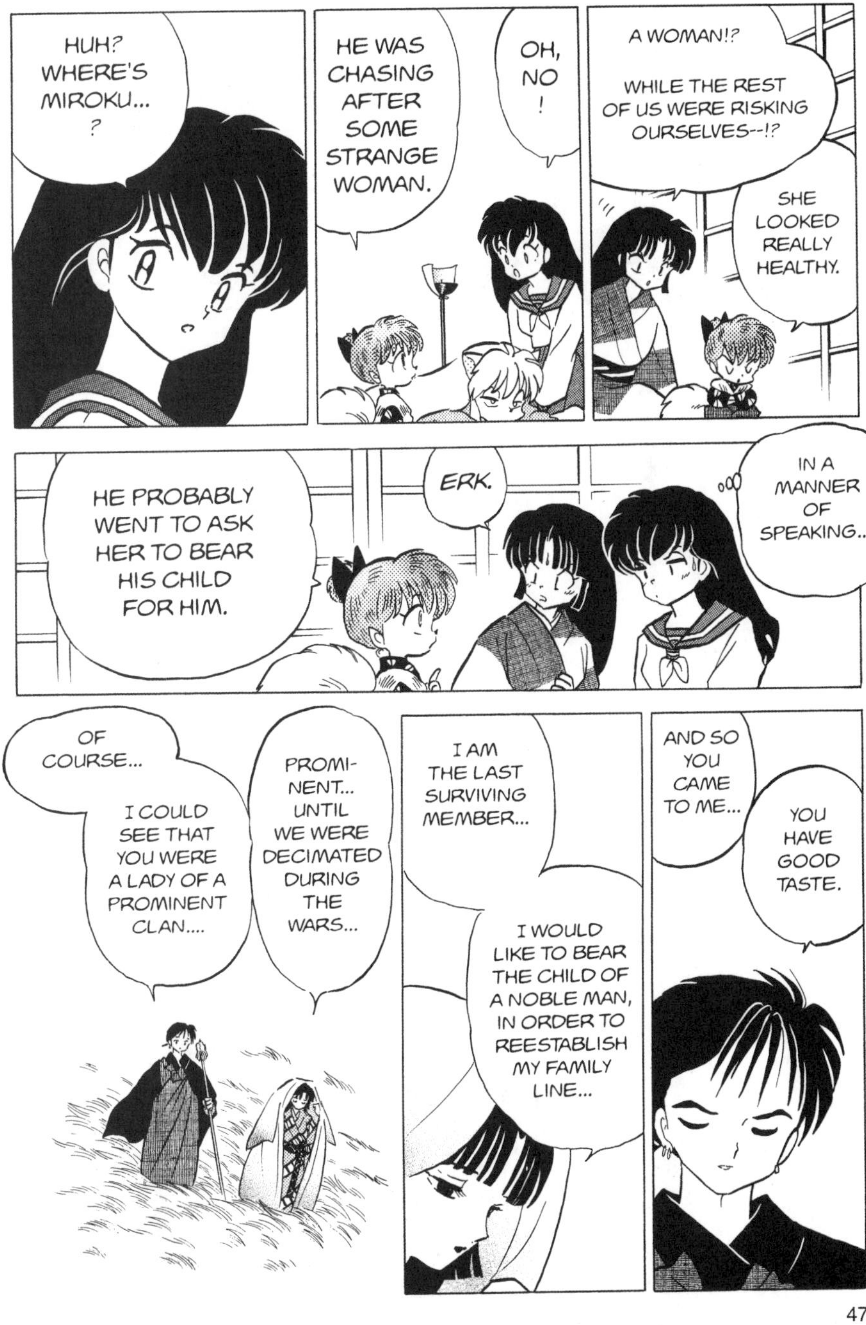
HUH? WHERE'S MIROKU...?
HE WAS CHASING AFTER SOME STRANGE WOMAN.
OH, NO!
A WOMAN!? WHILE THE REST OF US WERE RISKING OURSELVES--!?
SHE LOOKED REALLY HEALTHY.
HE PROBABLY WENT TO ASK HER TO BEAR HIS CHILD FOR HIM.
ERK.
IN A MANNER OF SPEAKING....
OF COURSE...
I COULD SEE THAT YOU WERE A LADY OF A PROMINENT CLAN....
PROMI-NENT... UNTIL WE WERE DECIMATED DURING THE WARS...
I AM THE LAST SURVIVING MEMBER...
I WOULD LIKE TO BEAR THE CHILD OF A NOBLE MAN, IN ORDER TO REESTABLISH MY FAMILY LINE...
AND SO YOU CAME TO ME...
YOU HAVE GOOD TASTE.

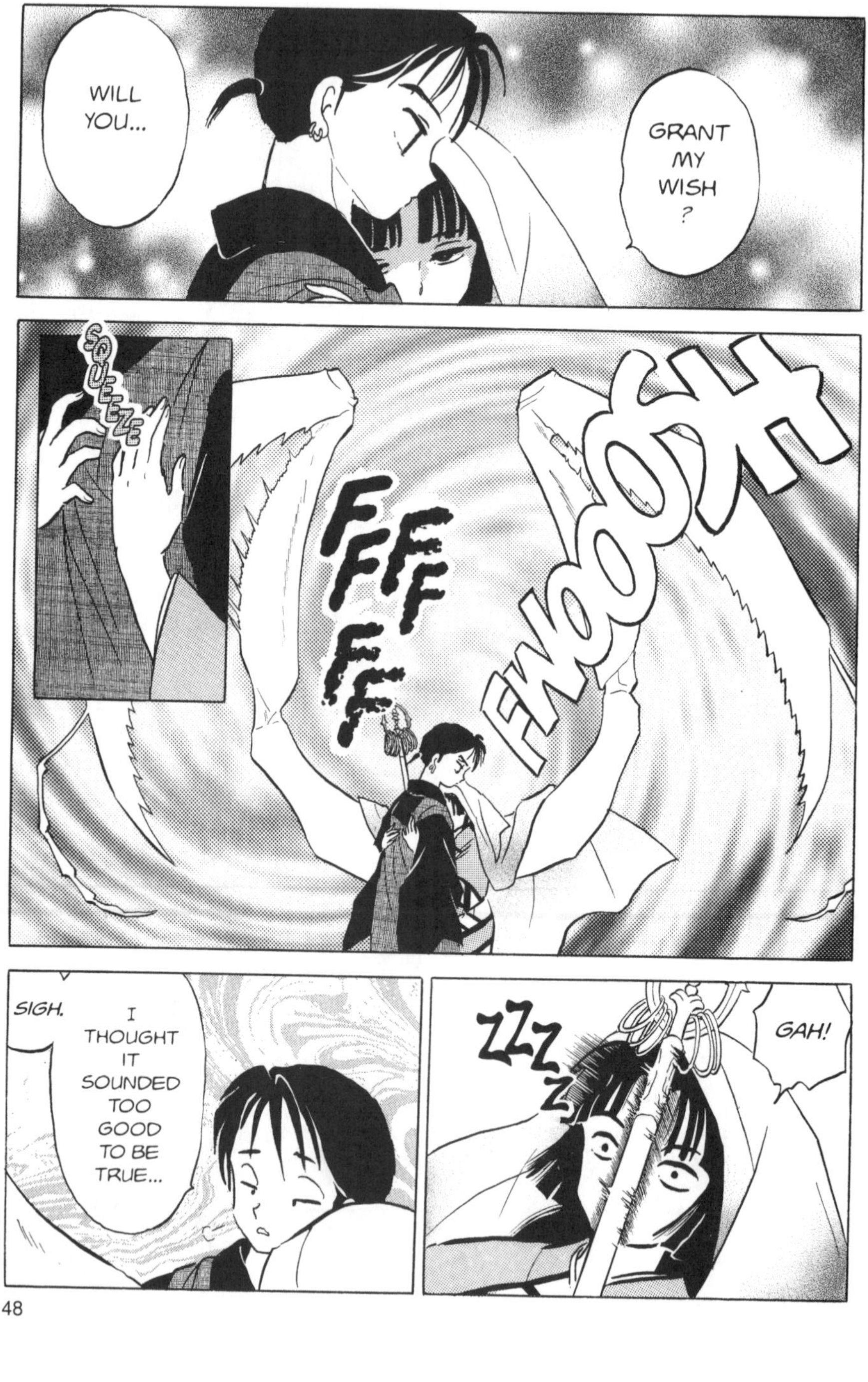
WILL YOU...
GRANT MY WISH?
SQUEEZE
FFFFFF
FWOOOSH
SIGH.
I THOUGHT IT SOUNDED TOO GOOD TO BE TRUE...
ZZZZ
GAH!

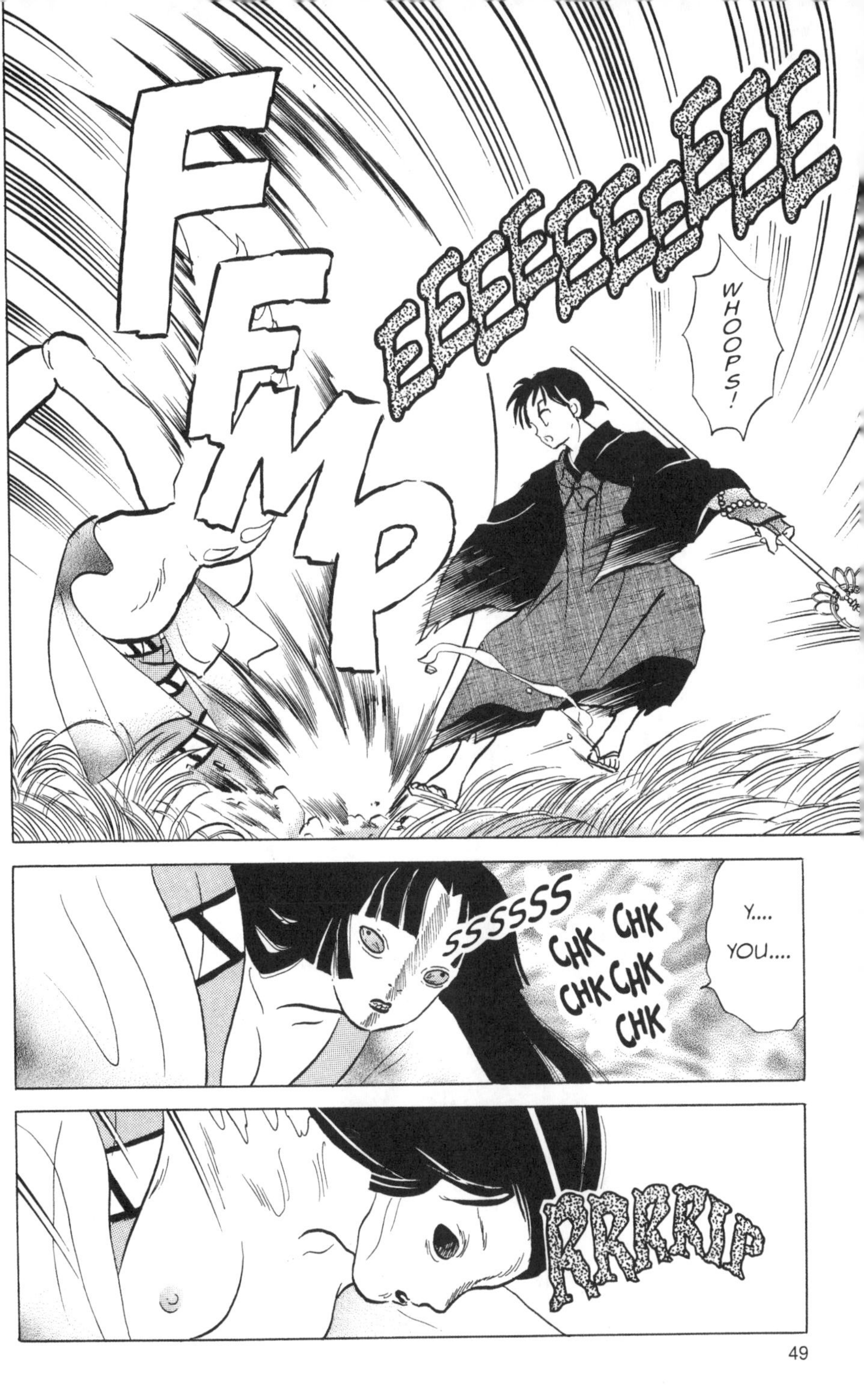
WHOOPS!
EEEEEEEEEE
FFMP
Y.... YOU....
SSSSSS
CHK CHK CHK CHK CHK
RRRRIP

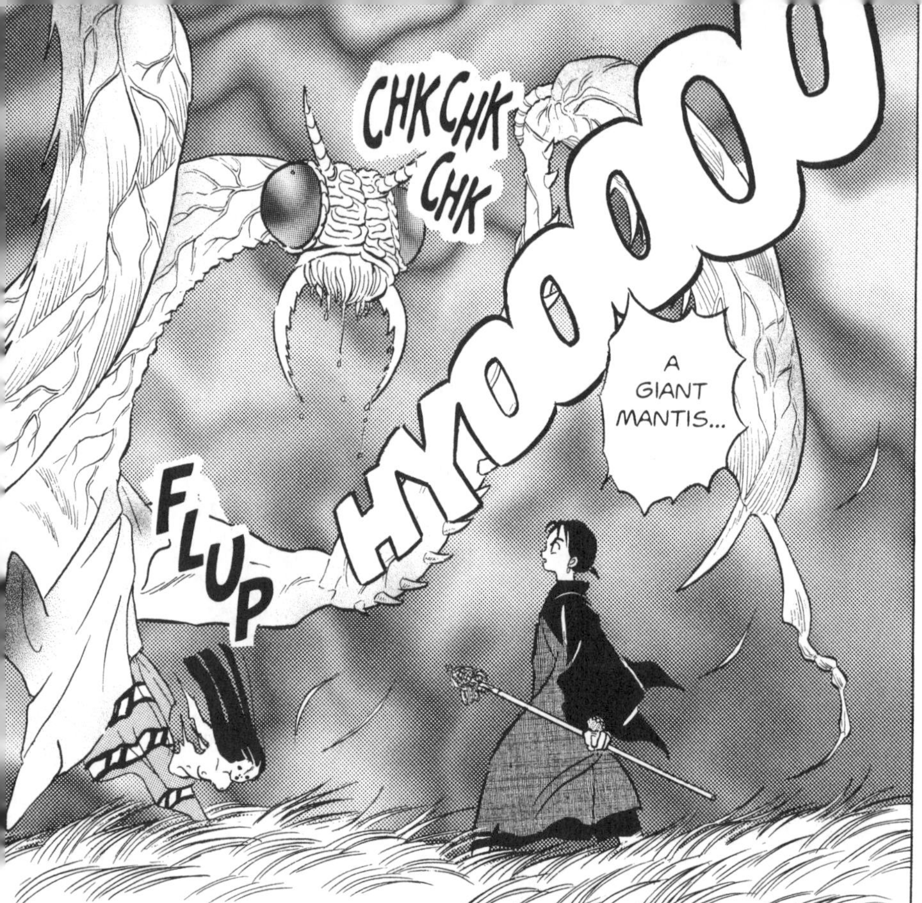
CHK CHK
CHK
HYOOOOOO
A GIANT MANTIS...
FLUP
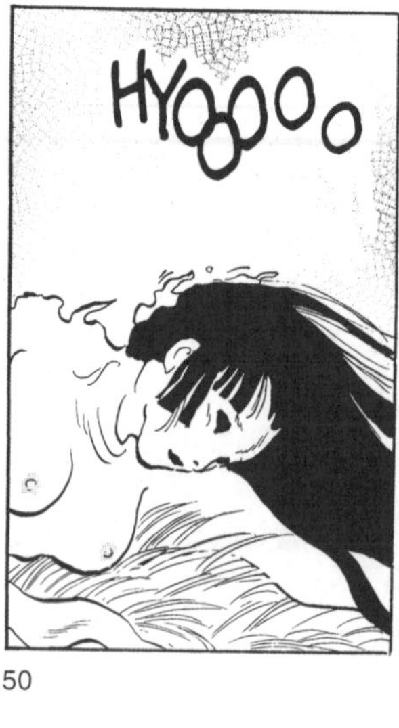
HYOOOOO
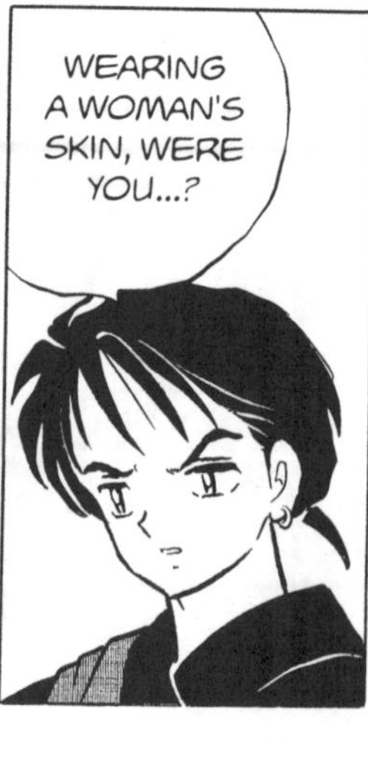
WEARING A WOMAN'S SKIN, WERE YOU...?
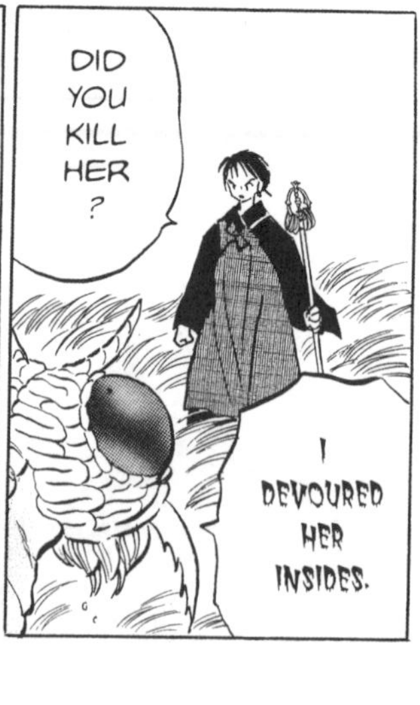
DID YOU KILL HER?
I DEVOURED HER INSIDES.

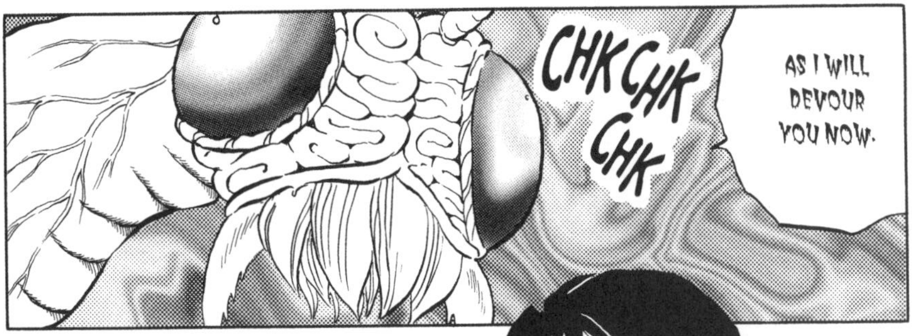
AS I WILL DEVOUR YOU NOW.
CHK CHK CHK

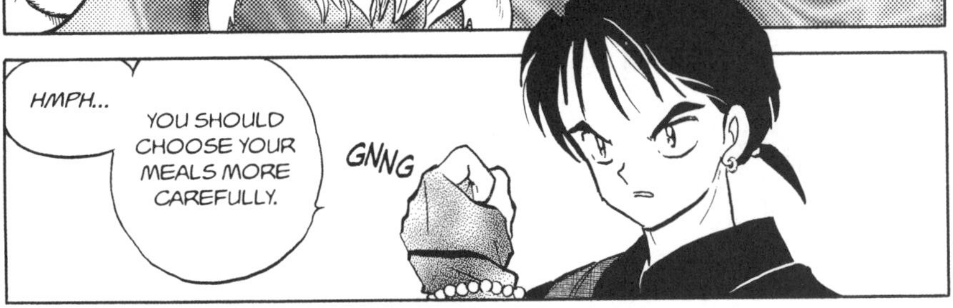
GNNG
HMPH... YOU SHOULD CHOOSE YOUR MEALS MORE CAREFULLY.

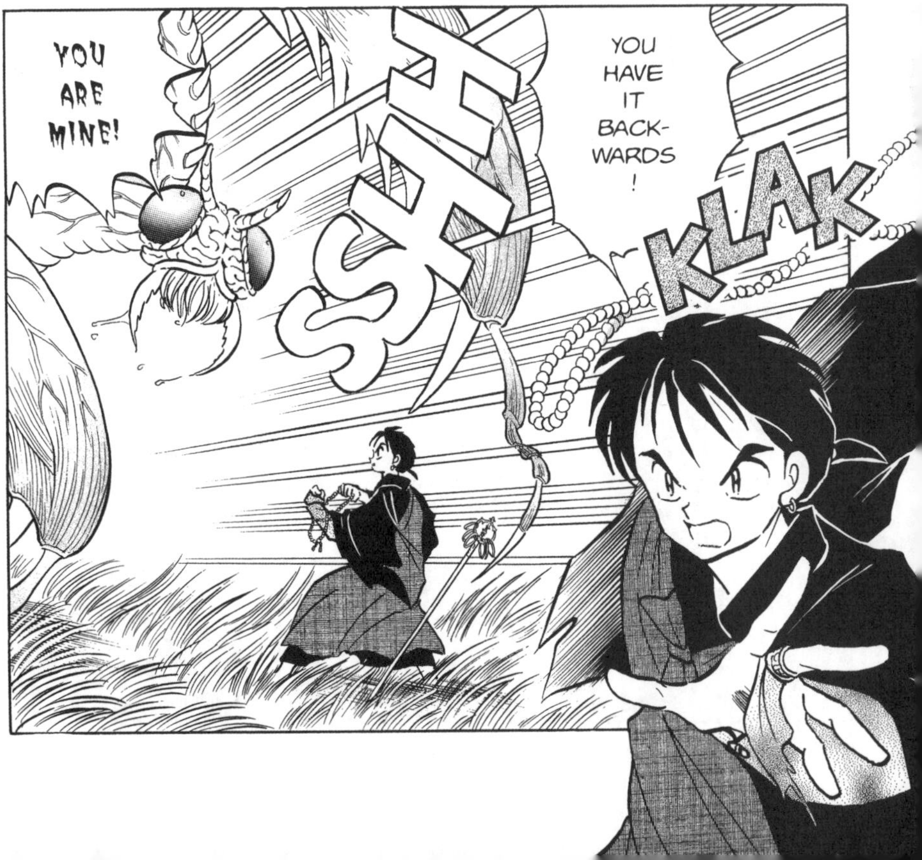
KLAK
YOU HAVE IT BACKWARDS!
SSHH
YOU ARE MINE!

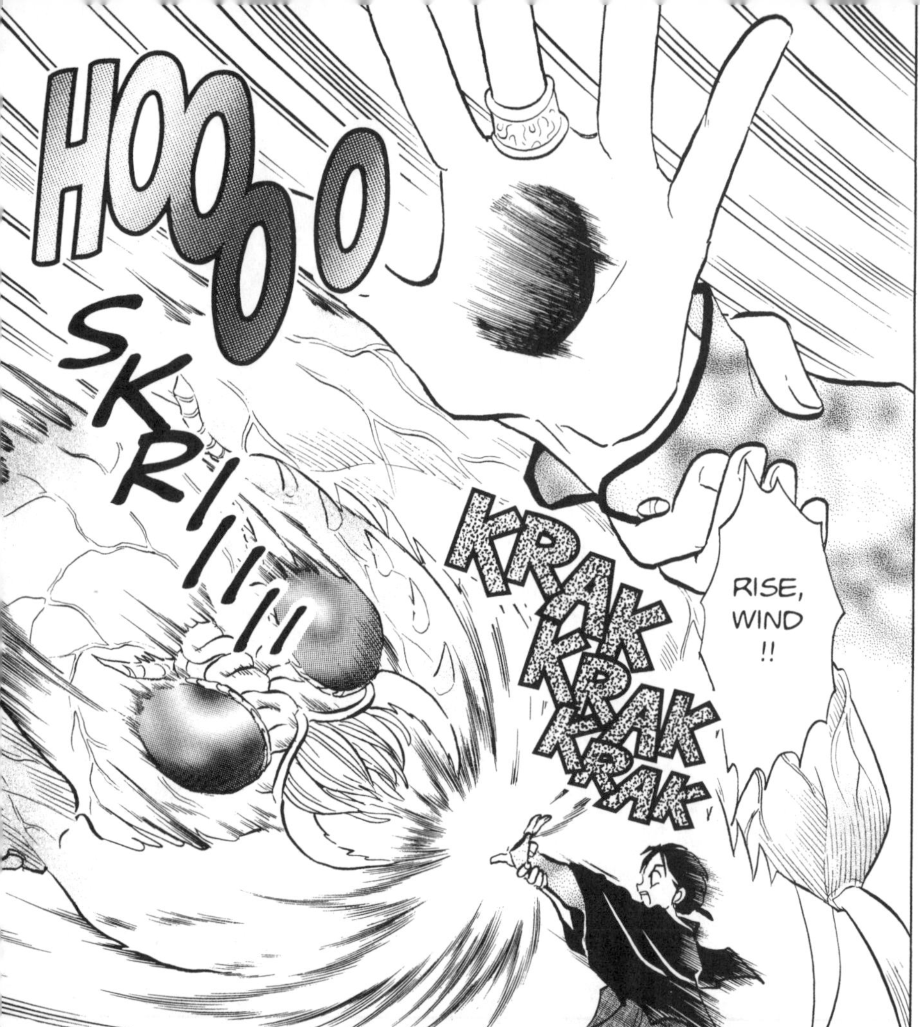
HOOOOO
SKRIIIIII
KRAK KRAK KRAK KRAK
RISE, WIND !!
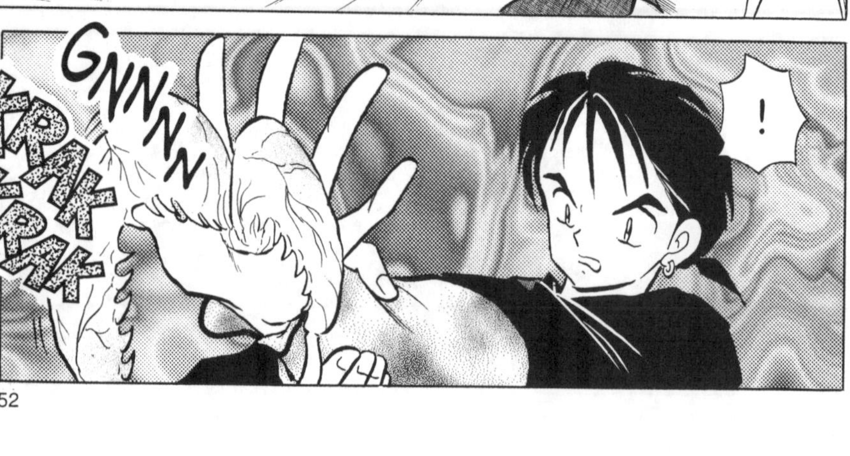
!
GNNNNN
KRAK KRAK

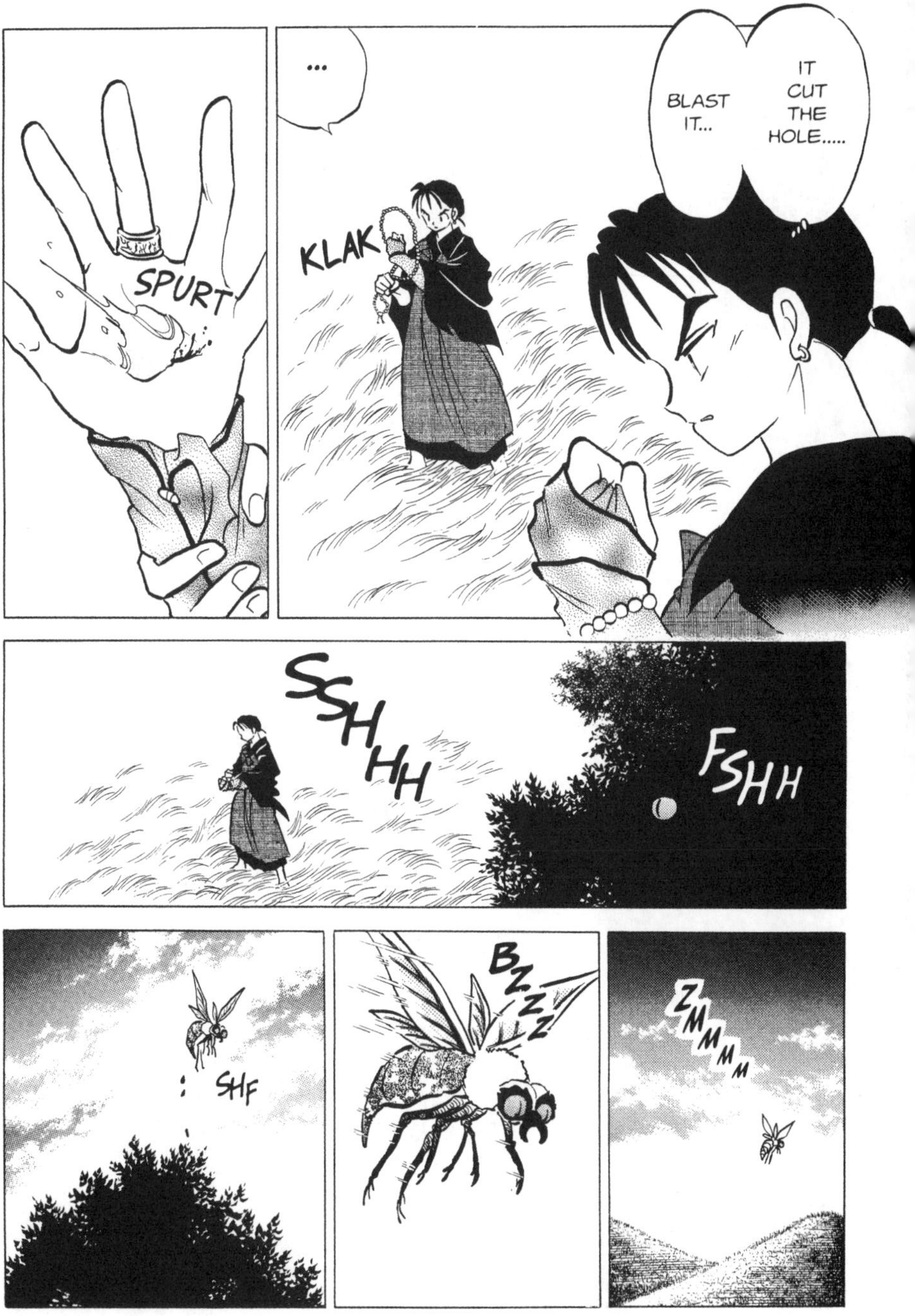
BLAST IT...
IT CUT THE HOLE.....
...
KLAK
SPURT
FSHH
SSHHHH
ZMMMM
BZZZ
SHF

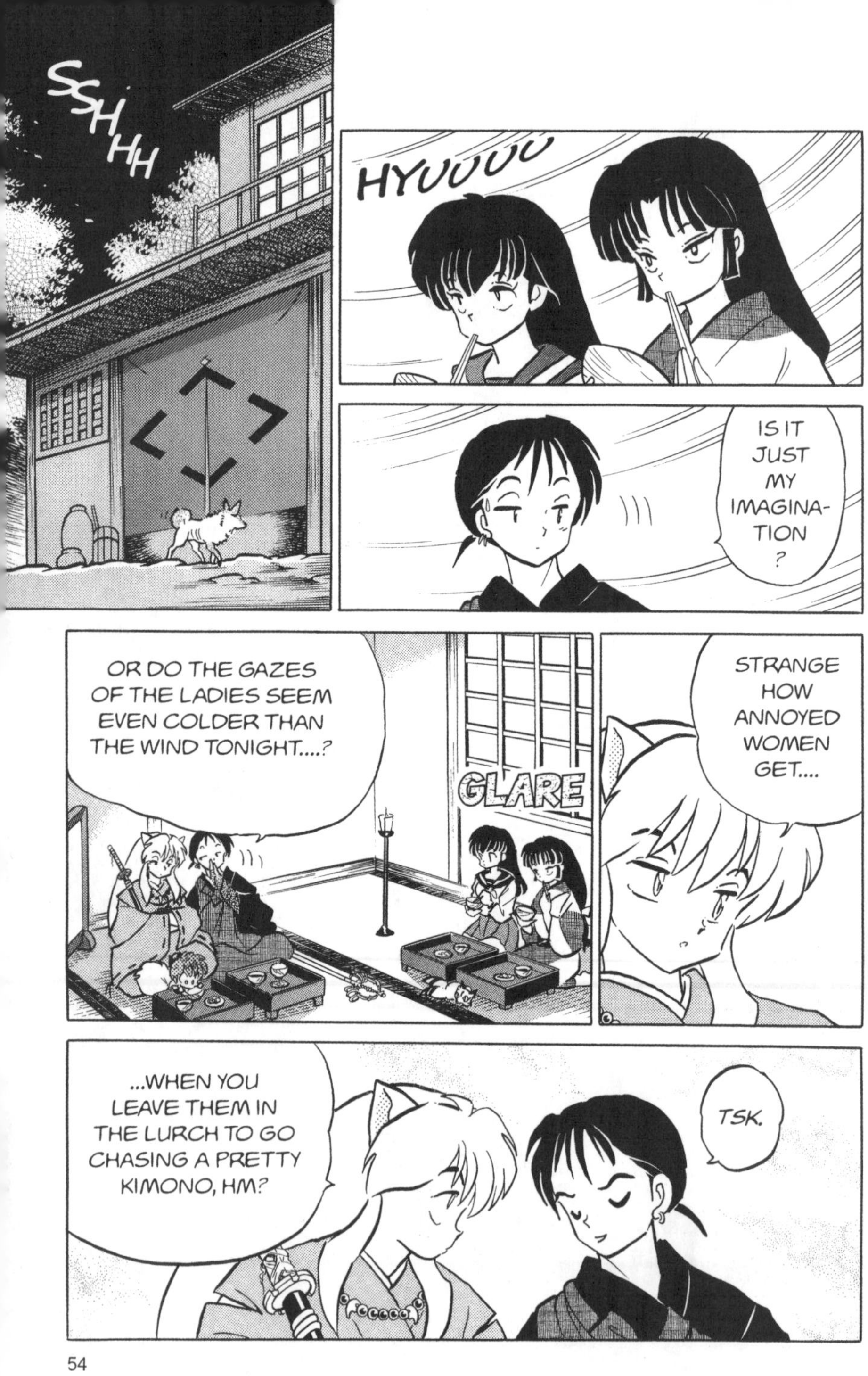
SSHHH
HYUUUU
IS IT JUST MY IMAGINATION?
OR DO THE GAZES OF THE LADIES SEEM EVEN COLDER THAN THE WIND TONIGHT....?
GLARE
STRANGE HOW ANNOYED WOMEN GET....
...WHEN YOU LEAVE THEM IN THE LURCH TO GO CHASING A PRETTY KIMONO, HM?
TSK.

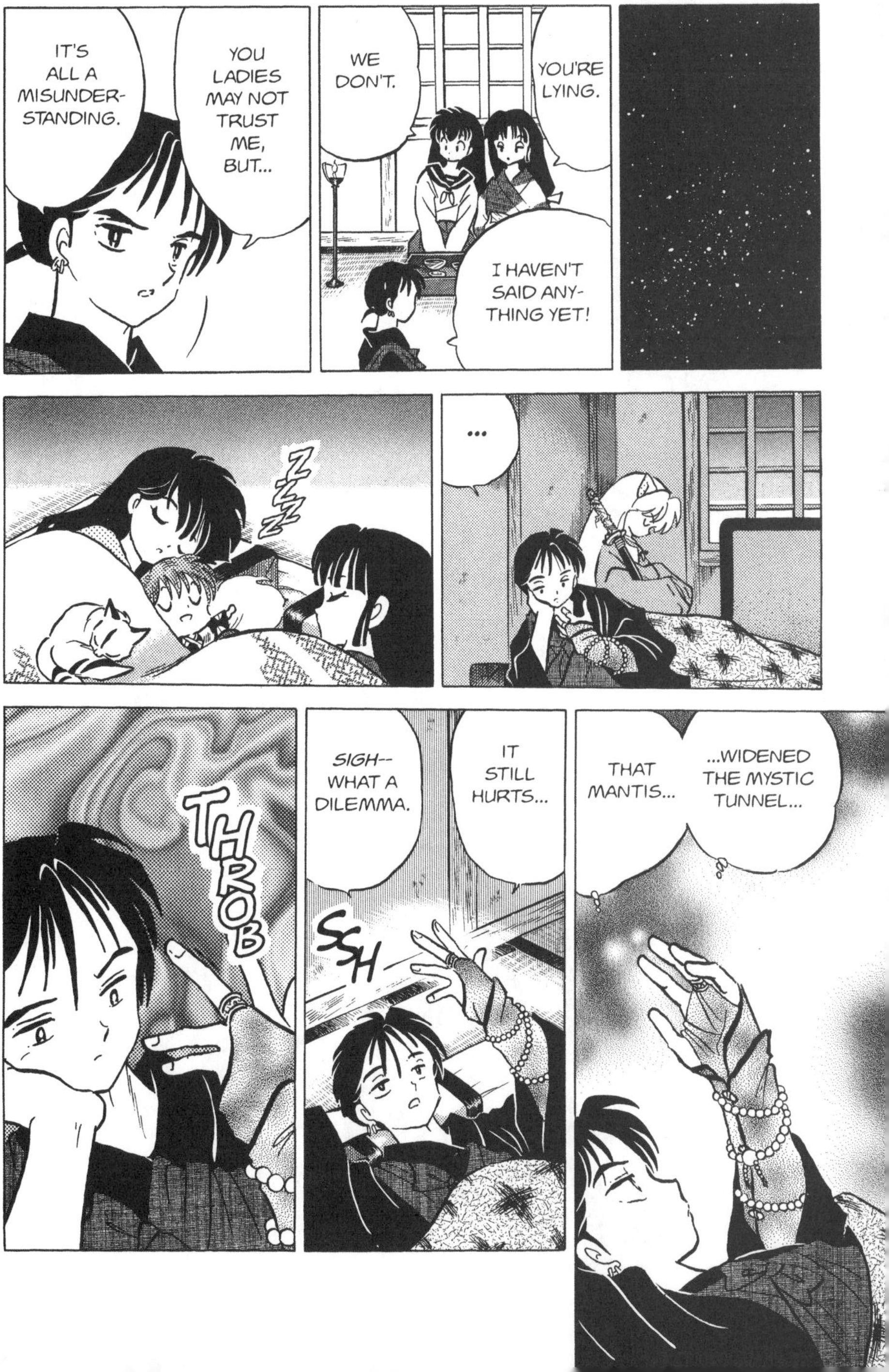
IT'S ALL A MISUNDER-STANDING.
YOU LADIES MAY NOT TRUST ME, BUT...
WE DON'T.
YOU'RE LYING.
I HAVEN'T SAID ANY-THING YET!
ZZZ
...
THROB
SIGH-- WHAT A DILEMMA.
IT STILL HURTS...
SSH
THAT MANTIS...
...WIDENED THE MYSTIC TUNNEL...

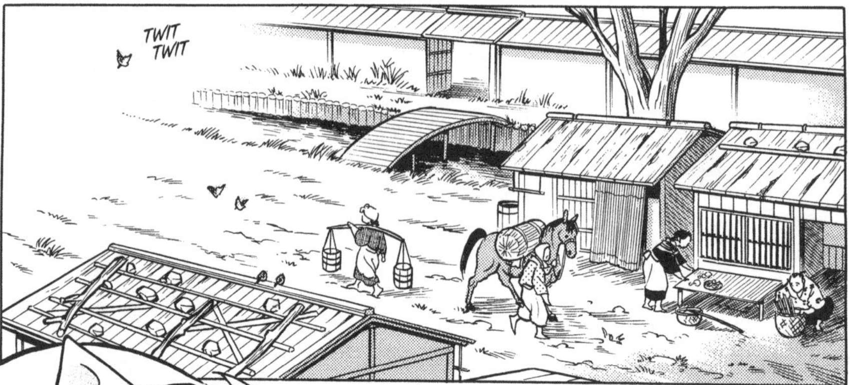
TWIT
TWIT

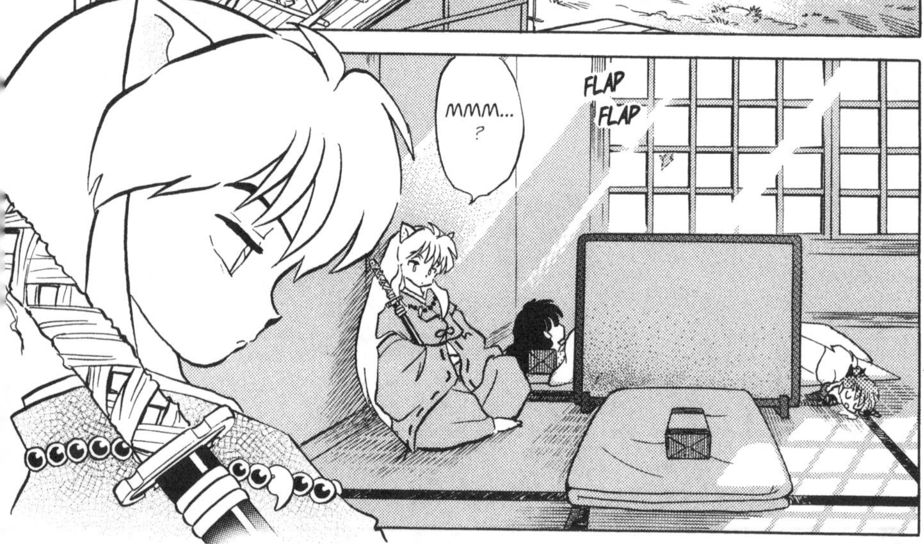
FLAP
FLAP
MMM... ?

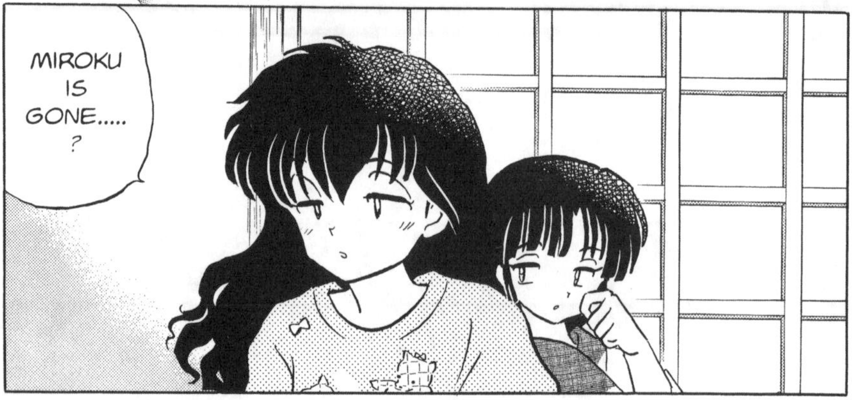
MIROKU IS GONE..... ?

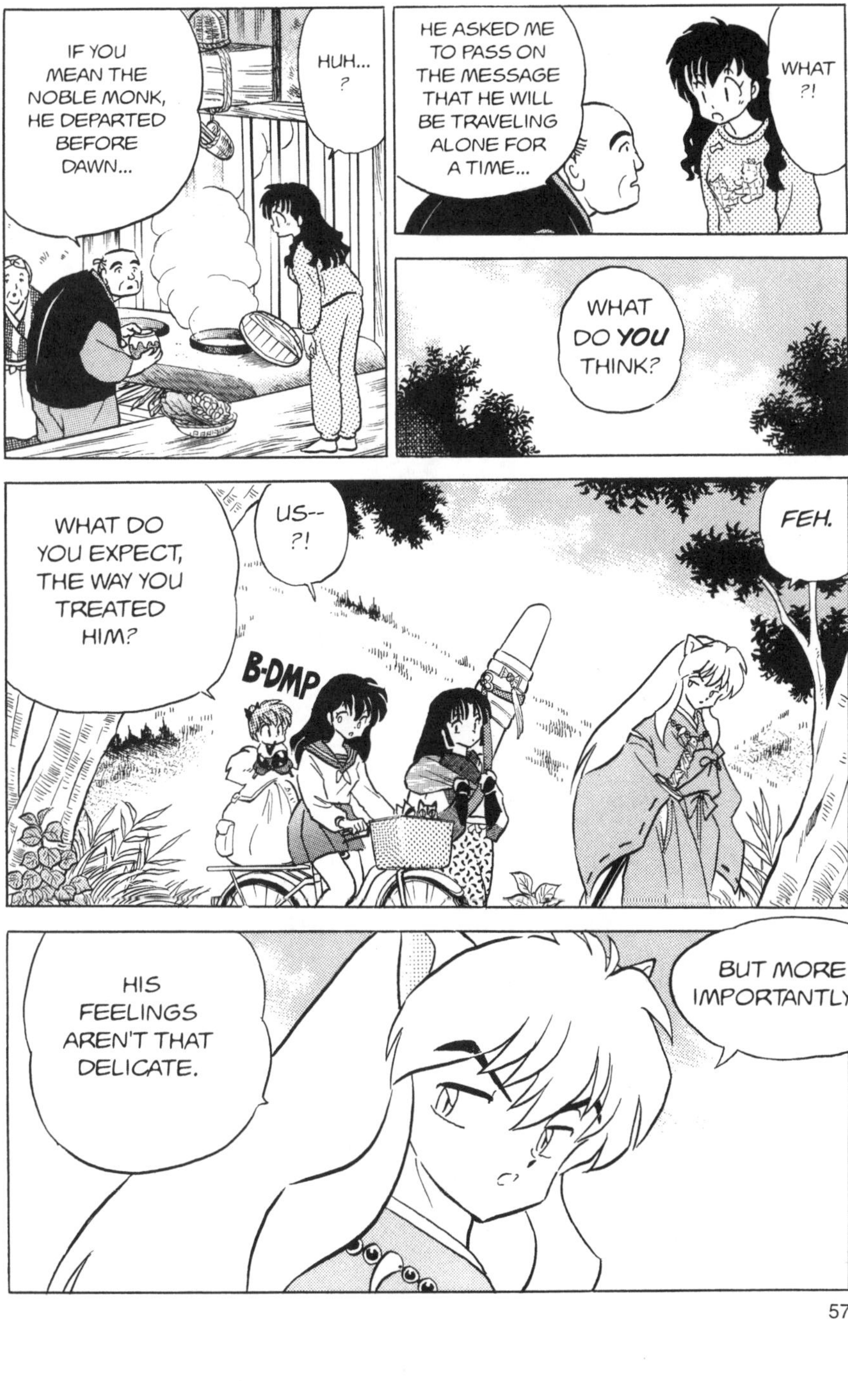
IF YOU MEAN THE NOBLE MONK, HE DEPARTED BEFORE DAWN...
HUH... ?
HE ASKED ME TO PASS ON THE MESSAGE THAT HE WILL BE TRAVELING ALONE FOR A TIME...
WHAT ?!
WHAT DO **YOU** THINK?
WHAT DO YOU EXPECT, THE WAY YOU TREATED HIM?
US-- ?!
B-DMP
FEH.
HIS FEELINGS AREN'T THAT DELICATE.
BUT MORE IMPORTANTLY....

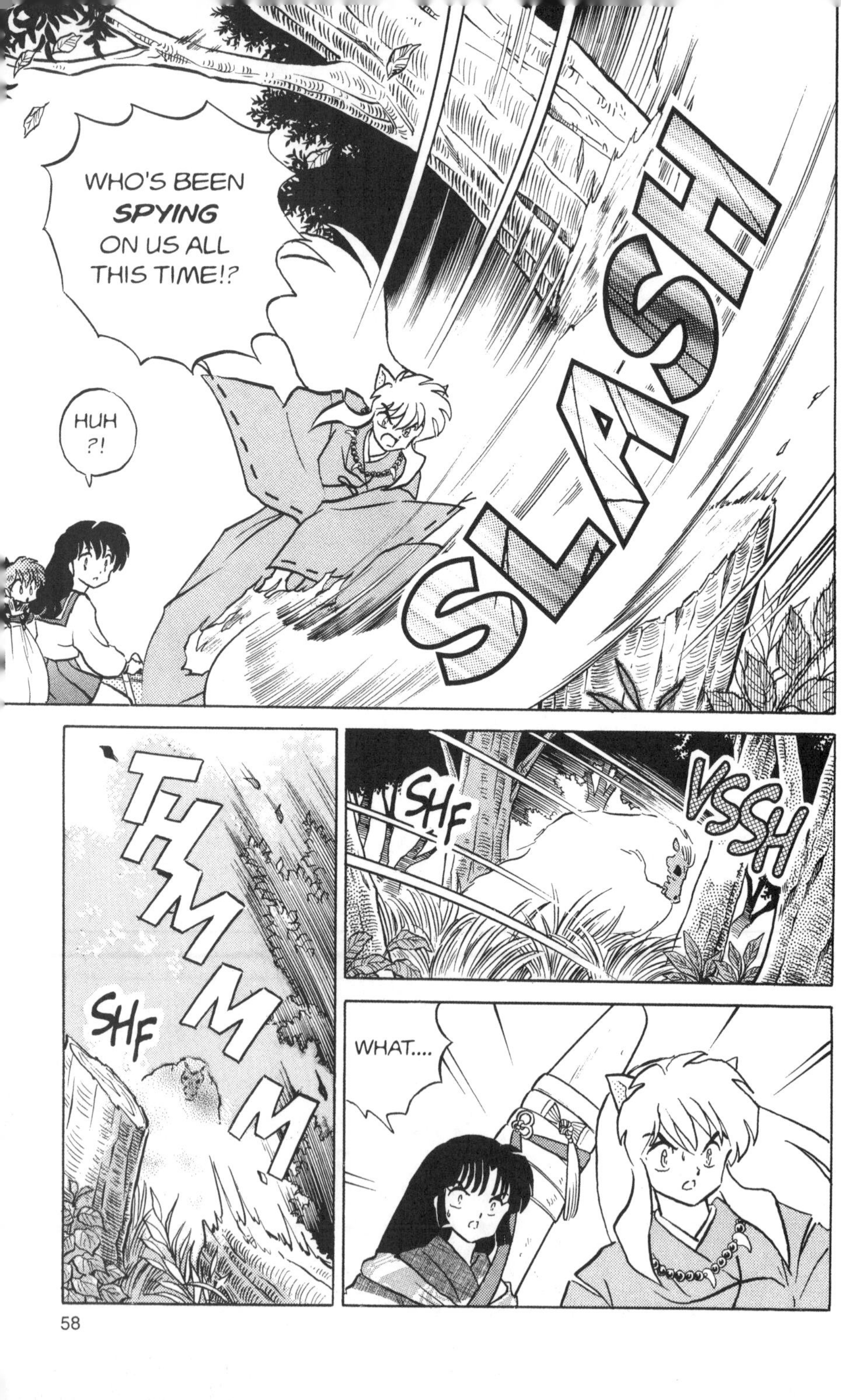
WHO'S BEEN **SPYING** ON US ALL THIS TIME!?
SLASH
HUH ?!
VSSH
SHF
WHAT....
THMMM
SHF

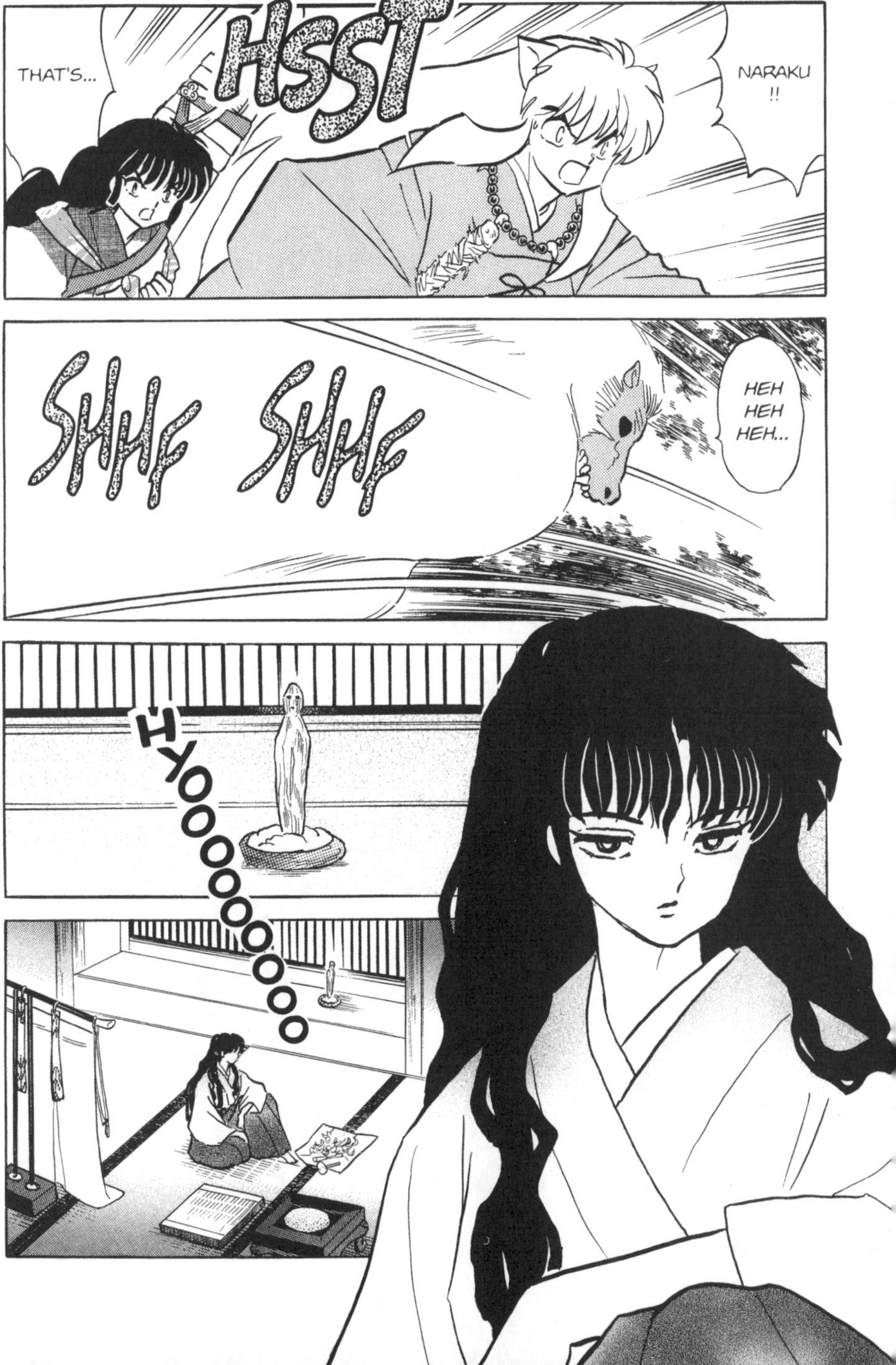
THAT'S...
HSST
NARAKU !!
SHHF SHHF
HEH HEH HEH...
HYOOOOOOOOOOOO

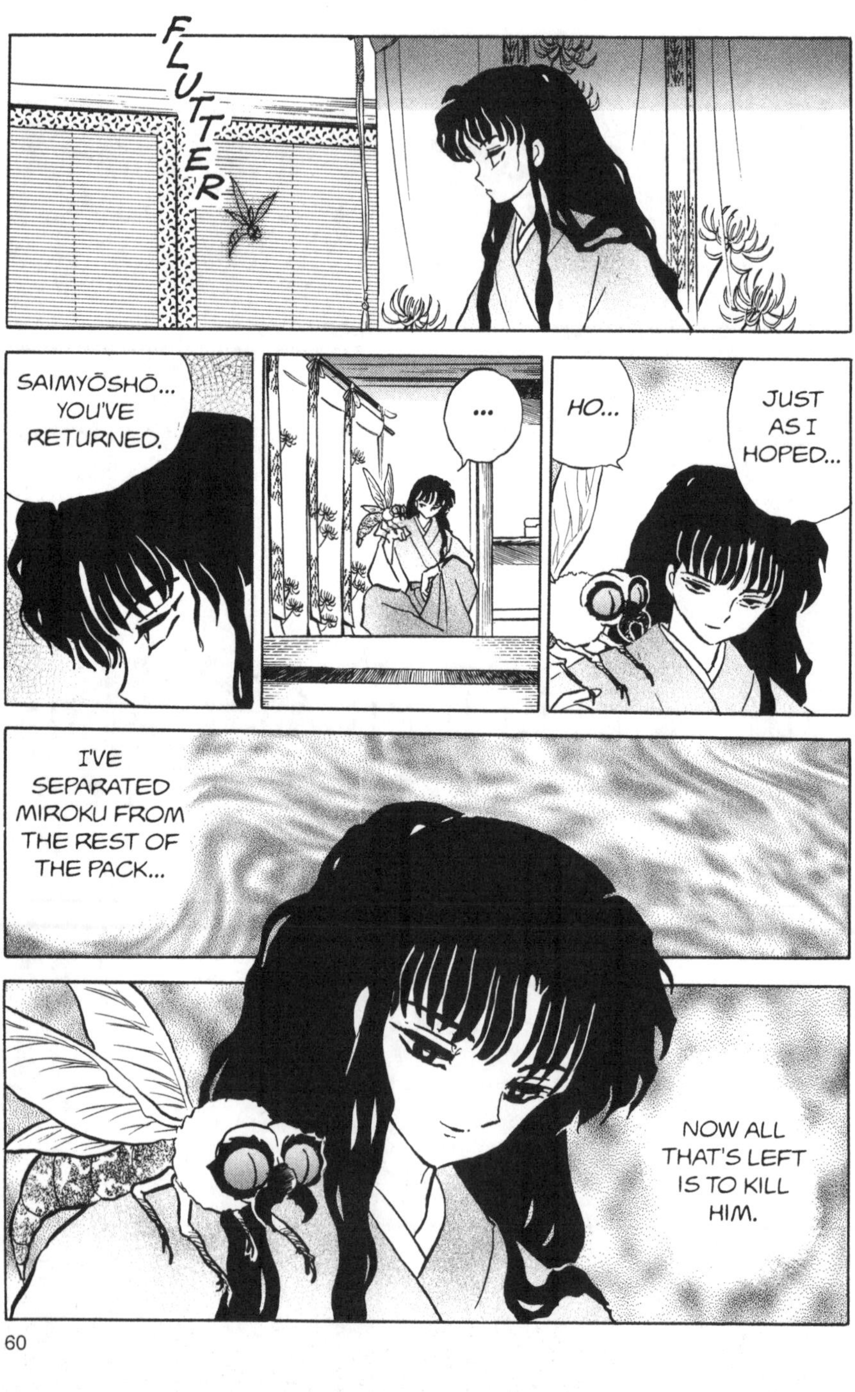
FLUTTER
SAIMYŌSHŌ... YOU'VE RETURNED.
...
HO...
JUST AS I HOPED...
I'VE SEPARATED MIROKU FROM THE REST OF THE PACK...
NOW ALL THAT'S LEFT IS TO KILL HIM.

SCROLL FOUR

THE TEMPLE OF INNOCENCE

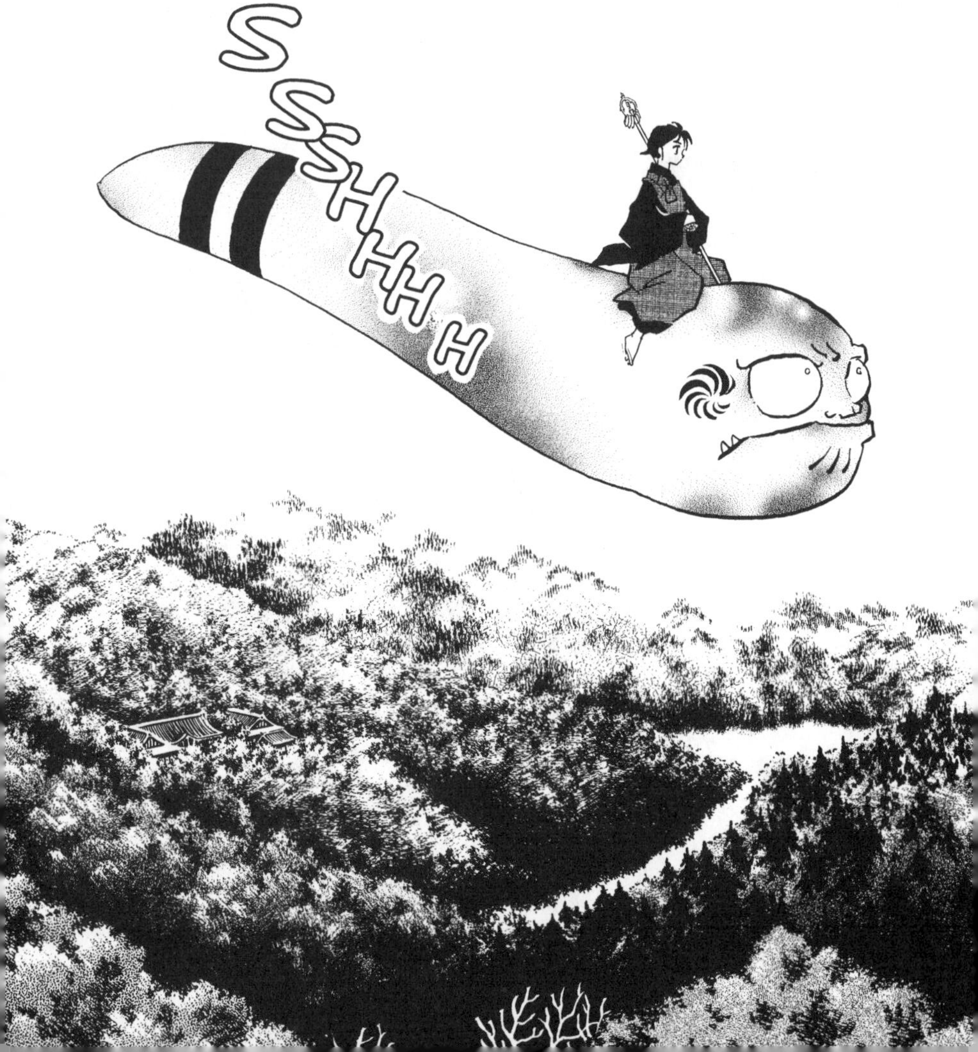
SSSHHHH

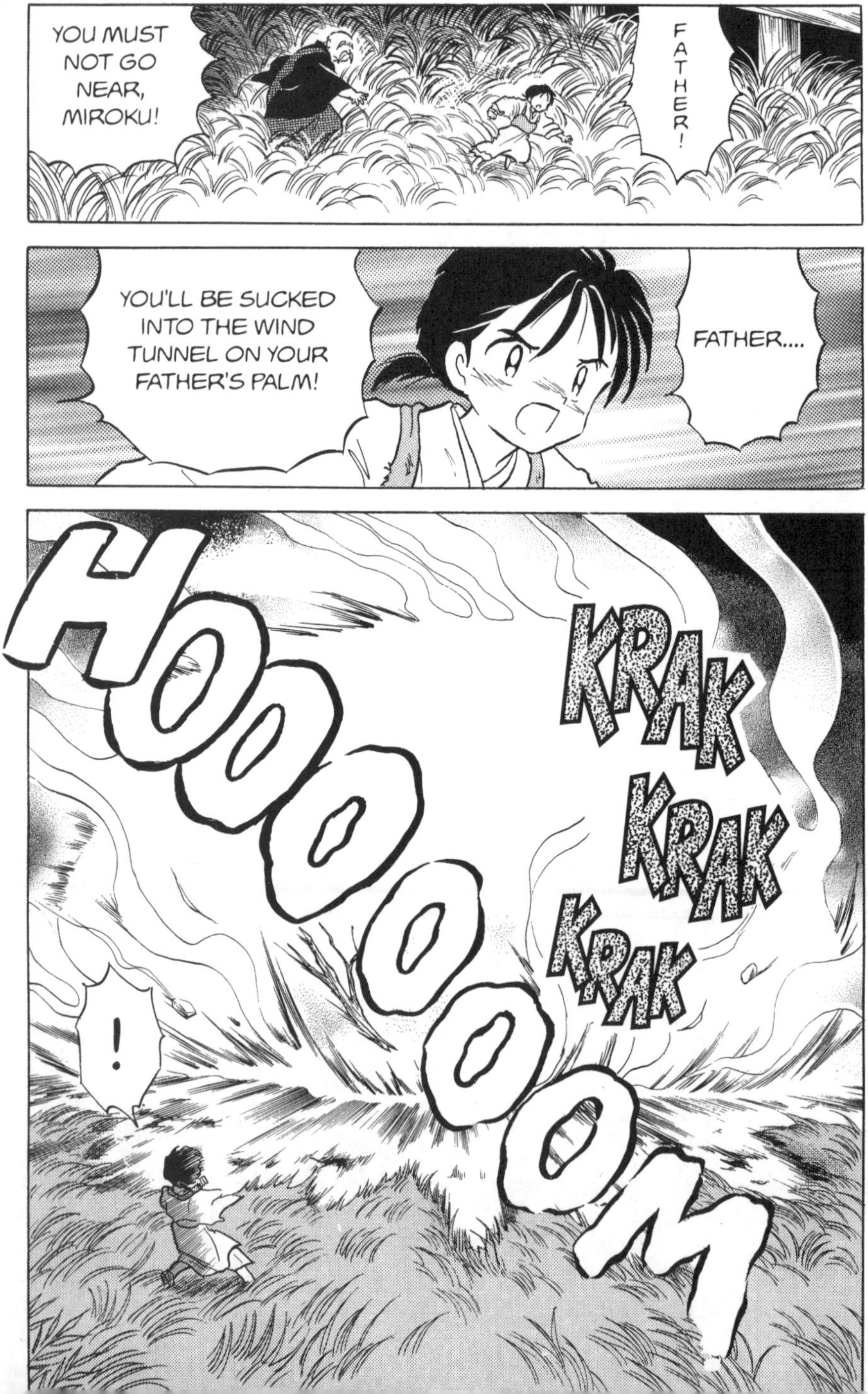
FATHER!
YOU MUST NOT GO NEAR, MIROKU!
FATHER....
YOU'LL BE SUCKED INTO THE WIND TUNNEL ON YOUR FATHER'S PALM!
KRAK KRAK KRAK
HOOOOOOM
!

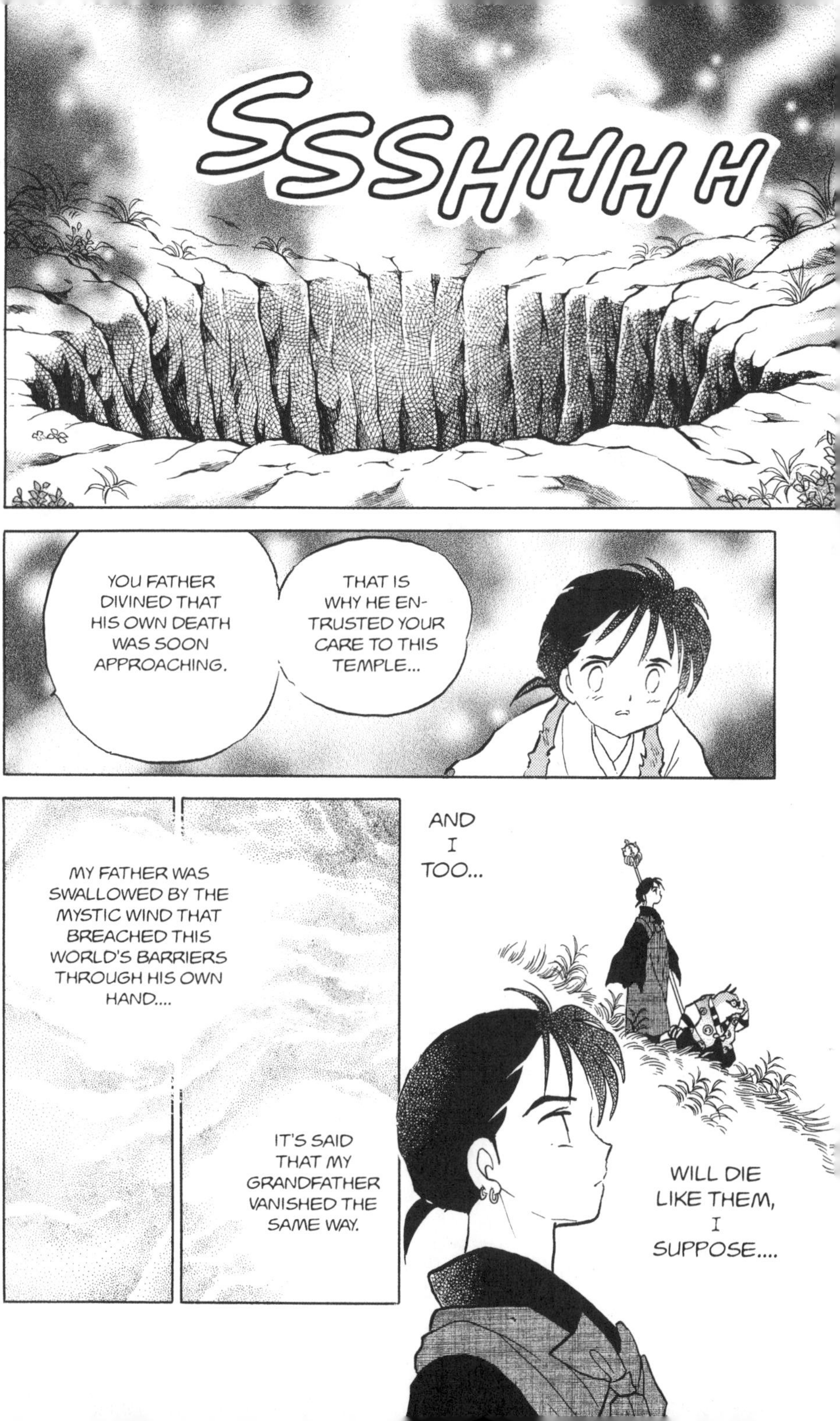
SSSHHH H
THAT IS WHY HE ENTRUSTED YOUR CARE TO THIS TEMPLE...
YOU FATHER DIVINED THAT HIS OWN DEATH WAS SOON APPROACHING.
AND I TOO...
WILL DIE LIKE THEM, I SUPPOSE....
MY FATHER WAS SWALLOWED BY THE MYSTIC WIND THAT BREACHED THIS WORLD'S BARRIERS THROUGH HIS OWN HAND....
IT'S SAID THAT MY GRANDFATHER VANISHED THE SAME WAY.

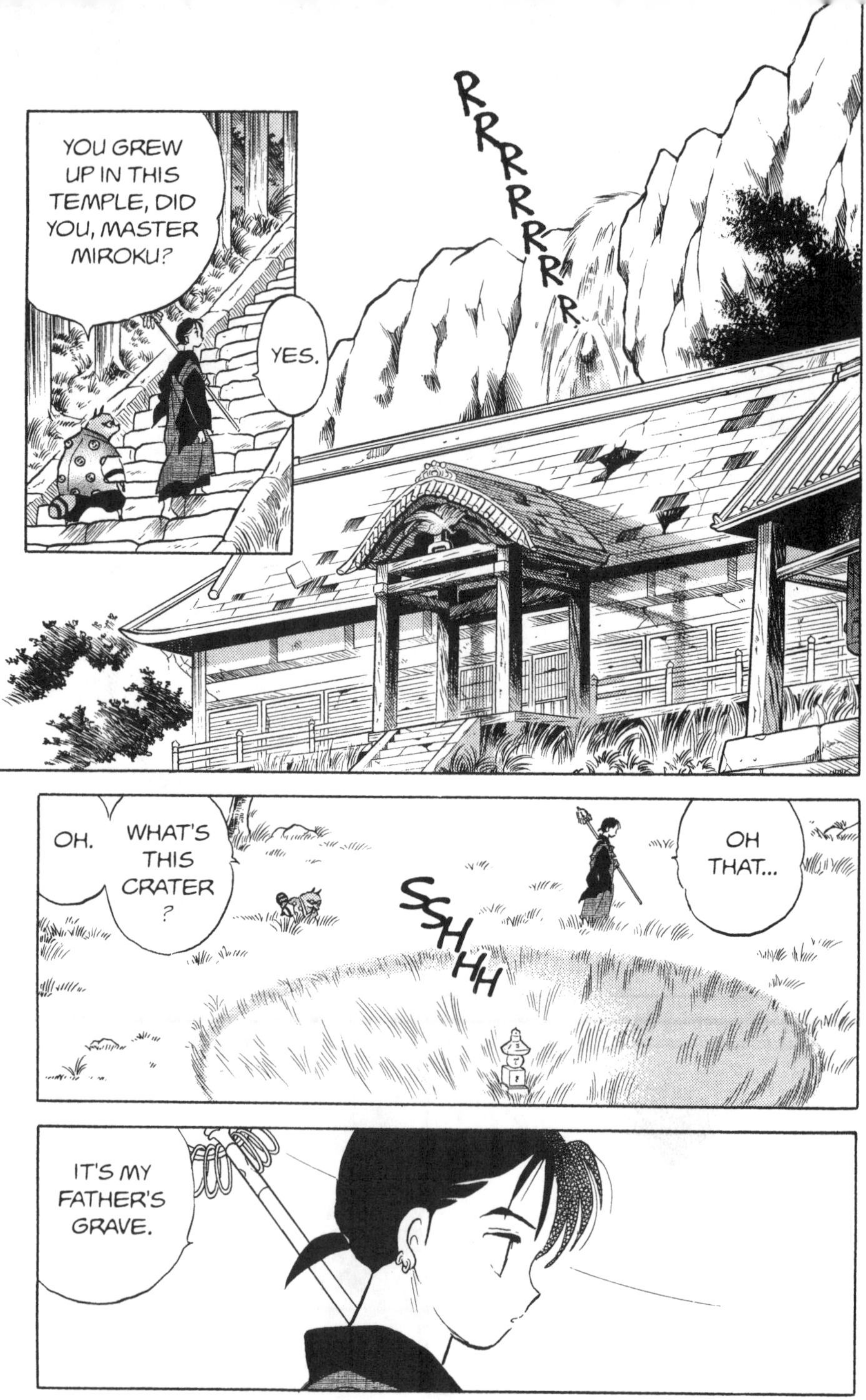
YOU GREW UP IN THIS TEMPLE, DID YOU, MASTER MIROKU?
YES.
RRRRRRRR
OH.
WHAT'S THIS CRATER?
SSHHH
OH THAT...
IT'S MY FATHER'S GRAVE.

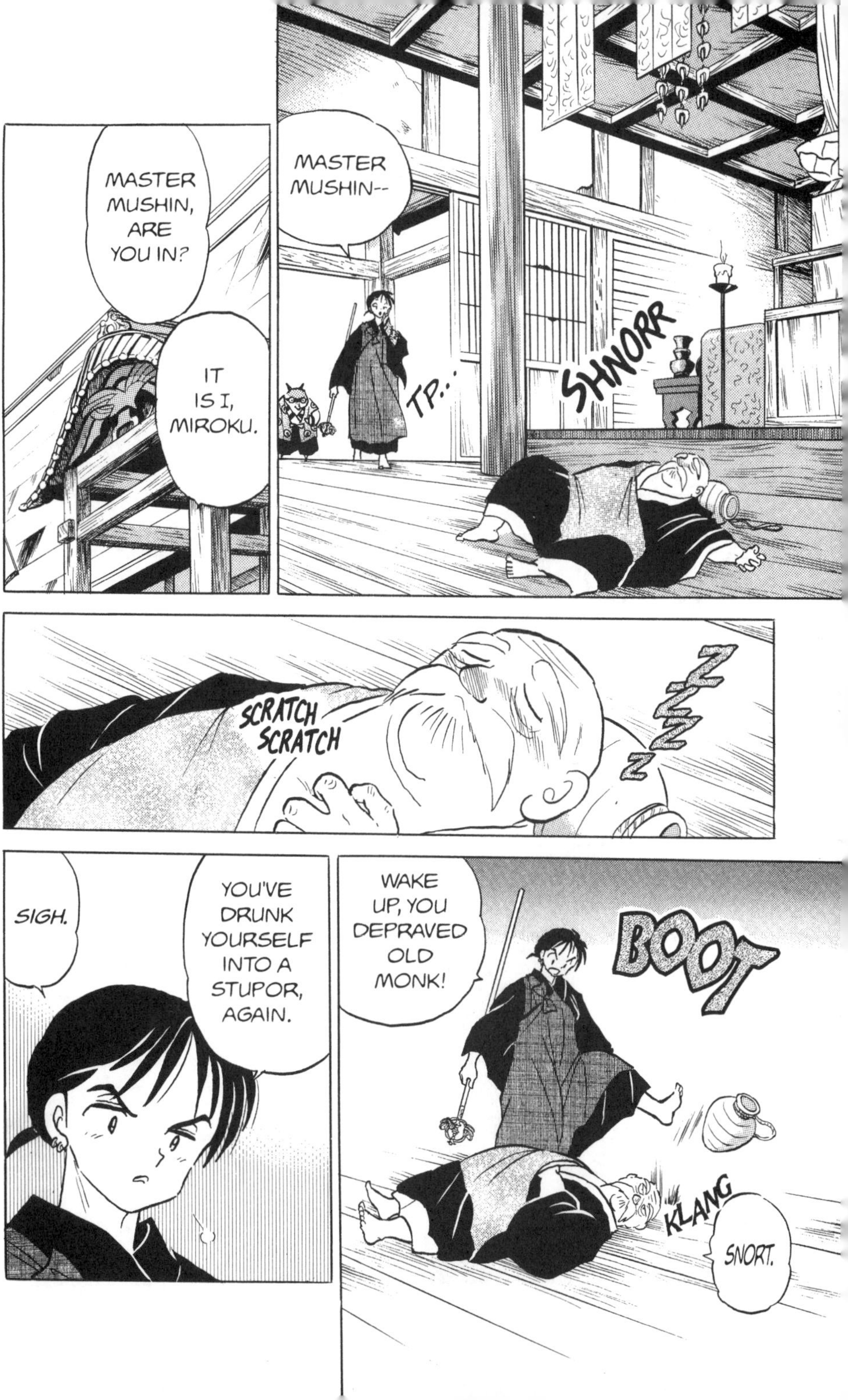
MASTER MUSHIN, ARE YOU IN?
IT IS I, MIROKU.
MASTER MUSHIN--
TP...
SHNORR
SCRATCH SCRATCH
ZZZZZ
SIGH.
YOU'VE DRUNK YOURSELF INTO A STUPOR, AGAIN.
WAKE UP, YOU DEPRAVED OLD MONK!
BOOT
KLANG
SNORT.

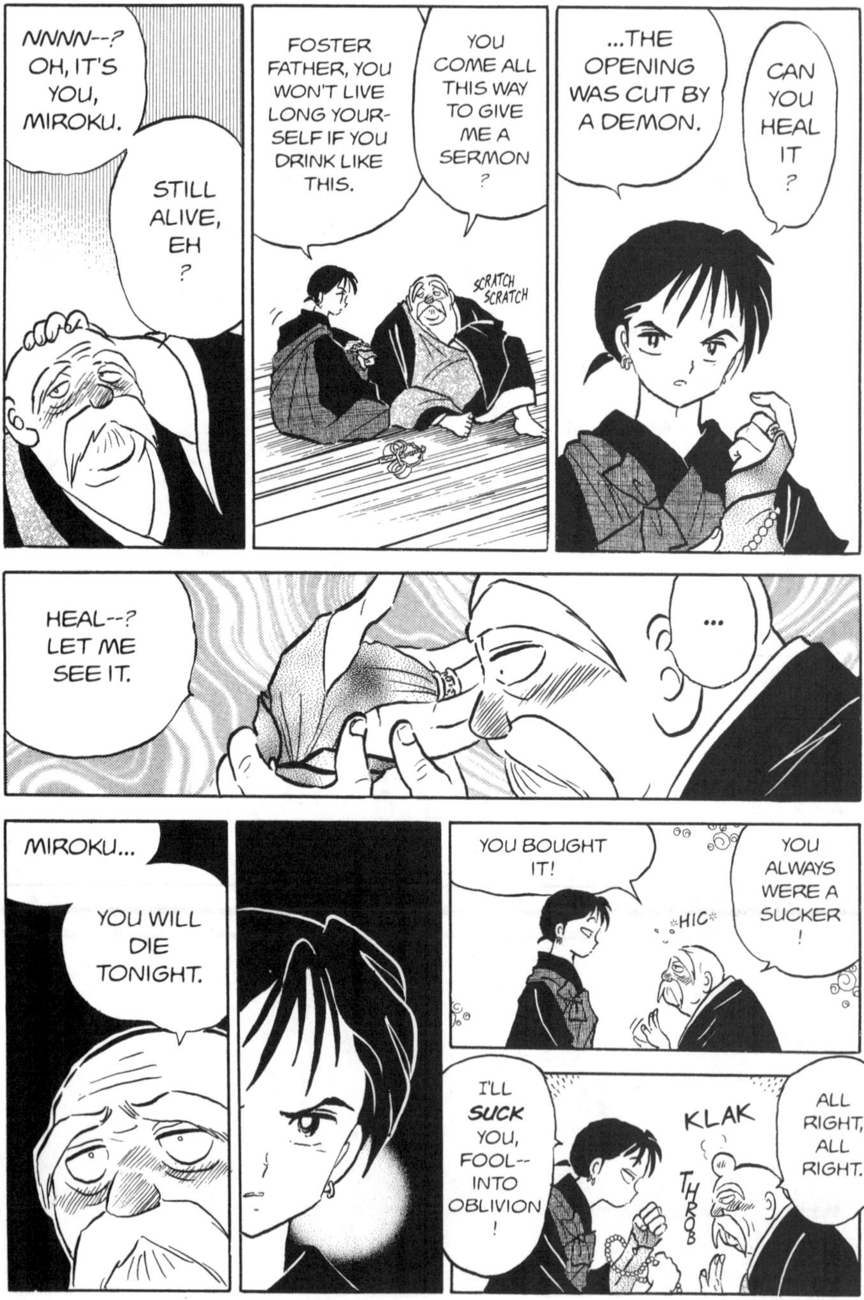
NNNN--? OH, IT'S YOU, MIROKU.
STILL ALIVE, EH ?
FOSTER FATHER, YOU WON'T LIVE LONG YOURSELF IF YOU DRINK LIKE THIS.
YOU COME ALL THIS WAY TO GIVE ME A SERMON ?
SCRATCH SCRATCH
...THE OPENING WAS CUT BY A DEMON.
CAN YOU HEAL IT ?
HEAL--? LET ME SEE IT.
...
MIROKU...
YOU WILL DIE TONIGHT.
YOU BOUGHT IT!
HIC
YOU ALWAYS WERE A SUCKER !
I'LL **SUCK** YOU, FOOL-- INTO OBLIVION !
KLAK
THROB
ALL RIGHT, ALL RIGHT.

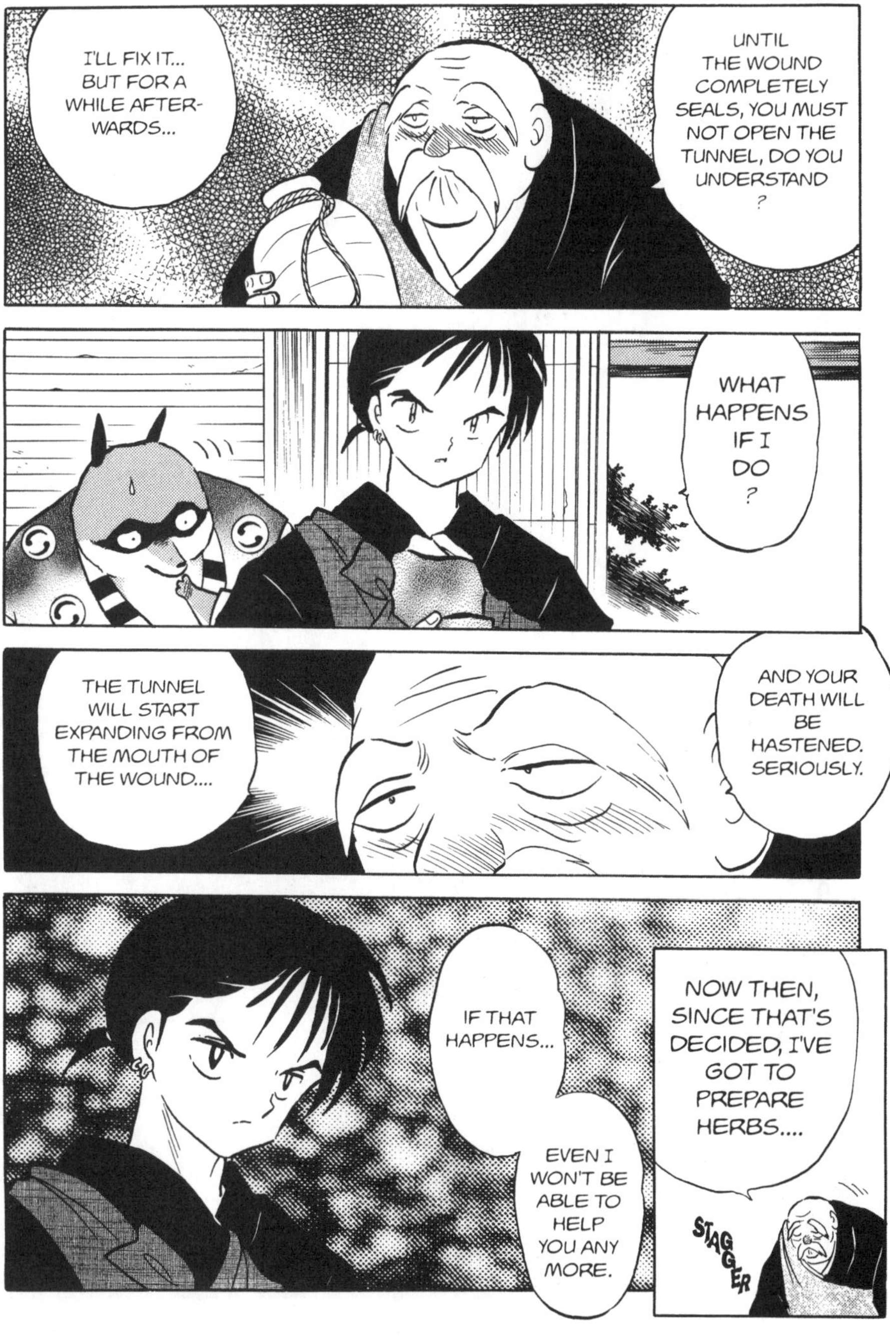
I'LL FIX IT... BUT FOR A WHILE AFTER-WARDS...
UNTIL THE WOUND COMPLETELY SEALS, YOU MUST NOT OPEN THE TUNNEL, DO YOU UNDERSTAND ?
WHAT HAPPENS IF I DO ?
THE TUNNEL WILL START EXPANDING FROM THE MOUTH OF THE WOUND....
AND YOUR DEATH WILL BE HASTENED. SERIOUSLY.
IF THAT HAPPENS...
EVEN I WON'T BE ABLE TO HELP YOU ANY MORE.
NOW THEN, SINCE THAT'S DECIDED, I'VE GOT TO PREPARE HERBS....
STAGGER

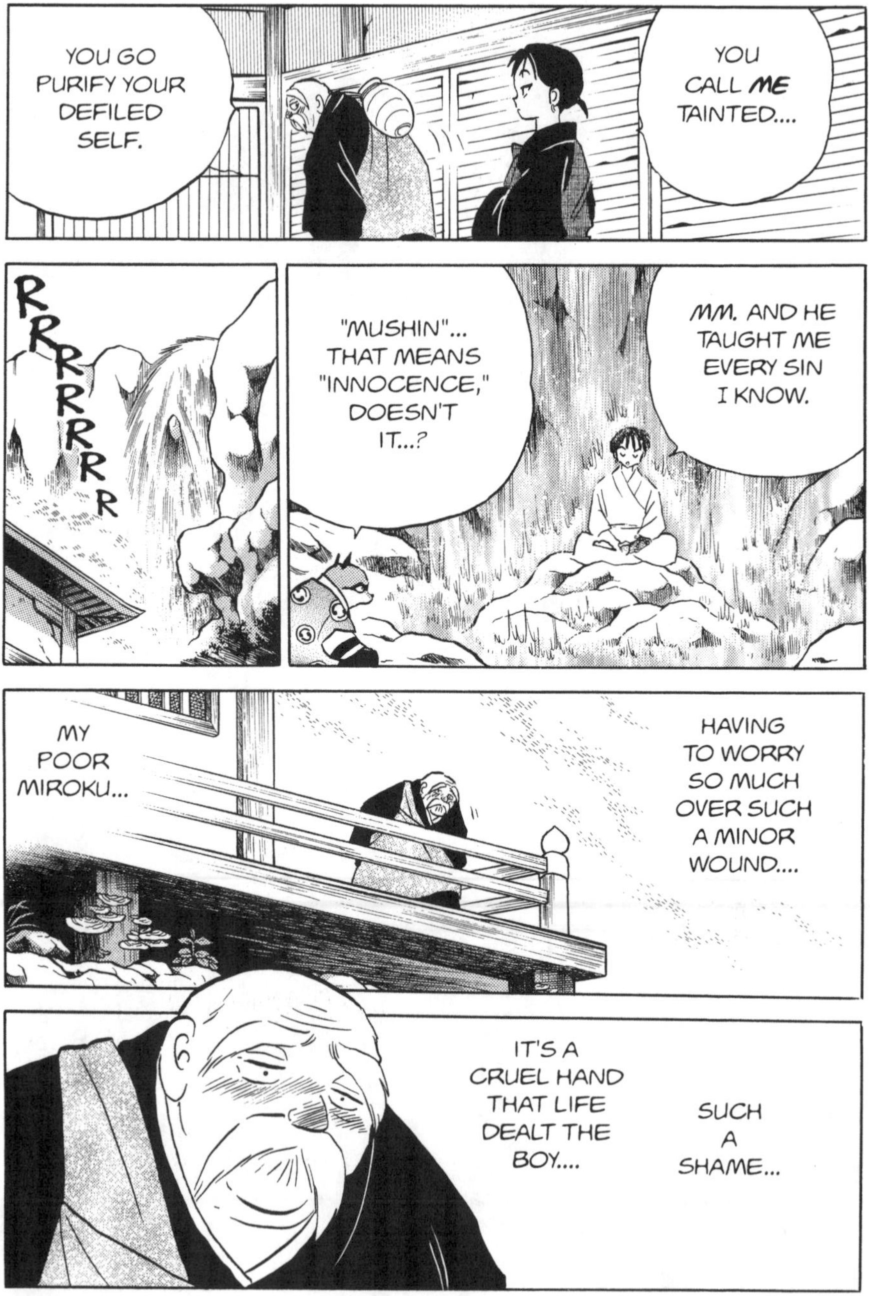
YOU GO PURIFY YOUR DEFILED SELF.
YOU CALL **ME** TAINTED....
RRRRRRR
"MUSHIN"... THAT MEANS "INNOCENCE," DOESN'T IT...?
MM. AND HE TAUGHT ME EVERY SIN I KNOW.
MY POOR MIROKU...
HAVING TO WORRY SO MUCH OVER SUCH A MINOR WOUND....
IT'S A CRUEL HAND THAT LIFE DEALT THE BOY....
SUCH A SHAME...

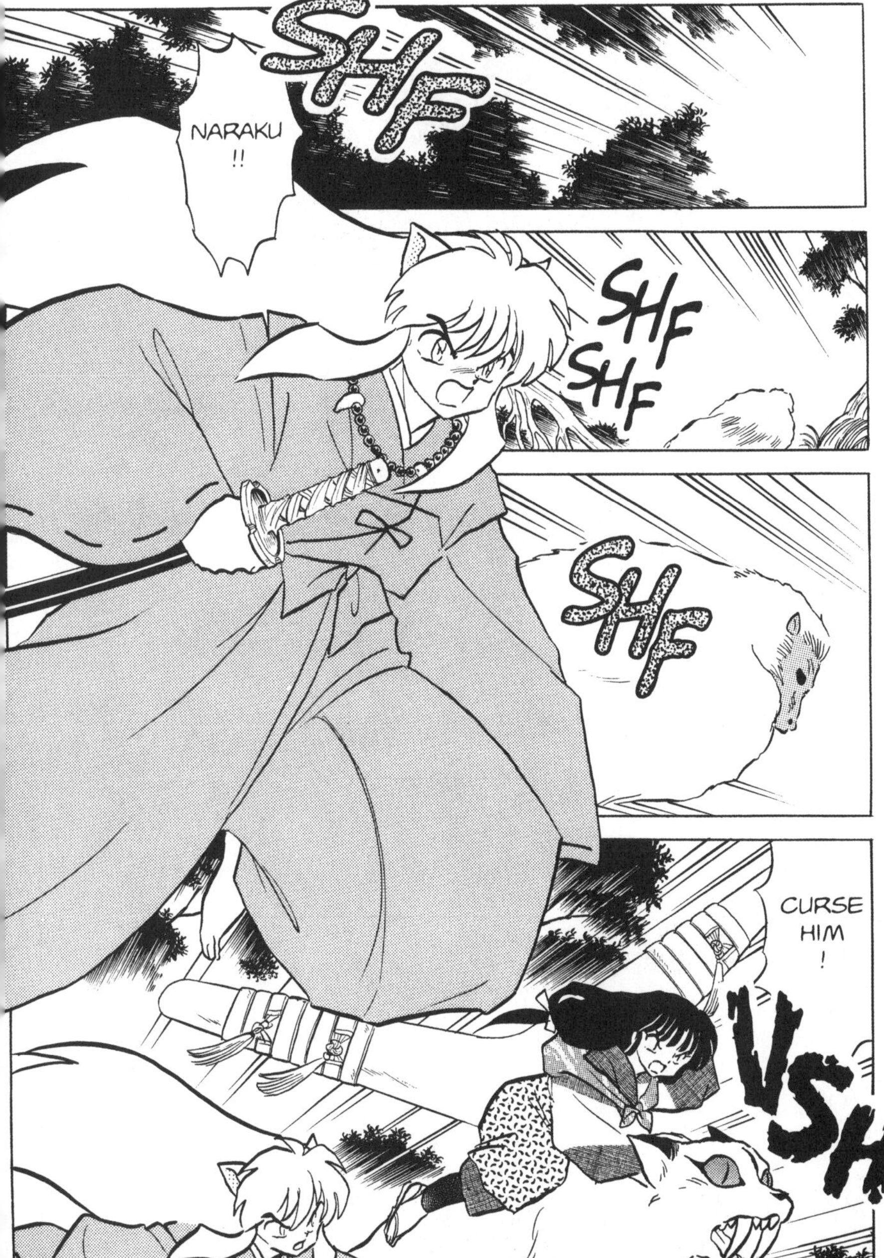
SHF
NARAKU !!
SHF SHF
SHF
CURSE HIM !
VSH

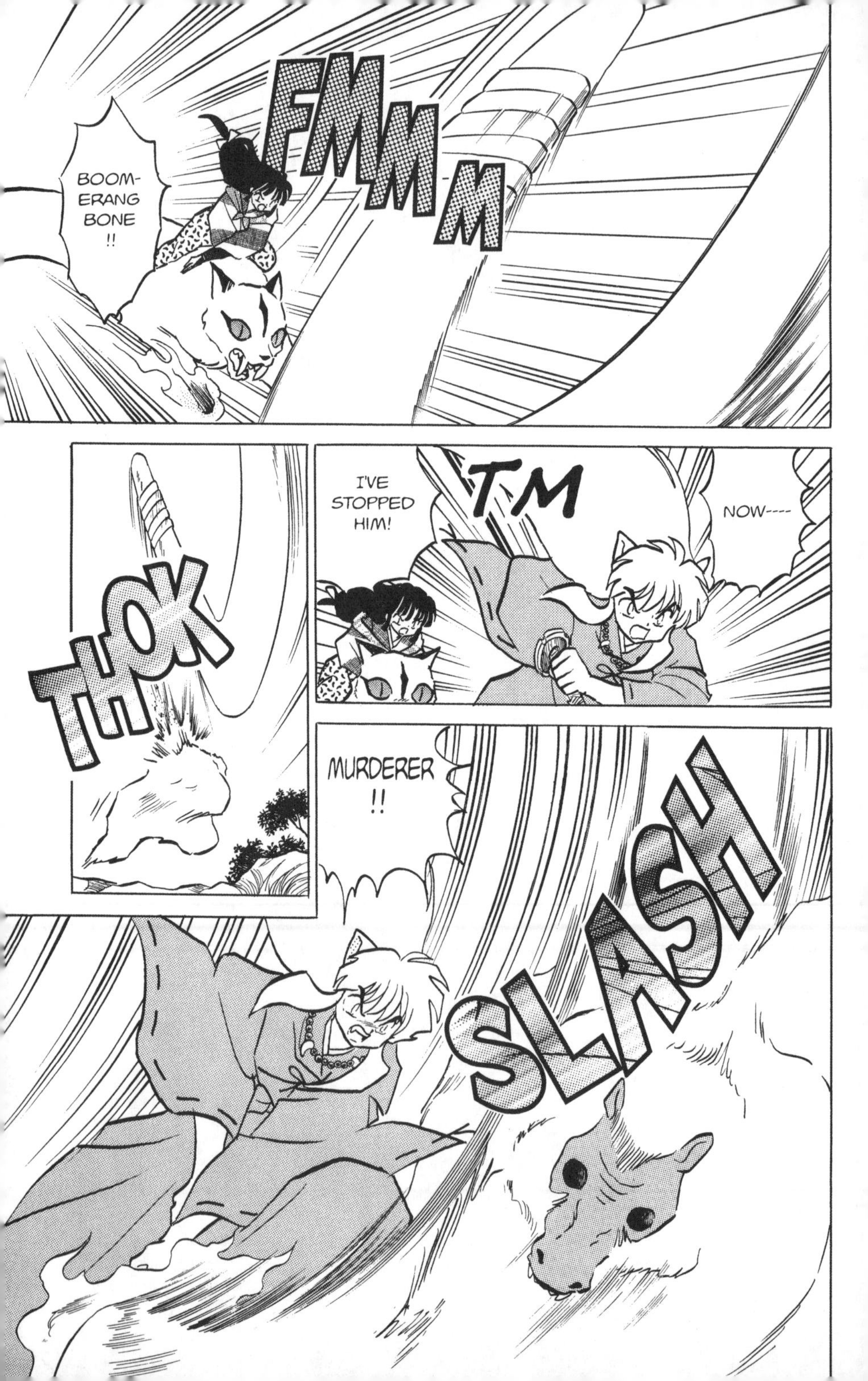
BOOM-
ERANG
BONE
!!
FMMMM
NOW----
TM
I'VE
STOPPED
HIM!
SLASH
MURDERER
!!
THOK

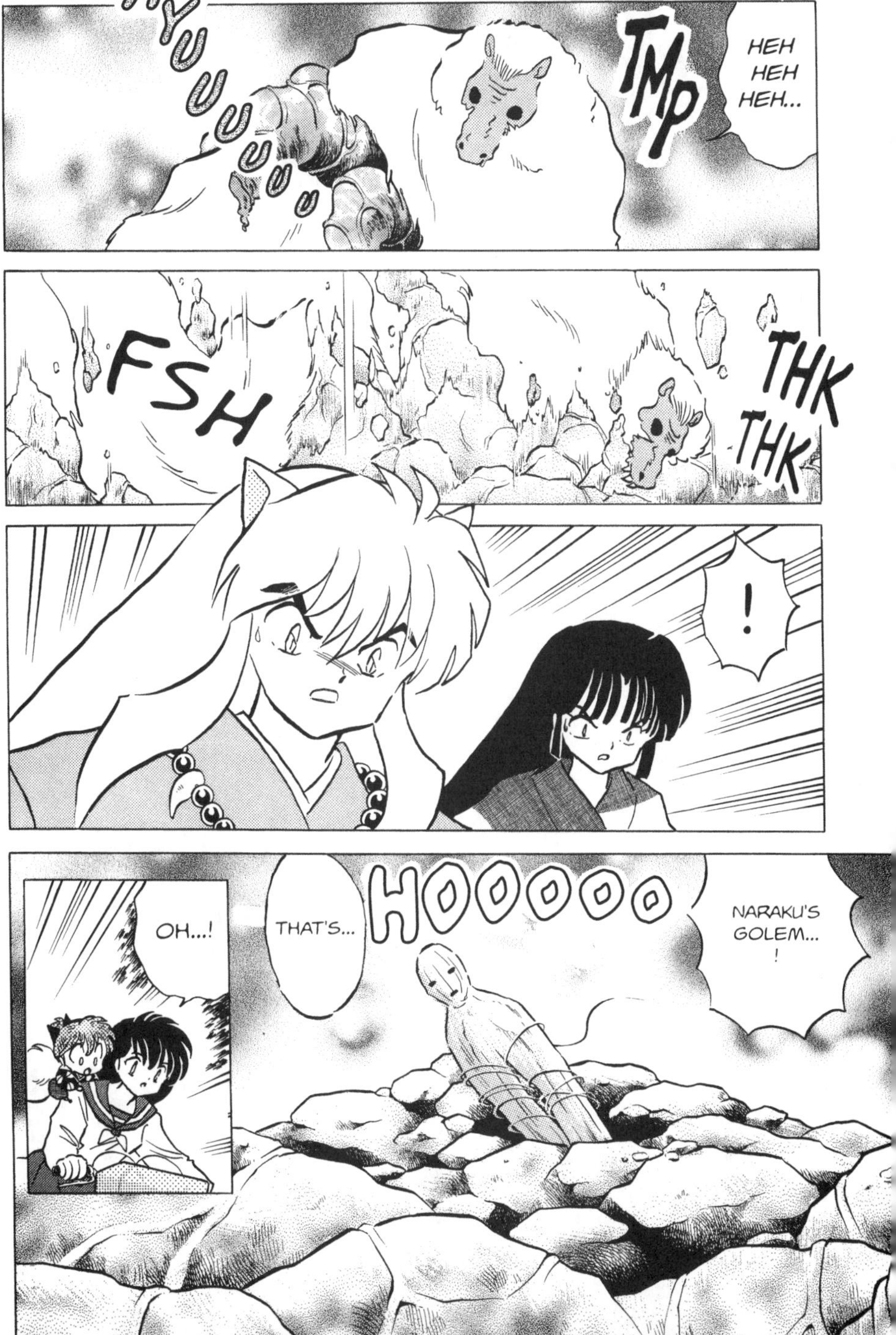
HEH HEH HEH...
TMP
HYUUUUUUU
THK THK
FSH
!
NARAKU'S GOLEM... !
HOOOOO
THAT'S...
OH...!

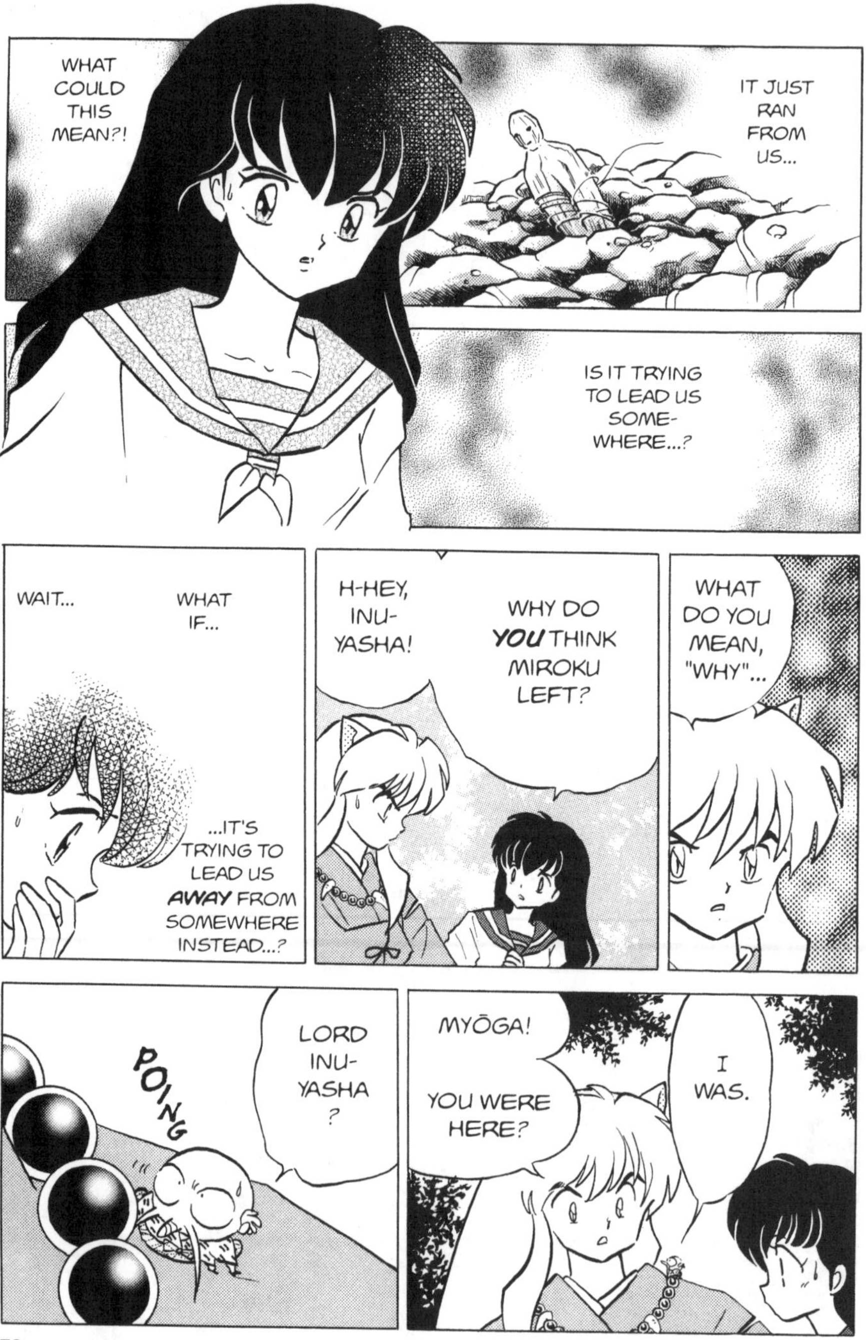
WHAT COULD THIS MEAN?!
IT JUST RAN FROM US...
IS IT TRYING TO LEAD US SOME- WHERE...?
WAIT...
WHAT IF...
...IT'S TRYING TO LEAD US AWAY FROM SOMEWHERE INSTEAD...?
H-HEY, INU- YASHA!
WHY DO YOU THINK MIROKU LEFT?
WHAT DO YOU MEAN, "WHY"...
POING
LORD INU- YASHA ?
MYŌGA!
YOU WERE HERE?
I WAS.

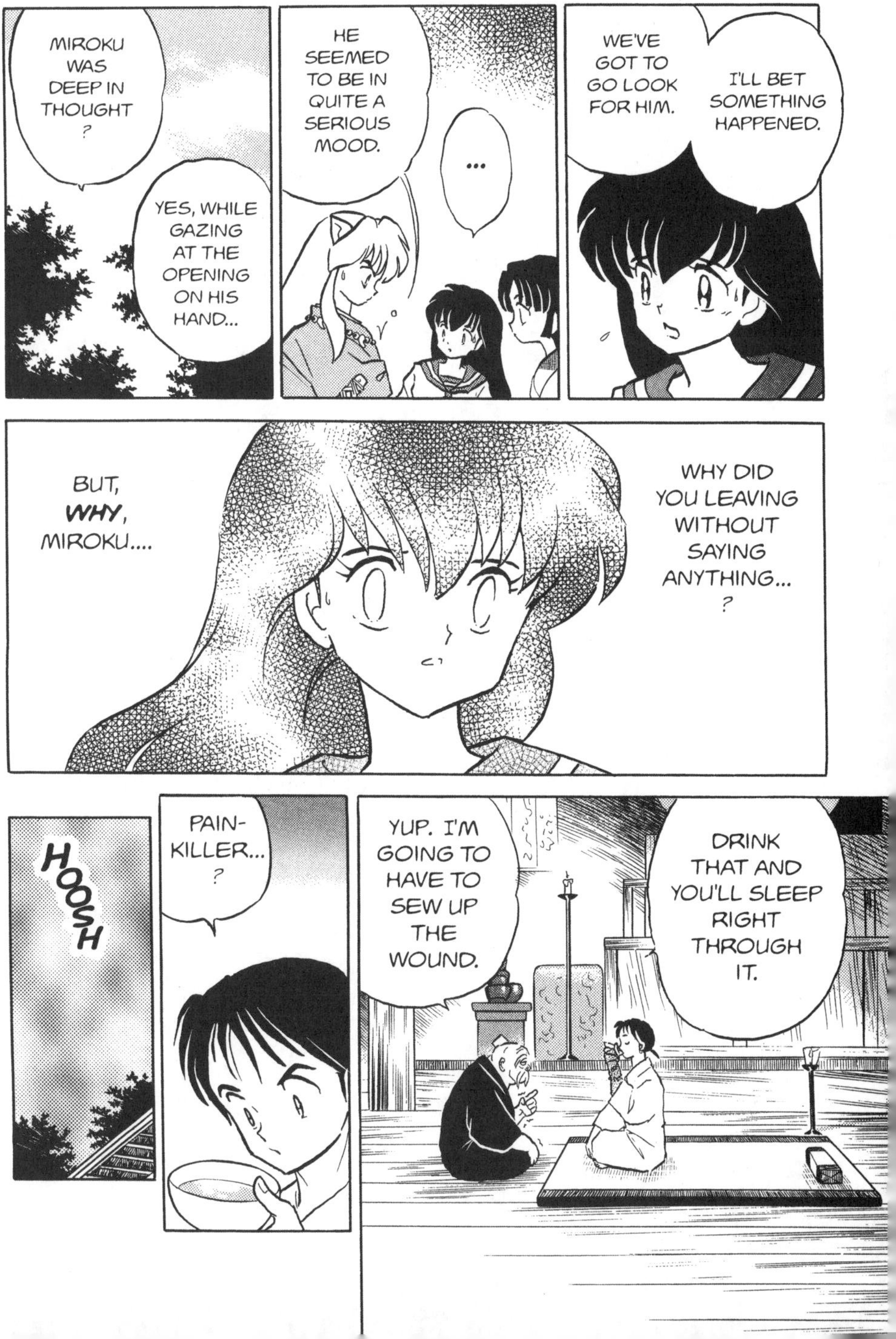
MIROKU WAS DEEP IN THOUGHT?
YES, WHILE GAZING AT THE OPENING ON HIS HAND...
HE SEEMED TO BE IN QUITE A SERIOUS MOOD.
...
WE'VE GOT TO GO LOOK FOR HIM.
I'LL BET SOMETHING HAPPENED.
BUT, *WHY*, MIROKU....
WHY DID YOU LEAVING WITHOUT SAYING ANYTHING...?
HOOSH
PAIN-KILLER...?
YUP. I'M GOING TO HAVE TO SEW UP THE WOUND.
DRINK THAT AND YOU'LL SLEEP RIGHT THROUGH IT.

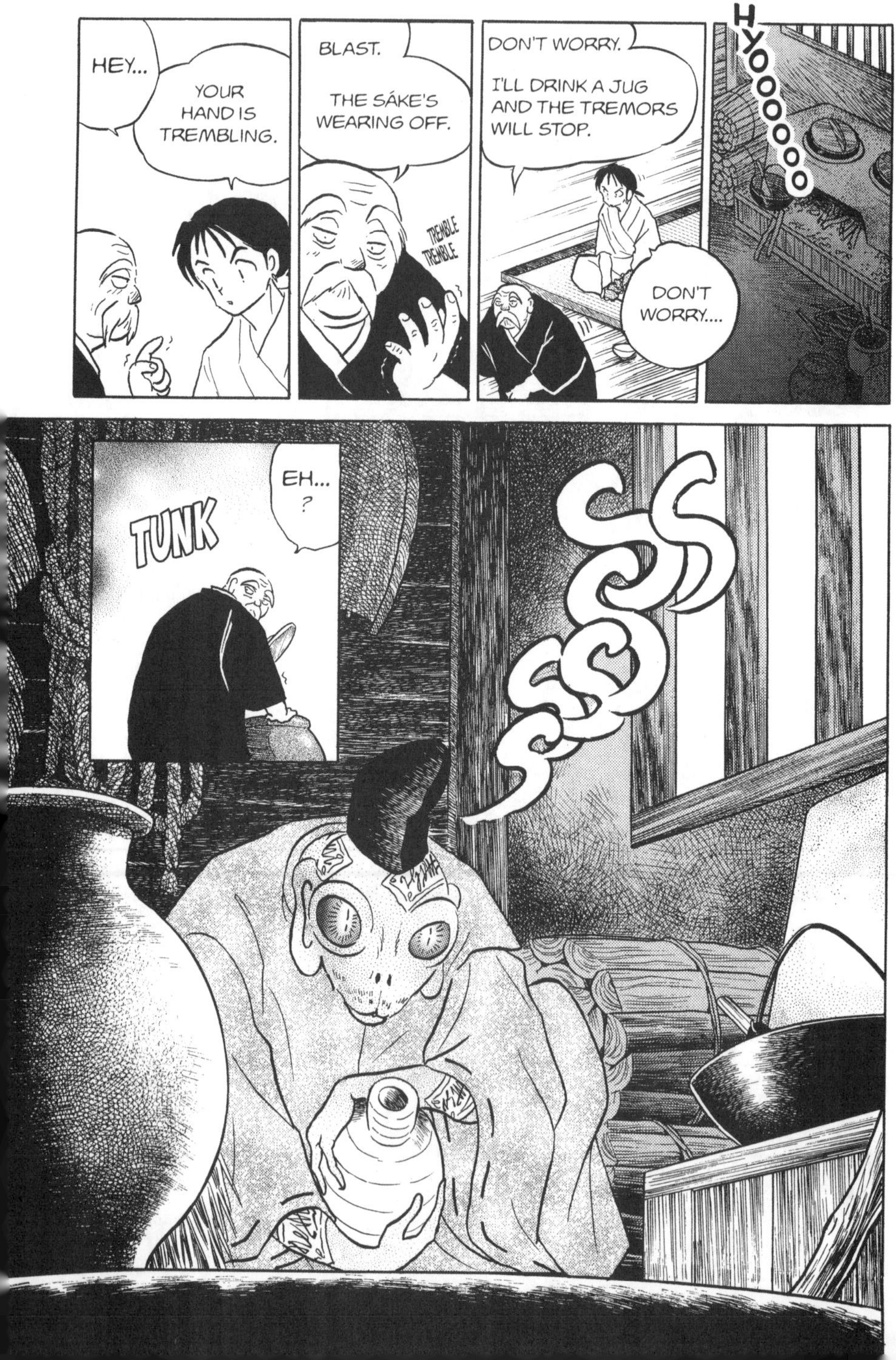
HEY...
YOUR HAND IS TREMBLING.
BLAST.
THE SÁKE'S WEARING OFF.
TREMBLE TREMBLE
DON'T WORRY.
I'LL DRINK A JUG AND THE TREMORS WILL STOP.
DON'T WORRY....
HYOOOOOO
TUNK
EH... ?
SSSSSS

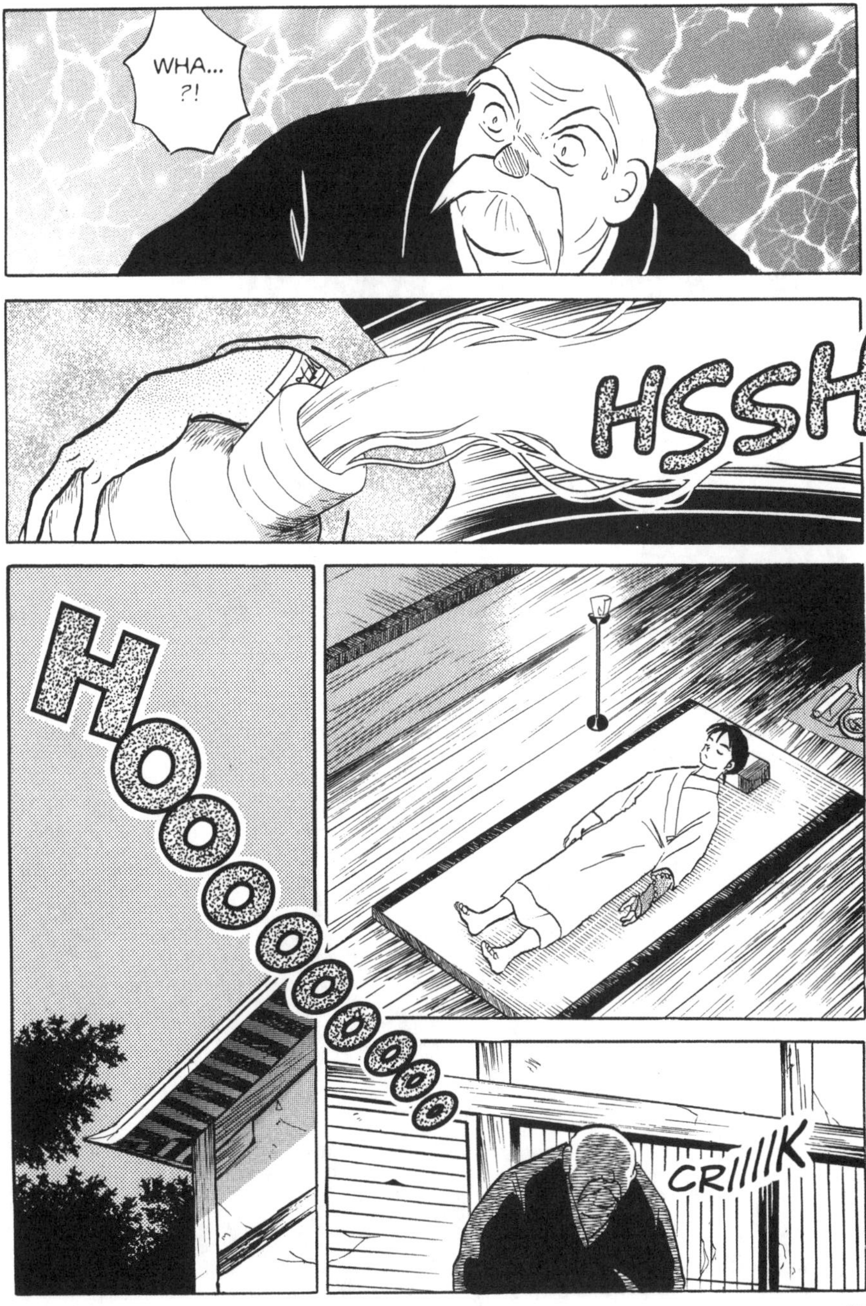
WHA... ?!
HSSH
HOOOOOOOOOO
CRIIIIK

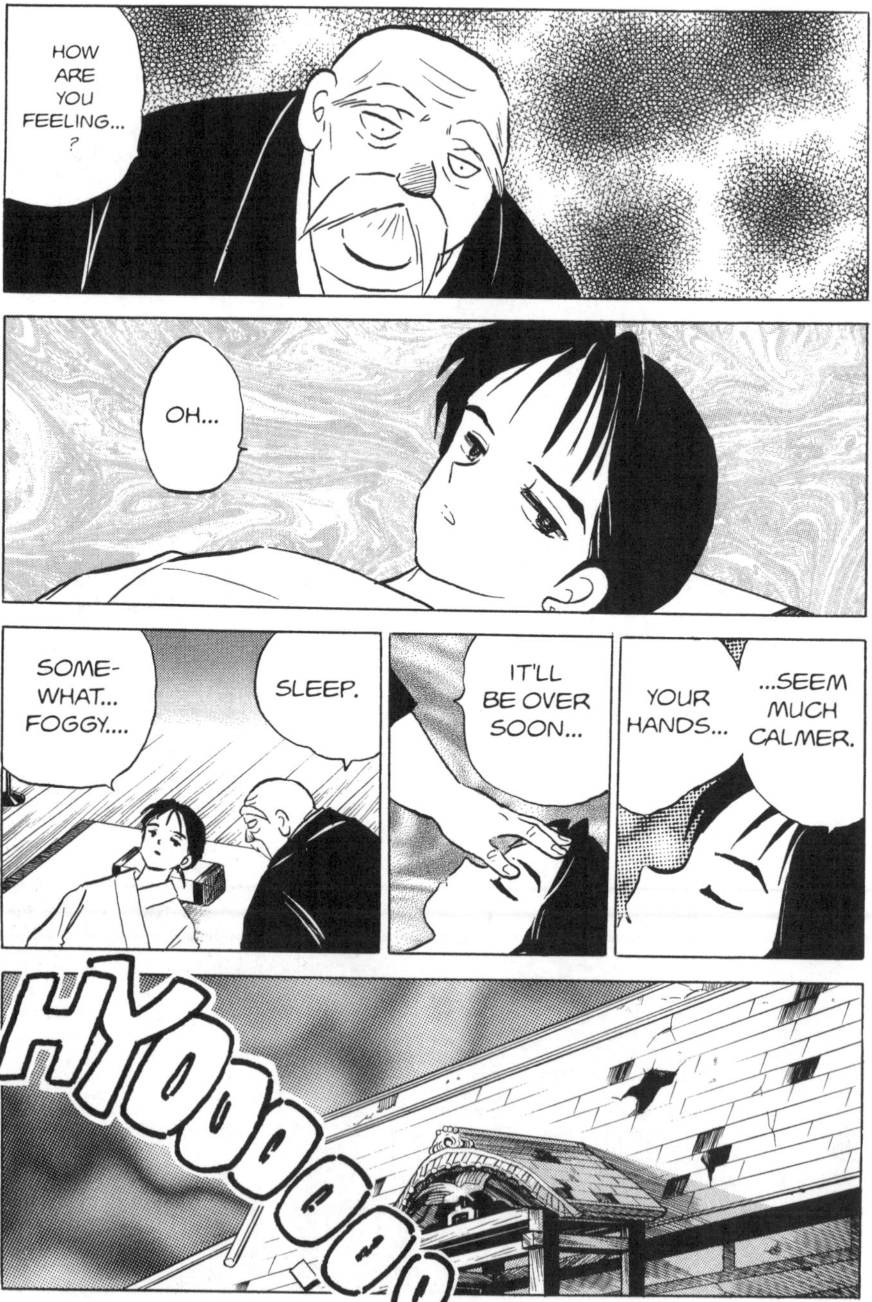
HOW ARE YOU FEELING... ?
OH...
SOME-WHAT... FOGGY....
SLEEP.
IT'LL BE OVER SOON...
YOUR HANDS...
...SEEM MUCH CALMER.
HYOOOOOO

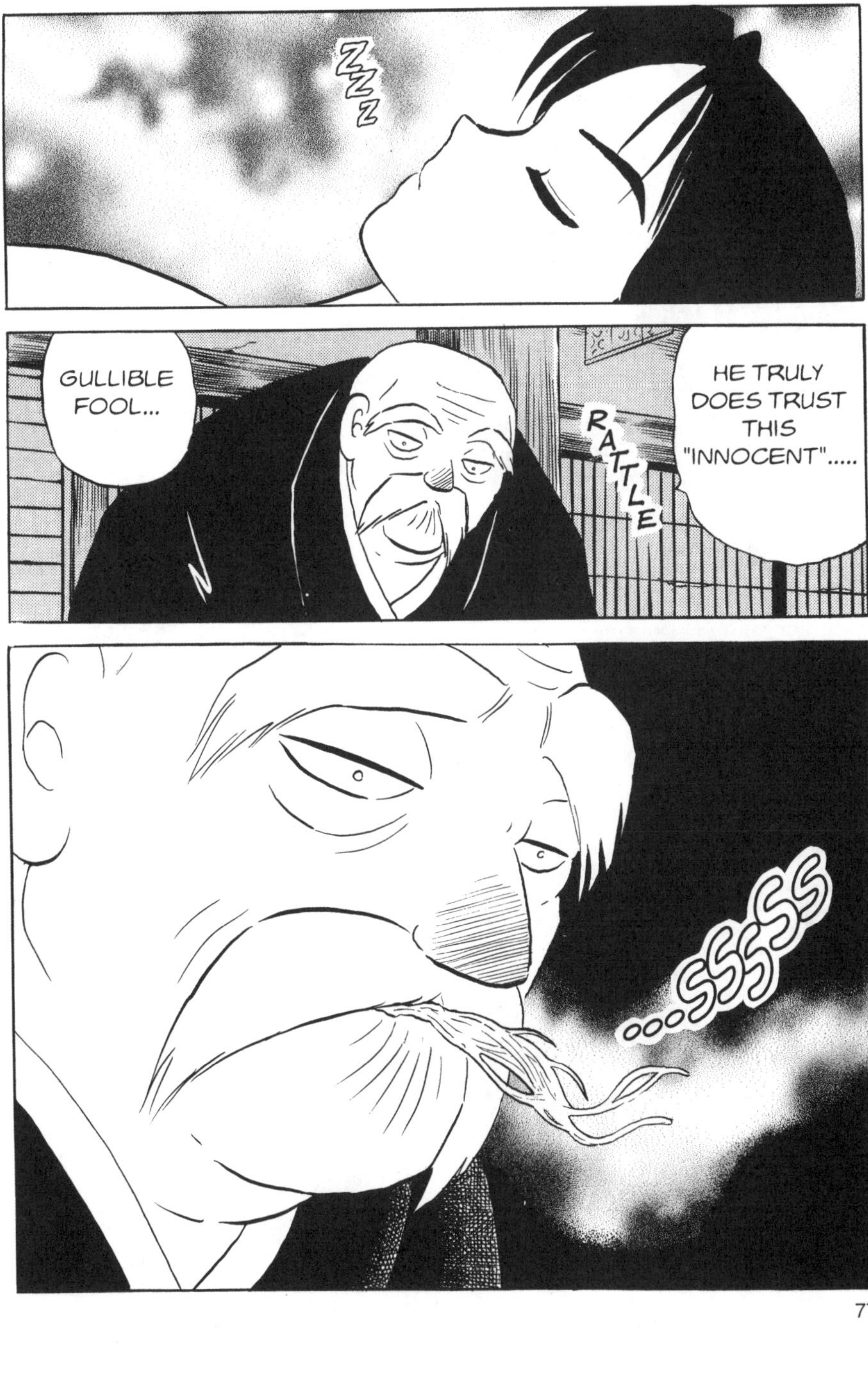
ZZZ
HE TRULY DOES TRUST THIS "INNOCENT".....
RATTLE
GULLIBLE FOOL...
...SSSSS

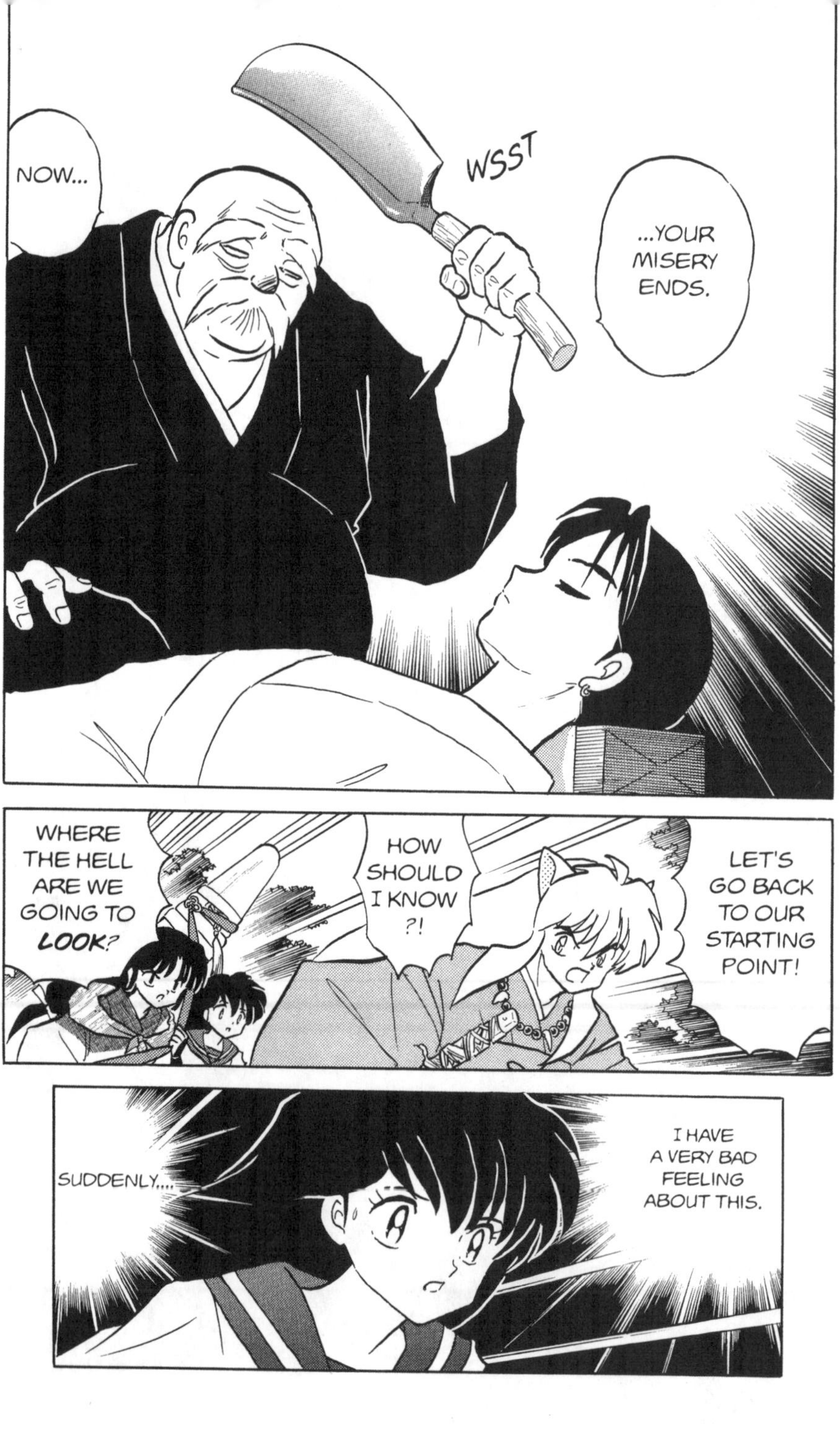
NOW...
WSST
...YOUR MISERY ENDS.
WHERE THE HELL ARE WE GOING TO *LOOK*?
HOW SHOULD I KNOW ?!
LET'S GO BACK TO OUR STARTING POINT!
SUDDENLY....
I HAVE A VERY BAD FEELING ABOUT THIS.

SCROLL FIVE

TO THE RESCUE

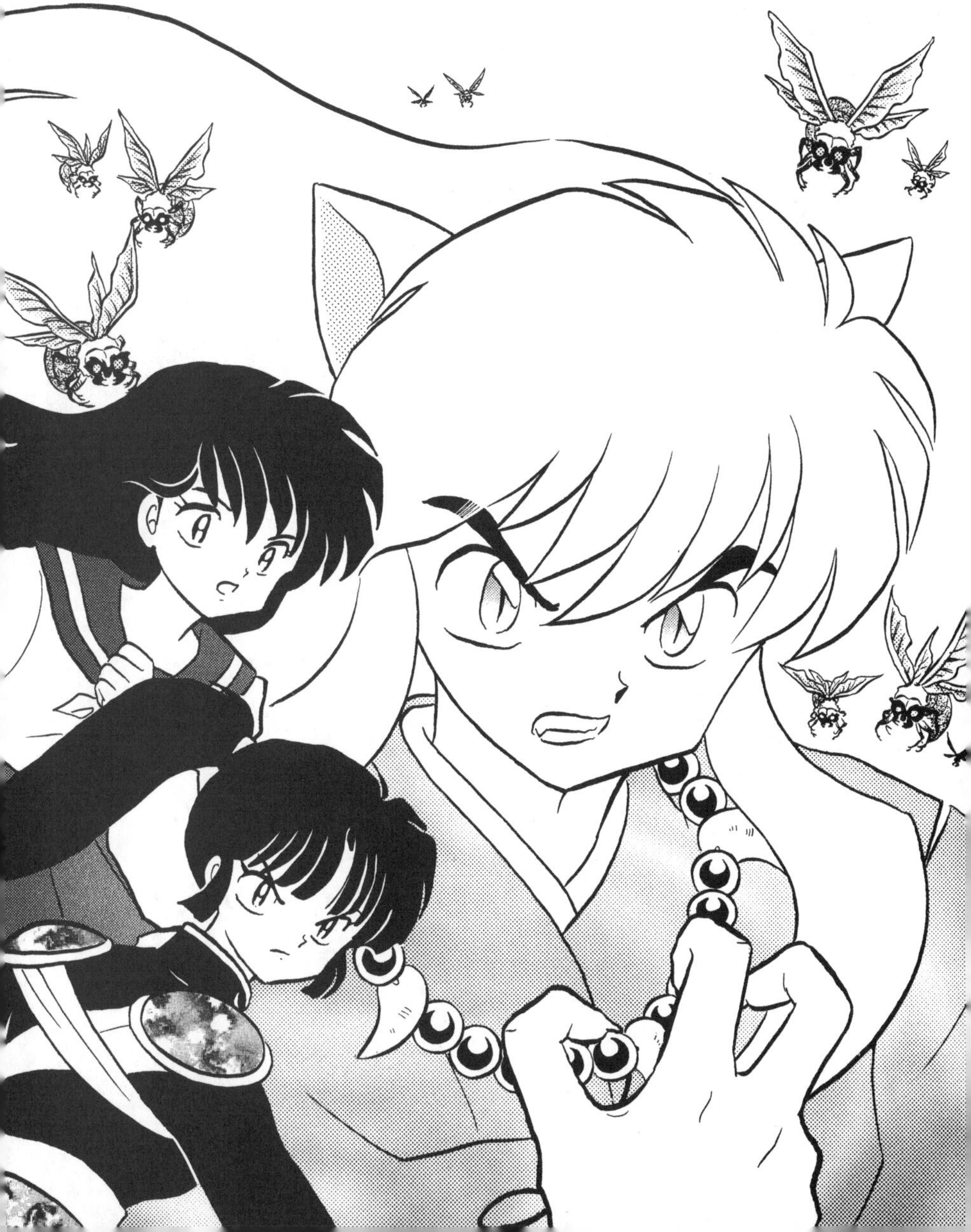

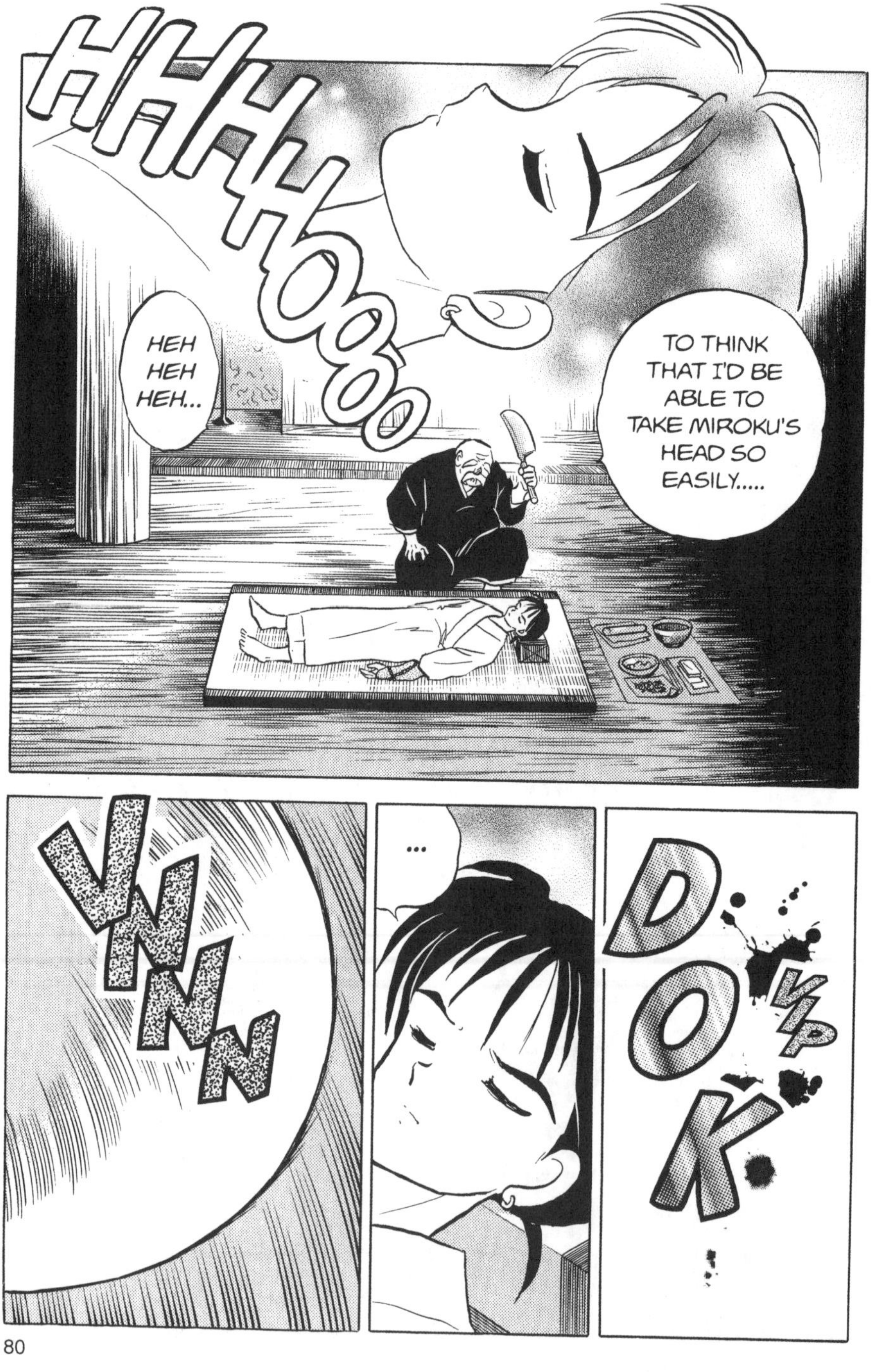
HHHHHOOOO
TO THINK THAT I'D BE ABLE TO TAKE MIROKU'S HEAD SO EASILY.....
HEH HEH HEH...
DOK
...
VNNN

HO...

STILL AWAKE, EH...?

YOU...

WHO **ARE** YOU?

WHAT ARE YOU TALKING ABOUT?

I'M YOUR FOSTER FATHER, MUSHIN.

SLITHER

HE'S BEING MANIPULATED BY... *SOMETHING!*

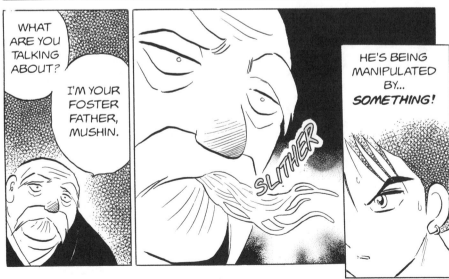

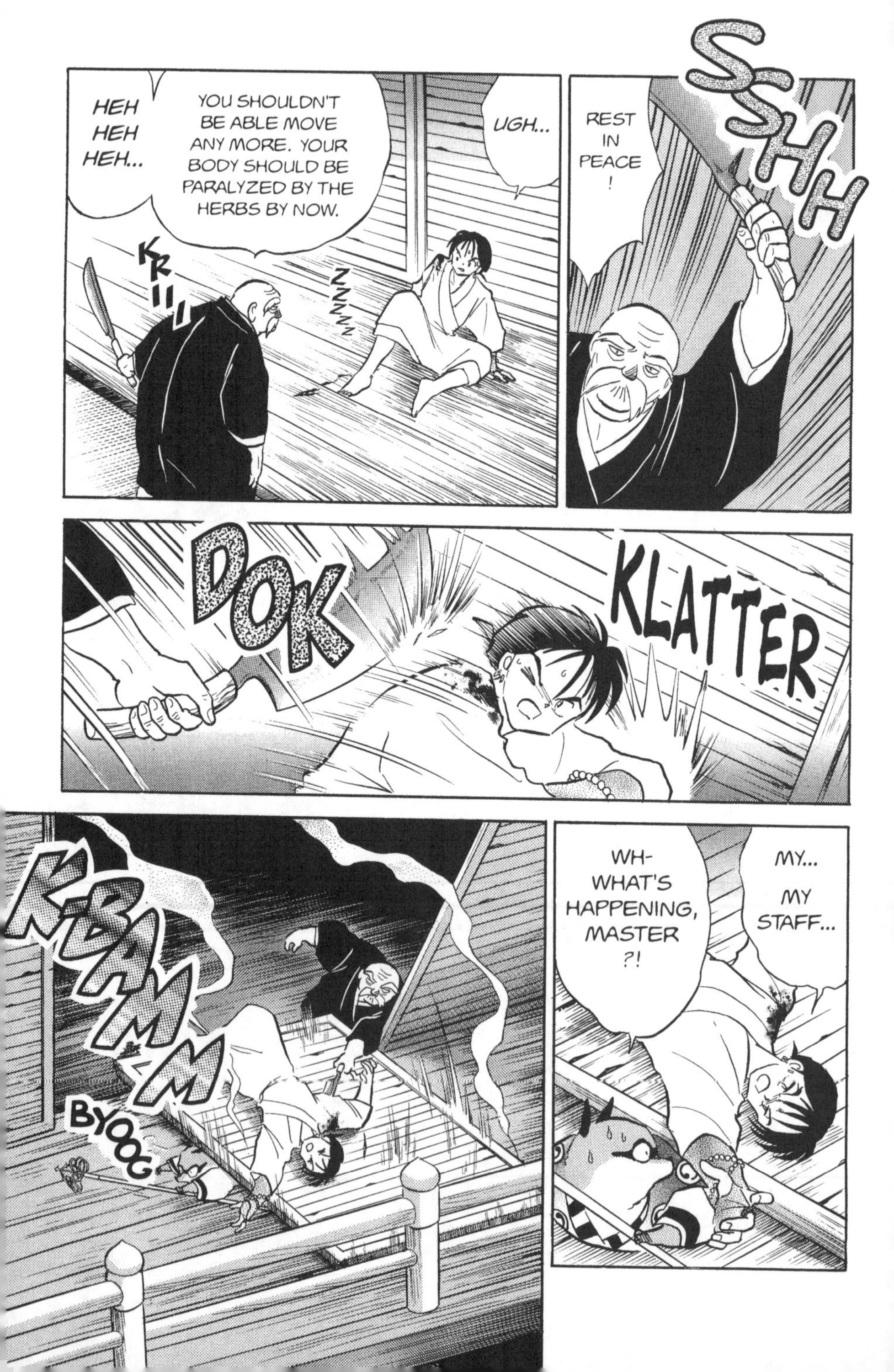
SSHH
REST IN PEACE!
UGH...
HEH HEH HEH...
YOU SHOULDN'T BE ABLE MOVE ANY MORE. YOUR BODY SHOULD BE PARALYZED BY THE HERBS BY NOW.
KRIII
ZZZZZ
KLATTER
DOK
MY... MY STAFF...
WH-WHAT'S HAPPENING, MASTER?!
K-BAMMM
BYOOG

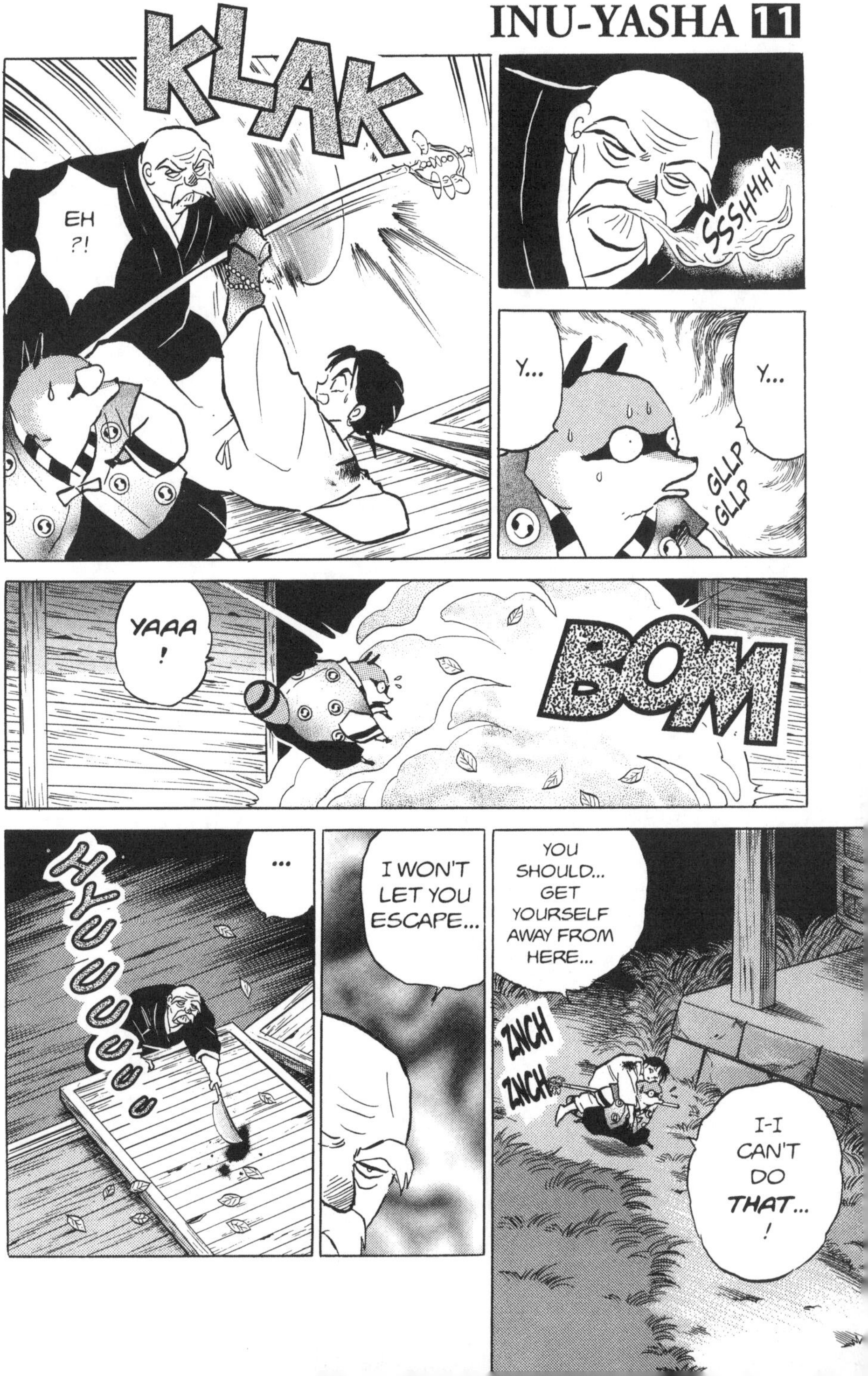
SSSHHHH
Y...
Y...
GLLP GLLP
KLAK
EH ?!
BOM
YAAA !
YOU SHOULD... GET YOURSELF AWAY FROM HERE...
ZNCH ZNCH
I-I CAN'T DO *THAT*... !
I WON'T LET YOU ESCAPE...
...
HYUUUUUU

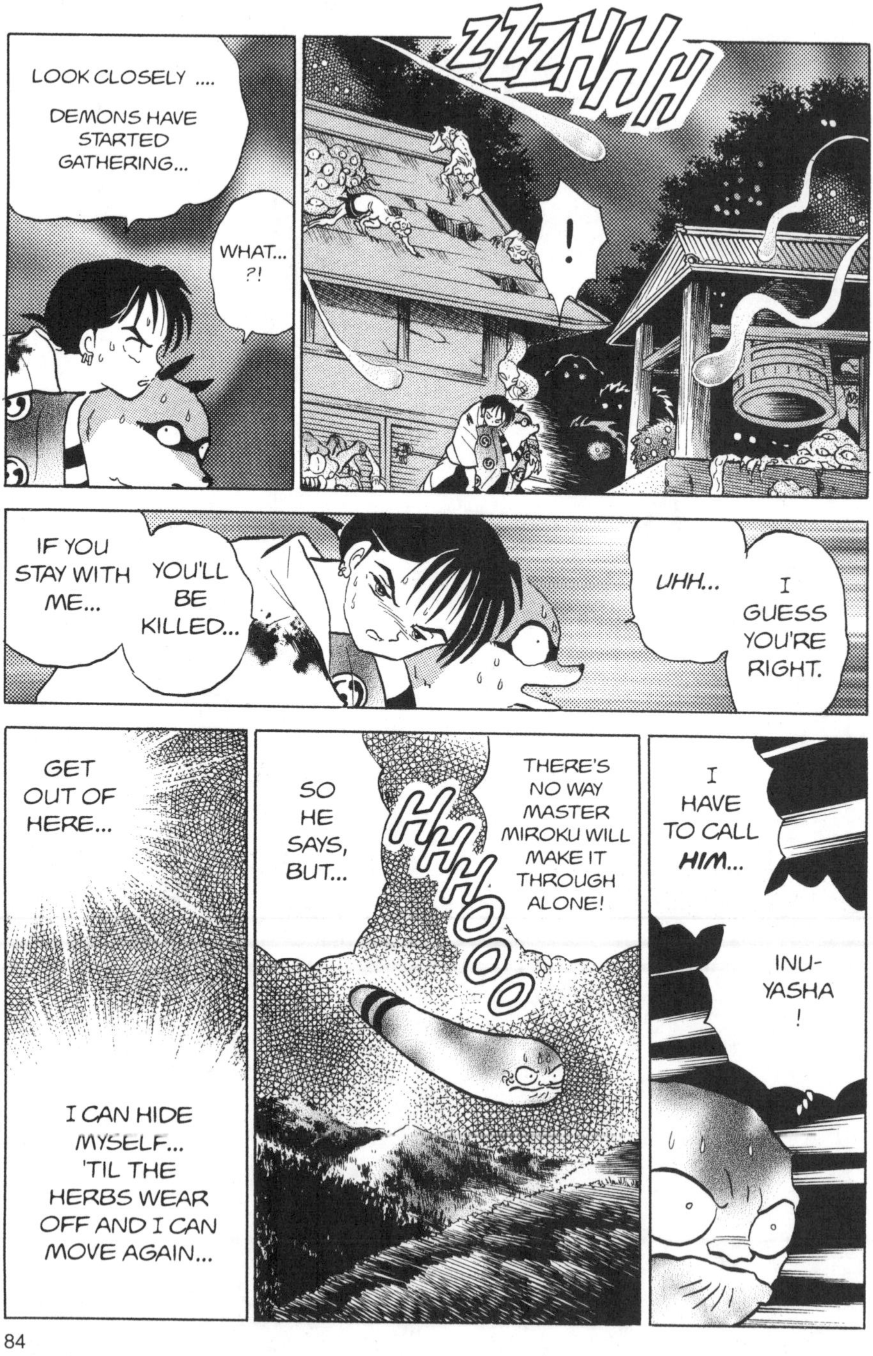
LOOK CLOSELY ....
DEMONS HAVE STARTED GATHERING...
WHAT... ?!
ZZZHHHH
!
IF YOU STAY WITH ME...
YOU'LL BE KILLED...
UHH...
I GUESS YOU'RE RIGHT.
GET OUT OF HERE...
I CAN HIDE MYSELF... 'TIL THE HERBS WEAR OFF AND I CAN MOVE AGAIN...
SO HE SAYS, BUT...
THERE'S NO WAY MASTER MIROKU WILL MAKE IT THROUGH ALONE!
HHHOOO
I HAVE TO CALL HIM...
INU-YASHA !

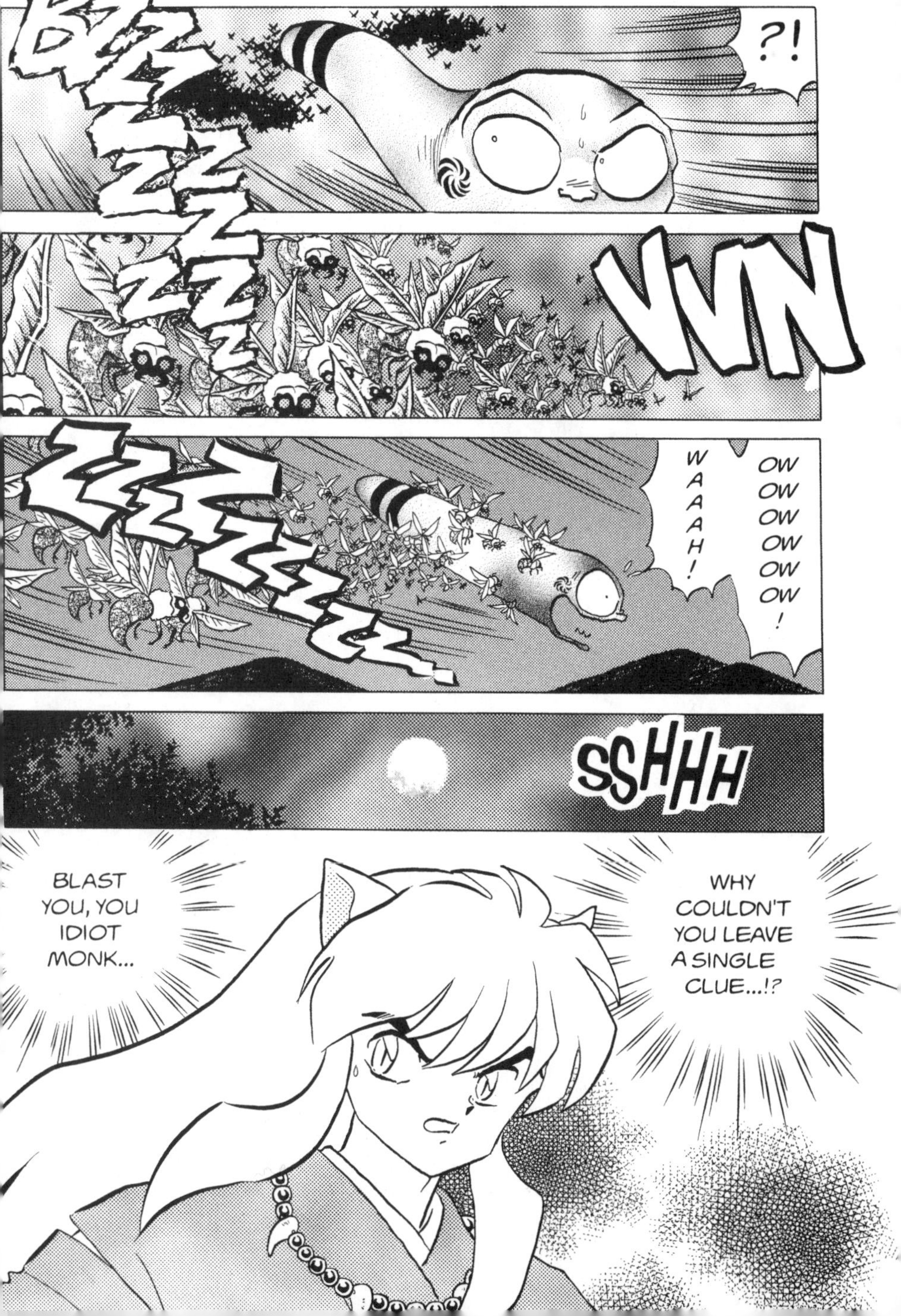
?!
VVN
OW OW OW OW OW OW!
WAAAAH!
SSHHH
WHY COULDN'T YOU LEAVE A SINGLE CLUE...!?
BLAST YOU, YOU IDIOT MONK...

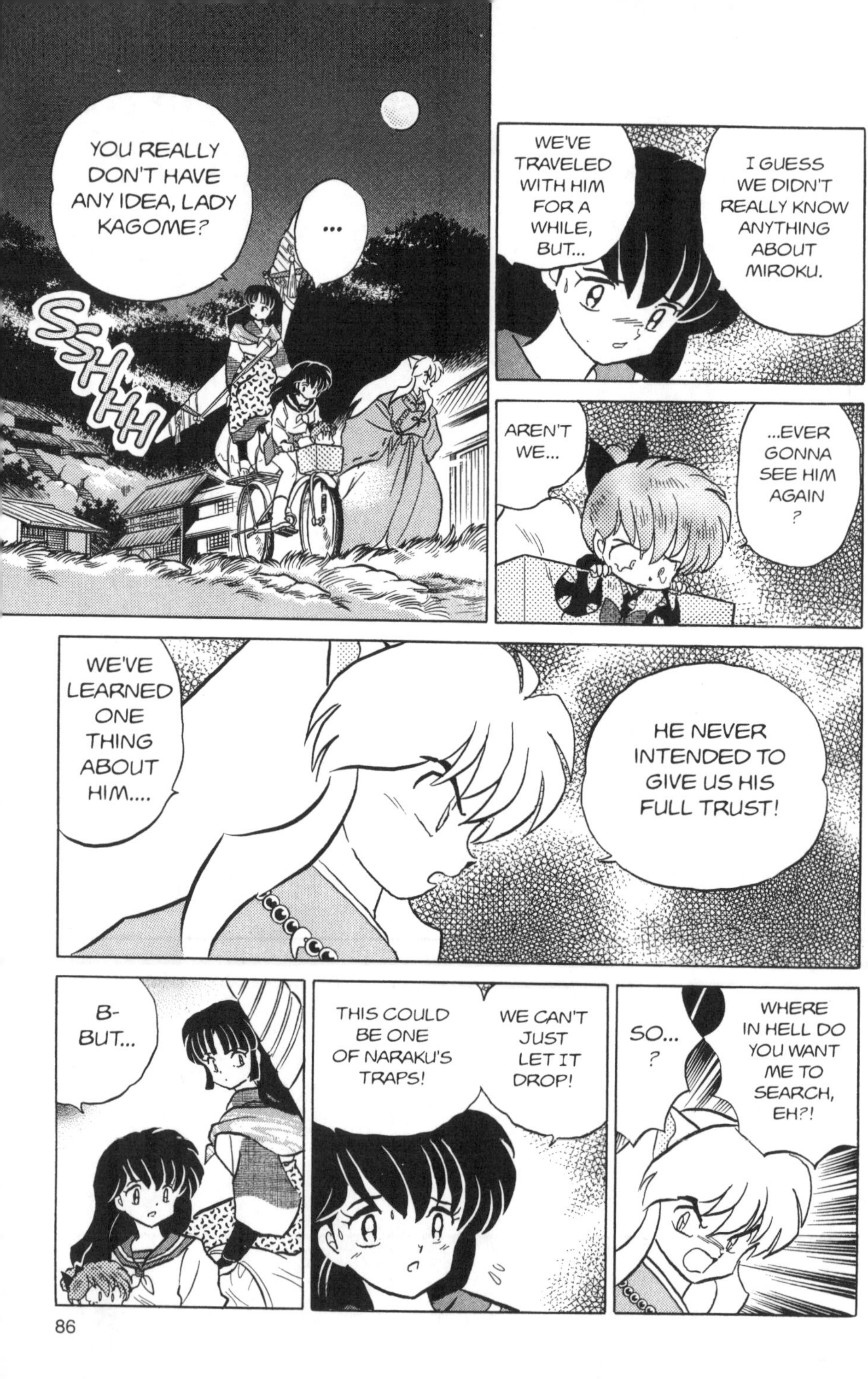
YOU REALLY DON'T HAVE ANY IDEA, LADY KAGOME?
...
SSHHH
WE'VE TRAVELED WITH HIM FOR A WHILE, BUT...
I GUESS WE DIDN'T REALLY KNOW ANYTHING ABOUT MIROKU.
AREN'T WE...
...EVER GONNA SEE HIM AGAIN ?
WE'VE LEARNED ONE THING ABOUT HIM....
HE NEVER INTENDED TO GIVE US HIS FULL TRUST!
B- BUT...
THIS COULD BE ONE OF NARAKU'S TRAPS!
WE CAN'T JUST LET IT DROP!
SO... ?
WHERE IN HELL DO YOU WANT ME TO SEARCH, EH?!

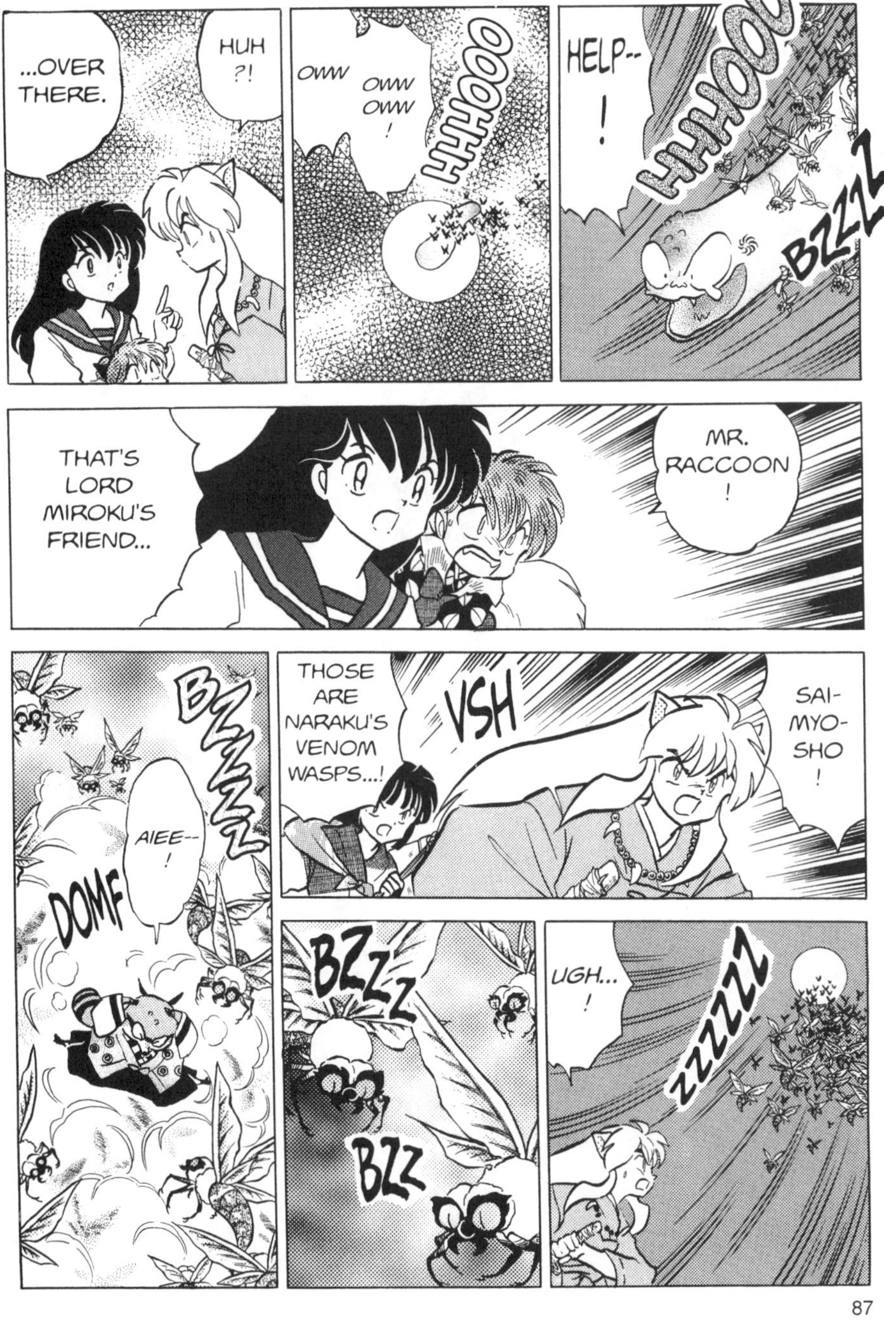
HELP-- !
HHHOOOO
BZZZ
OWW OWW !
OWW
HHHOOOO
HUH ?!
...OVER THERE.
MR. RACCOON !
THAT'S LORD MIROKU'S FRIEND...
SAI-MYO-SHO !
VSH
THOSE ARE NARAKU'S VENOM WASPS...!
UGH... !
ZZZZZZ
BZZZ
BZZ
BZZZZZ
AIEE-- !
DOMF

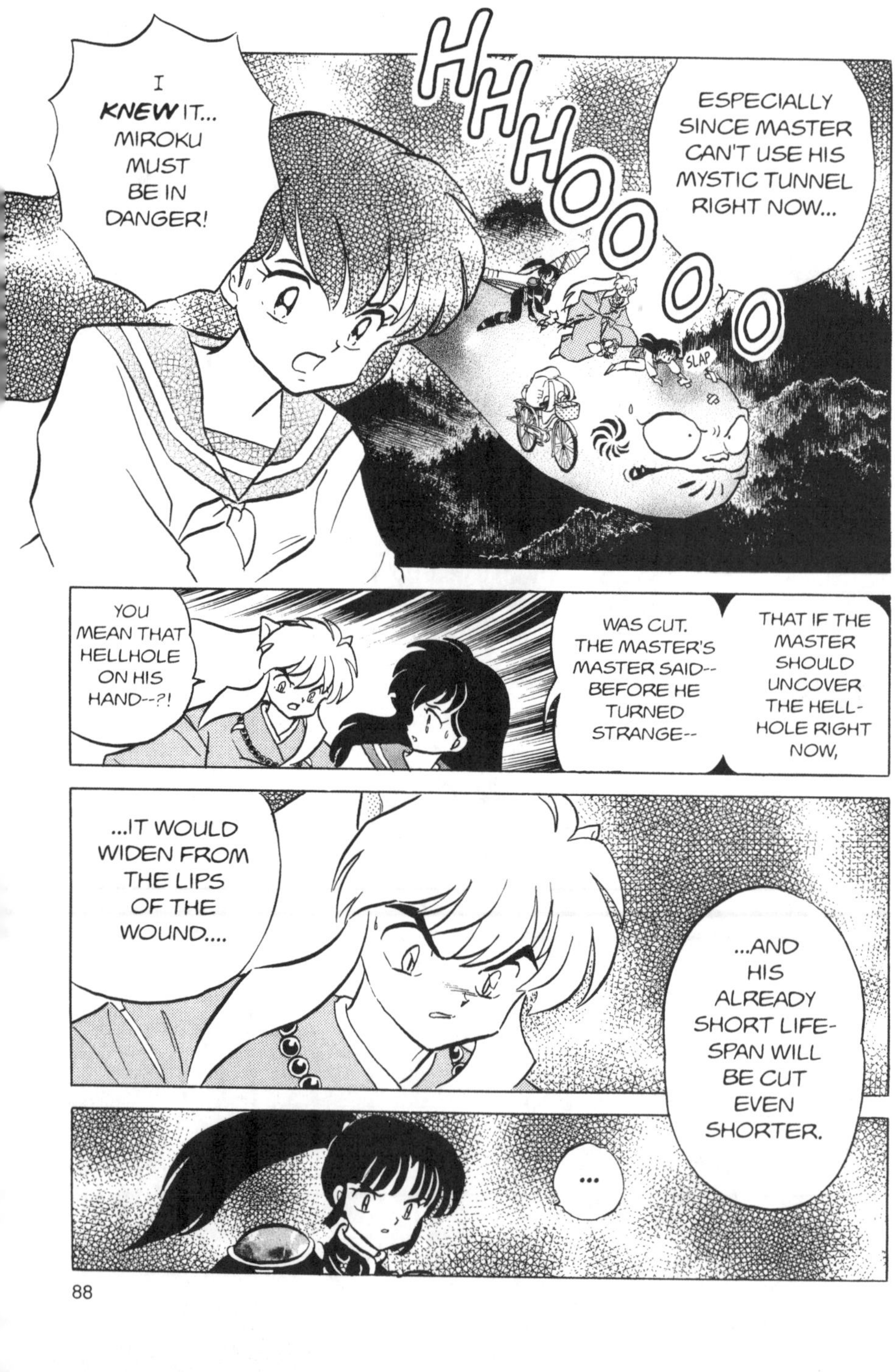
I KNEW IT... MIROKU MUST BE IN DANGER!
HHHOOOOOO
SLAP
ESPECIALLY SINCE MASTER CAN'T USE HIS MYSTIC TUNNEL RIGHT NOW...
YOU MEAN THAT HELLHOLE ON HIS HAND--?!
WAS CUT. THE MASTER'S MASTER SAID-- BEFORE HE TURNED STRANGE--
THAT IF THE MASTER SHOULD UNCOVER THE HELL-HOLE RIGHT NOW,
...IT WOULD WIDEN FROM THE LIPS OF THE WOUND....
...AND HIS ALREADY SHORT LIFE-SPAN WILL BE CUT EVEN SHORTER.
...

!
BZZZ
INU-YASHA, THERE ARE SAIMYOSHO ABOUT....
THOUGH THEY DON'T SEEM POISED TO ATTACK US.....
THEY'RE ON RECONNAIS-SANCE...
THEY'RE SPYING ON US...
SSHHH
WHERE IS THAT MONK..?!
SHHOOOO
I WILL TEAR HIM LIMB FROM LIMB...!
I DO NOT SEE HIM...
PERHAPS HE HAS RAISED A SHIELD...
SSSHHH
FIND HIM...
HE MUST BE NEARBY!

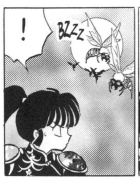

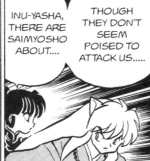

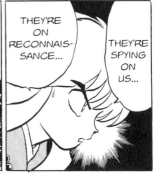

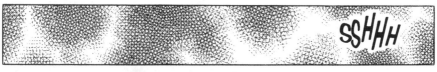

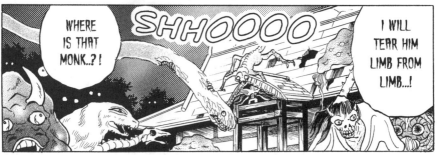

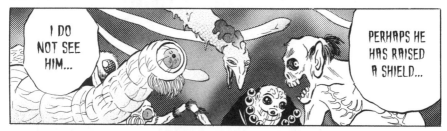

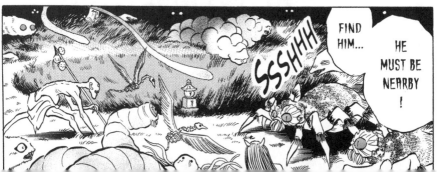

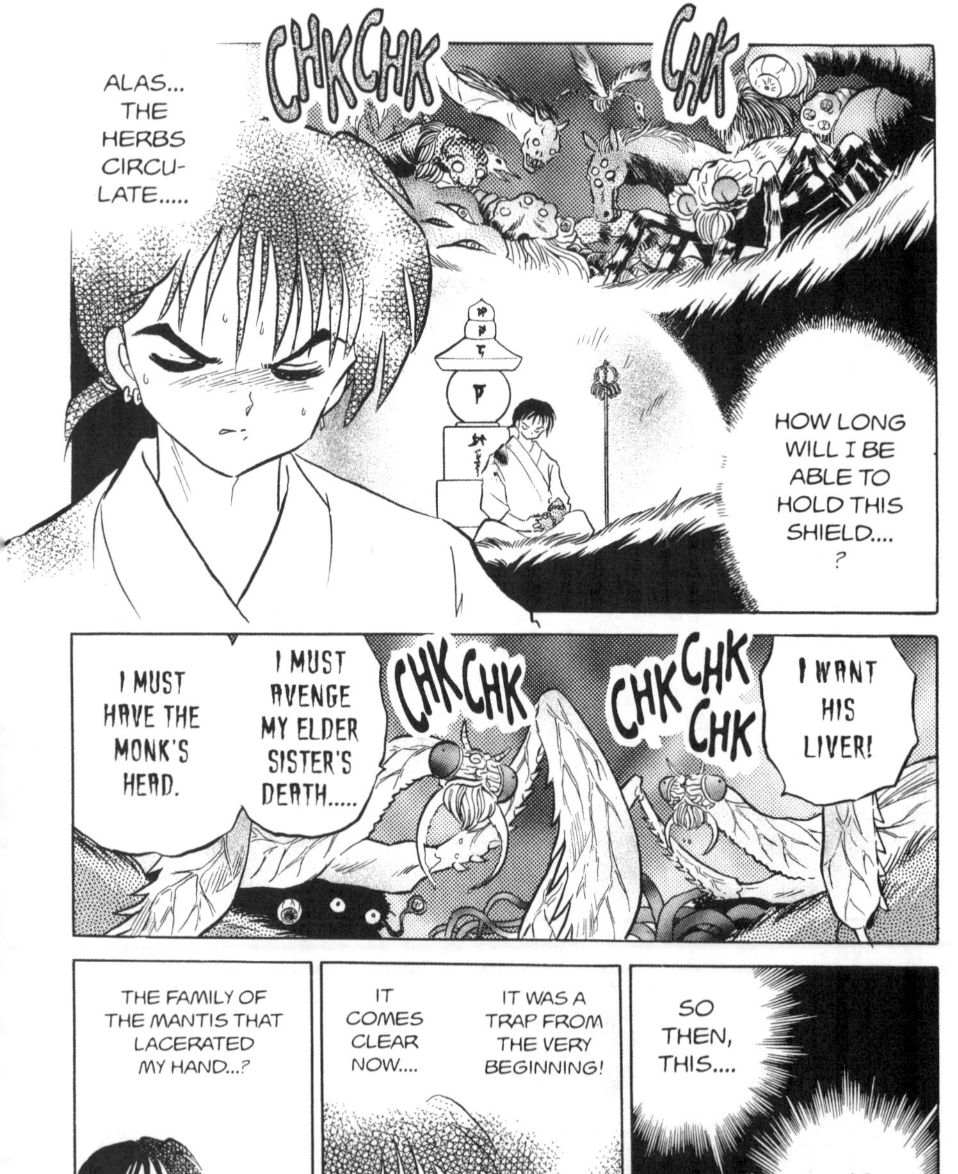
CHKCHK
ALAS... THE HERBS CIRCULATE.....
CHK
HOW LONG WILL I BE ABLE TO HOLD THIS SHIELD....?
I MUST HAVE THE MONK'S HEAD.
I MUST AVENGE MY ELDER SISTER'S DEATH.....
CHKCHK
CHKCHK CHK CHK
I WANT HIS LIVER!
THE FAMILY OF THE MANTIS THAT LACERATED MY HAND...?
IT COMES CLEAR NOW....
IT WAS A TRAP FROM THE VERY BEGINNING!
SO THEN, THIS....
...IS WHERE I DIE.

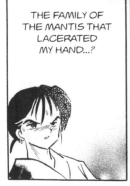

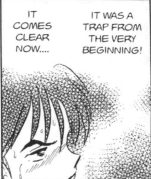

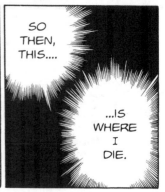

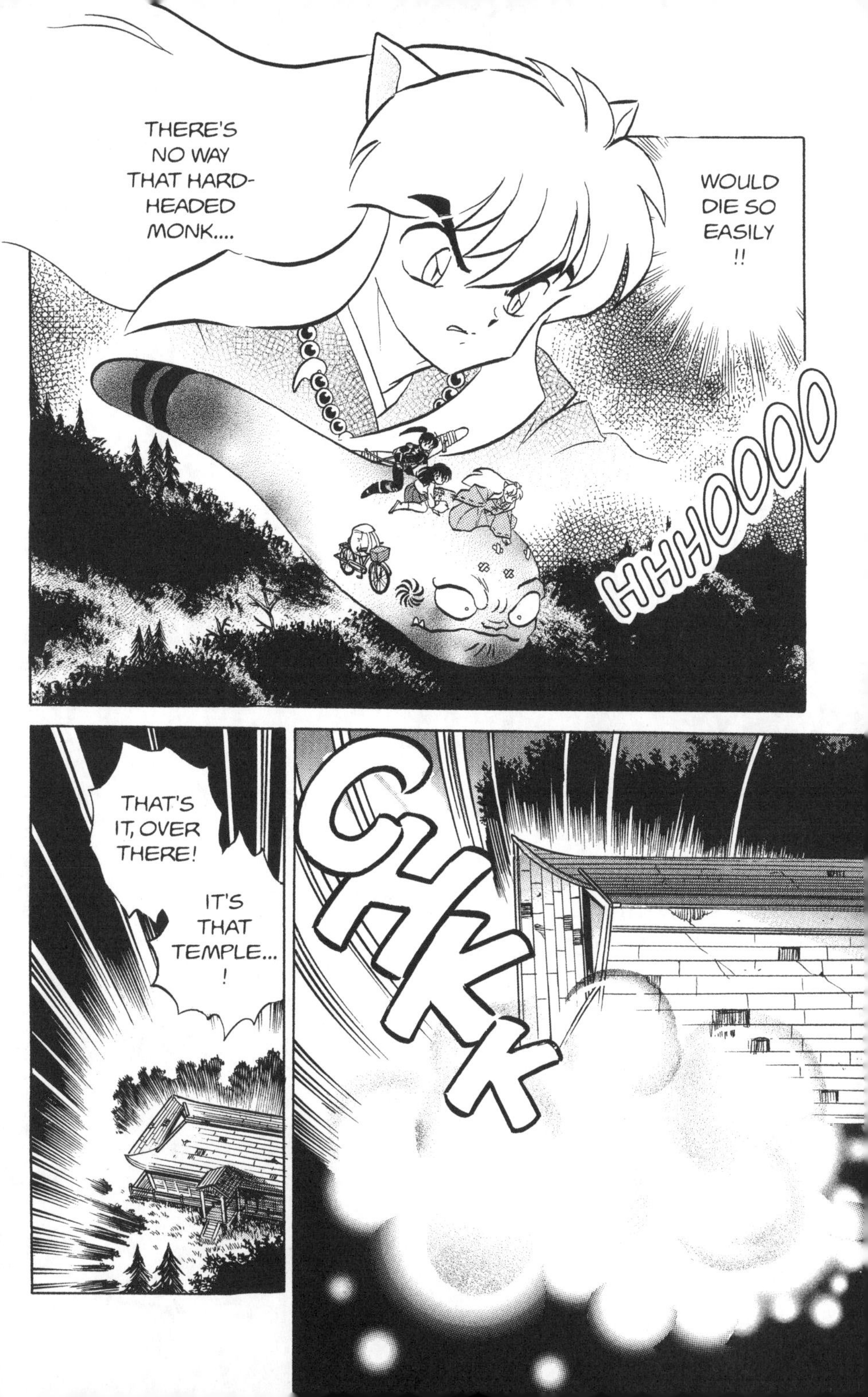
THERE'S NO WAY THAT HARD-HEADED MONK....
WOULD DIE SO EASILY !!
HHHOOOO
THAT'S IT, OVER THERE!
IT'S THAT TEMPLE... !
CHKK

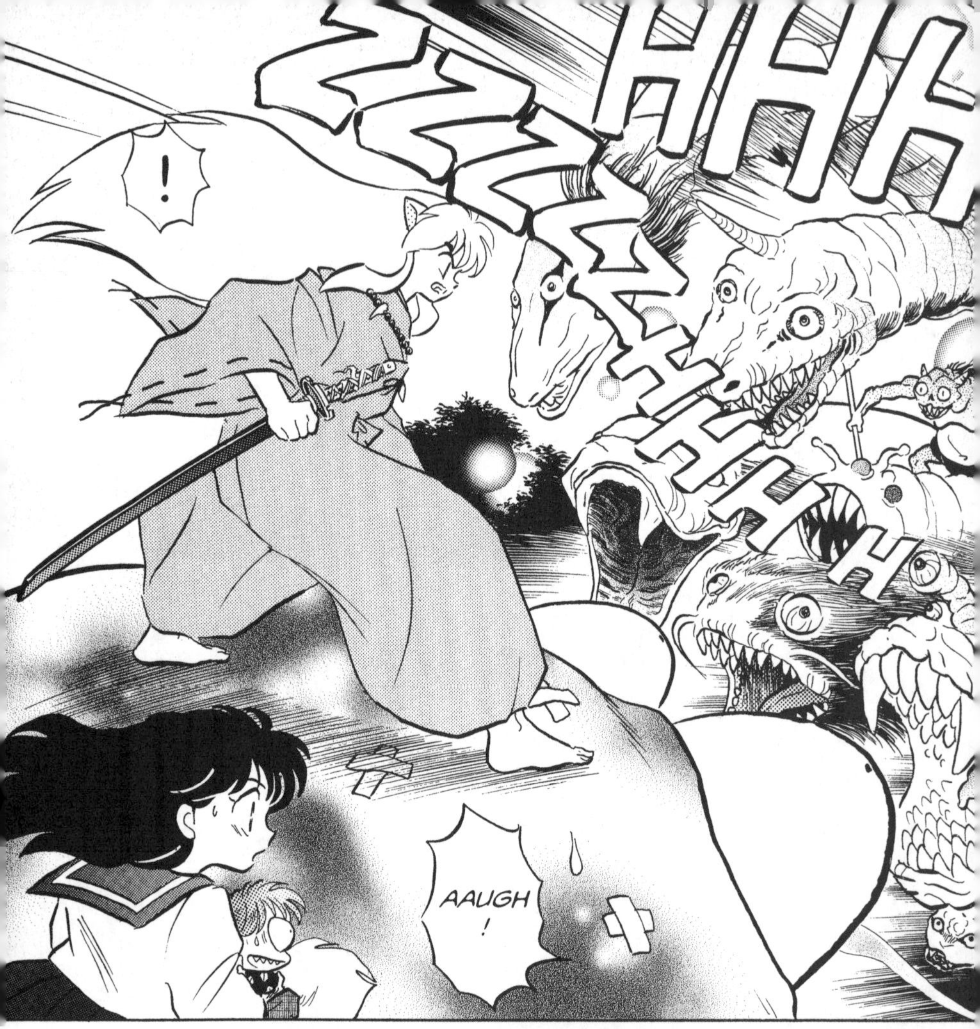
HHHH
!
AAUGH!

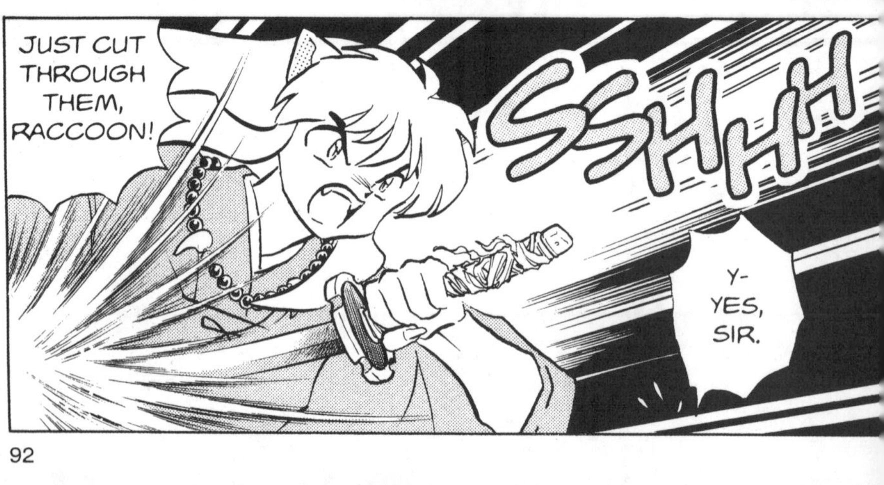
SSHHHH
JUST CUT THROUGH THEM, RACCOON!
Y- YES, SIR.

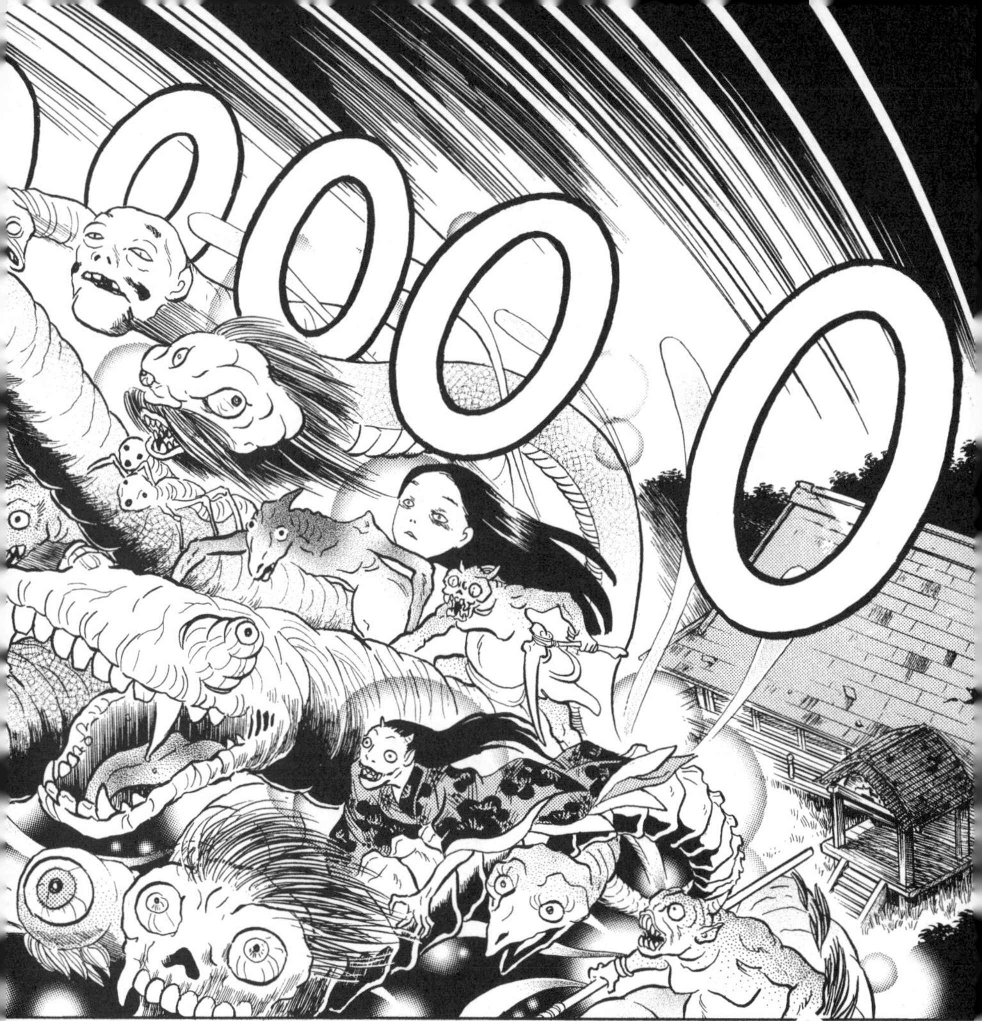
OOOOOO
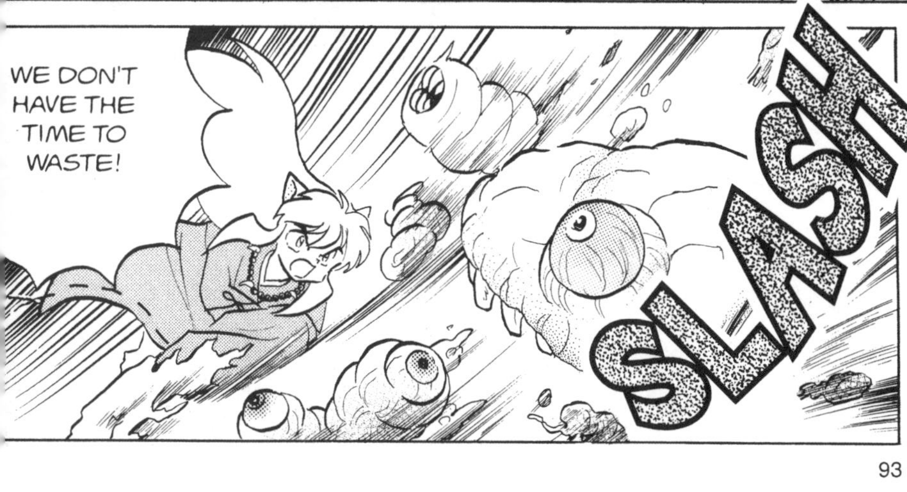
WE DON'T HAVE THE TIME TO WASTE!
SLASH

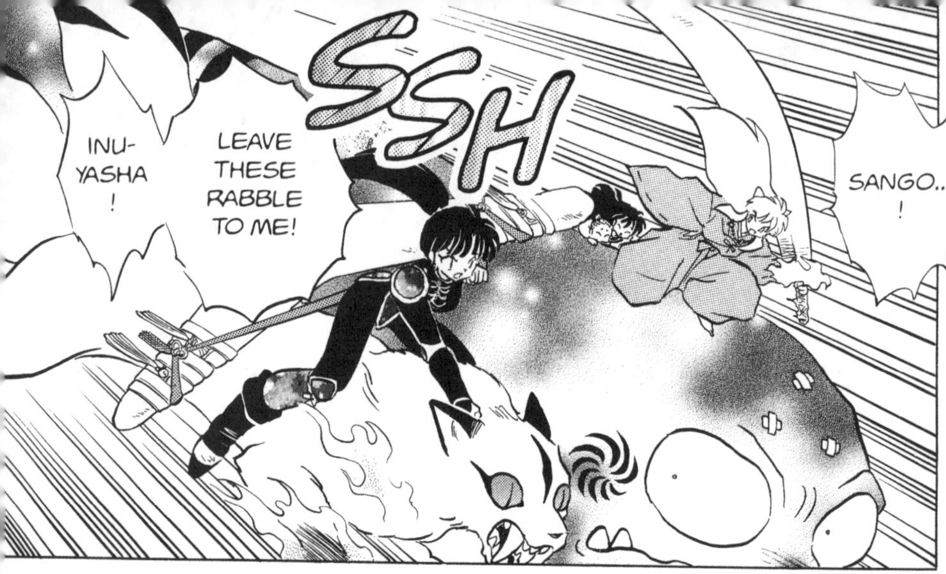
SSH
INU-YASHA!
LEAVE THESE RABBLE TO ME!
SANGO...!
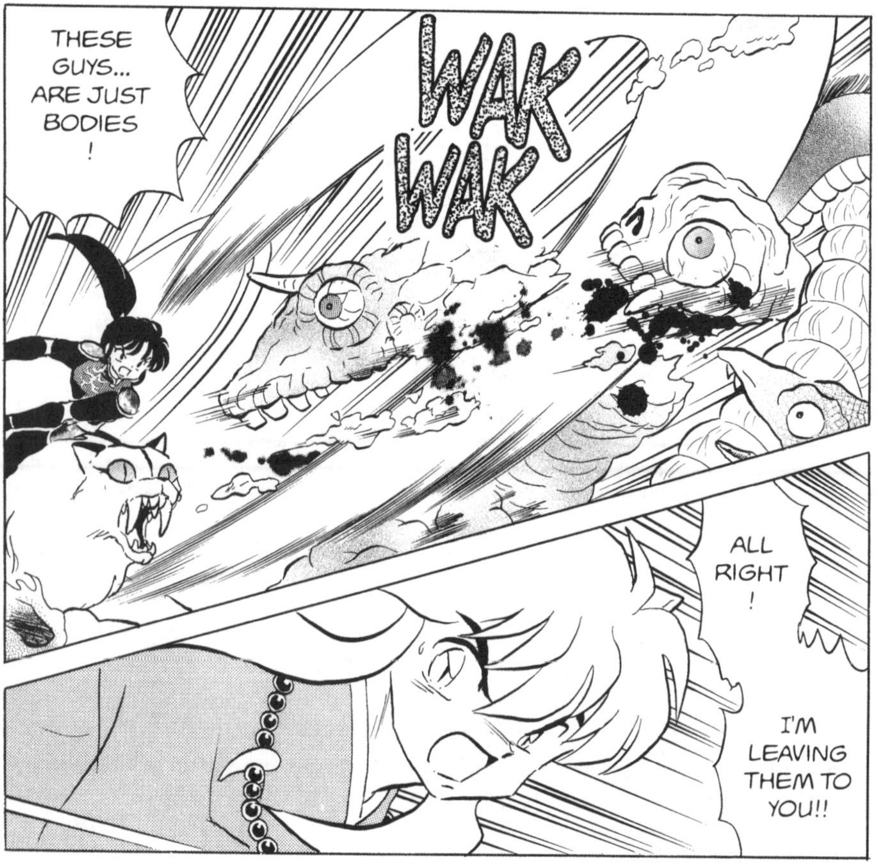
WAK WAK
THESE GUYS... ARE JUST BODIES!
ALL RIGHT!
I'M LEAVING THEM TO YOU!!

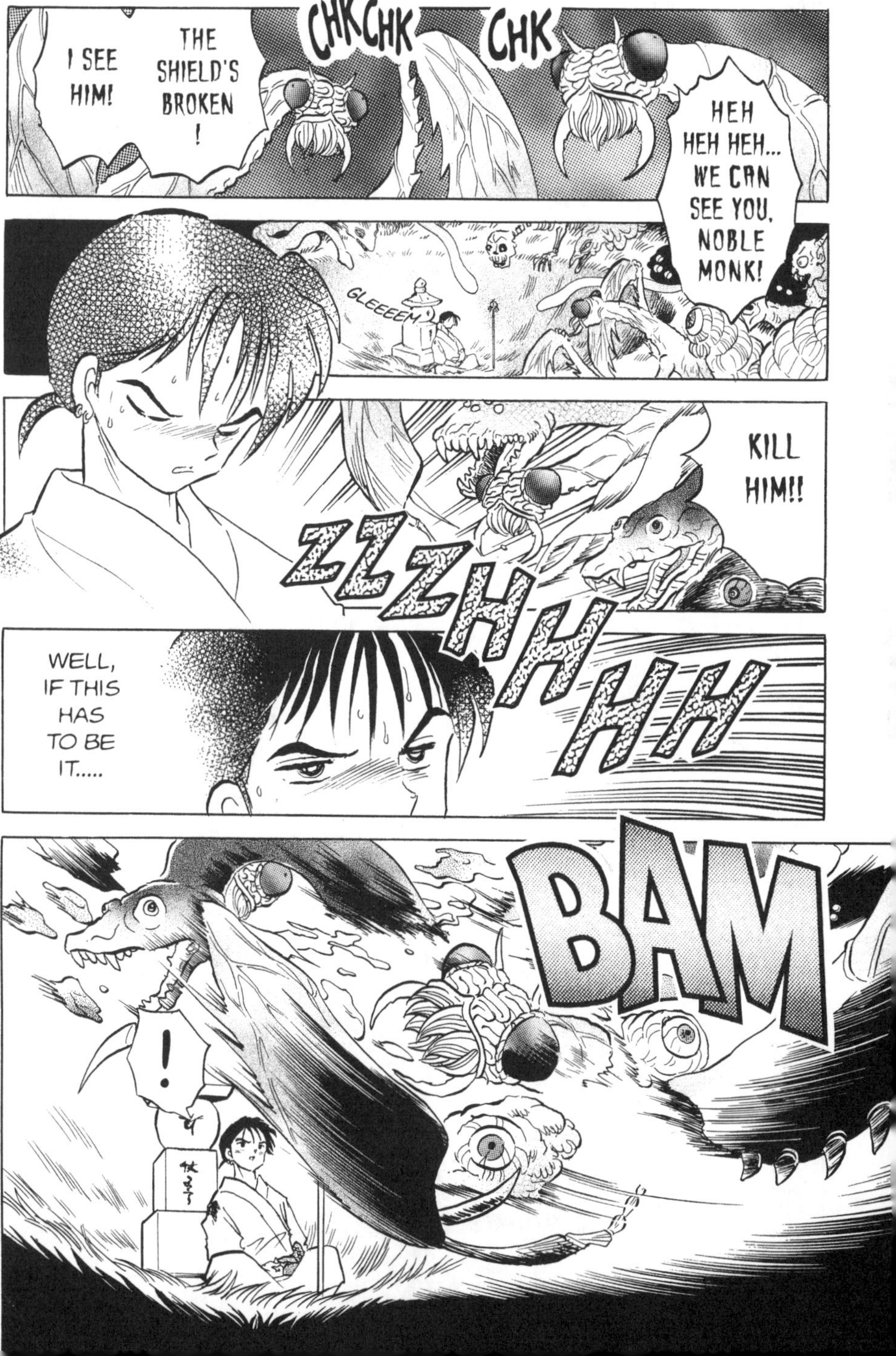
CHK CHK
CHK
THE SHIELD'S BROKEN!
I SEE HIM!
HEH HEH HEH... WE CAN SEE YOU, NOBLE MONK!
GLEEEEM
KILL HIM!!
ZZZHHHHH
WELL, IF THIS HAS TO BE IT.....
BAM
!

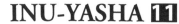

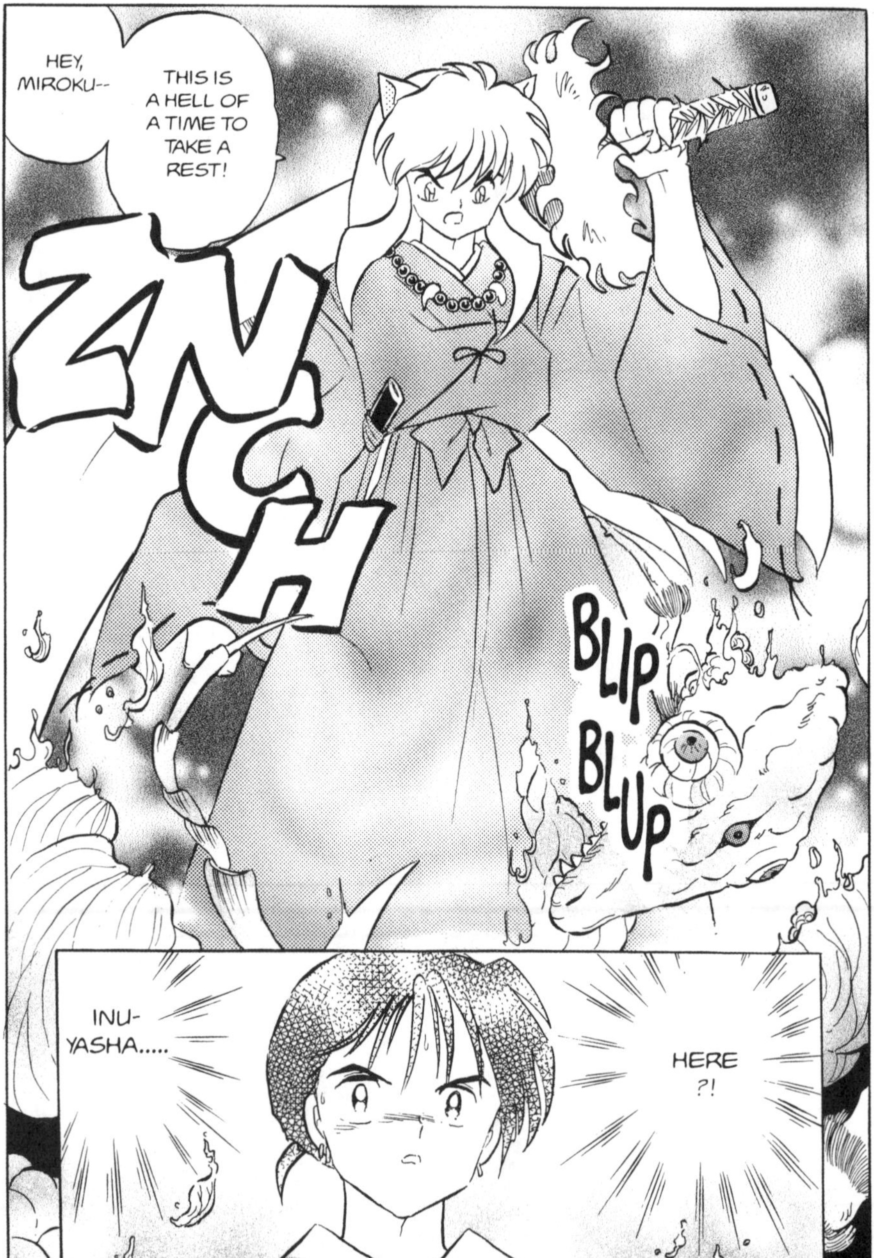
HEY, MIROKU--
THIS IS A HELL OF A TIME TO TAKE A REST!
ZNCH
BLIP BLUP
HERE ?!
INU-YASHA.....

SCROLL SIX

URN GRUBS

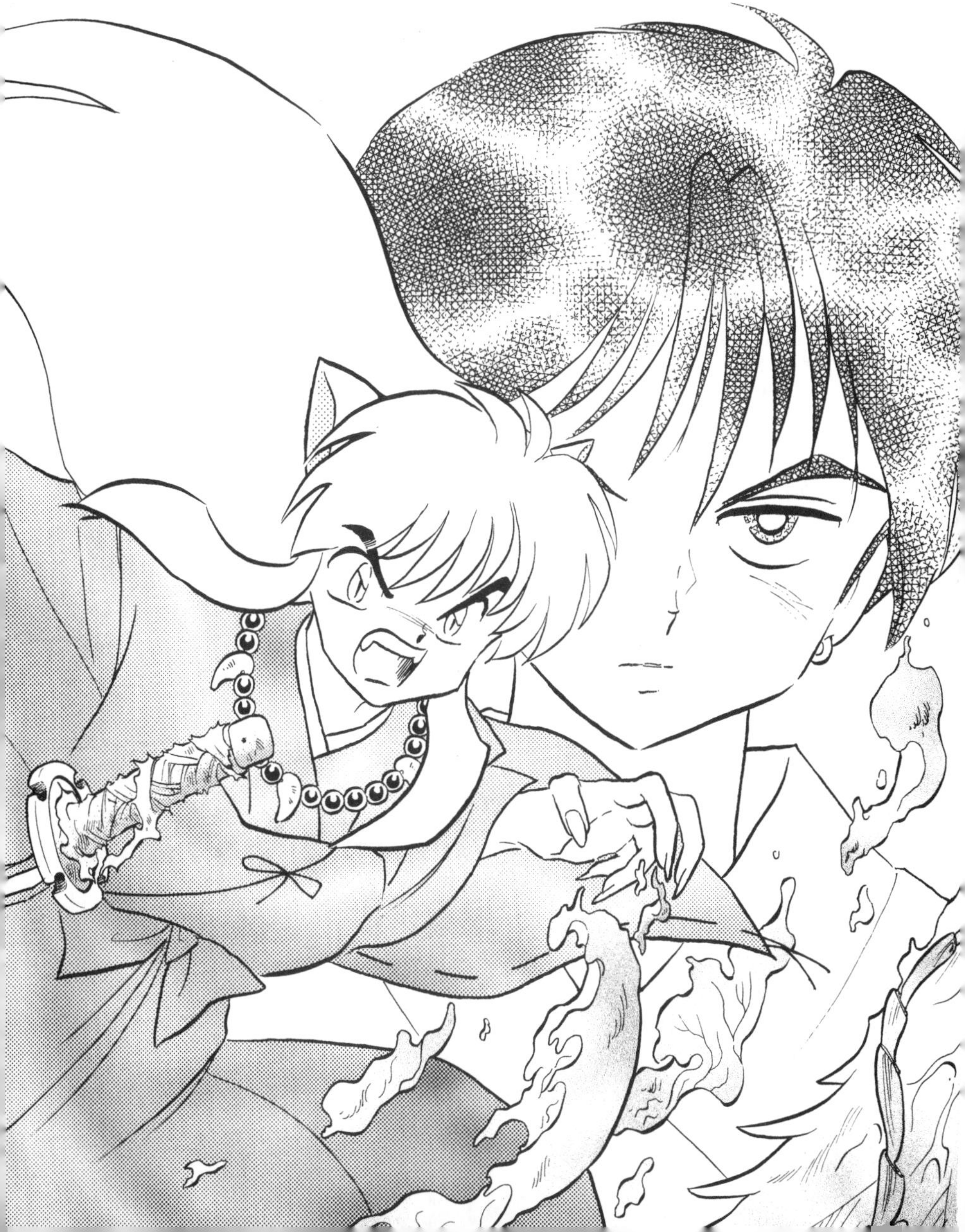

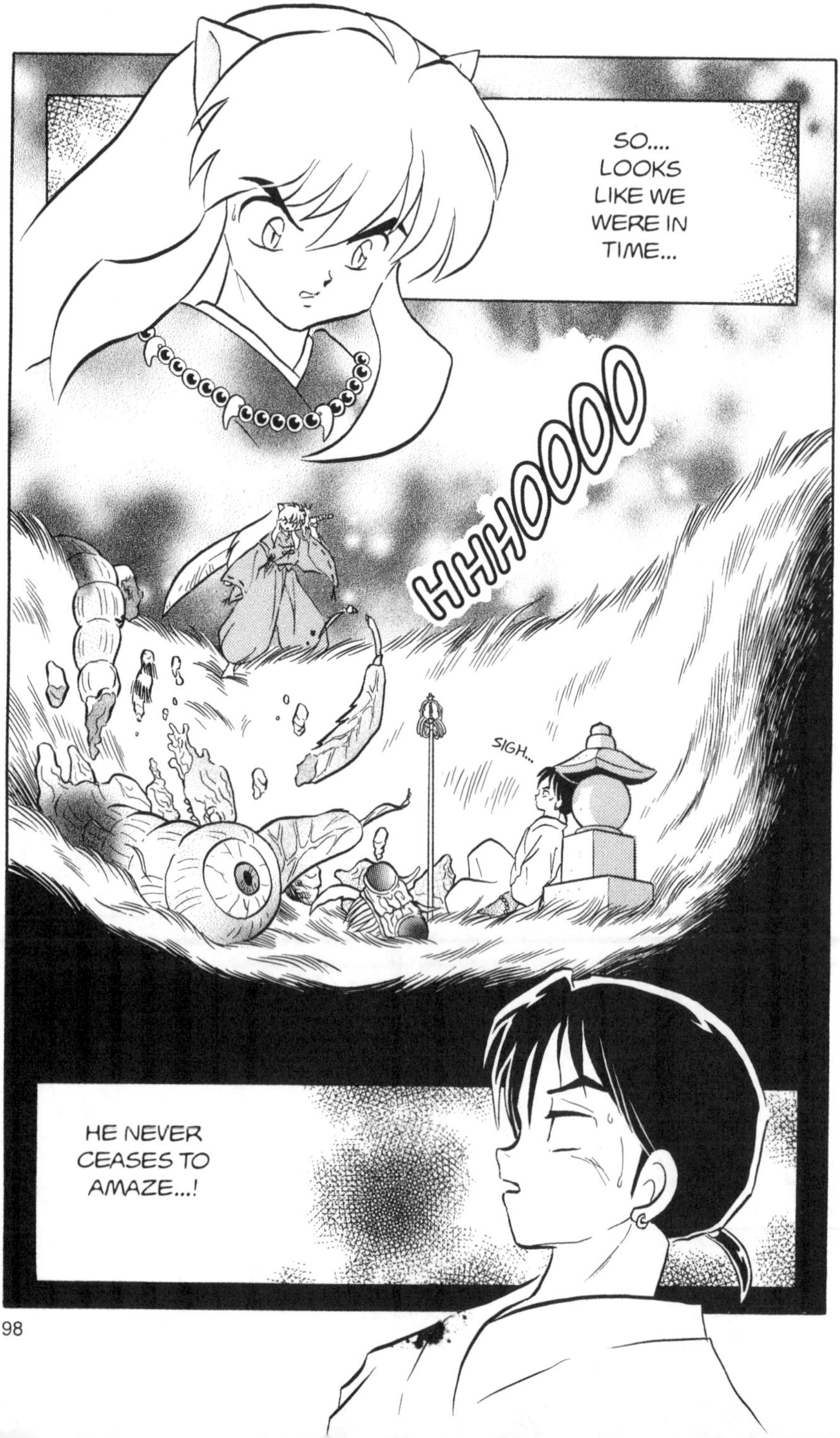
SO.... LOOKS LIKE WE WERE IN TIME...
HHHOOOO
SIGH...
HE NEVER CEASES TO AMAZE...!

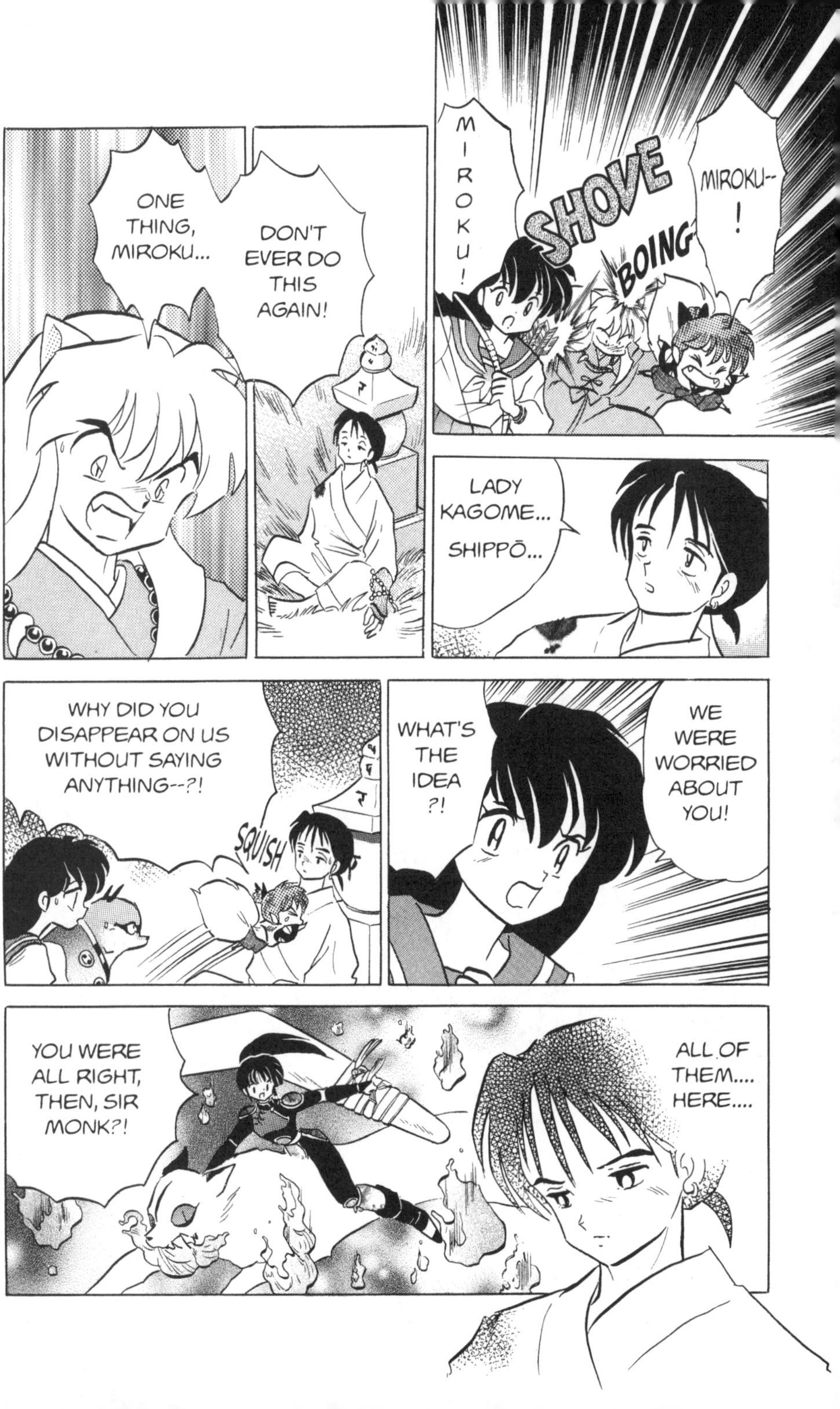
MIROKU-- !
SHOVE
BOING
MIROKU!
LADY KAGOME... SHIPPŌ...
ONE THING, MIROKU...
DON'T EVER DO THIS AGAIN!
WE WERE WORRIED ABOUT YOU!
WHAT'S THE IDEA ?!
WHY DID YOU DISAPPEAR ON US WITHOUT SAYING ANYTHING--?!
SQUISH
ALL OF THEM.... HERE....
YOU WERE ALL RIGHT, THEN, SIR MONK?!

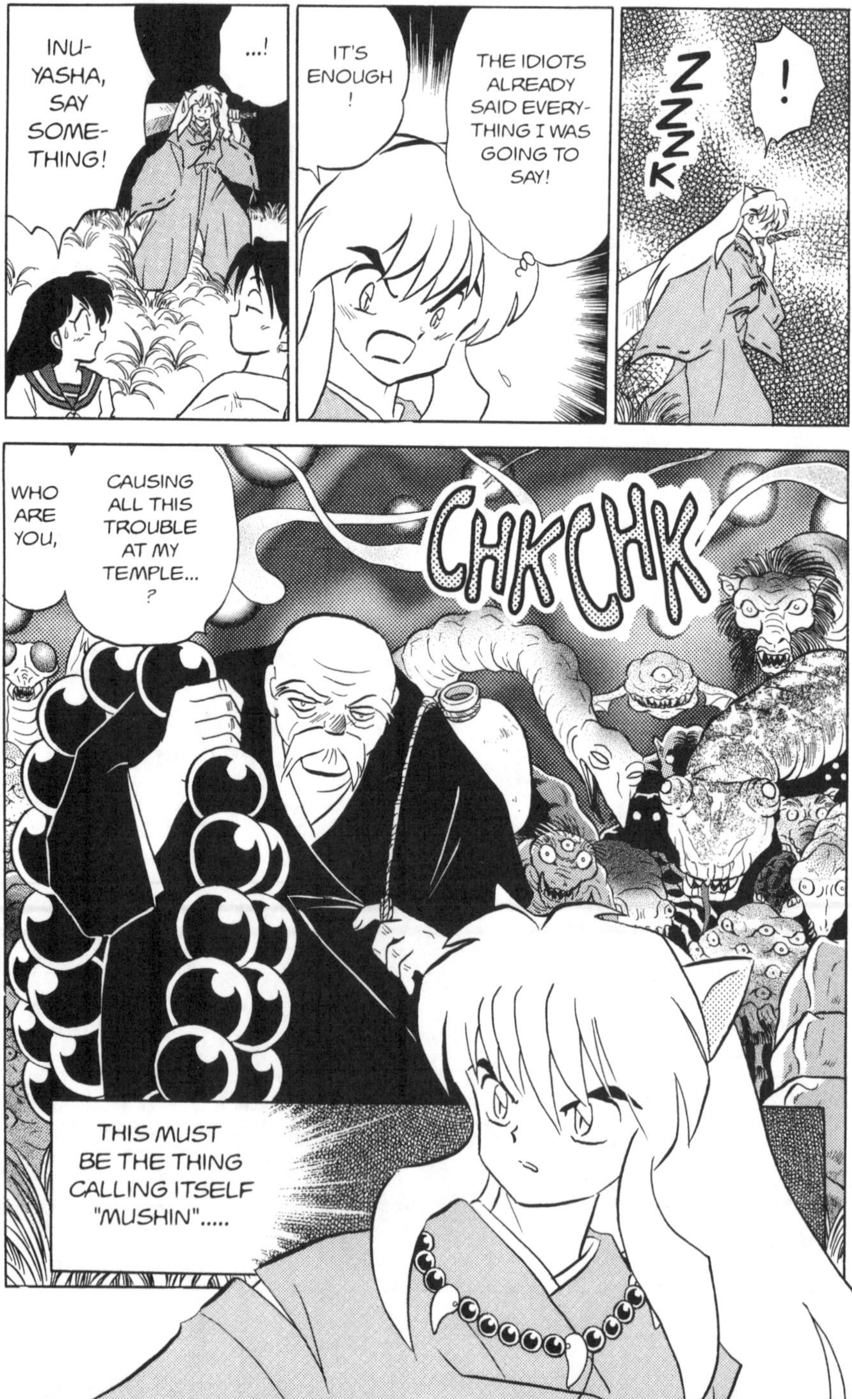
INU-YASHA, SAY SOME-THING!
...!
IT'S ENOUGH!
THE IDIOTS ALREADY SAID EVERY-THING I WAS GOING TO SAY!
ZZZK
!
WHO ARE YOU,
CAUSING ALL THIS TROUBLE AT MY TEMPLE...?
CHKCHK
THIS MUST BE THE THING CALLING ITSELF "MUSHIN".....

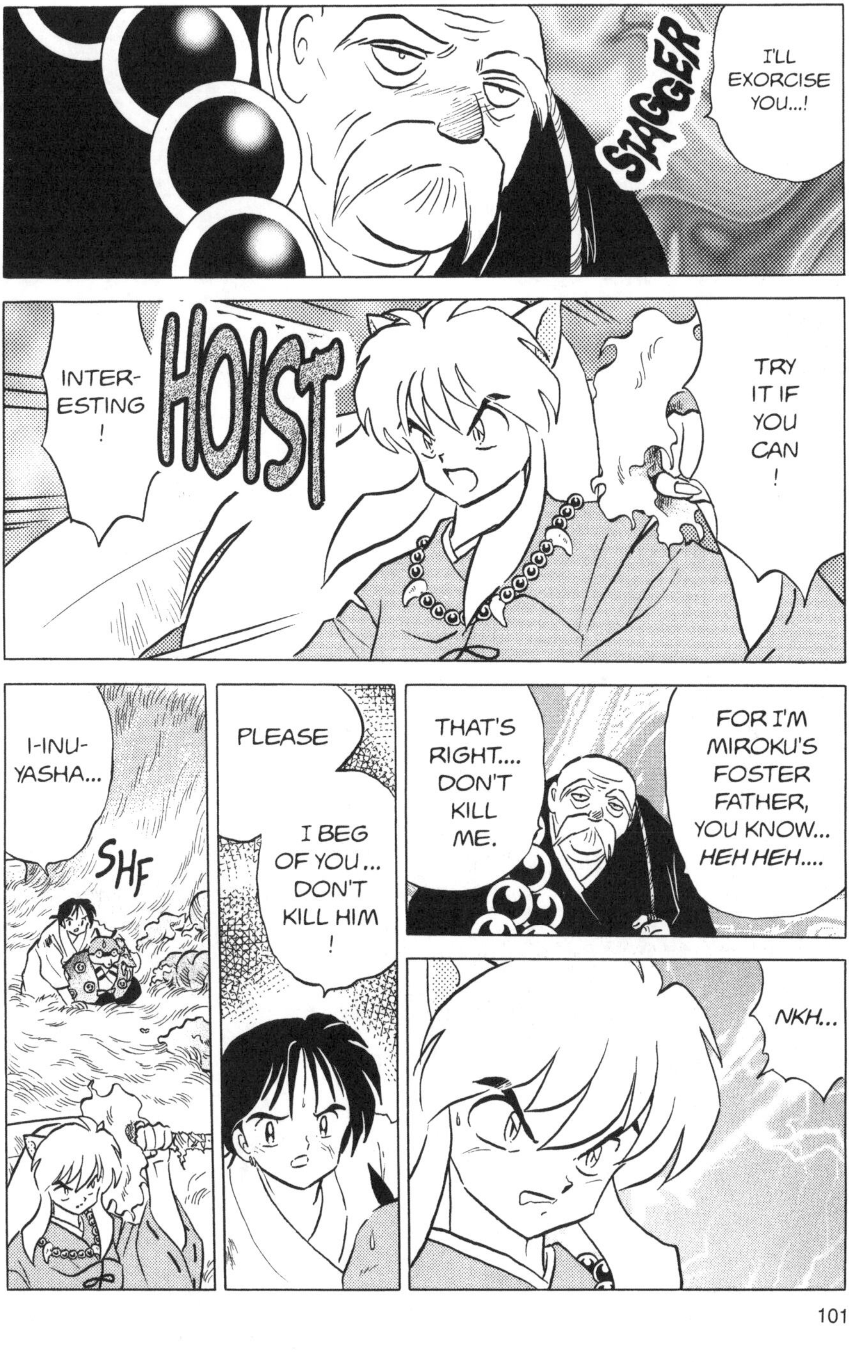
STAGGER
I'LL EXORCISE YOU...!
INTER-ESTING!
HOIST
TRY IT IF YOU CAN!
I-INU-YASHA...
SHF
PLEASE
I BEG OF YOU... DON'T KILL HIM!
THAT'S RIGHT.... DON'T KILL ME.
FOR I'M MIROKU'S FOSTER FATHER, YOU KNOW... HEH HEH....
NKH...

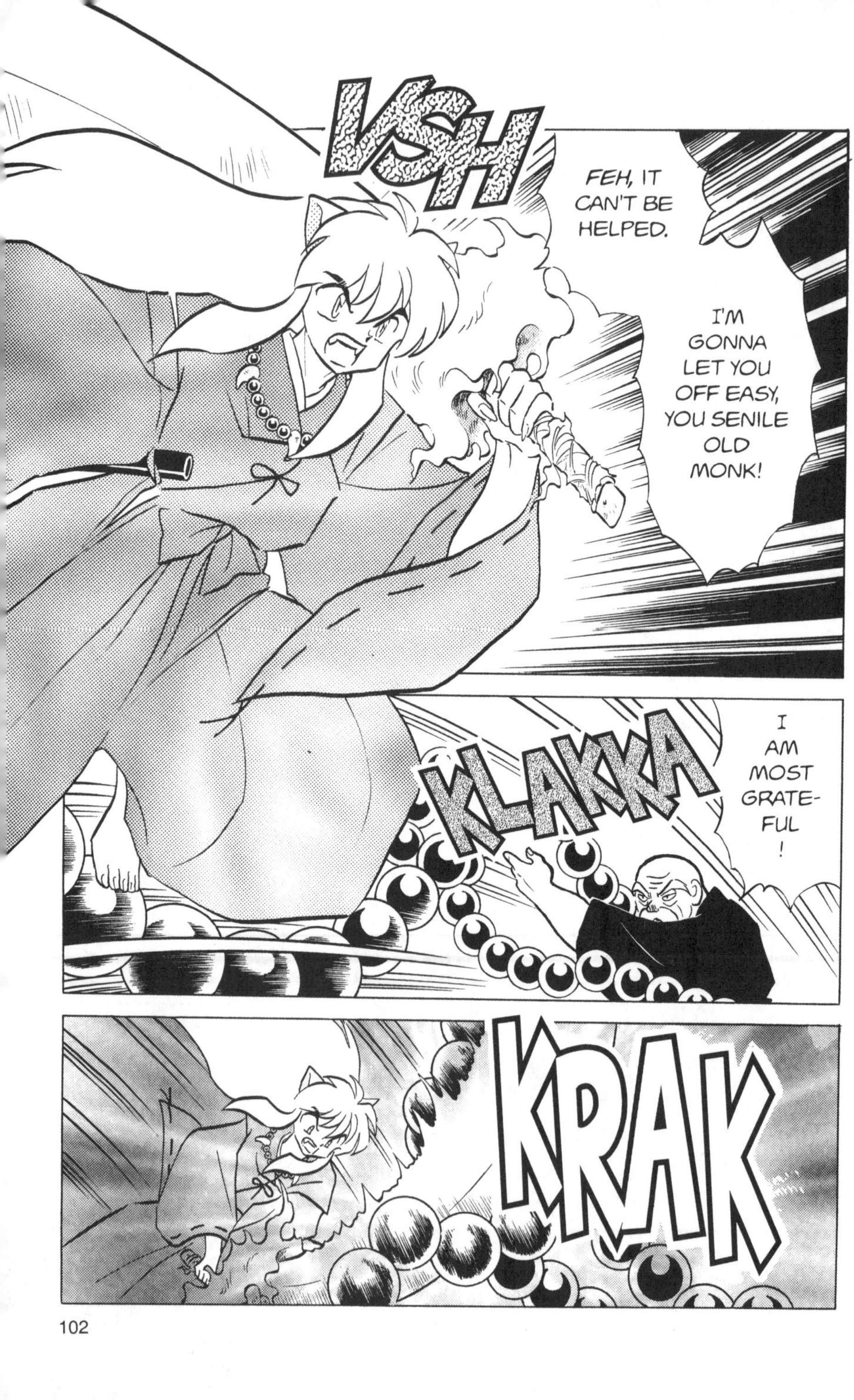
VSH
FEH, IT CAN'T BE HELPED.
I'M GONNA LET YOU OFF EASY, YOU SENILE OLD MONK!
I AM MOST GRATE-FUL!
KLAKKA
KRAK

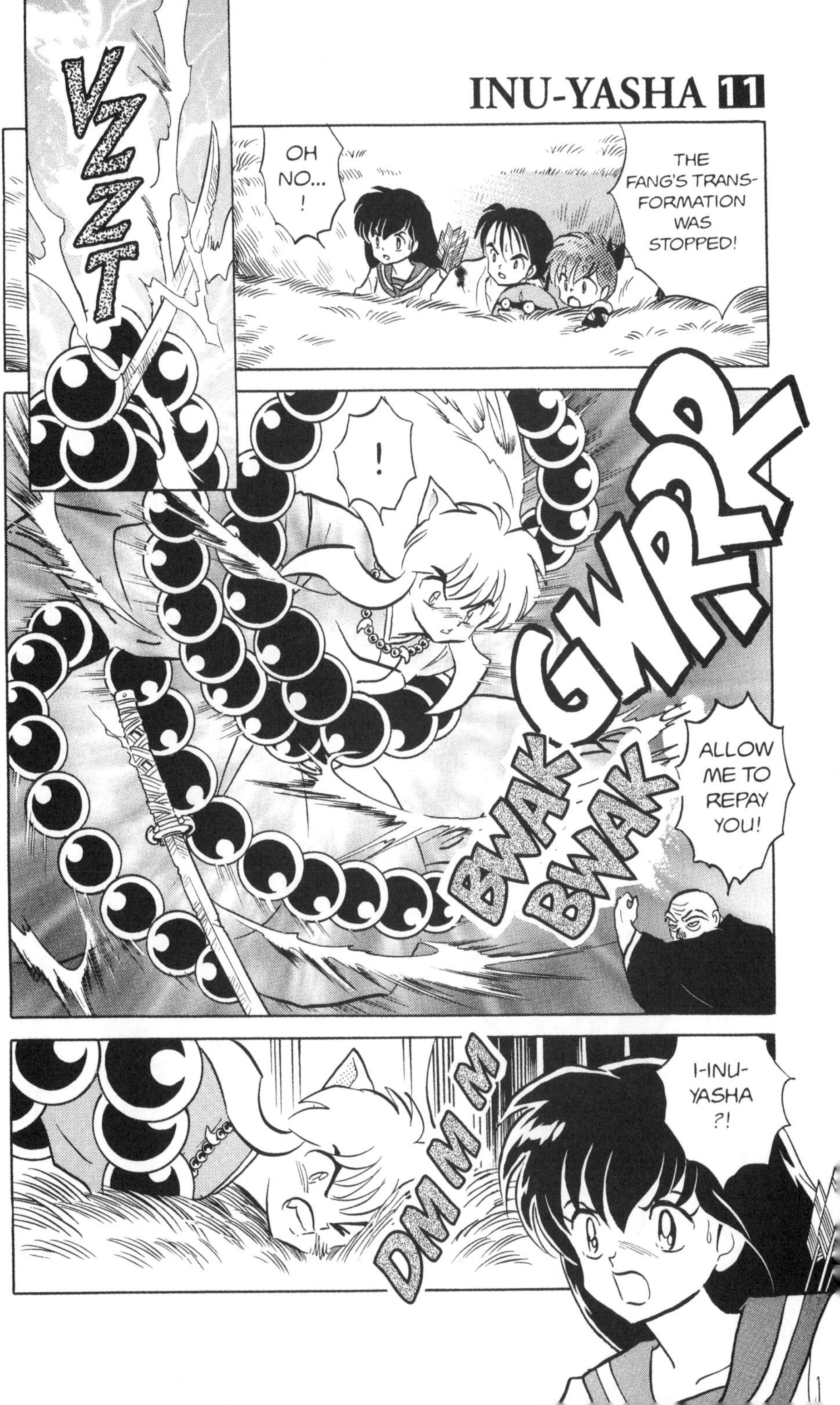
THE FANG'S TRANS-FORMATION WAS STOPPED!
OH NO... !
VZZT
GWRRR
!
ALLOW ME TO REPAY YOU!
BWAK BWAK
I-INU-YASHA ?!
DMMM

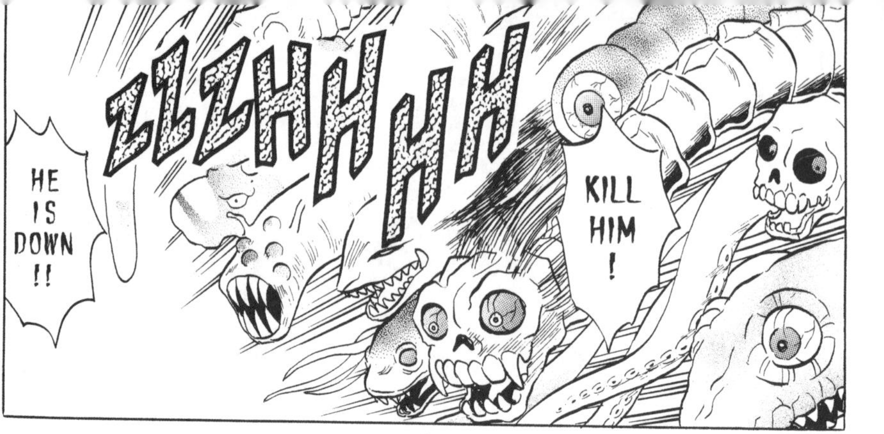
KILL HIM !
ZZZHHHHH
HE IS DOWN !!
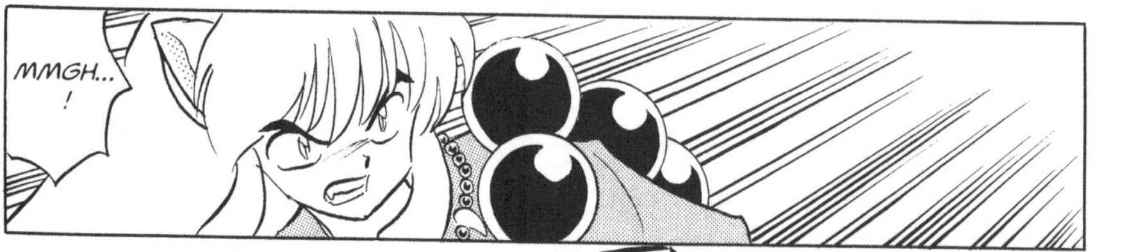
MMGH... !
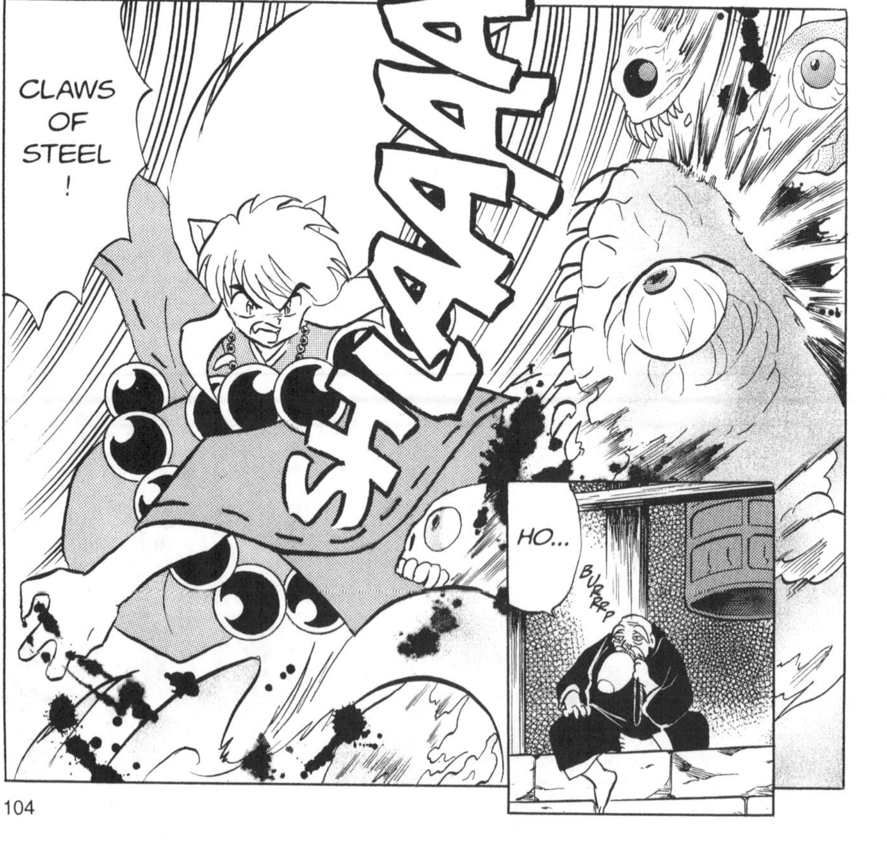
CLAWS OF STEEL !
SHAAAA
HO...
BURRRP

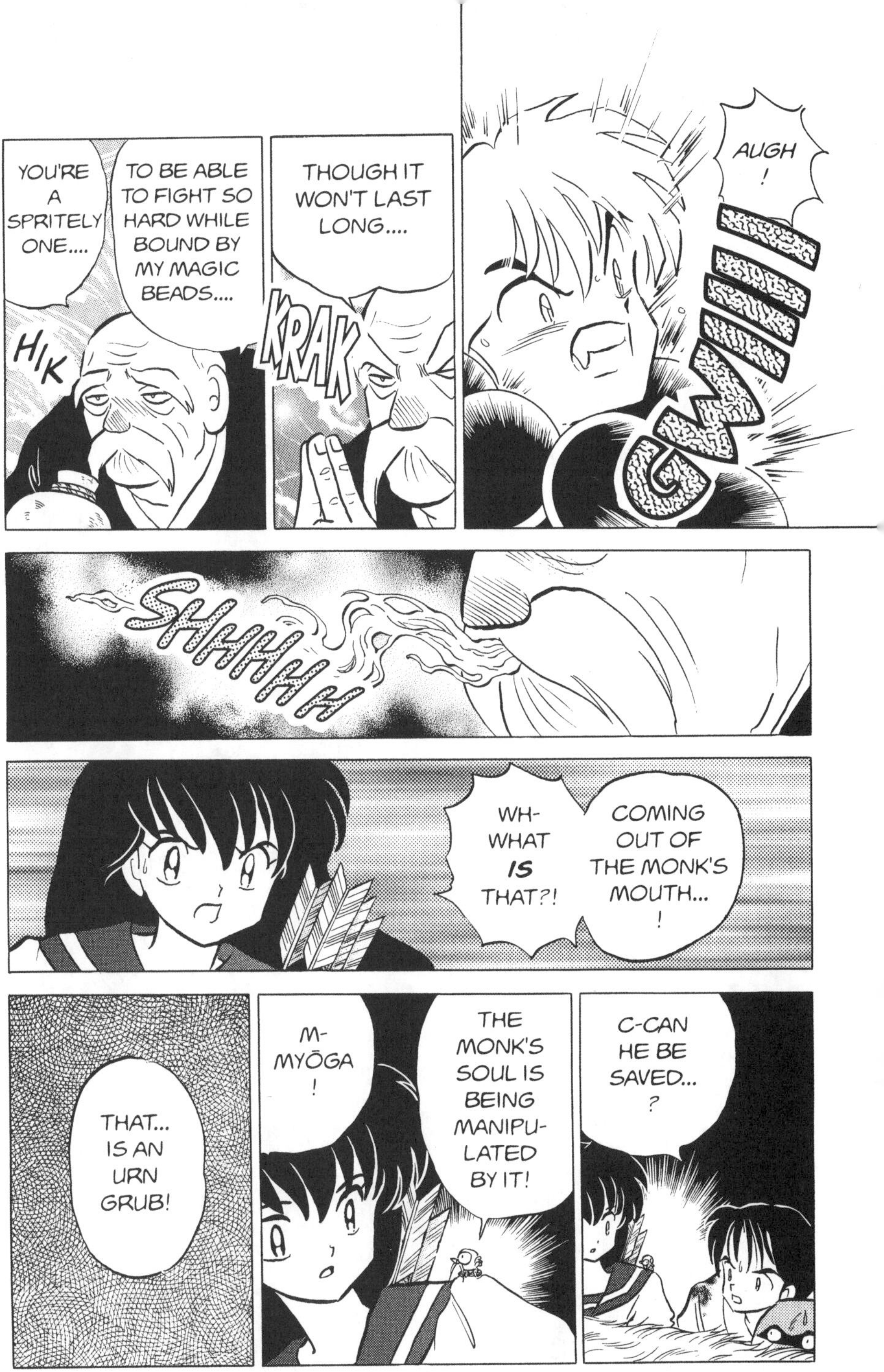
YOU'RE A SPRITELY ONE....
TO BE ABLE TO FIGHT SO HARD WHILE BOUND BY MY MAGIC BEADS....
HIK
THOUGH IT WON'T LAST LONG....
KRAK
AUGH!
GWIIIIK
SHHHHHH
WH- WHAT *IS* THAT?!
COMING OUT OF THE MONK'S MOUTH...!
THAT... IS AN URN GRUB!
M- MYŌGA!
THE MONK'S SOUL IS BEING MANIPU- LATED BY IT!
C-CAN HE BE SAVED...?

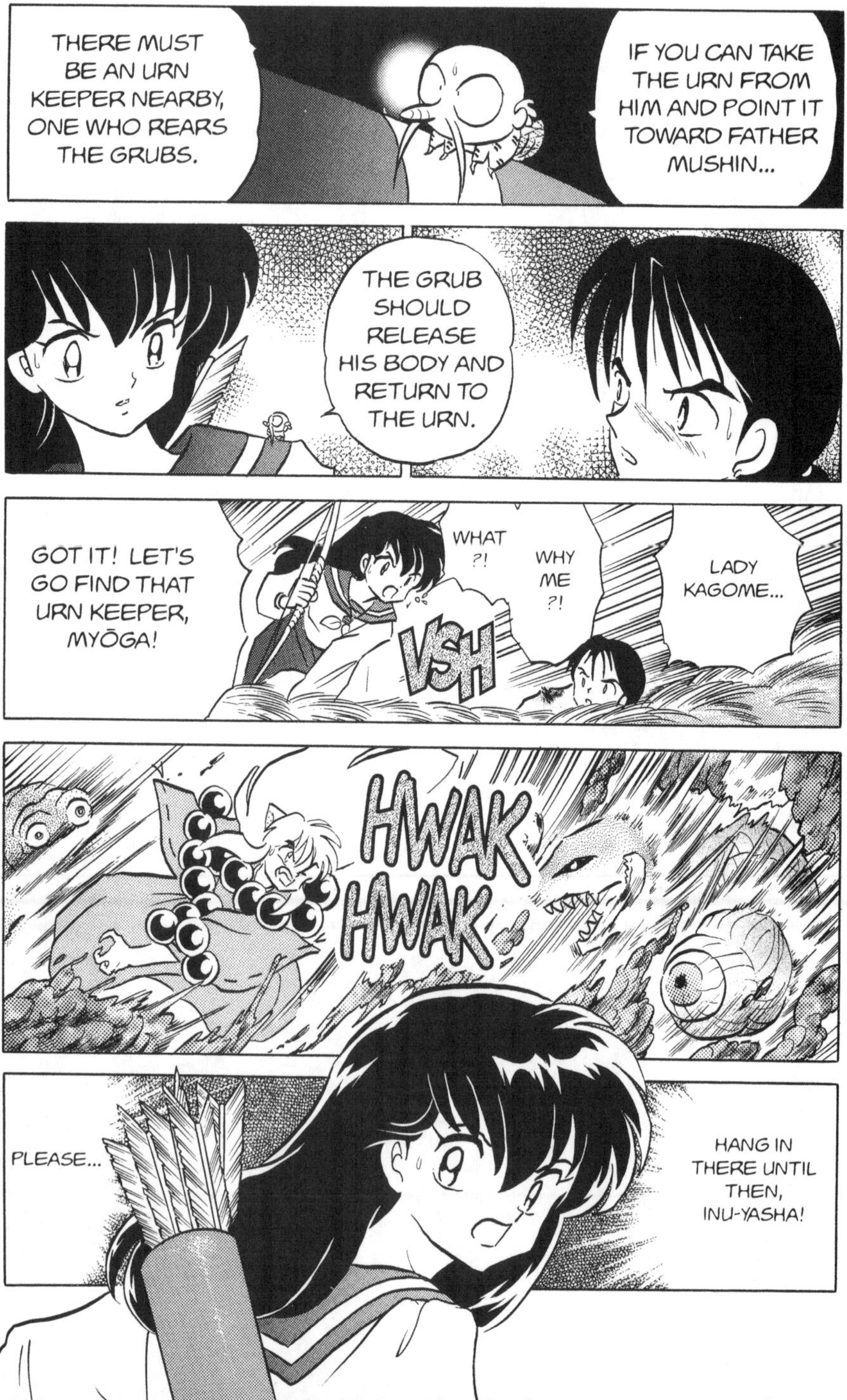
THERE MUST BE AN URN KEEPER NEARBY, ONE WHO REARS THE GRUBS.
IF YOU CAN TAKE THE URN FROM HIM AND POINT IT TOWARD FATHER MUSHIN...
THE GRUB SHOULD RELEASE HIS BODY AND RETURN TO THE URN.
GOT IT! LET'S GO FIND THAT URN KEEPER, MYŌGA!
WHAT ?!
WHY ME ?!
VSH
LADY KAGOME...
HWAK HWAK
PLEASE...
HANG IN THERE UNTIL THEN, INU-YASHA!

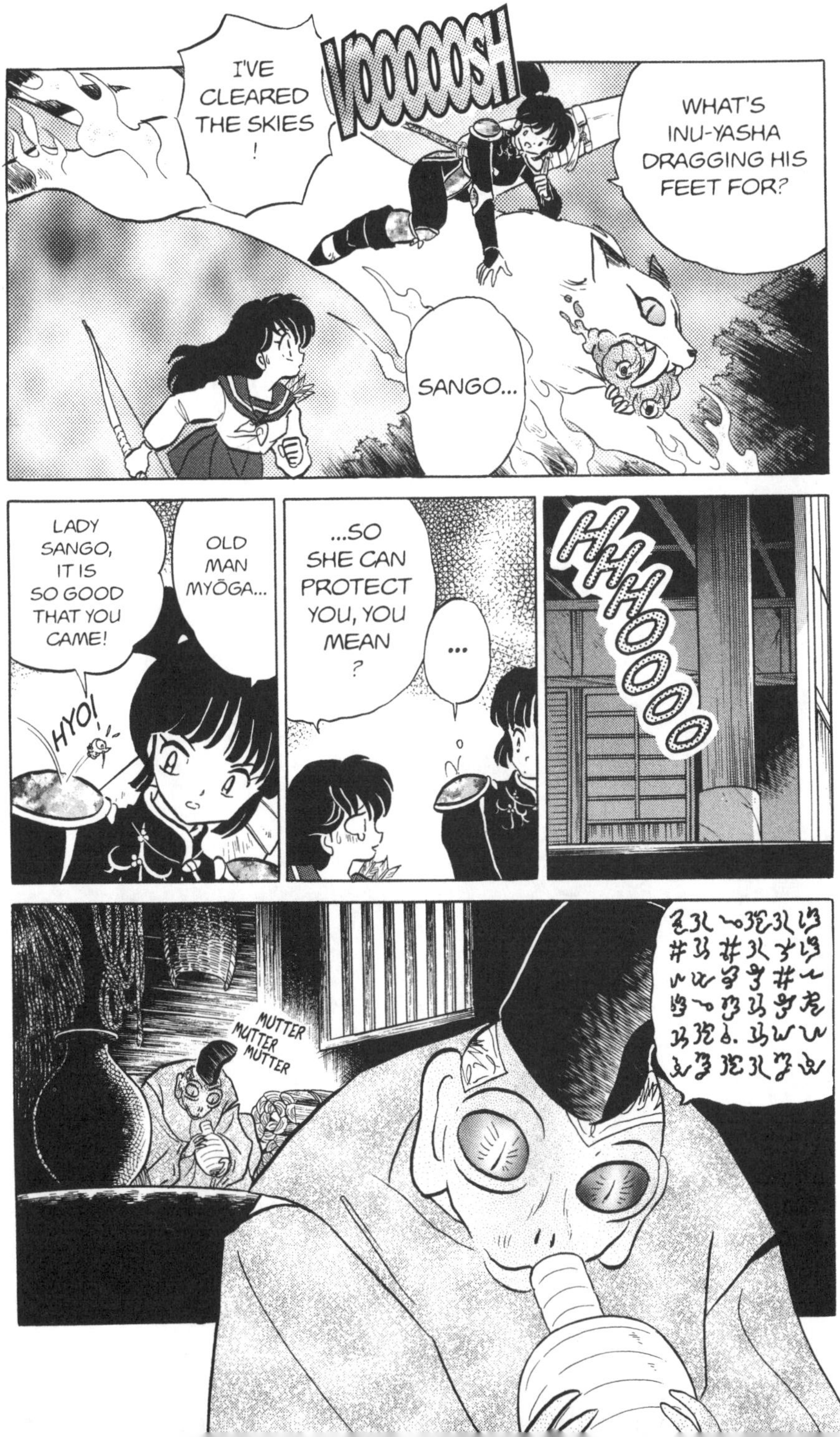
WHAT'S INU-YASHA DRAGGING HIS FEET FOR?
VOOOOOSH
I'VE CLEARED THE SKIES!
SANGO...
HHHOOOOO
...
...SO SHE CAN PROTECT YOU, YOU MEAN?
OLD MAN MYŌGA...
LADY SANGO, IT IS SO GOOD THAT YOU CAME!
HYO!
MUTTER MUTTER MUTTER

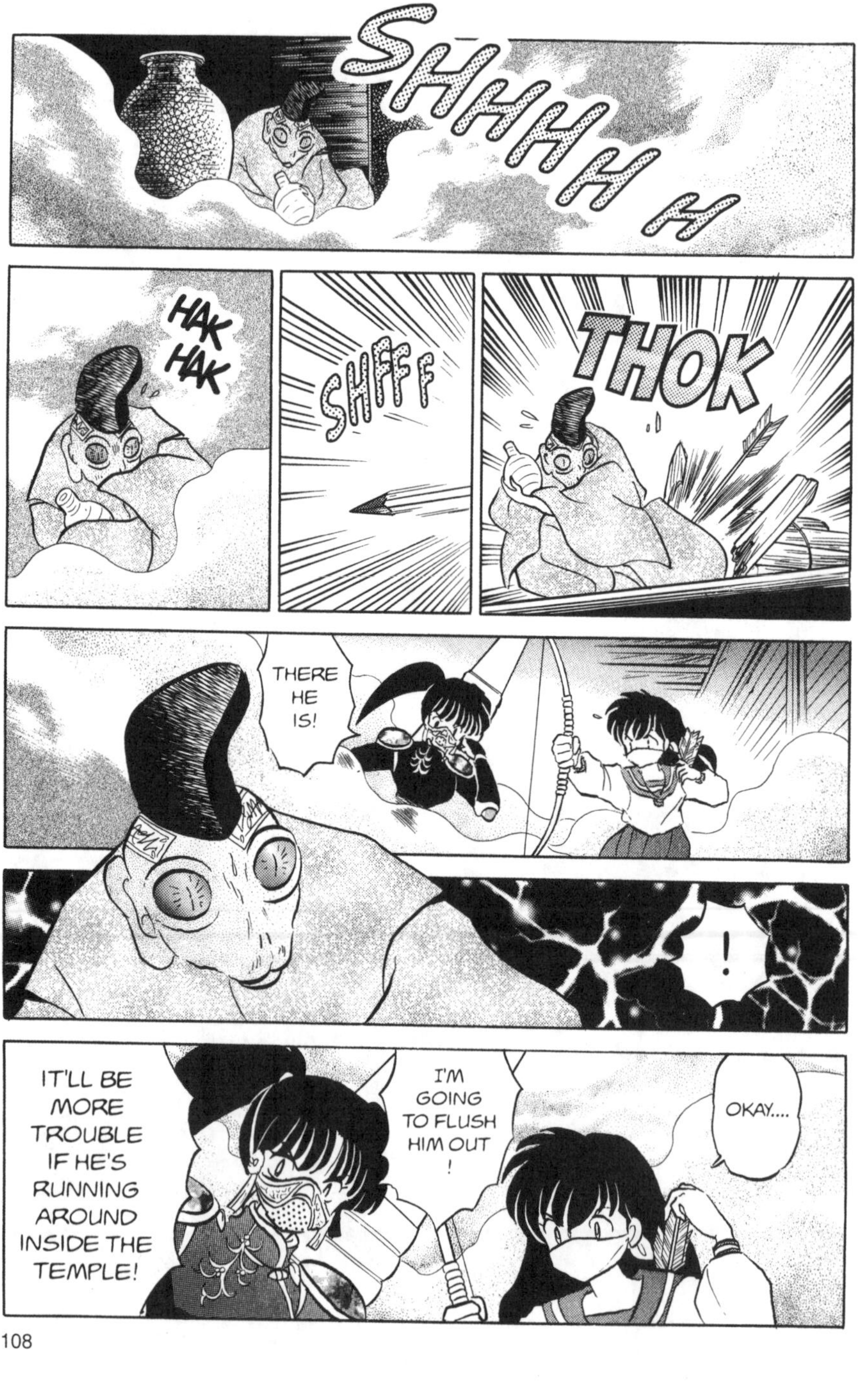
SHHHHH H
THOK
SHFFF
HAK HAK
THERE HE IS!
!
OKAY....
I'M GOING TO FLUSH HIM OUT!
IT'LL BE MORE TROUBLE IF HE'S RUNNING AROUND INSIDE THE TEMPLE!

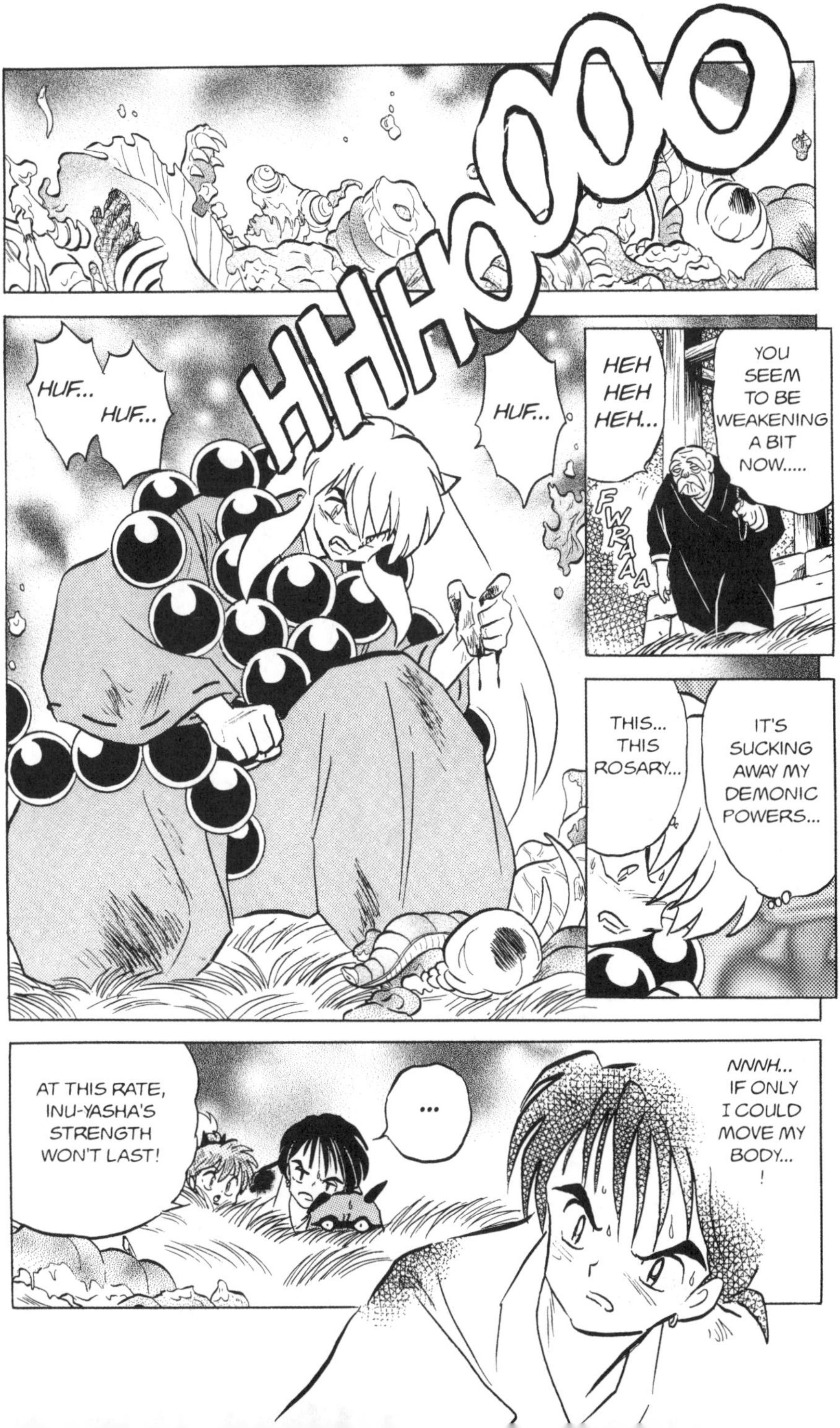
HHHOOOOOO
YOU SEEM TO BE WEAKENING A BIT NOW.....
HEH HEH HEH...
FWRAAA
IT'S SUCKING AWAY MY DEMONIC POWERS...
THIS... THIS ROSARY...
HUF...
HUF... HUF...
NNNH... IF ONLY I COULD MOVE MY BODY... !
...
AT THIS RATE, INU-YASHA'S STRENGTH WON'T LAST!

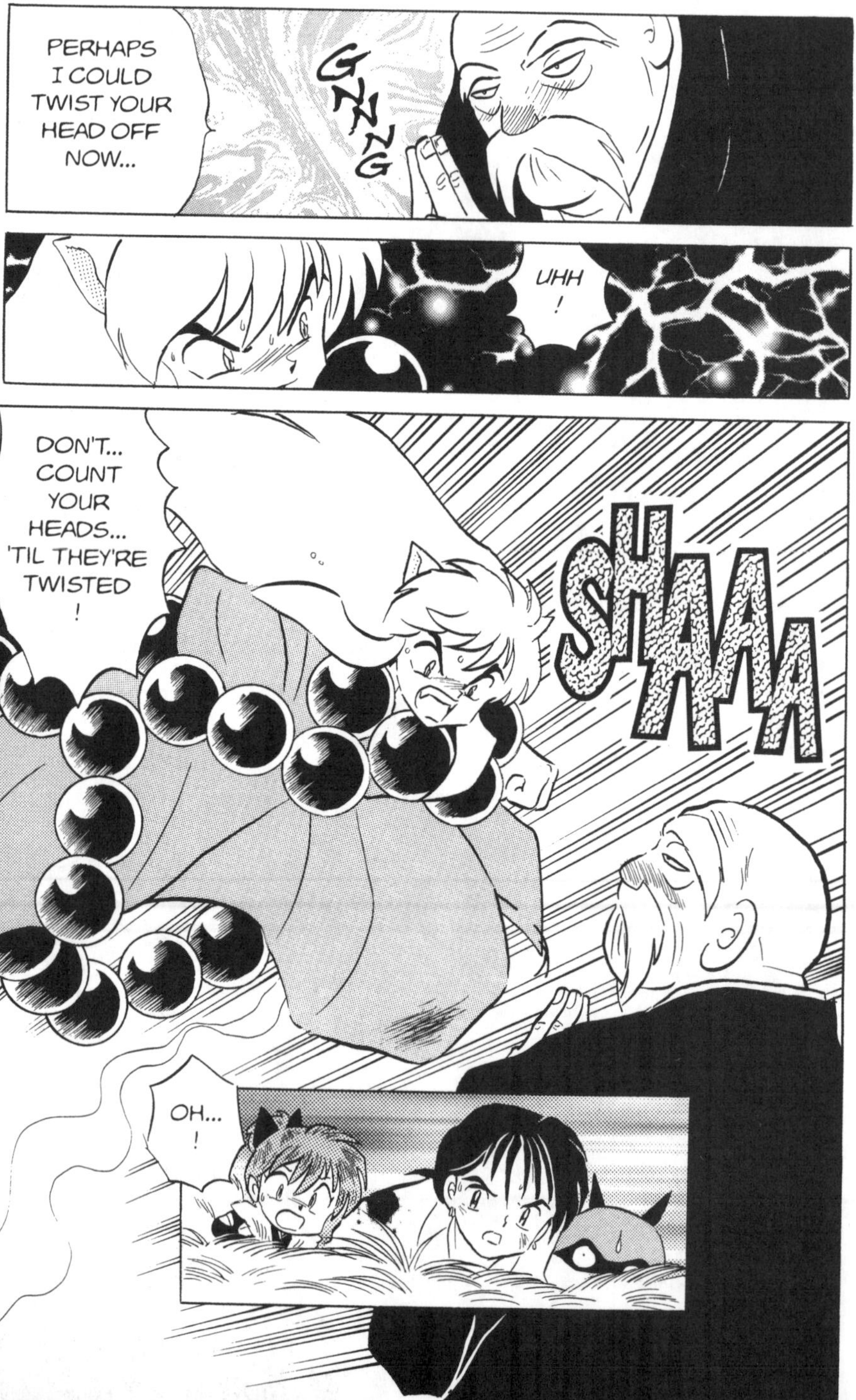
GNNG
PERHAPS I COULD TWIST YOUR HEAD OFF NOW...
UHH!
SHAAAA
DON'T... COUNT YOUR HEADS... 'TIL THEY'RE TWISTED!
OH...!

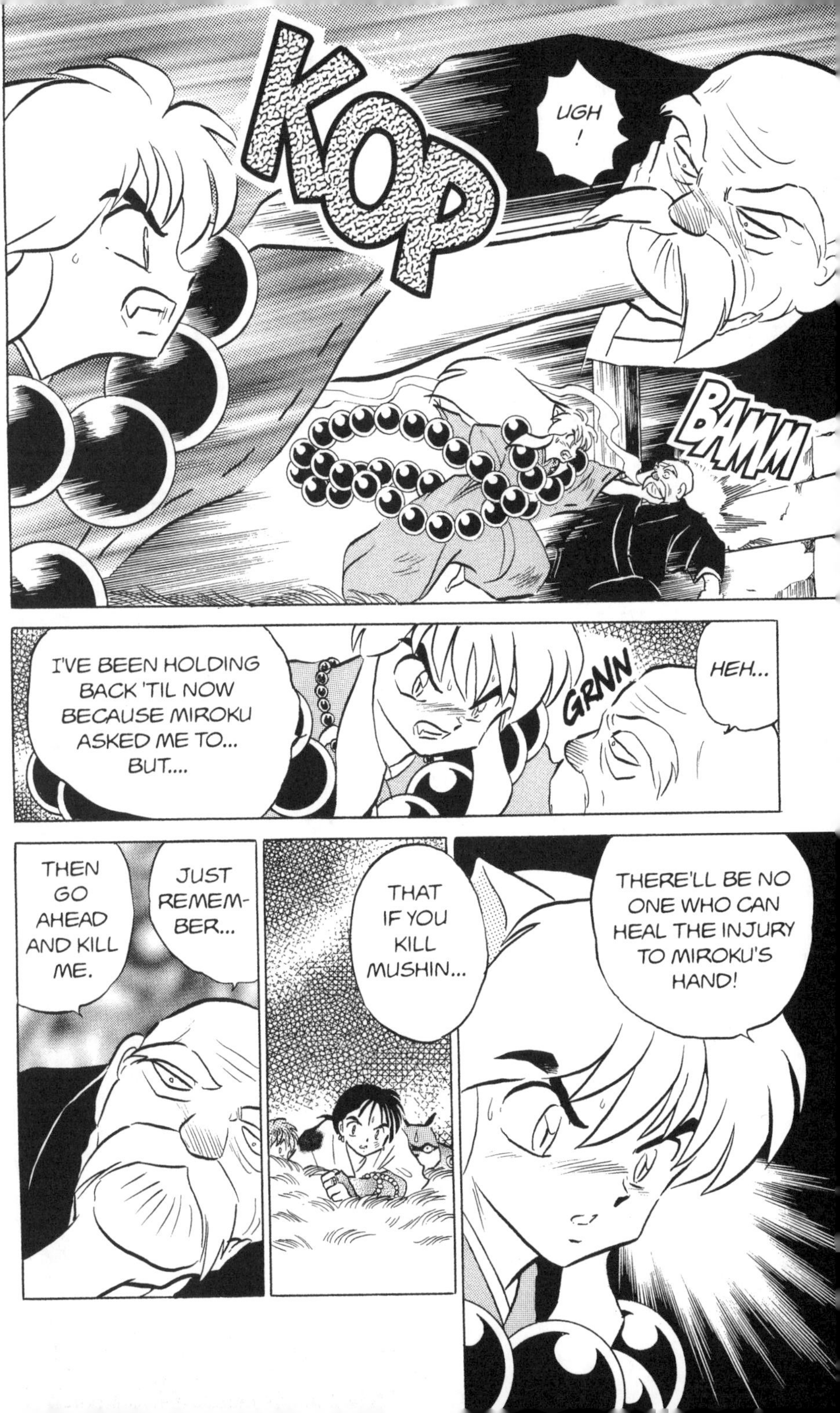
KOP
UGH !
BAMM
I'VE BEEN HOLDING BACK 'TIL NOW BECAUSE MIROKU ASKED ME TO... BUT....
GRNN
HEH...
THEN GO AHEAD AND KILL ME.
JUST REMEMBER...
THAT IF YOU KILL MUSHIN...
THERE'LL BE NO ONE WHO CAN HEAL THE INJURY TO MIROKU'S HAND!

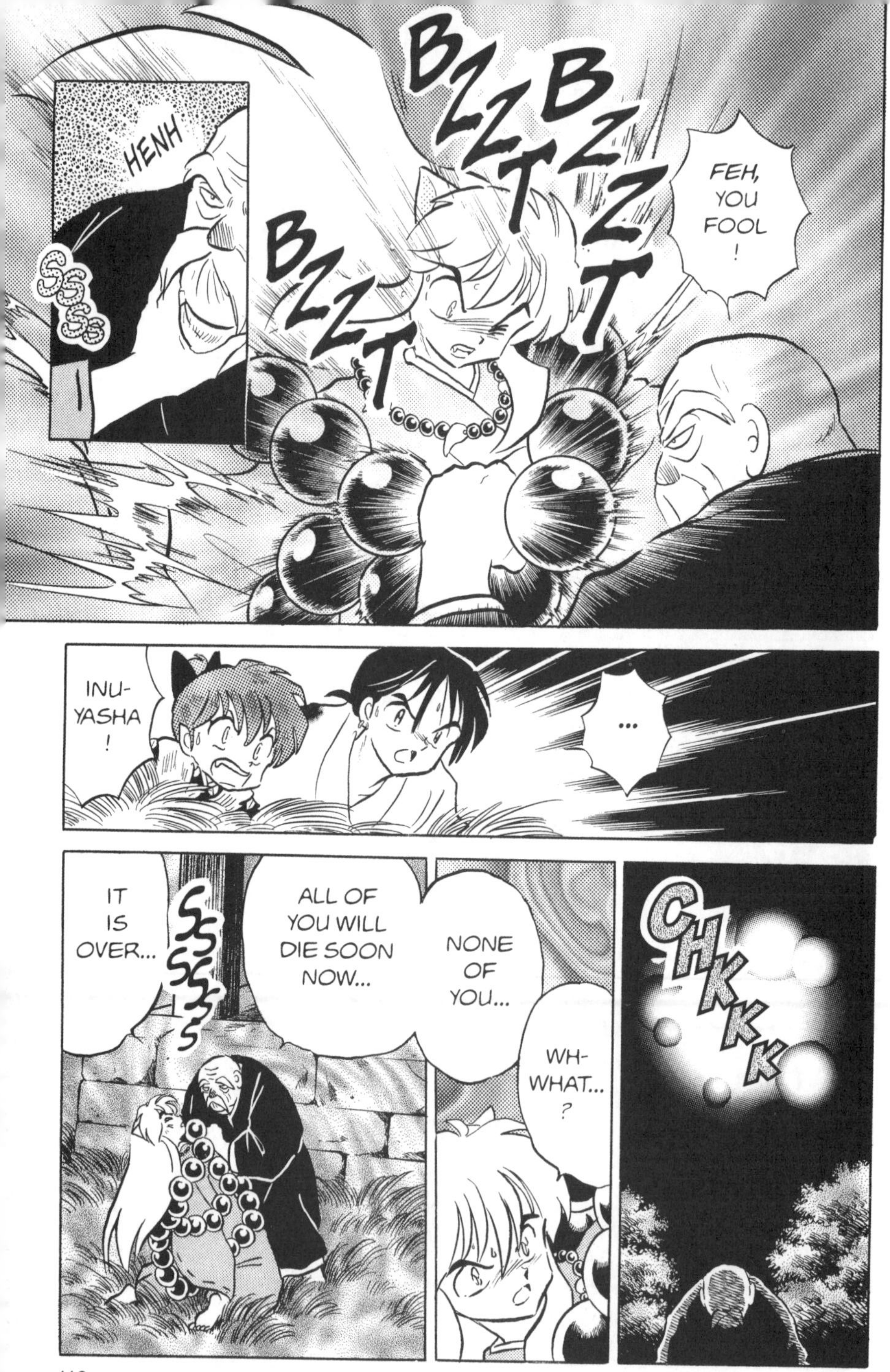
FEH, YOU FOOL!
BZZT
BZZT
BZZT
HENH
SSSS
...
INU-YASHA!
CHKKKK
NONE OF YOU...
WH-WHAT...?
ALL OF YOU WILL DIE SOON NOW...
IT IS OVER...
SSSSS

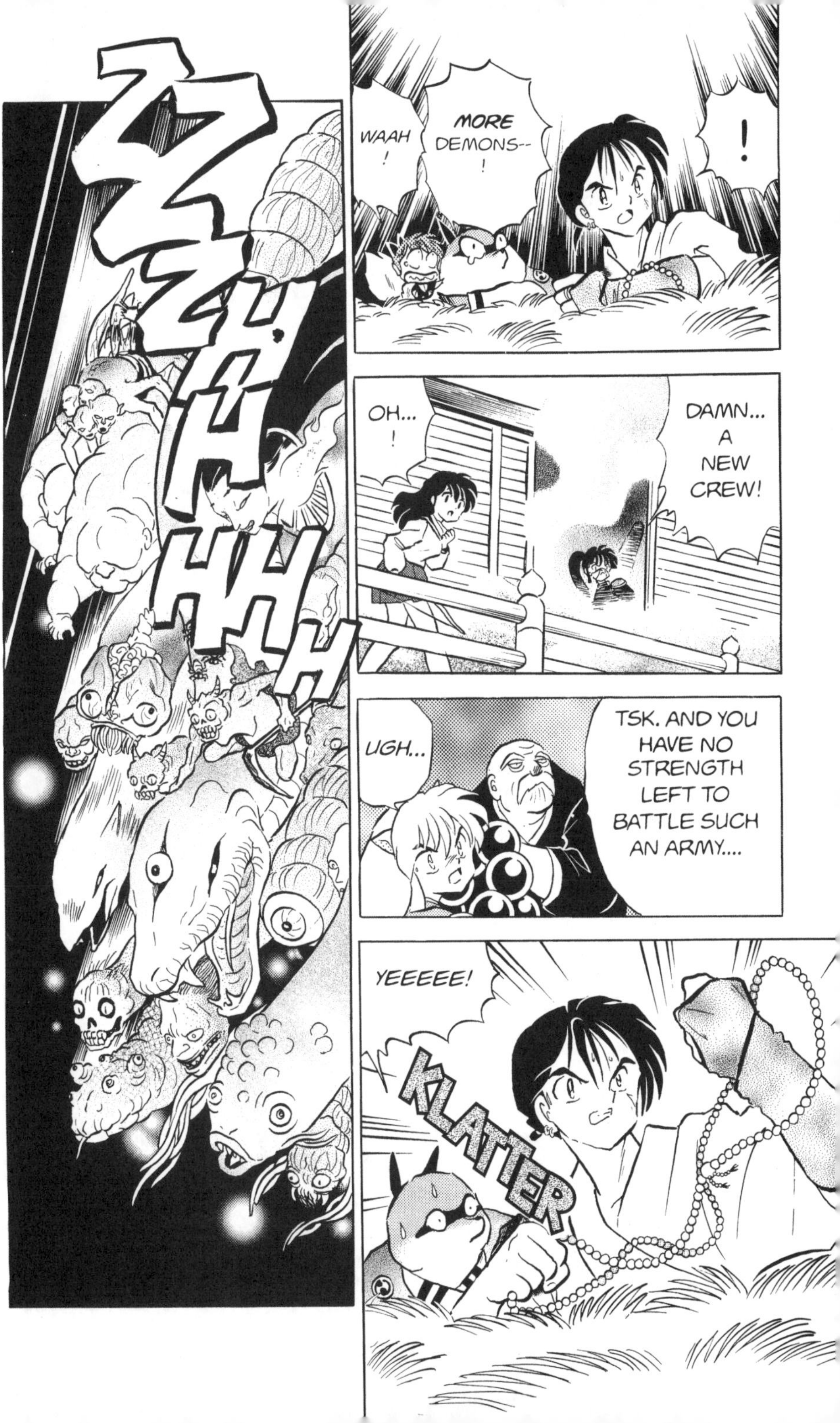
!
MORE DEMONS--!
WAAH!
DAMN... A NEW CREW!
OH...!
TSK. AND YOU HAVE NO STRENGTH LEFT TO BATTLE SUCH AN ARMY....
UGH...
YEEEEE!
KLATTER
ZZHHHHHHH

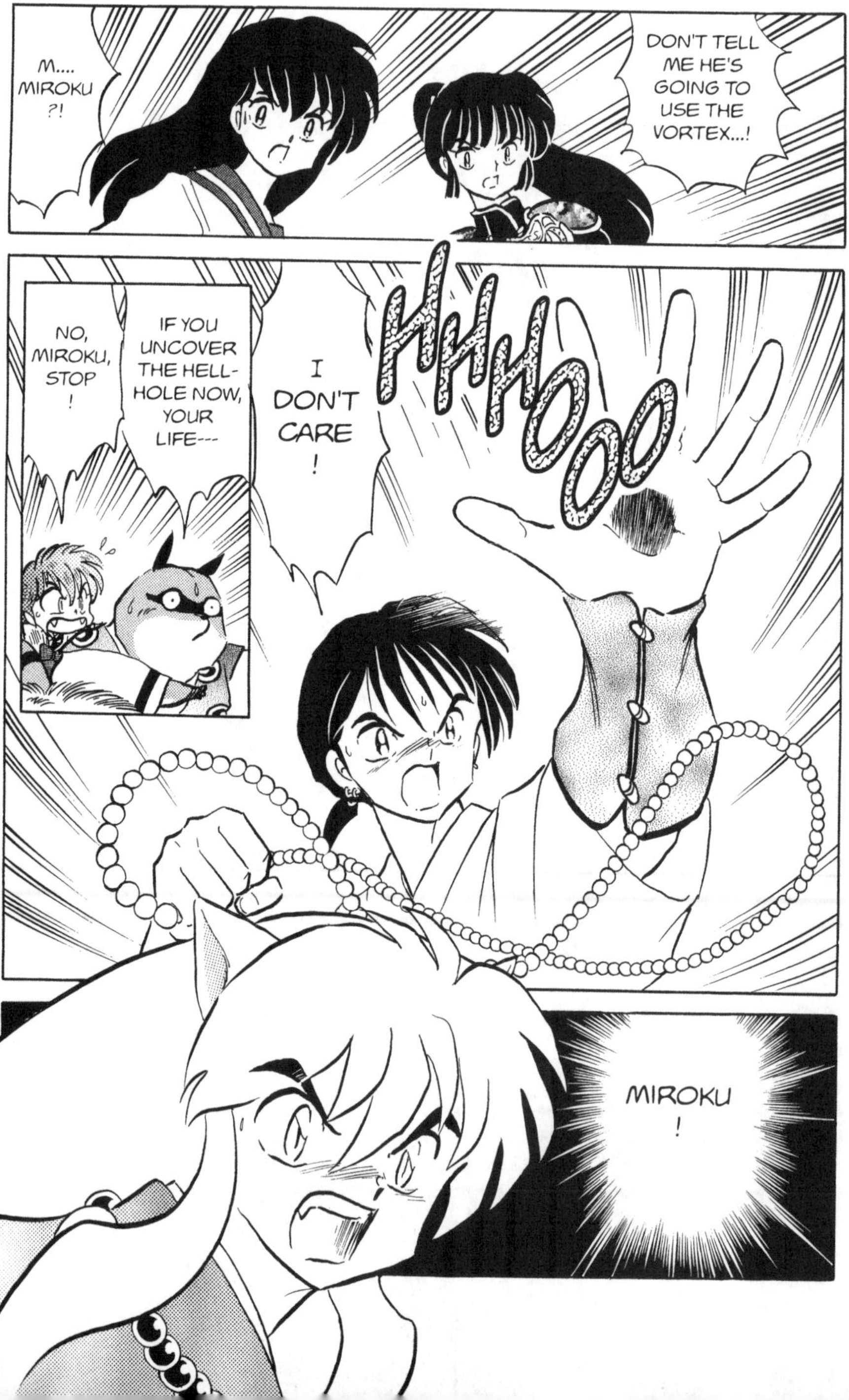
DON'T TELL ME HE'S GOING TO USE THE VORTEX...!
M.... MIROKU ?!
HHHOOO
I DON'T CARE !
IF YOU UNCOVER THE HELL-HOLE NOW, YOUR LIFE---
NO, MIROKU, STOP !
MIROKU !

SCROLL SEVEN

THE SPAN OF A LIFE

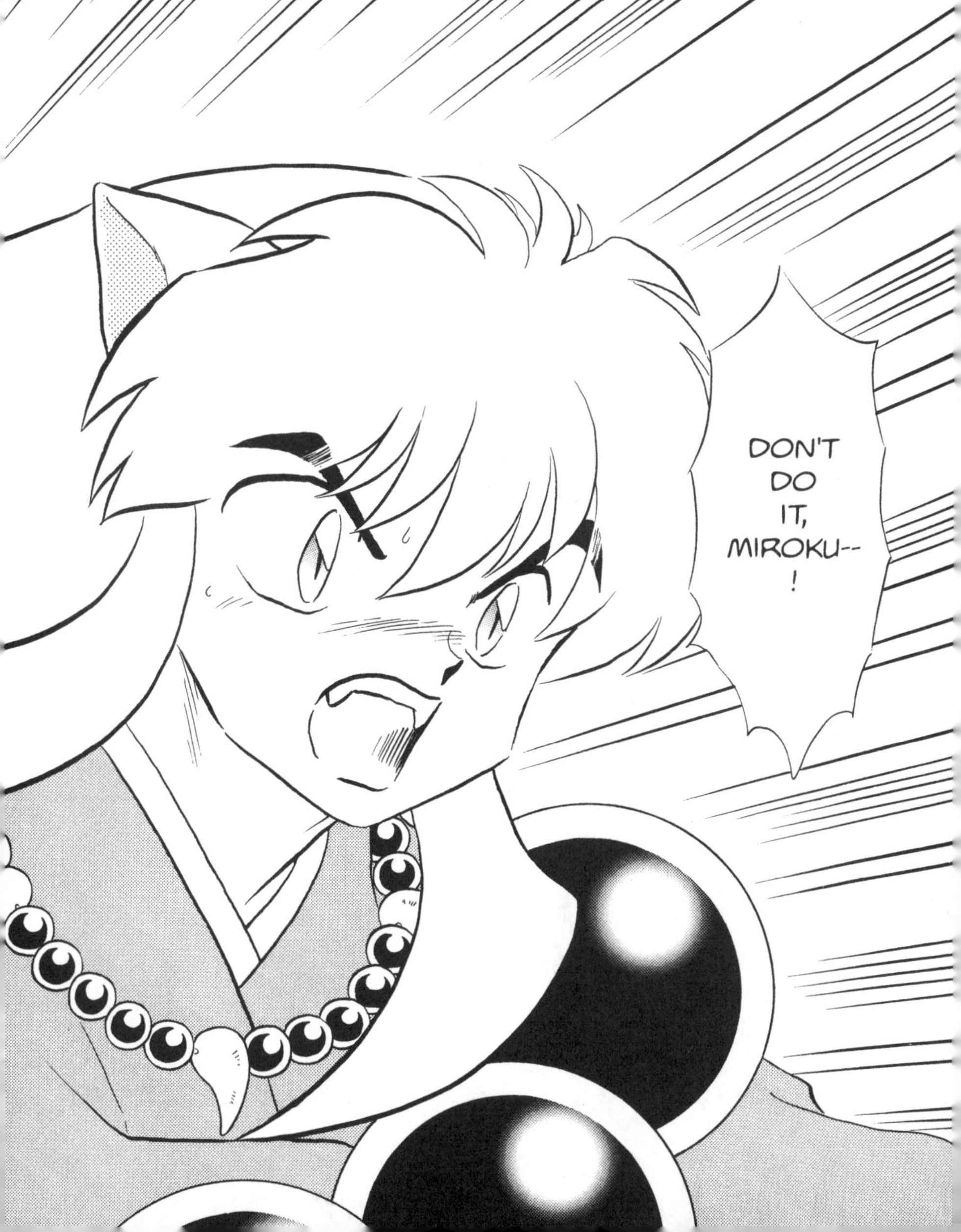
DON'T DO IT, MIROKU-- !

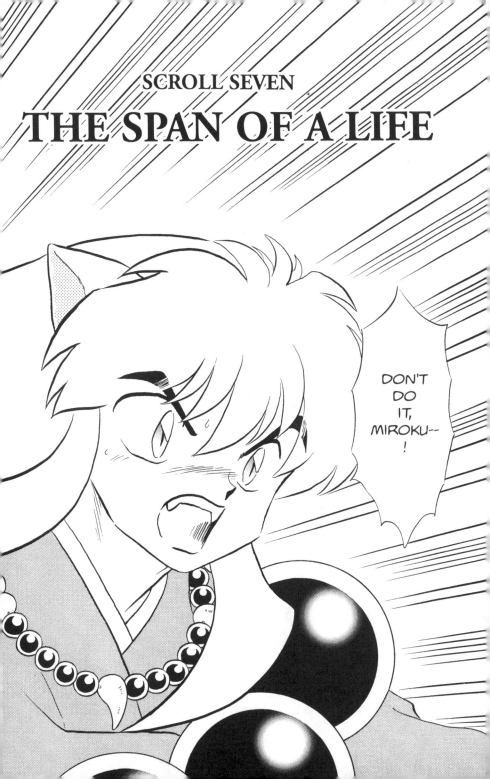

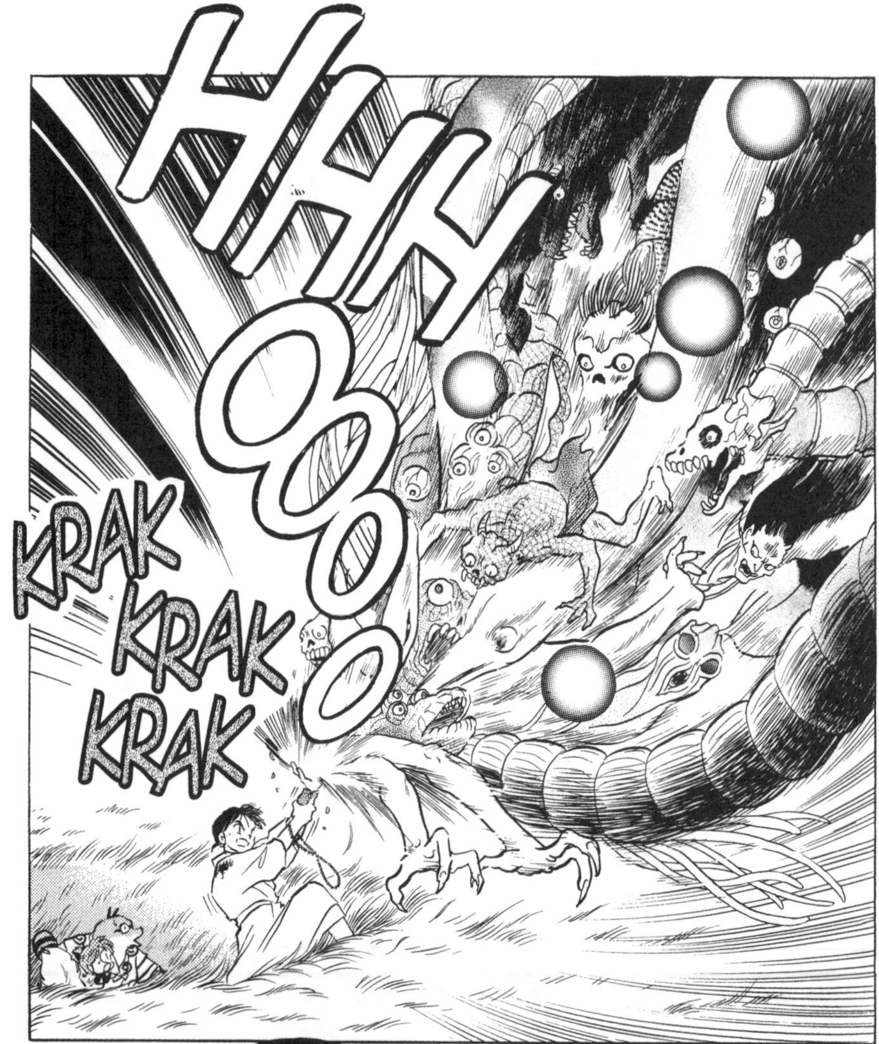
HHHOOOOO
KRAK KRAK KRAK

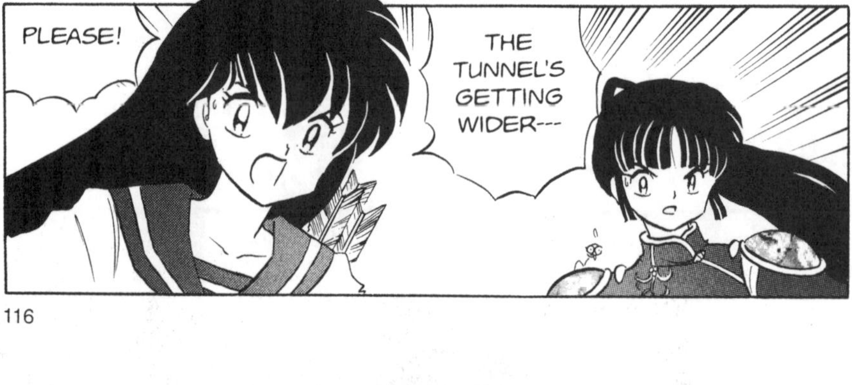
THE TUNNEL'S GETTING WIDER---
PLEASE!

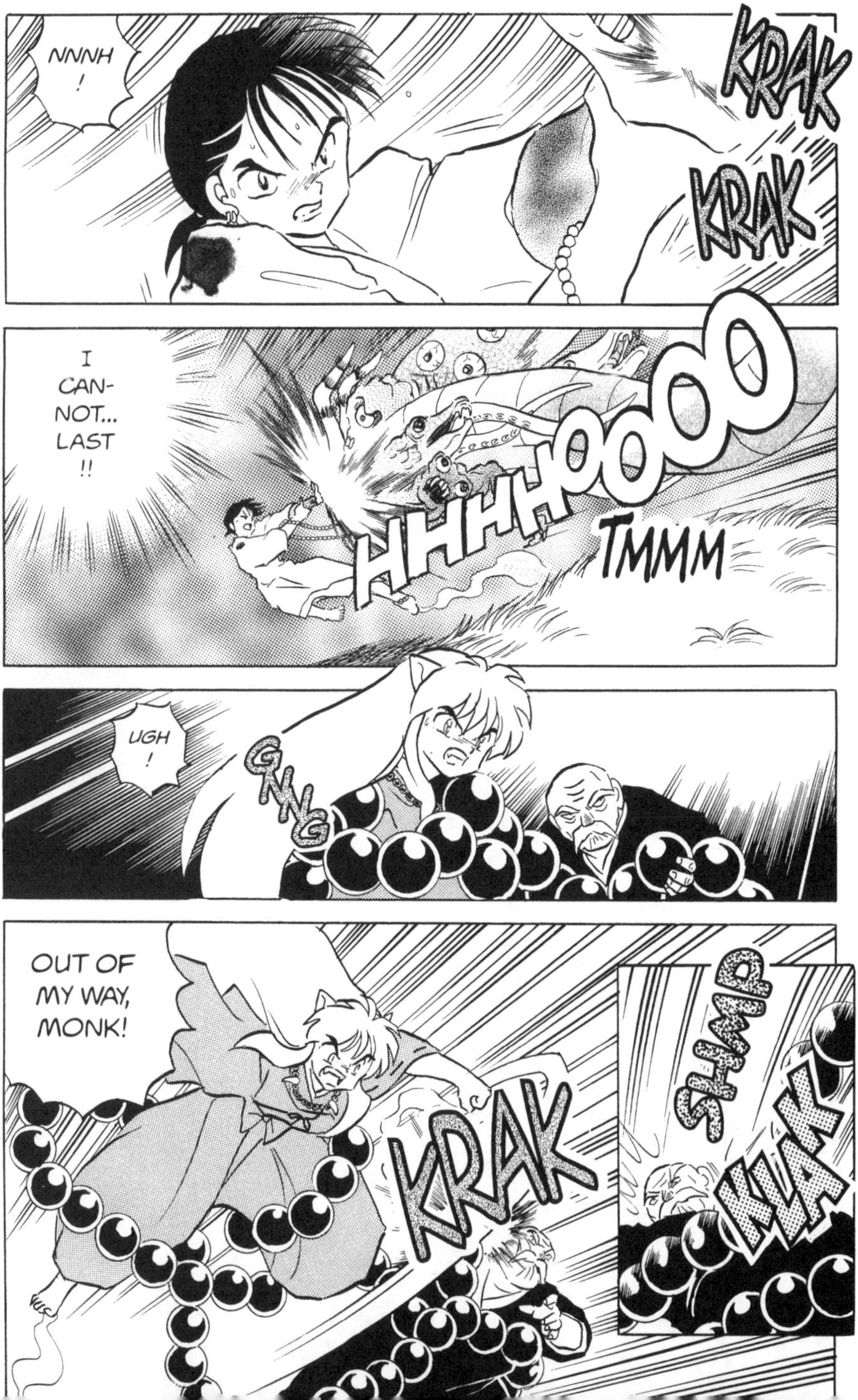
KRAK
KRAK
NNNH!
HHHHOOOOO
I CAN-NOT... LAST!!
TMMM
UGH!
GNNG
SHMP
KLAK
KRAK
OUT OF MY WAY, MONK!

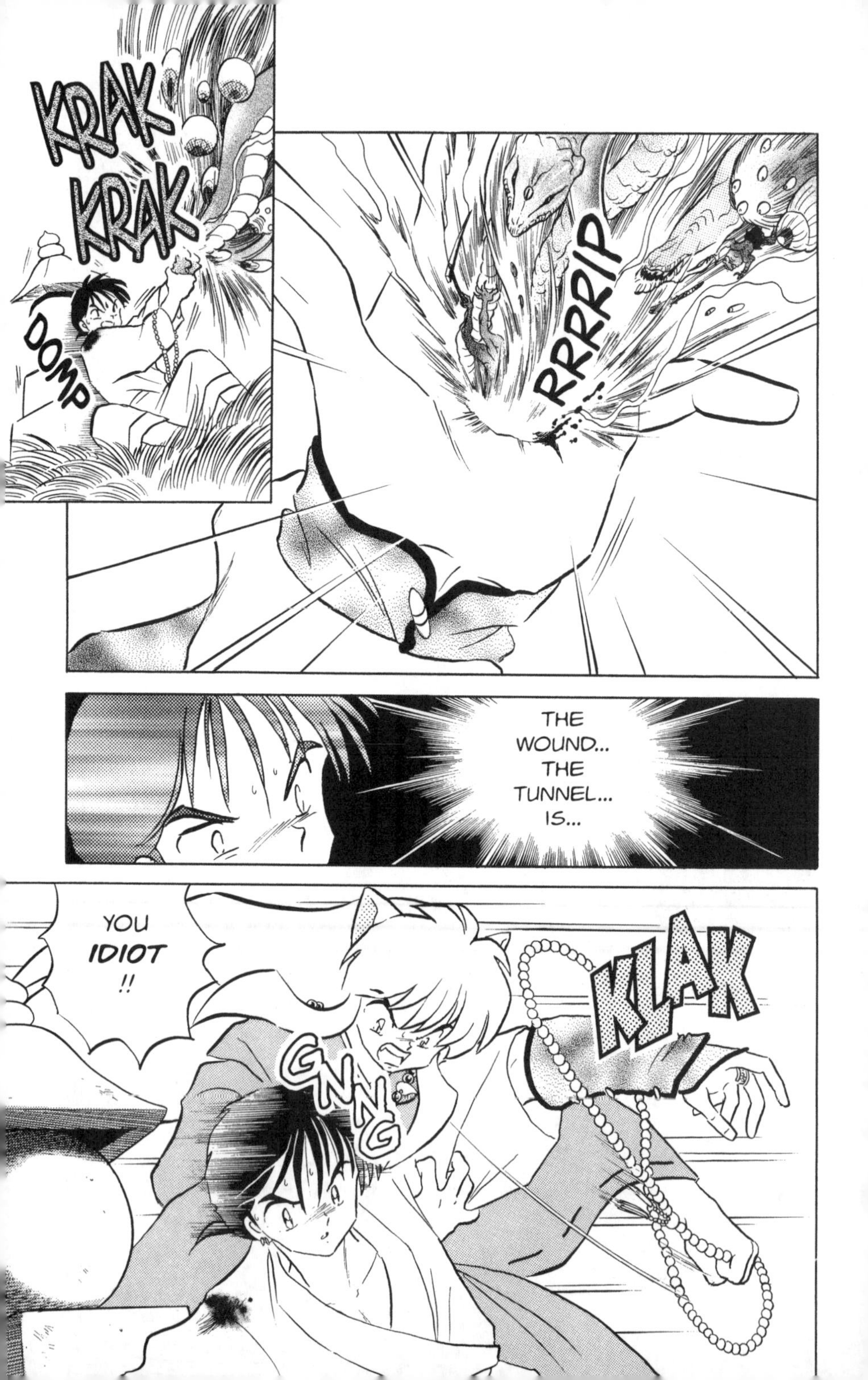
KRAK KRAK
DOMP
RRRRIP
THE WOUND... THE TUNNEL... IS...
YOU IDIOT !!
KLAK
GNNG

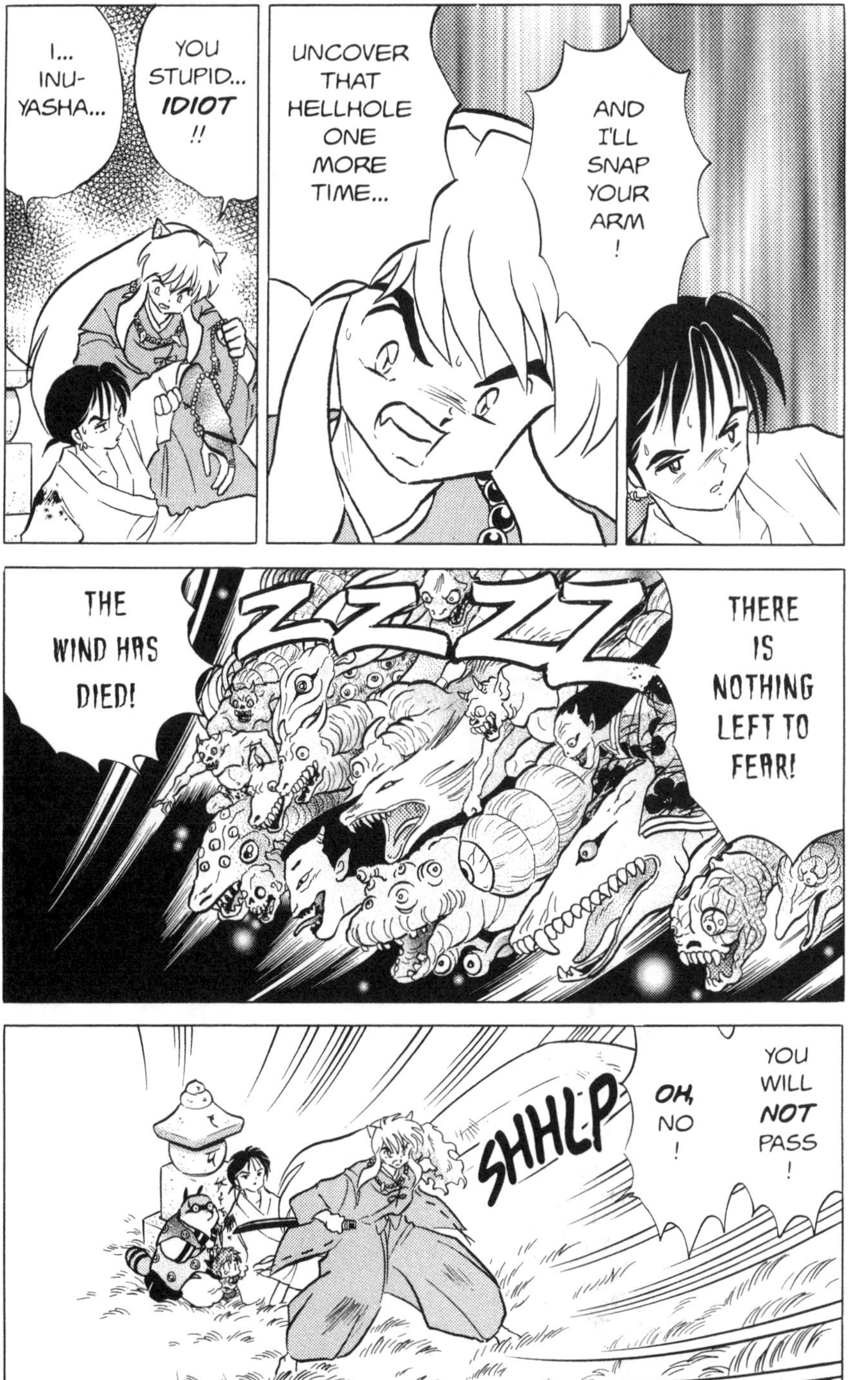
I... INU-YASHA...
YOU STUPID... IDIOT!!
UNCOVER THAT HELLHOLE ONE MORE TIME...
AND I'LL SNAP YOUR ARM!
THE WIND HAS DIED!
ZZZZZ
THERE IS NOTHING LEFT TO FEAR!
SHHLP
OH, NO!
YOU WILL NOT PASS!

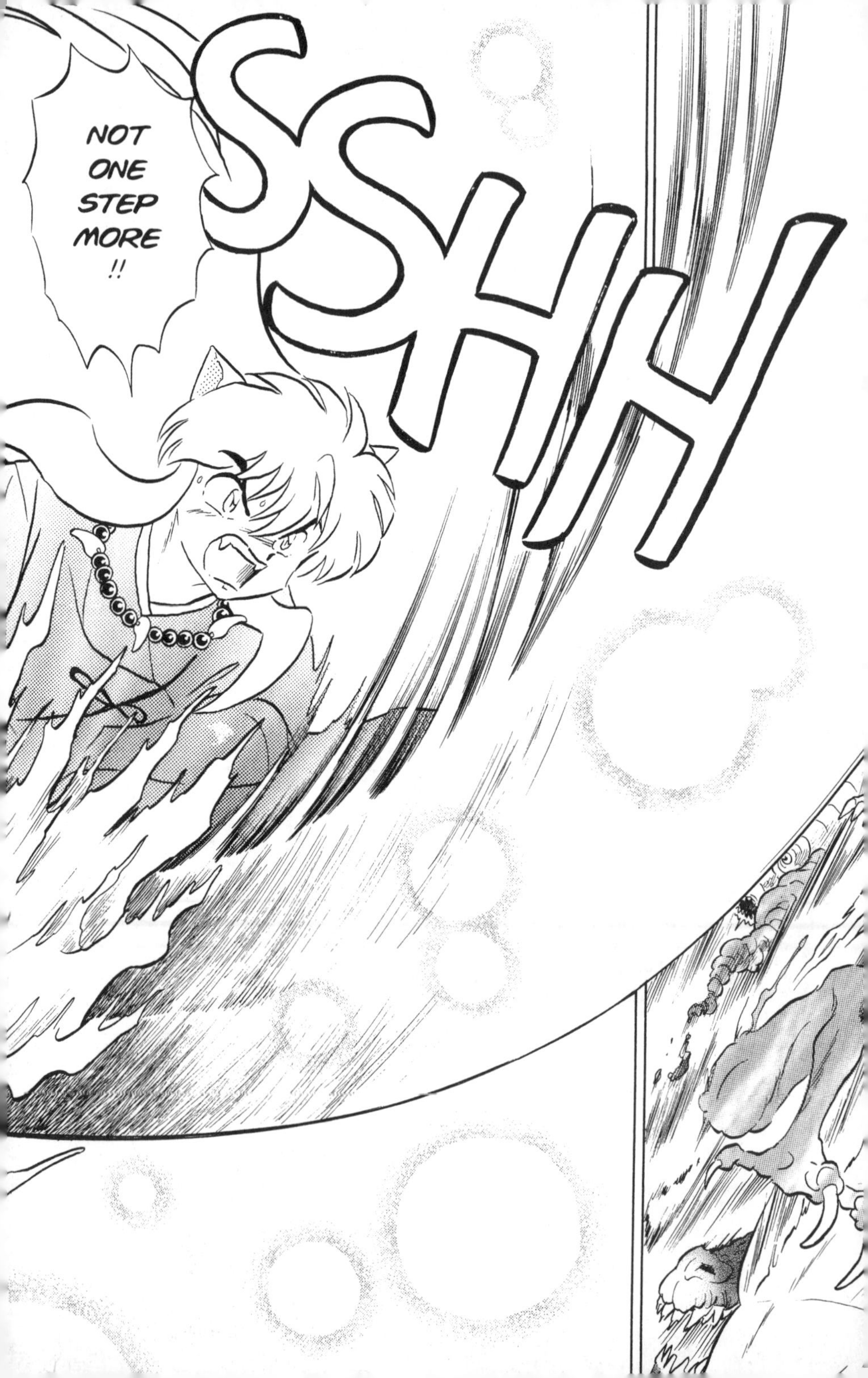
NOT ONE STEP MORE !!
SSHHH

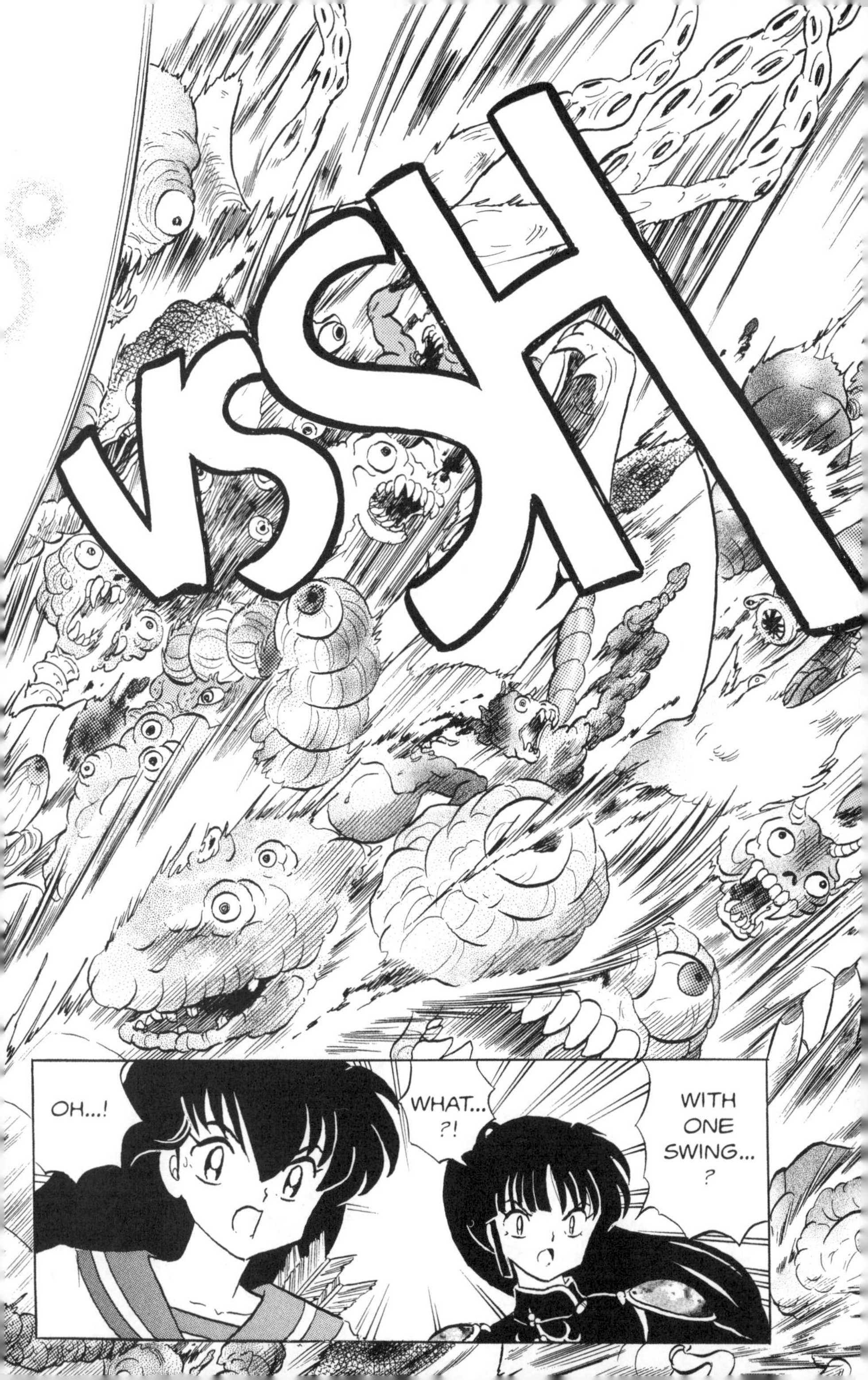
VSSH
WITH ONE SWING... ?
WHAT... ?!
OH...!

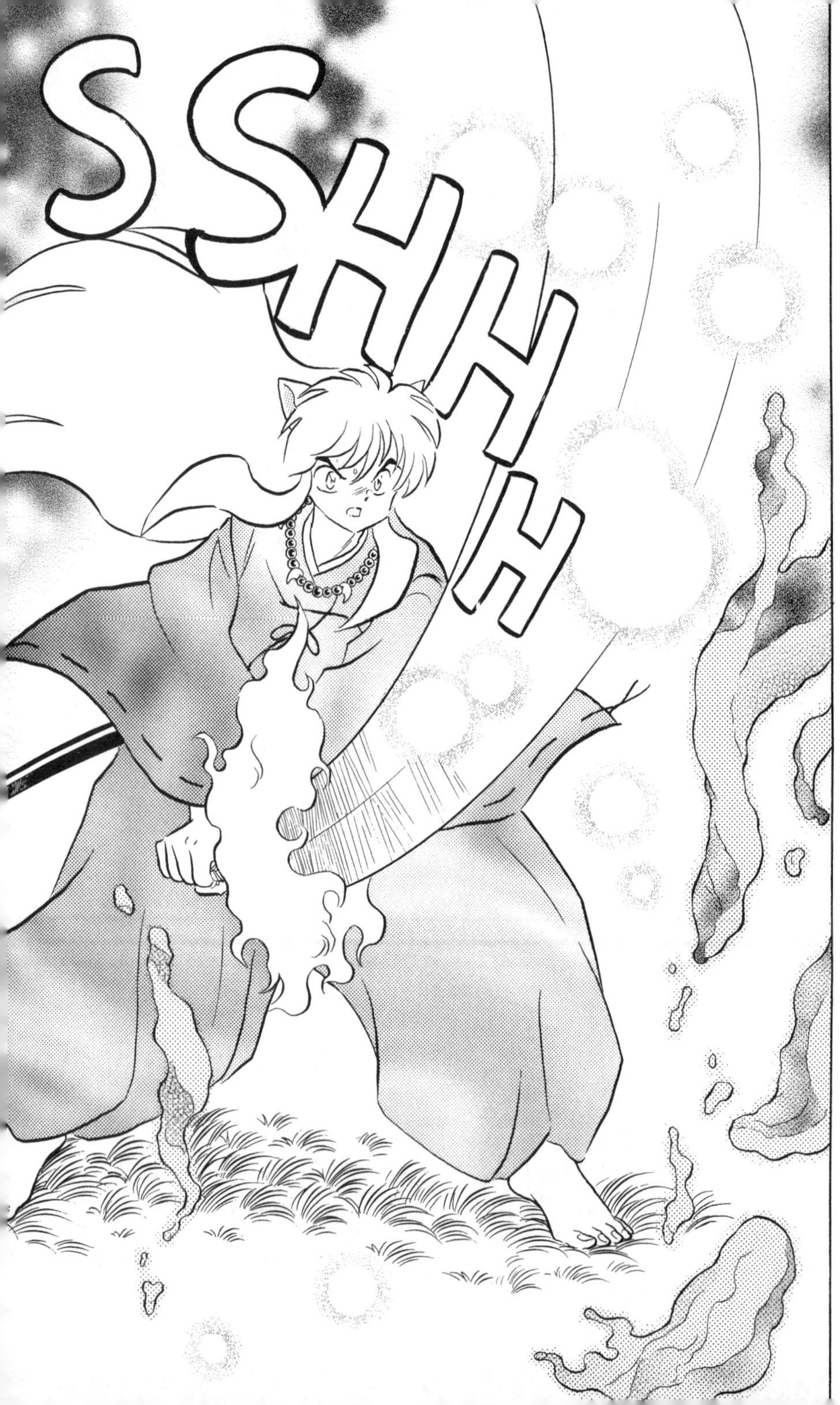
SSHHHH

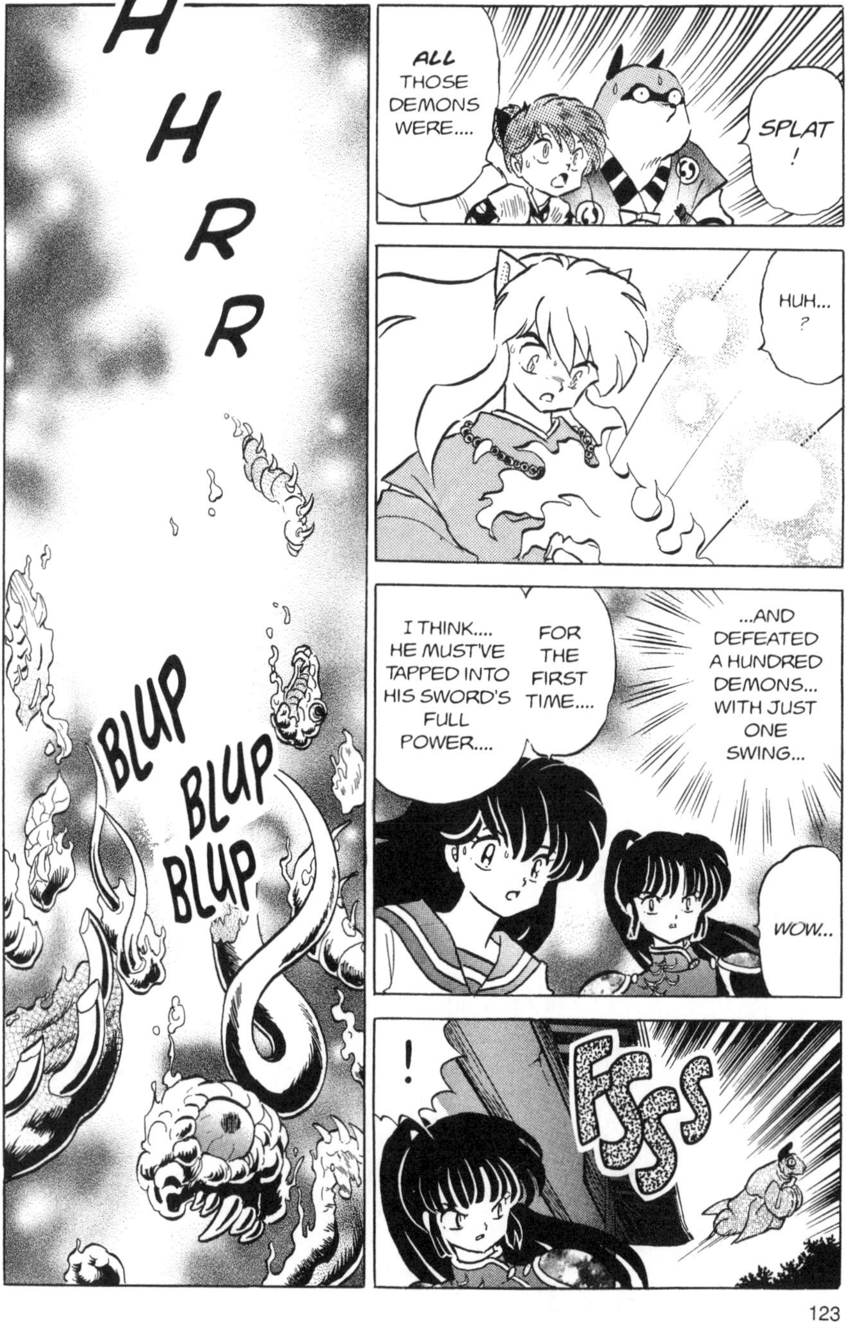
HHRR
BLUP BLUP BLUP
ALL THOSE DEMONS WERE....
SPLAT!
HUH...?
I THINK.... HE MUST'VE TAPPED INTO HIS SWORD'S FULL POWER....
FOR THE FIRST TIME....
...AND DEFEATED A HUNDRED DEMONS... WITH JUST ONE SWING...
WOW...
!
FSSS

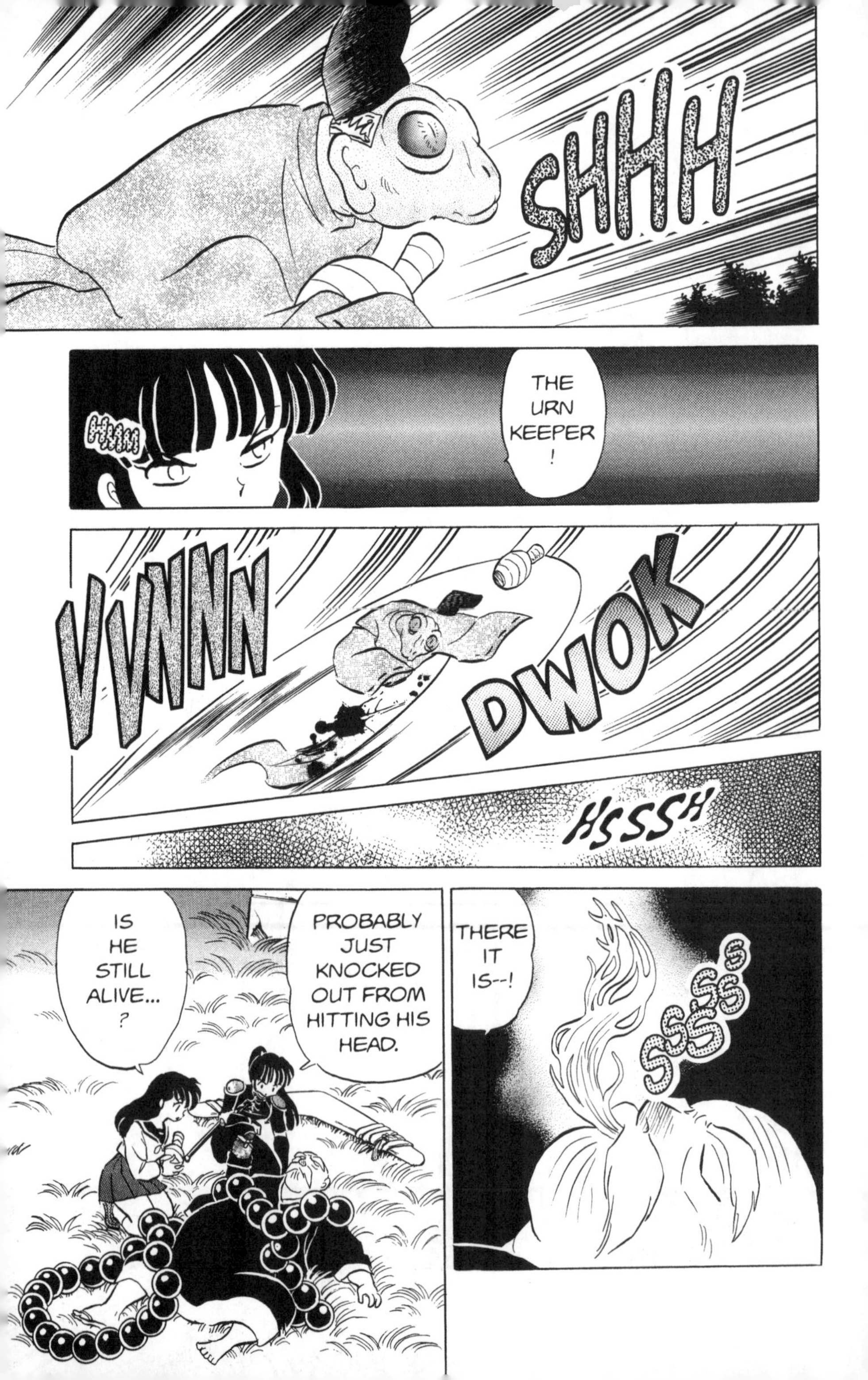
SHHH
THE URN KEEPER!
VVNNN
DWOK
HSSSH
THERE IT IS--!
SSSSS
IS HE STILL ALIVE...?
PROBABLY JUST KNOCKED OUT FROM HITTING HIS HEAD.

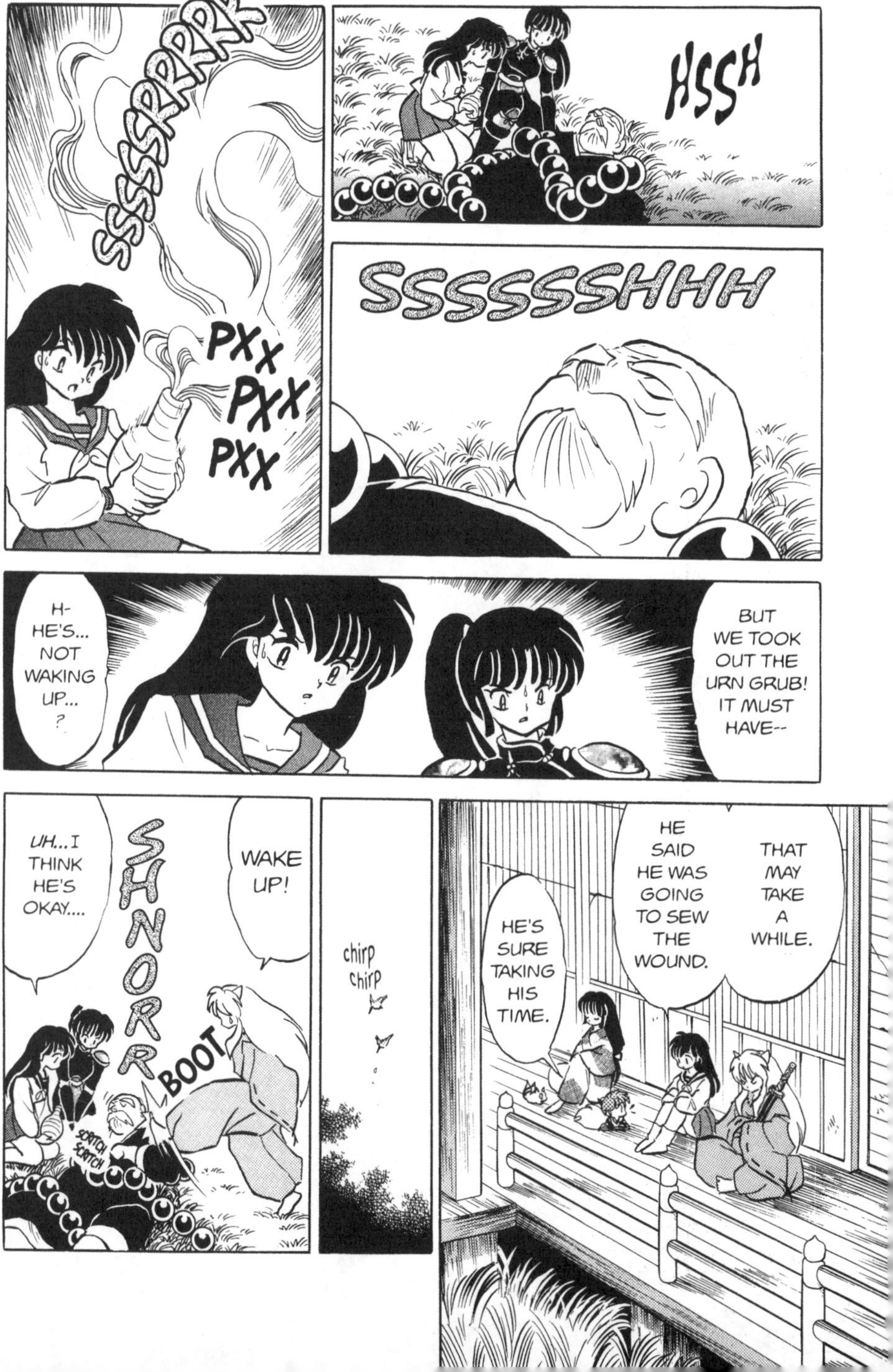
SSSSSRRRRR
PXX
PXX
PXX
HSSH
SSSSSSHHH
H- HE'S... NOT WAKING UP...?
BUT WE TOOK OUT THE URN GRUB! IT MUST HAVE--
UH...I THINK HE'S OKAY....
SHNORR
WAKE UP!
BOOT
SCRATCH SCRATCH
chirp chirp
HE'S SURE TAKING HIS TIME.
HE SAID HE WAS GOING TO SEW THE WOUND.
THAT MAY TAKE A WHILE.

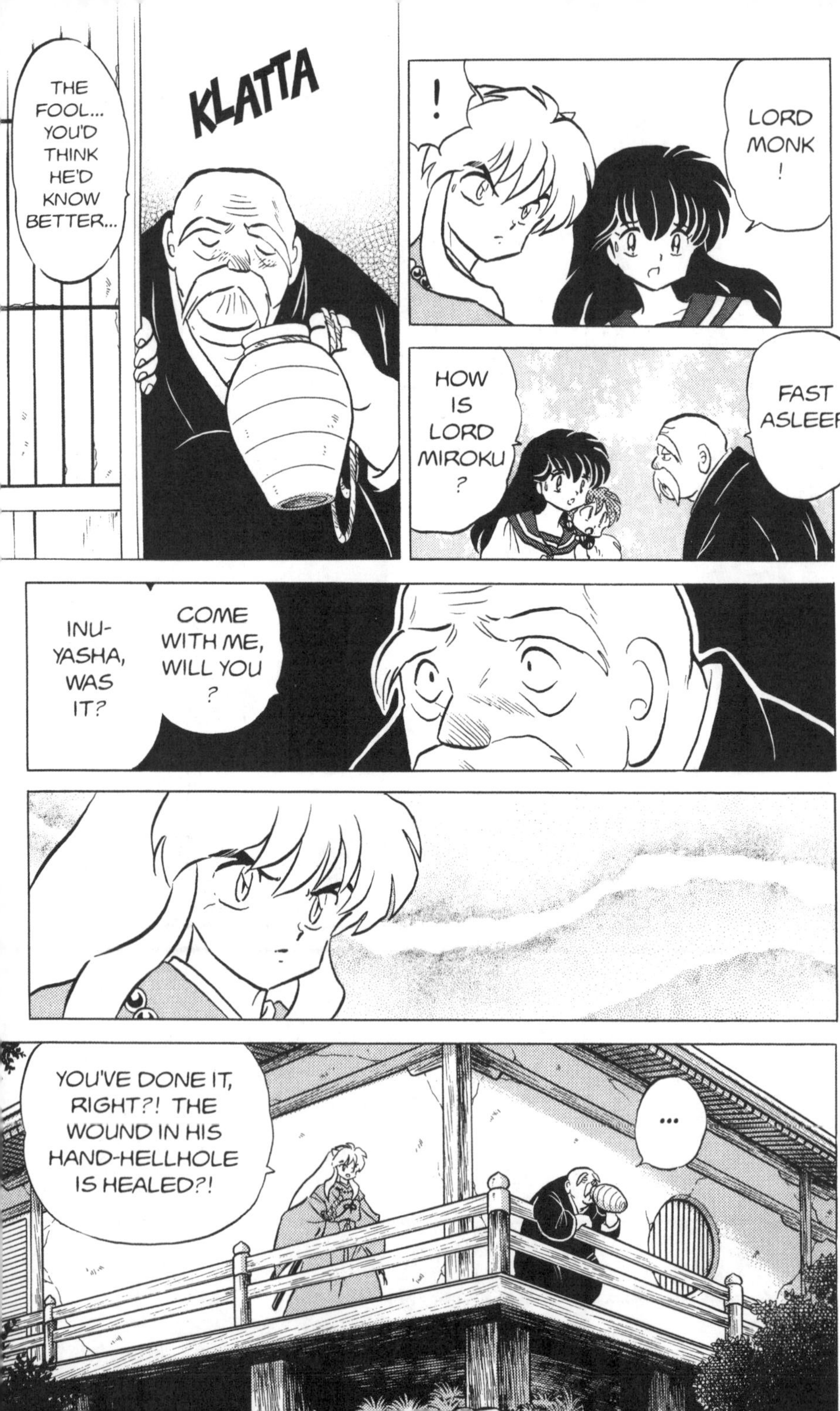
THE FOOL... YOU'D THINK HE'D KNOW BETTER...
KLATTA
!
LORD MONK!
HOW IS LORD MIROKU?
FAST ASLEEP.
INU-YASHA, WAS IT?
COME WITH ME, WILL YOU?
YOU'VE DONE IT, RIGHT?! THE WOUND IN HIS HAND-HELLHOLE IS HEALED?!
...

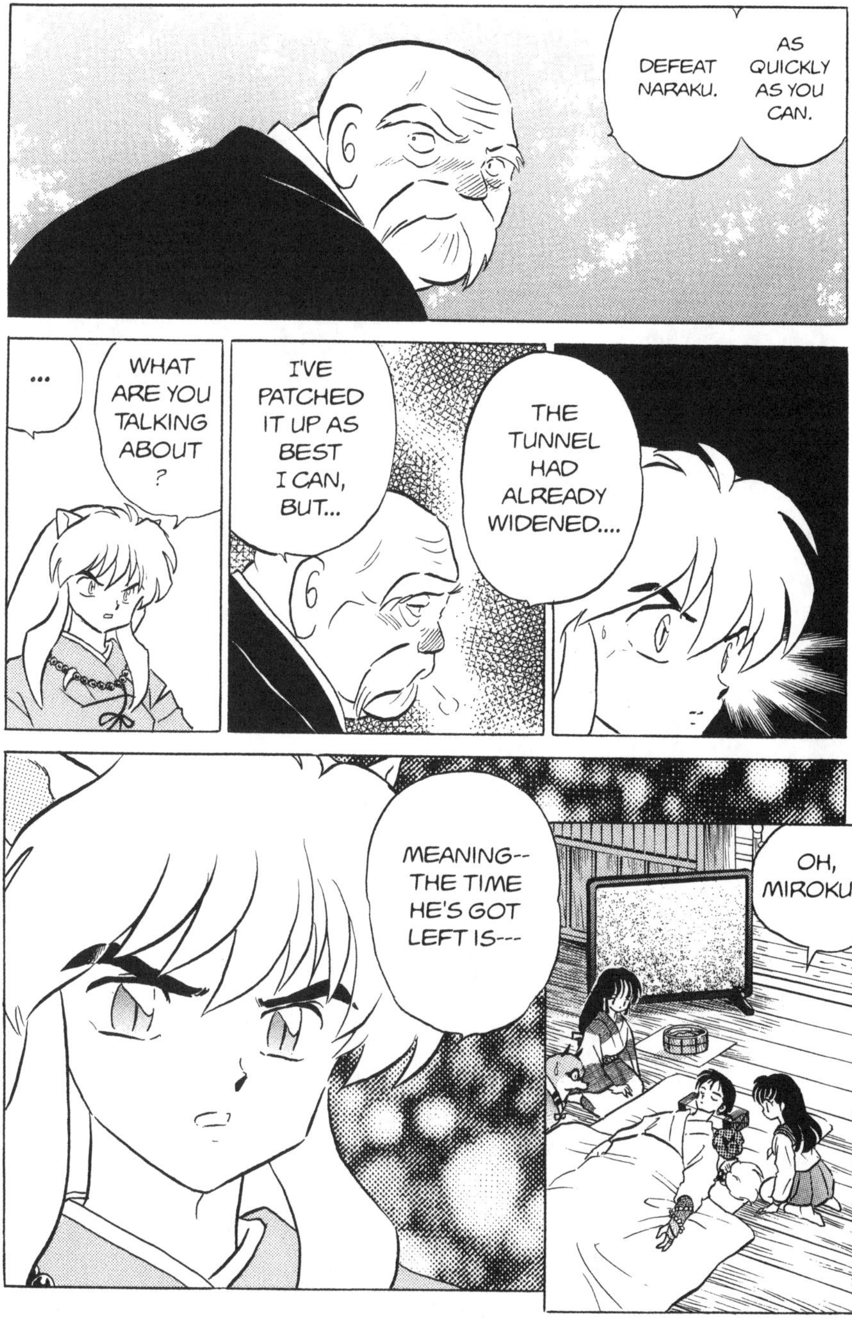
DEFEAT NARAKU. AS QUICKLY AS YOU CAN.
THE TUNNEL HAD ALREADY WIDENED....
I'VE PATCHED IT UP AS BEST I CAN, BUT...
WHAT ARE YOU TALKING ABOUT?
...
OH, MIROKU...
MEANING-- THE TIME HE'S GOT LEFT IS---

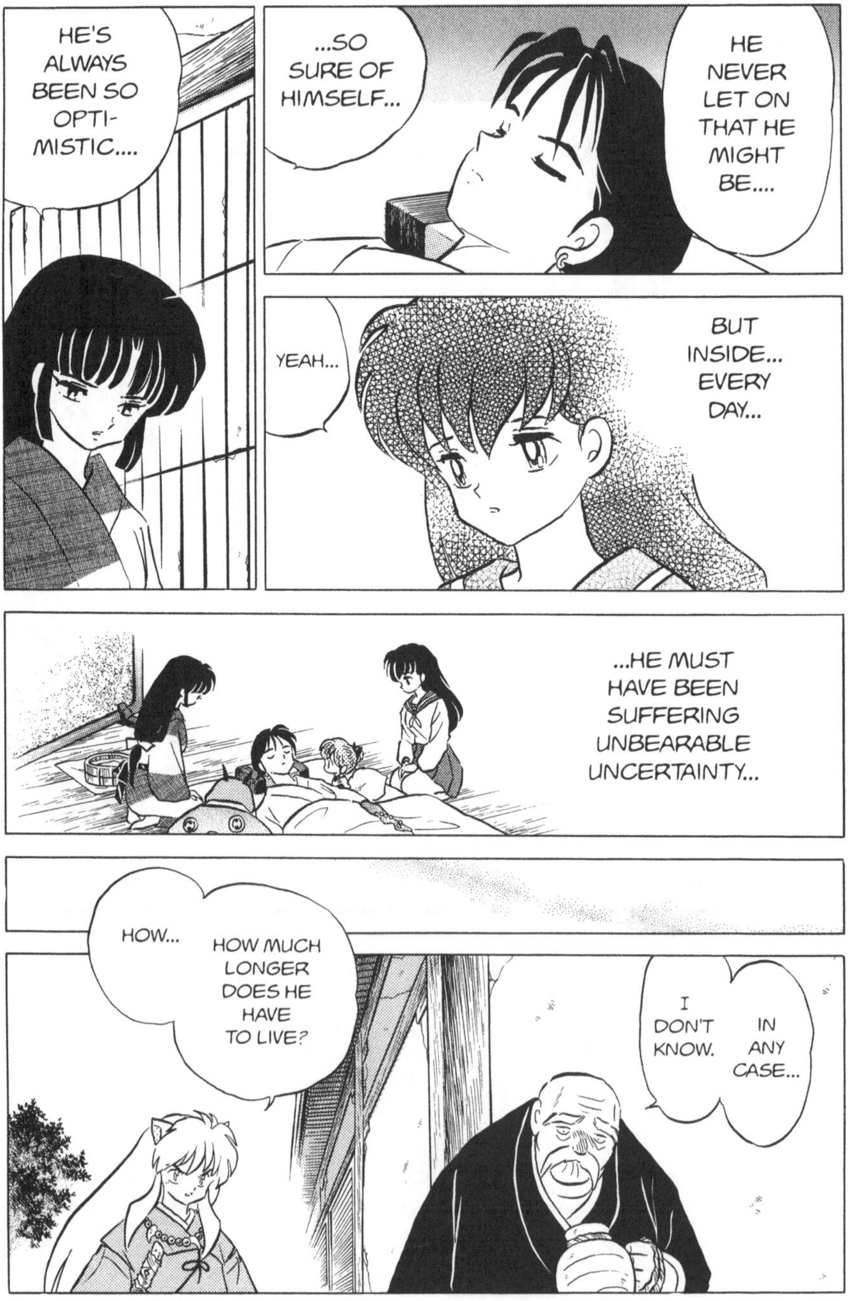
HE'S ALWAYS BEEN SO OPTI-MISTIC....
...SO SURE OF HIMSELF...
HE NEVER LET ON THAT HE MIGHT BE....
YEAH...
BUT INSIDE... EVERY DAY...
...HE MUST HAVE BEEN SUFFERING UNBEARABLE UNCERTAINTY...
HOW...
HOW MUCH LONGER DOES HE HAVE TO LIVE?
I DON'T KNOW.
IN ANY CASE...

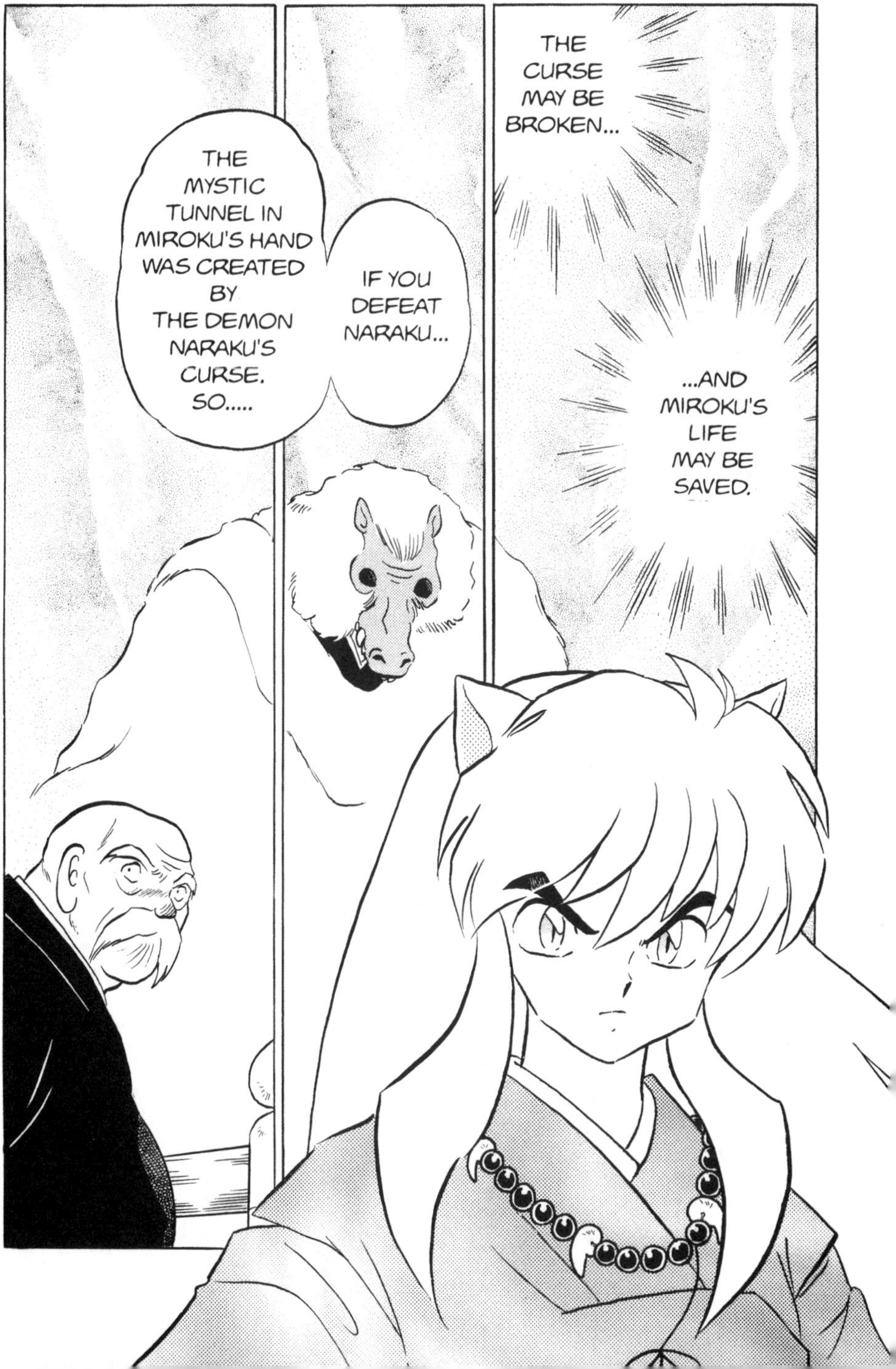
THE MYSTIC TUNNEL IN MIROKU'S HAND WAS CREATED BY THE DEMON NARAKU'S CURSE. SO.....
IF YOU DEFEAT NARAKU...
THE CURSE MAY BE BROKEN...
...AND MIROKU'S LIFE MAY BE SAVED.

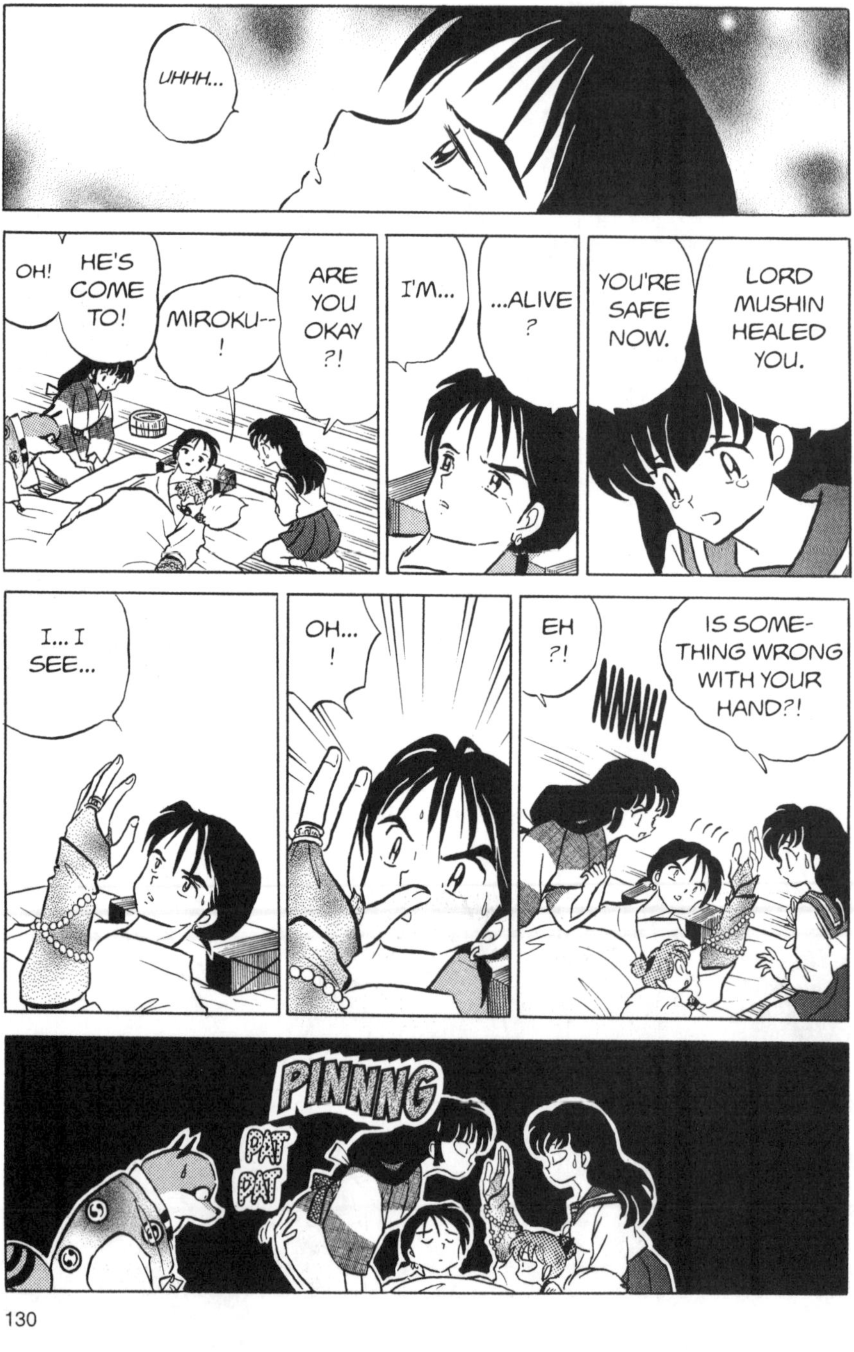
UHHH...
OH!
HE'S COME TO!
MIROKU--!
ARE YOU OKAY?!
I'M...
...ALIVE?
YOU'RE SAFE NOW.
LORD MUSHIN HEALED YOU.
I... I SEE...
OH...!
EH?!
NNNH
IS SOME-THING WRONG WITH YOUR HAND?!
PINNNG
PAT PAT

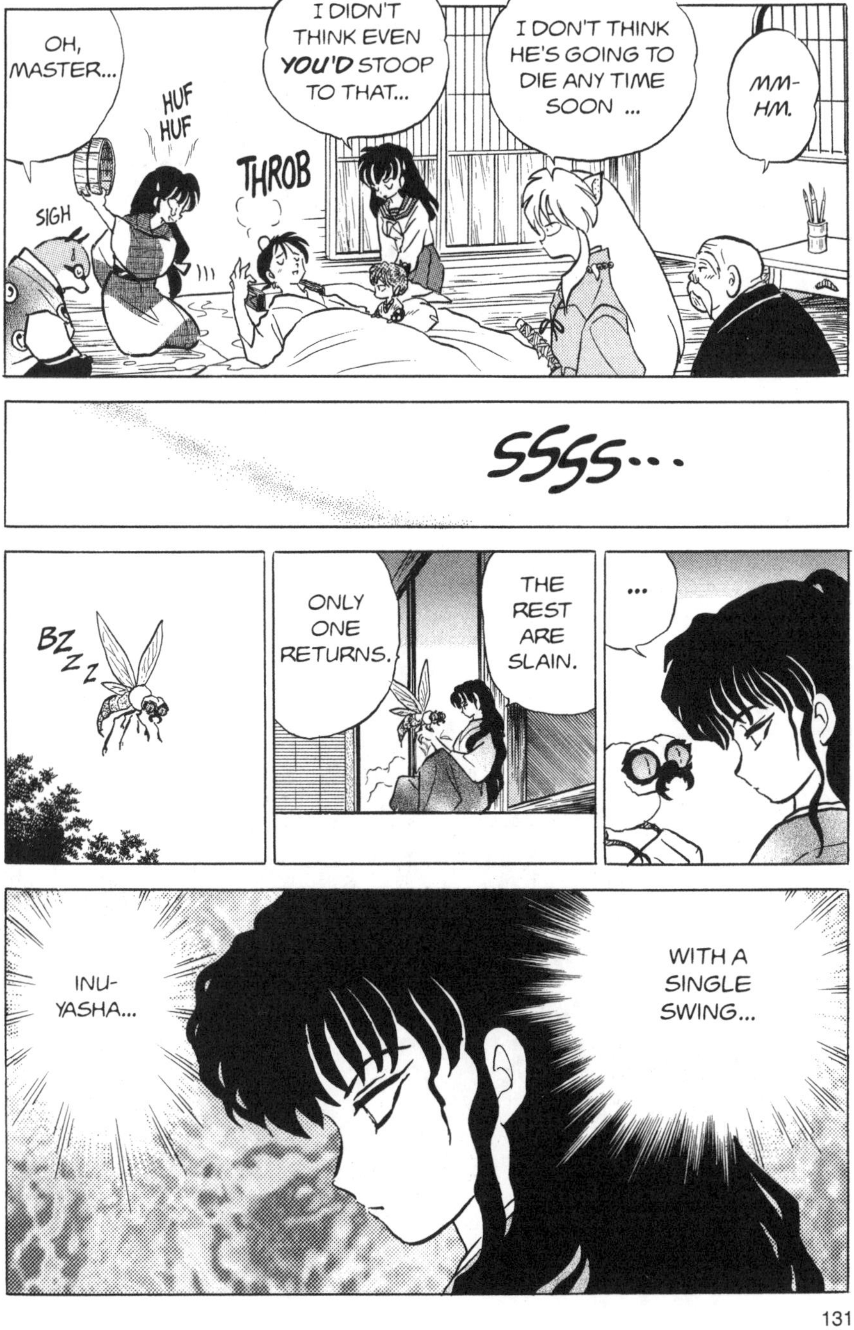
OH, MASTER...
SIGH
HUF HUF
THROB
I DIDN'T THINK EVEN YOU'D STOOP TO THAT...
I DON'T THINK HE'S GOING TO DIE ANY TIME SOON ...
MM-HM.
SSSS...
BZZZ
ONLY ONE RETURNS.
THE REST ARE SLAIN.
...
INU-YASHA...
WITH A SINGLE SWING...

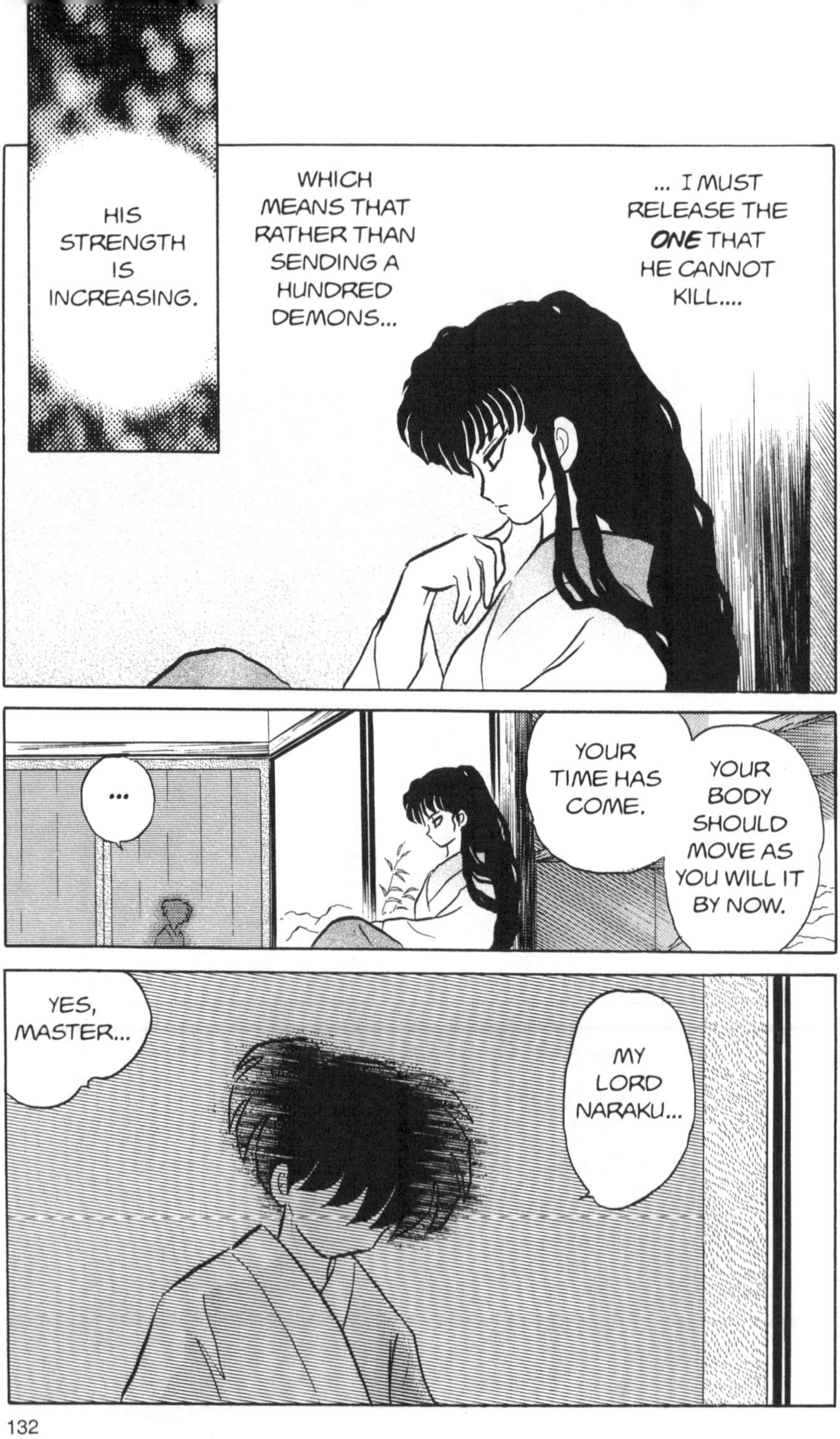
HIS STRENGTH IS INCREASING.
WHICH MEANS THAT RATHER THAN SENDING A HUNDRED DEMONS...
... I MUST RELEASE THE ***ONE*** THAT HE CANNOT KILL....
...
YOUR TIME HAS COME.
YOUR BODY SHOULD MOVE AS YOU WILL IT BY NOW.
YES, MASTER...
MY LORD NARAKU...

SCROLL EIGHT

KOHAKU

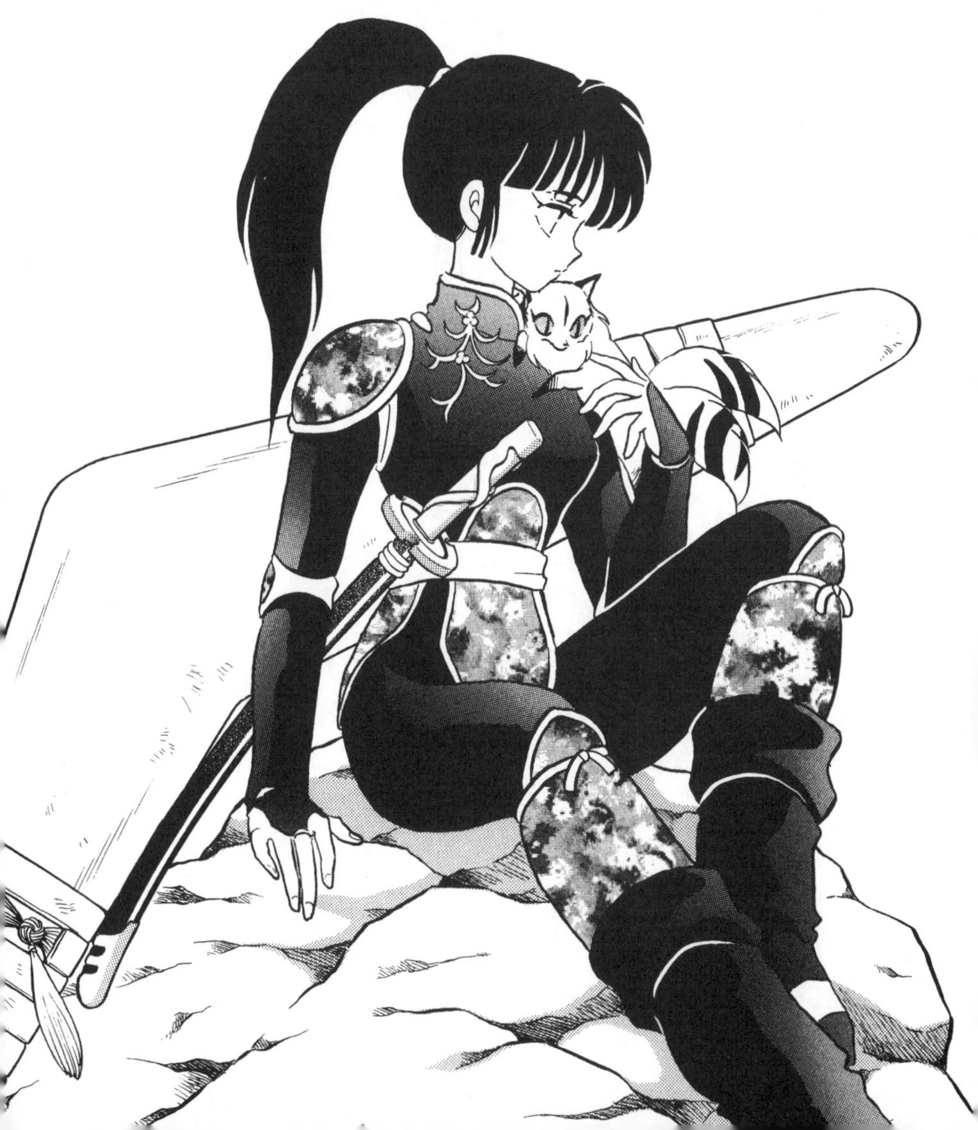

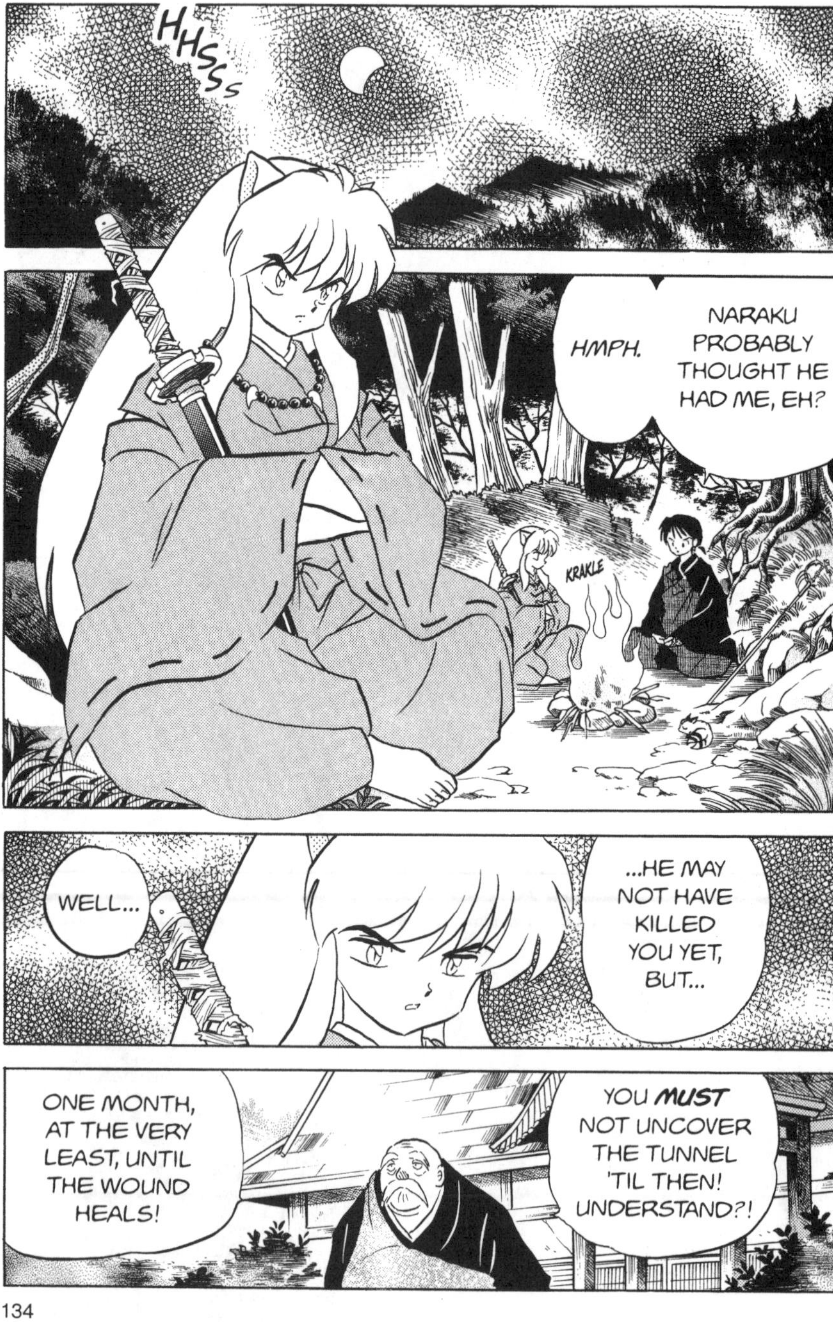
HHSSSS
HMPH.
NARAKU PROBABLY THOUGHT HE HAD ME, EH?
KRAKLE
WELL...
...HE MAY NOT HAVE KILLED YOU YET, BUT...
ONE MONTH, AT THE VERY LEAST, UNTIL THE WOUND HEALS!
YOU **MUST** NOT UNCOVER THE TUNNEL 'TIL THEN! UNDERSTAND?!

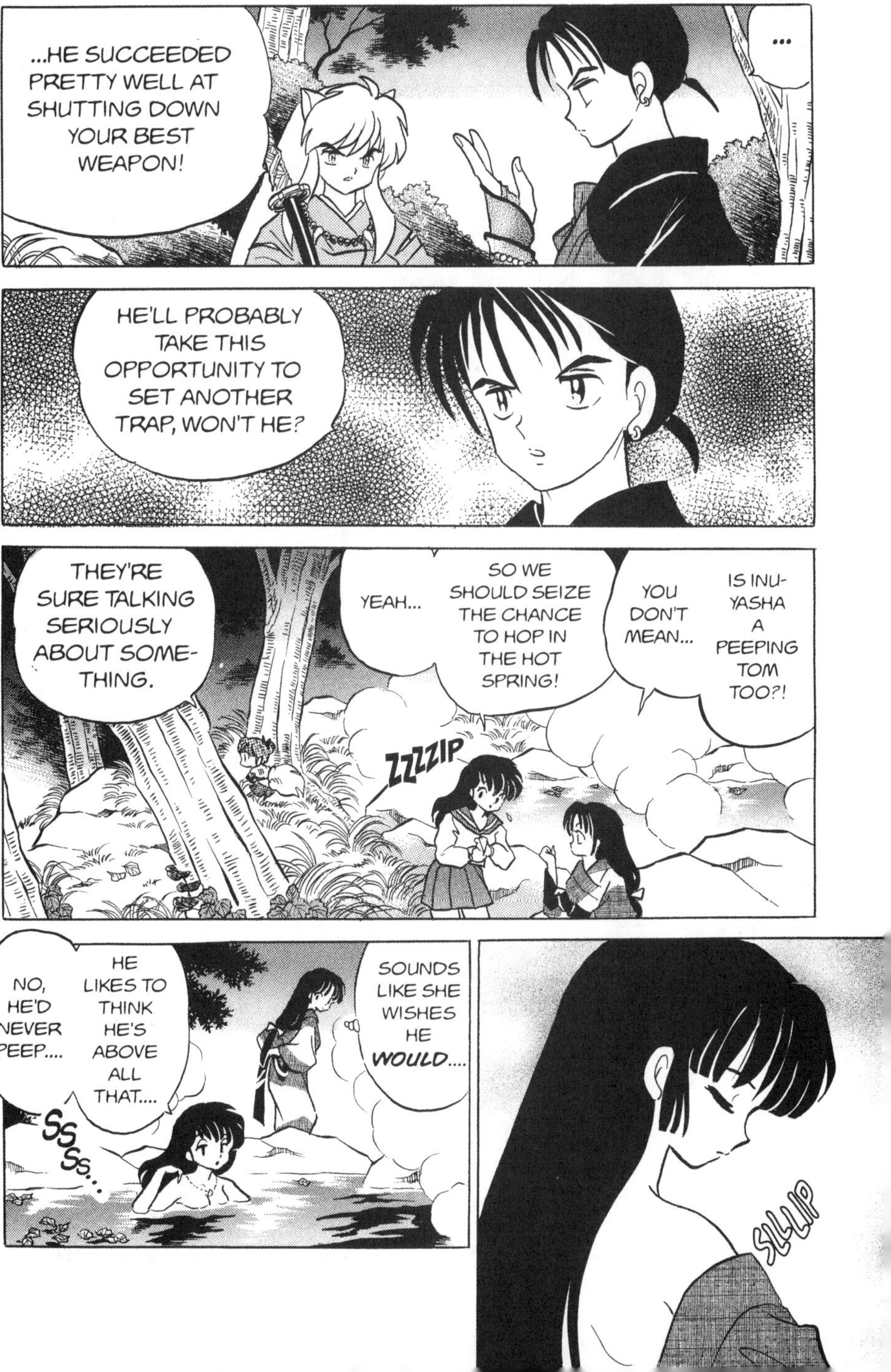
...HE SUCCEEDED PRETTY WELL AT SHUTTING DOWN YOUR BEST WEAPON!
...
HE'LL PROBABLY TAKE THIS OPPORTUNITY TO SET ANOTHER TRAP, WON'T HE?
THEY'RE SURE TALKING SERIOUSLY ABOUT SOME-THING.
YEAH...
SO WE SHOULD SEIZE THE CHANCE TO HOP IN THE HOT SPRING!
YOU DON'T MEAN...
IS INU-YASHA A PEEPING TOM TOO?!
ZZZZIP
NO, HE'D NEVER PEEP....
HE LIKES TO THINK HE'S ABOVE ALL THAT....
SOUNDS LIKE SHE WISHES HE *WOULD*....
SSSS...
SLLLIP

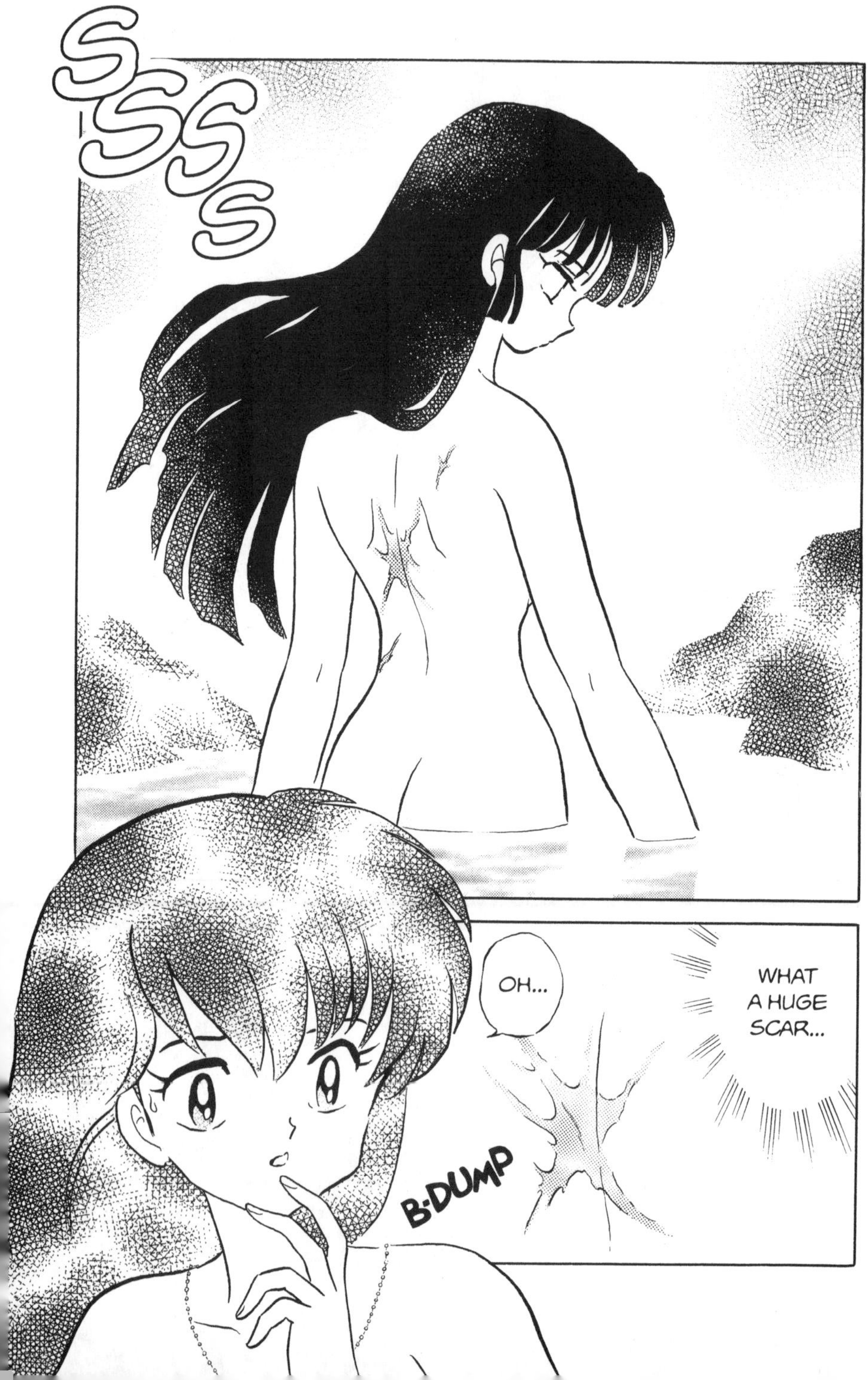
SSSS
WHAT A HUGE SCAR...
OH...
B-DUMP

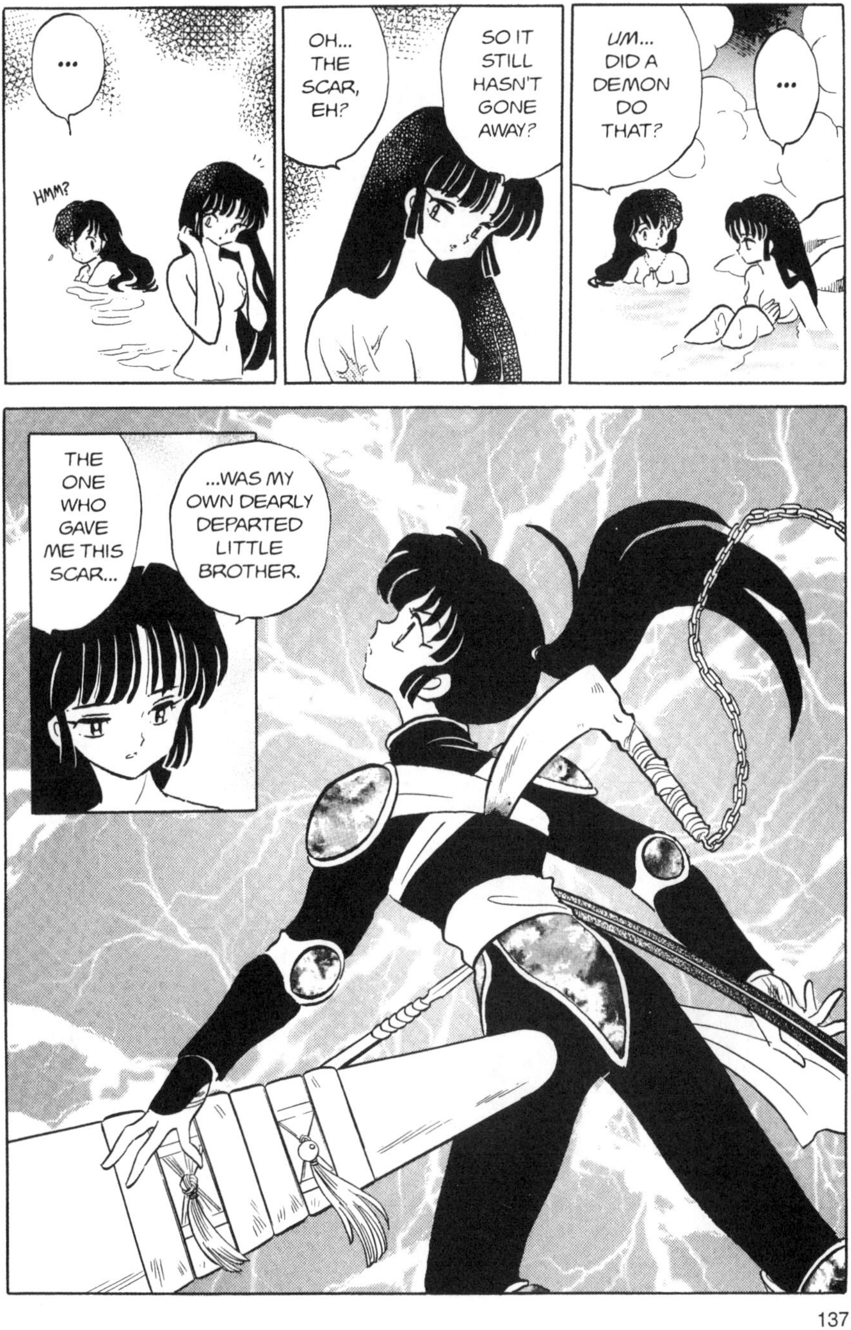
...
HMM?
OH... THE SCAR, EH?
SO IT STILL HASN'T GONE AWAY?
UM... DID A DEMON DO THAT?
...
THE ONE WHO GAVE ME THIS SCAR...
...WAS MY OWN DEARLY DEPARTED LITTLE BROTHER.

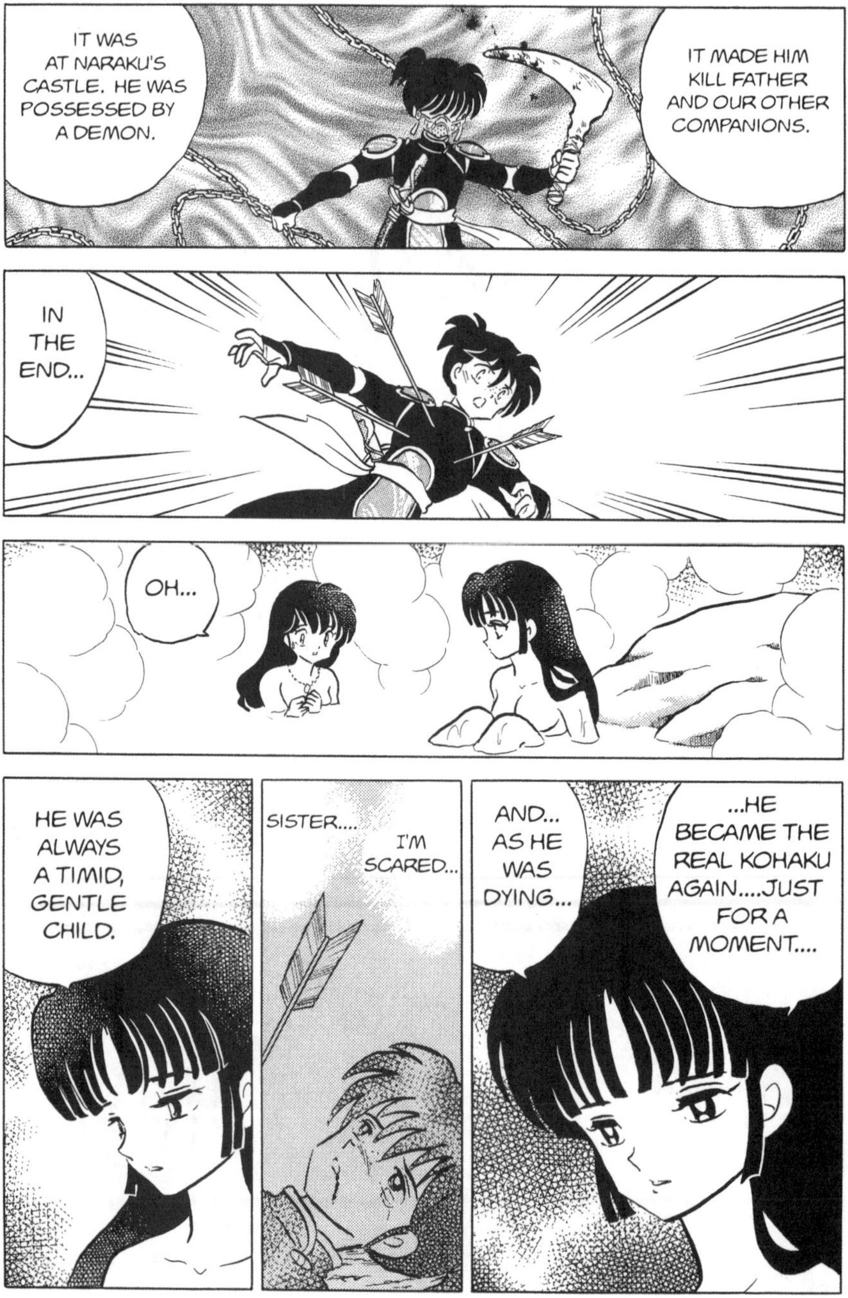
IT WAS AT NARAKU'S CASTLE. HE WAS POSSESSED BY A DEMON.
IT MADE HIM KILL FATHER AND OUR OTHER COMPANIONS.
IN THE END...
OH...
HE WAS ALWAYS A TIMID, GENTLE CHILD.
SISTER....
I'M SCARED...
AND... AS HE WAS DYING...
...HE BECAME THE REAL KOHAKU AGAIN....JUST FOR A MOMENT....

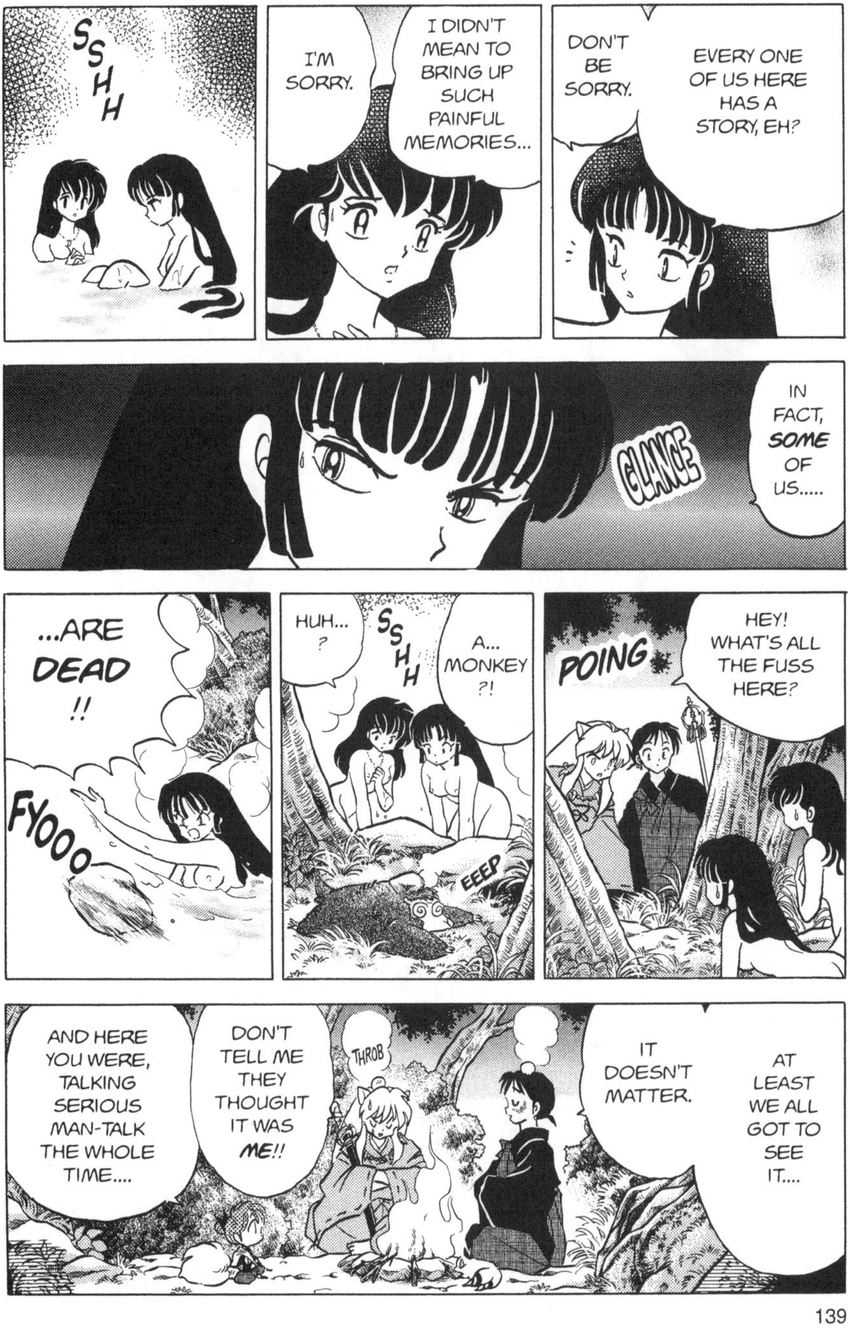
SSHH
I'M SORRY.
I DIDN'T MEAN TO BRING UP SUCH PAINFUL MEMORIES...
DON'T BE SORRY.
EVERY ONE OF US HERE HAS A STORY, EH?
GLANCE
IN FACT, SOME OF US.....
...ARE DEAD!!
FYOOO
HUH...?
SSHH
A... MONKEY?!
EEEP
POING
HEY! WHAT'S ALL THE FUSS HERE?
AND HERE YOU WERE, TALKING SERIOUS MAN-TALK THE WHOLE TIME....
DON'T TELL ME THEY THOUGHT IT WAS ME!!
THROB
IT DOESN'T MATTER.
AT LEAST WE ALL GOT TO SEE IT....

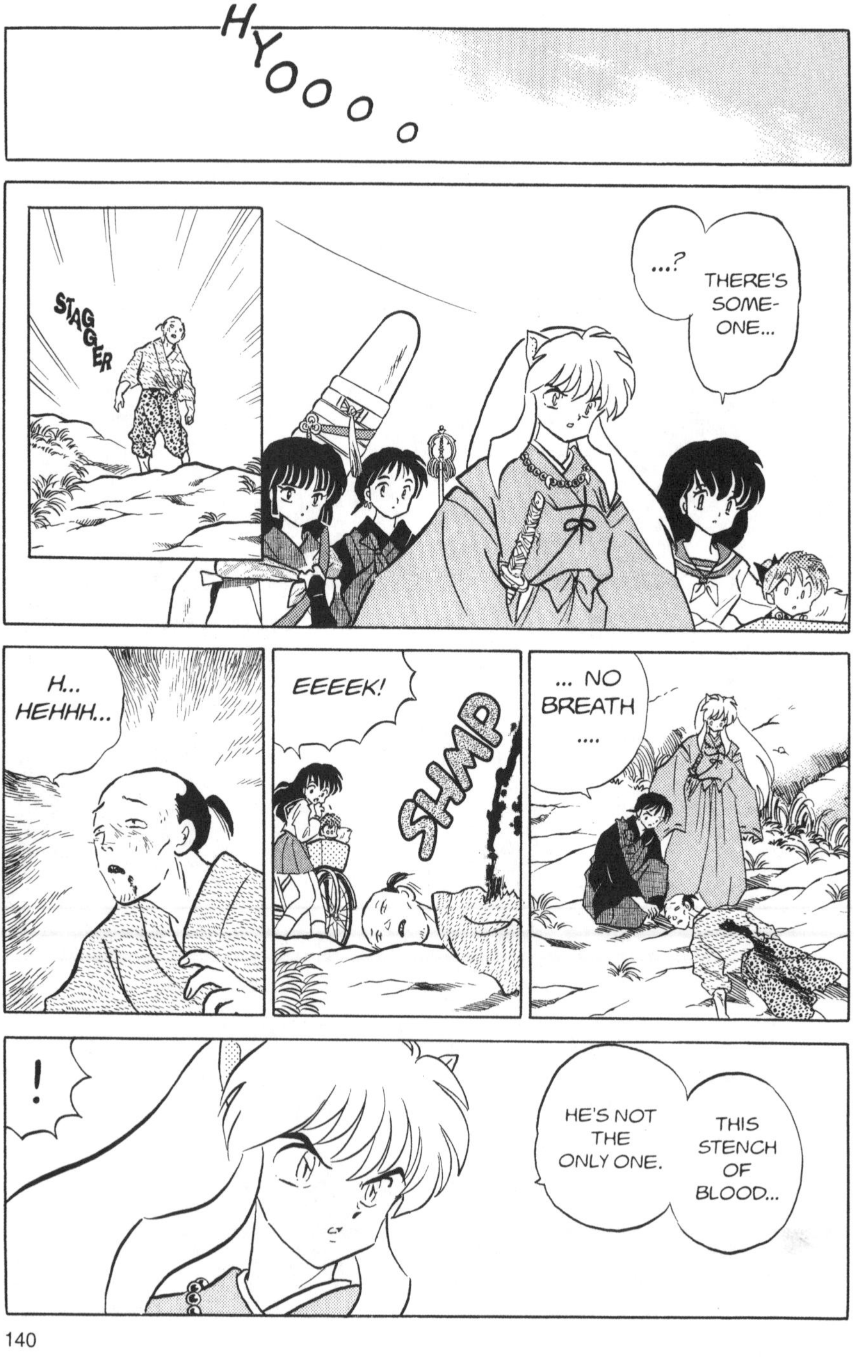
HYOOOOO
STAGGER
...?
THERE'S SOME-ONE...
H... HEHHH...
EEEEK!
SHMP
... NO BREATH ....
!
HE'S NOT THE ONLY ONE.
THIS STENCH OF BLOOD...

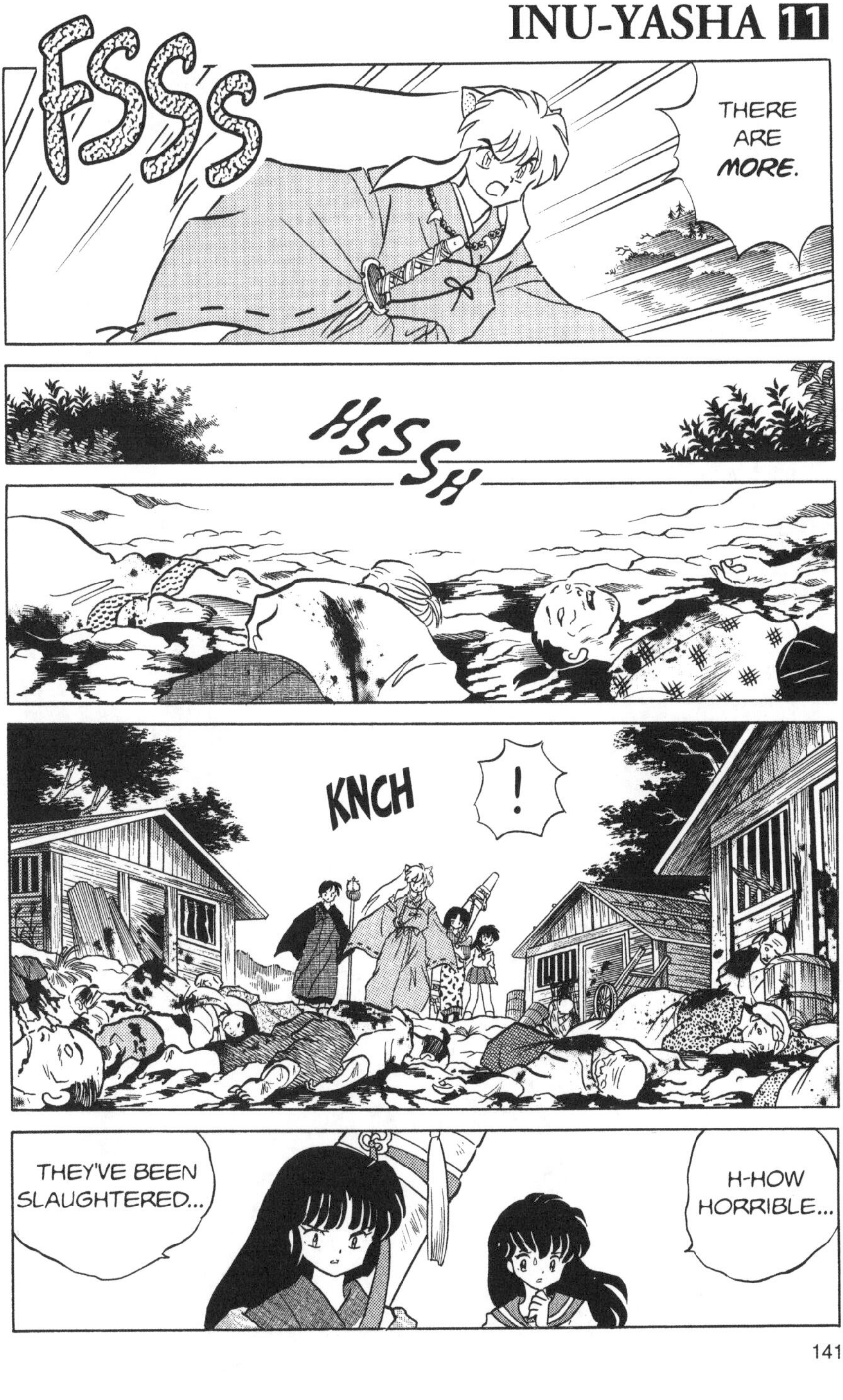
THERE ARE MORE.
FSSS
HSSSH
!
KNCH
H-HOW HORRIBLE...
THEY'VE BEEN SLAUGHTERED...

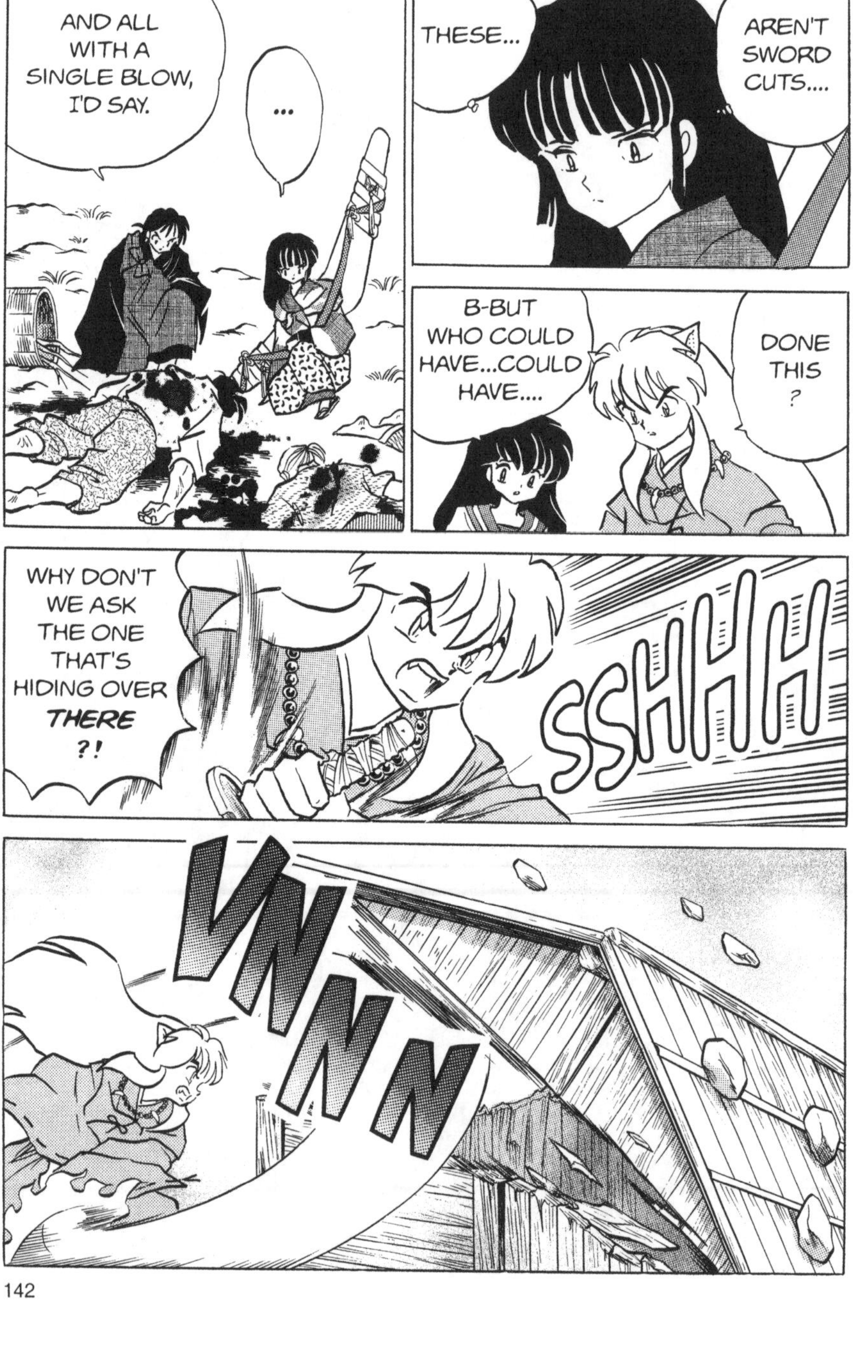
AND ALL WITH A SINGLE BLOW, I'D SAY.
...
THESE...
AREN'T SWORD CUTS....
B-BUT WHO COULD HAVE...COULD HAVE....
DONE THIS ?
WHY DON'T WE ASK THE ONE THAT'S HIDING OVER *THERE* ?!
SSHHH
VNNNN

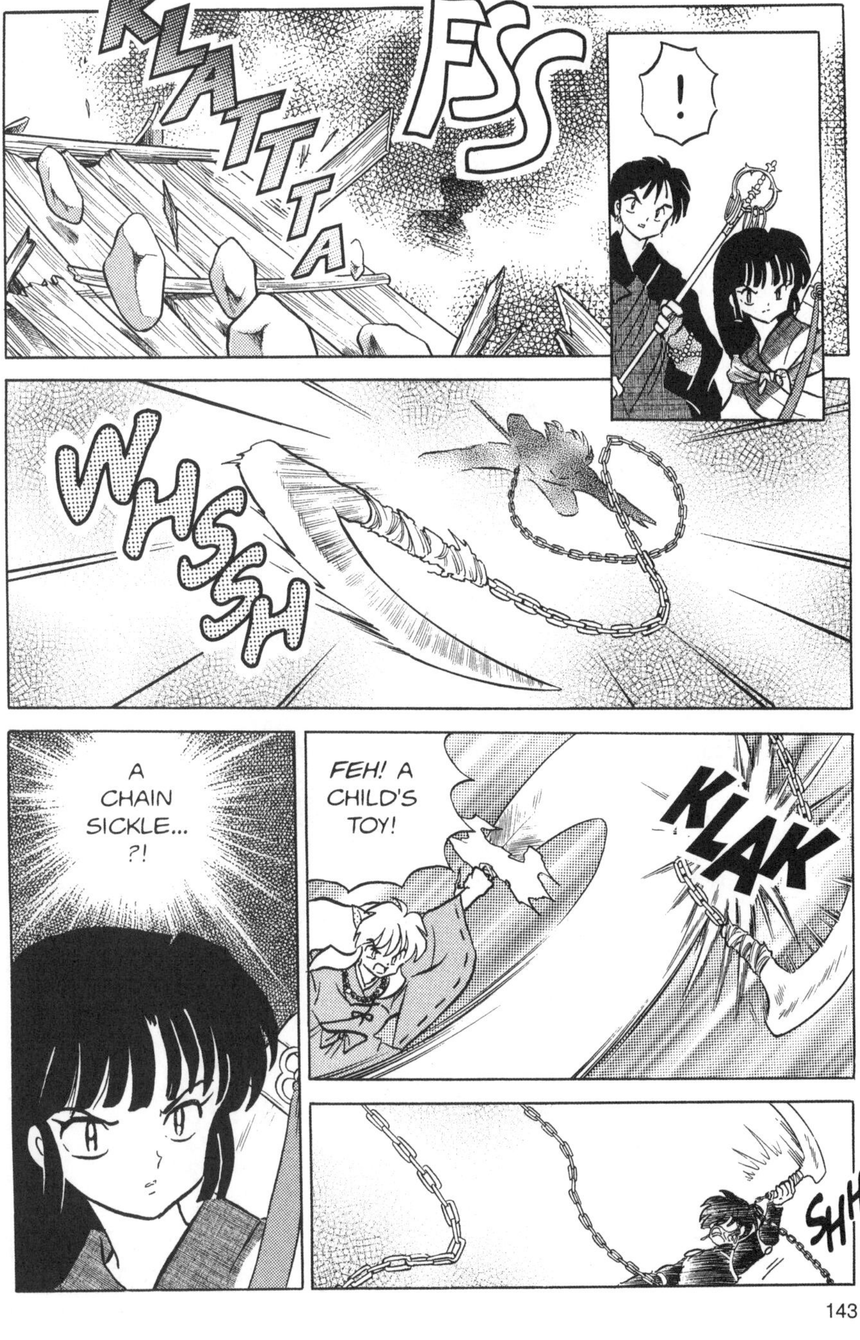
!
FSS
KLATTTTA
WHSSSH
FEH! A CHILD'S TOY!
KLAK
SHHP
A CHAIN SICKLE... ?!

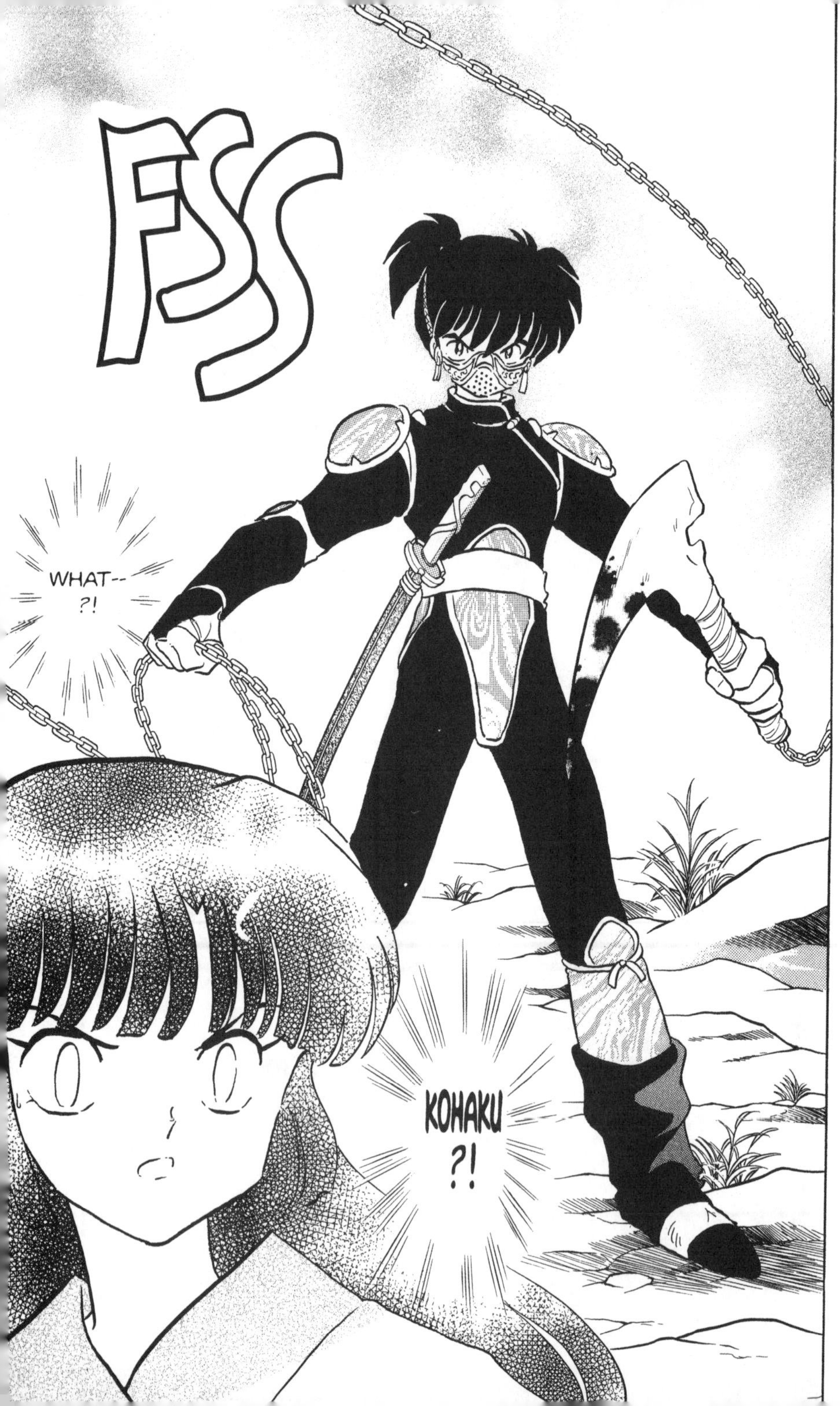
FSS
WHAT-- ?!
KOHAKU ?!

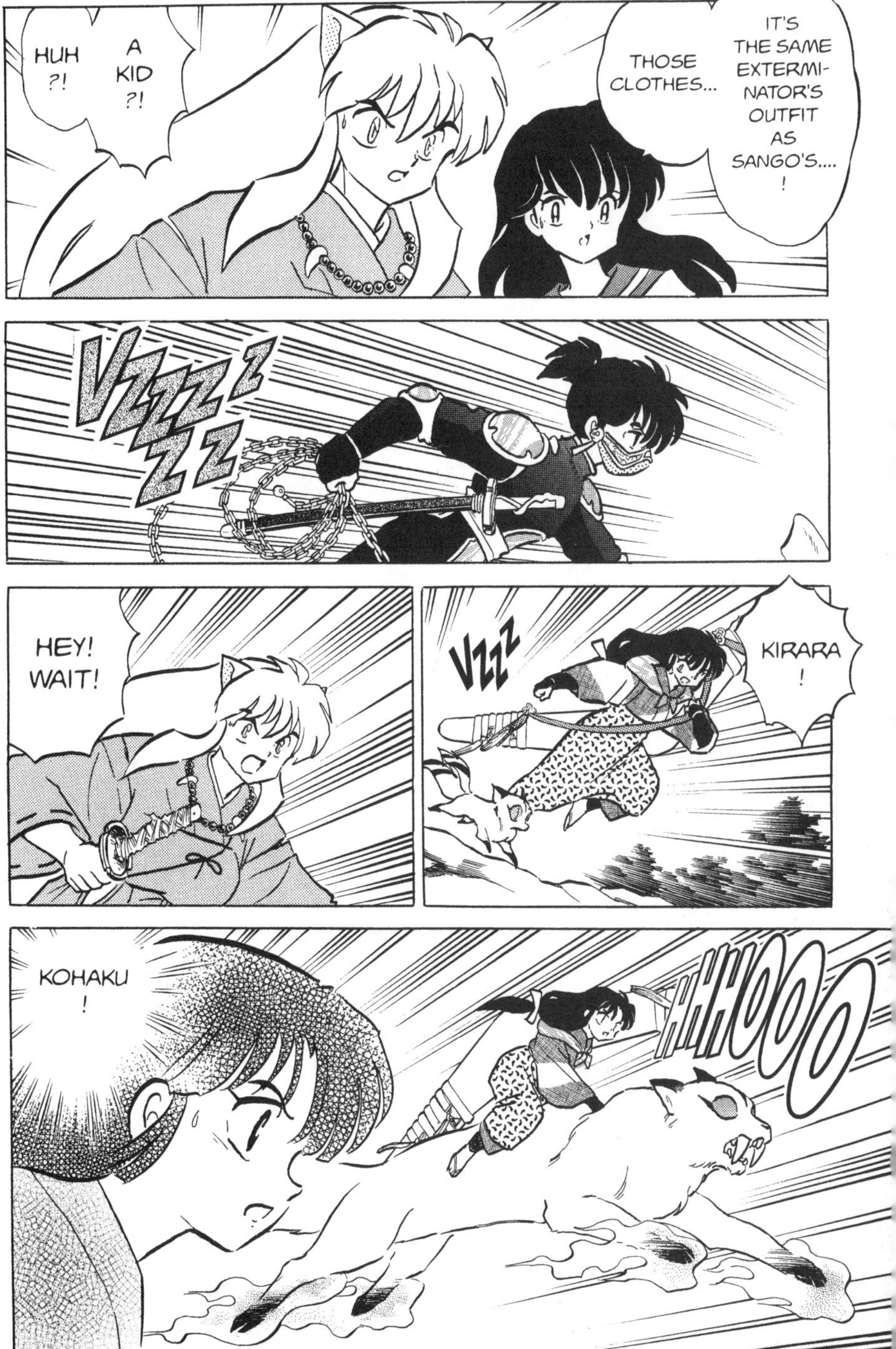
THOSE CLOTHES... IT'S THE SAME EXTERMI-NATOR'S OUTFIT AS SANGO'S....!
HUH?! A KID?!
VZZZZZZ
KIRARA!
VZZZ
HEY! WAIT!
HHOOOO
KOHAKU!

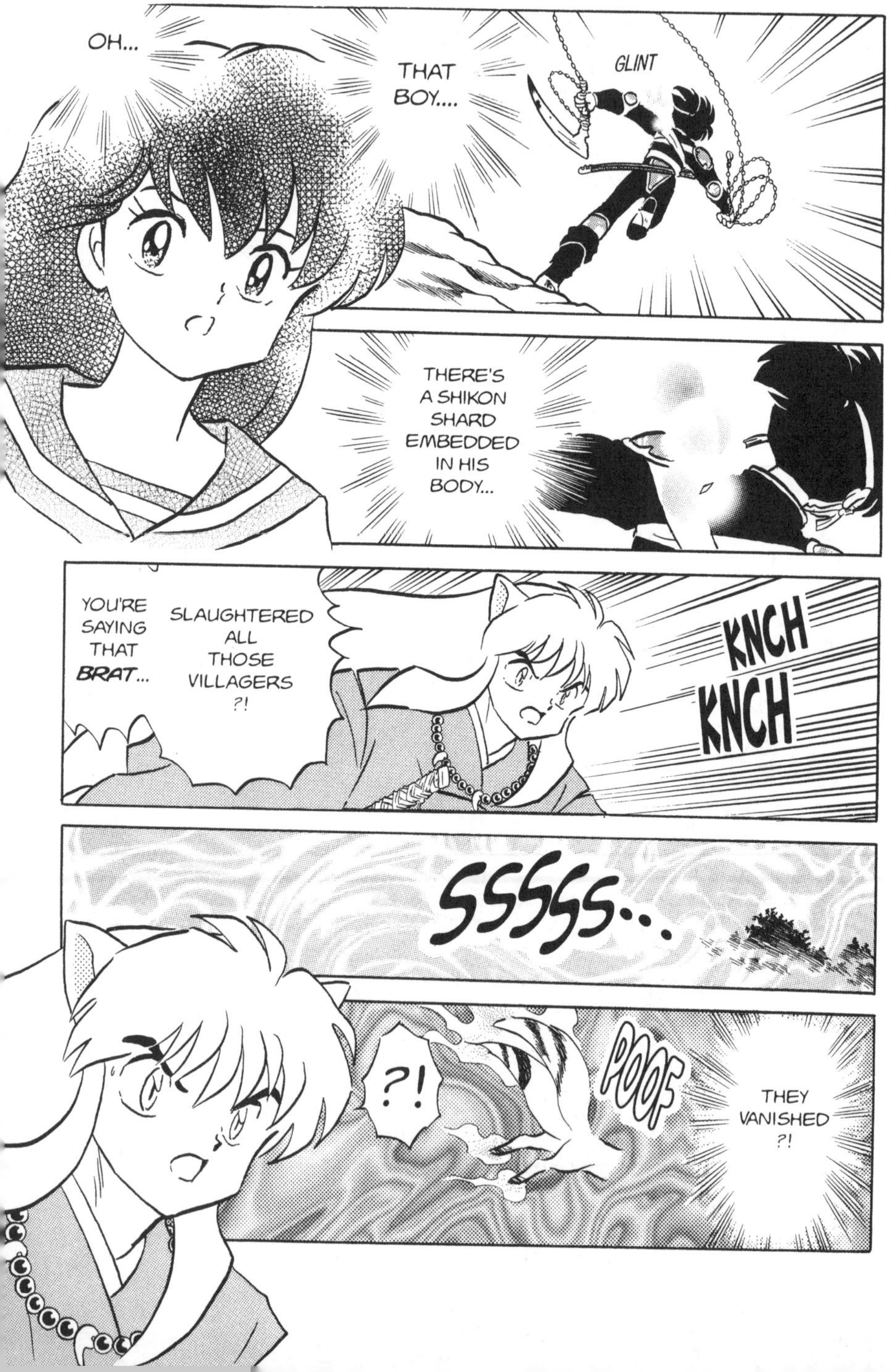
GLINT
OH...
THAT BOY....
THERE'S A SHIKON SHARD EMBEDDED IN HIS BODY...
KNCH KNCH
YOU'RE SAYING THAT *BRAT*...
SLAUGHTERED ALL THOSE VILLAGERS ?!
SSSSS...
THEY VANISHED ?!
POOF
?!

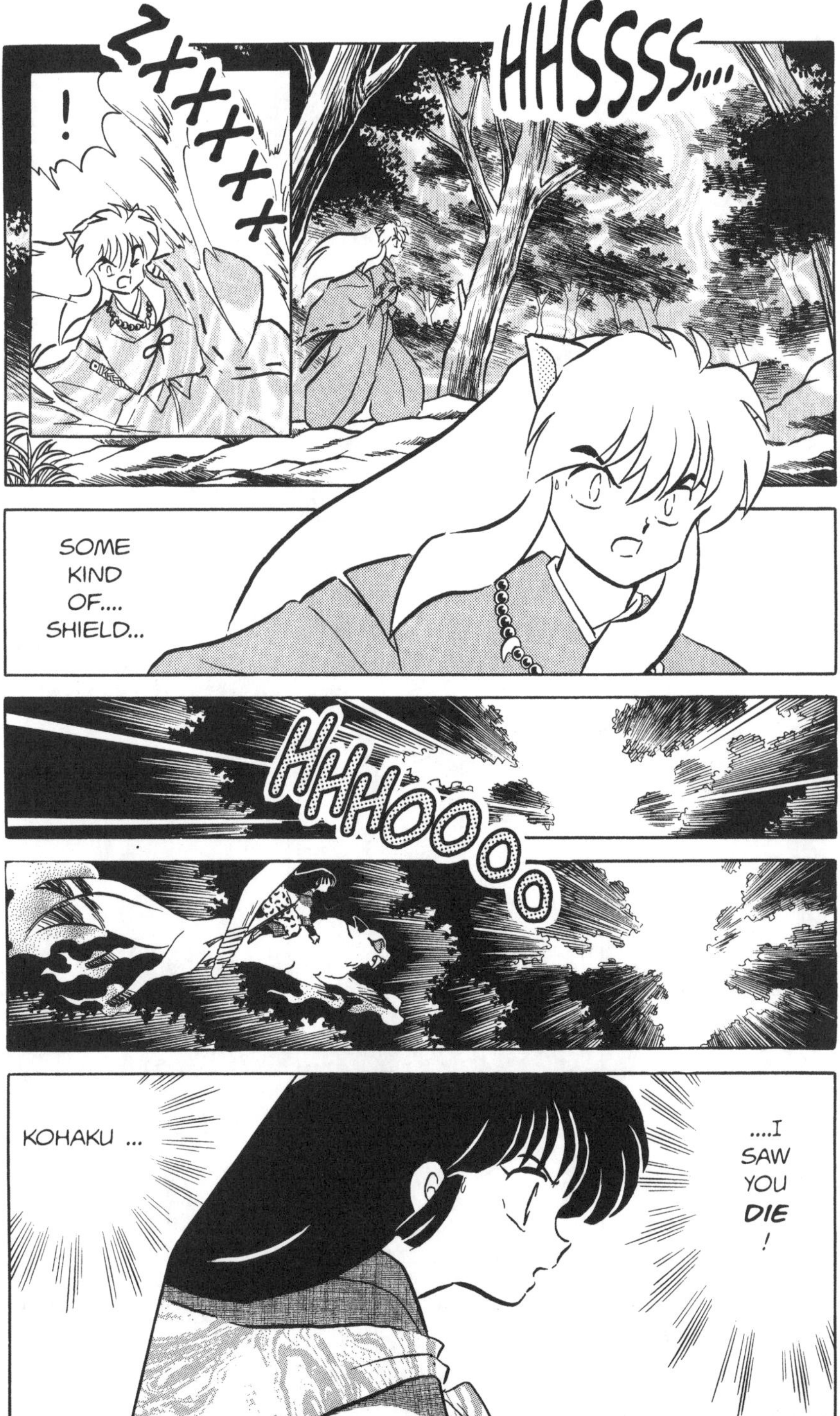
HHSSSS.....
ZZZZZZ
!
SOME KIND OF.... SHIELD...
HHHOOOOO
KOHAKU ...
....I SAW YOU DIE!

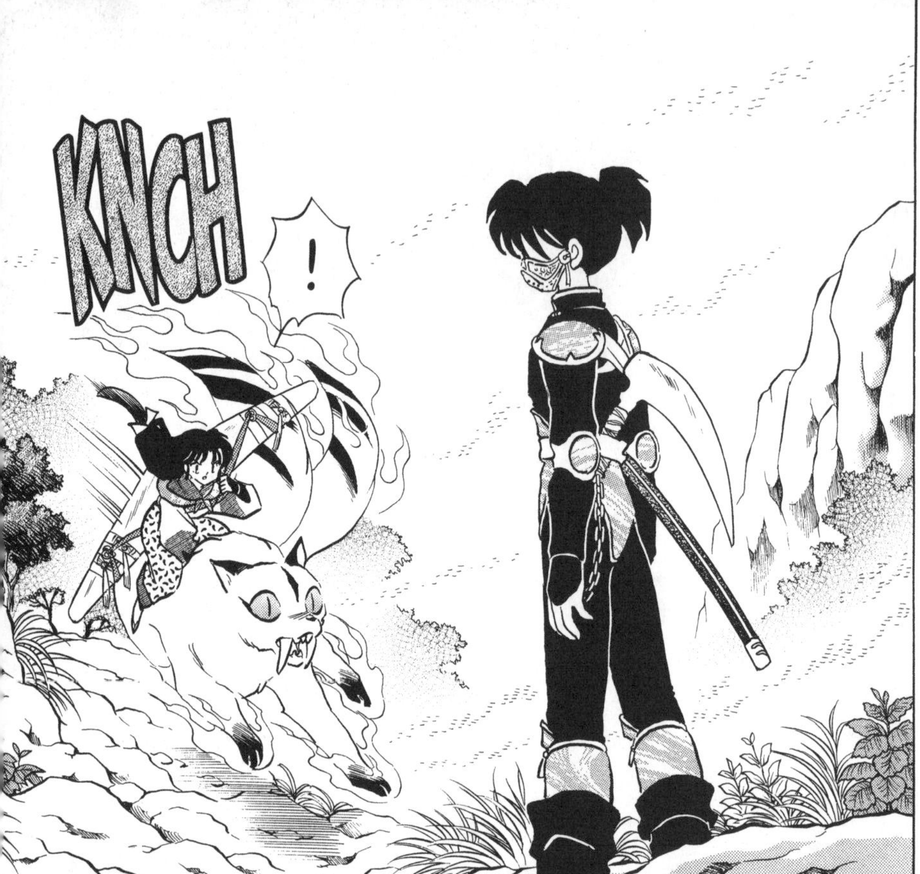
KNCH
!
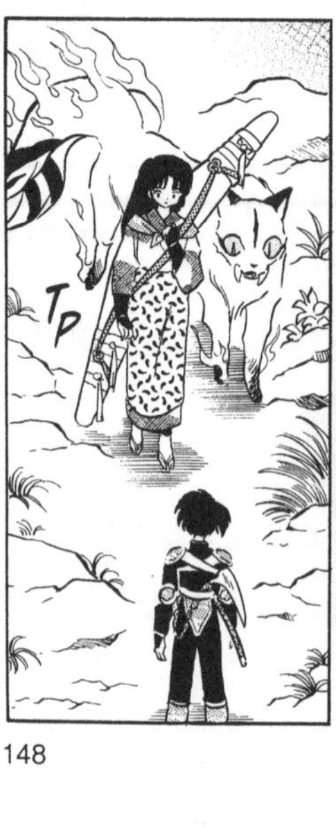
TP
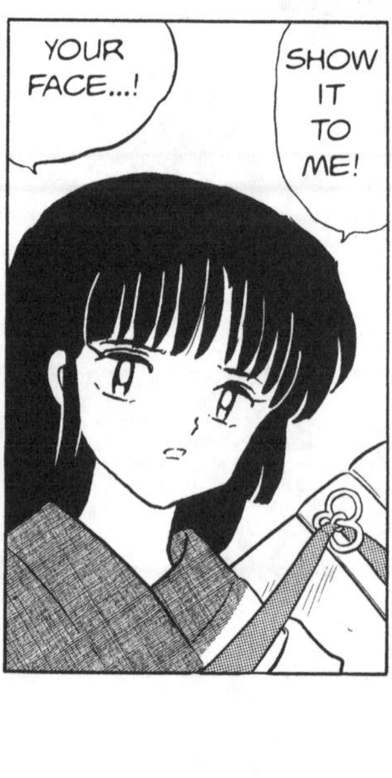
YOUR FACE...!
SHOW IT TO ME!
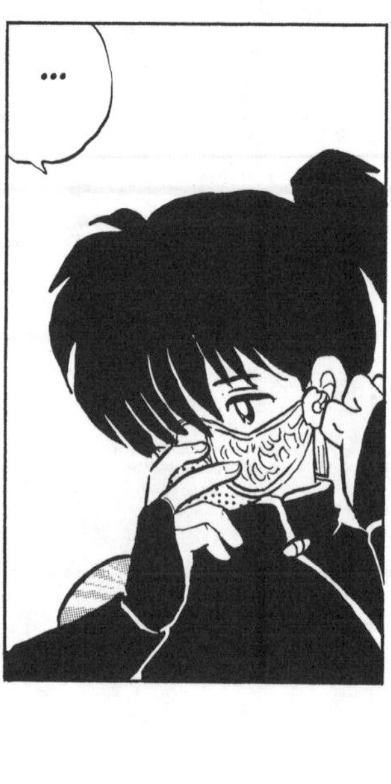
...

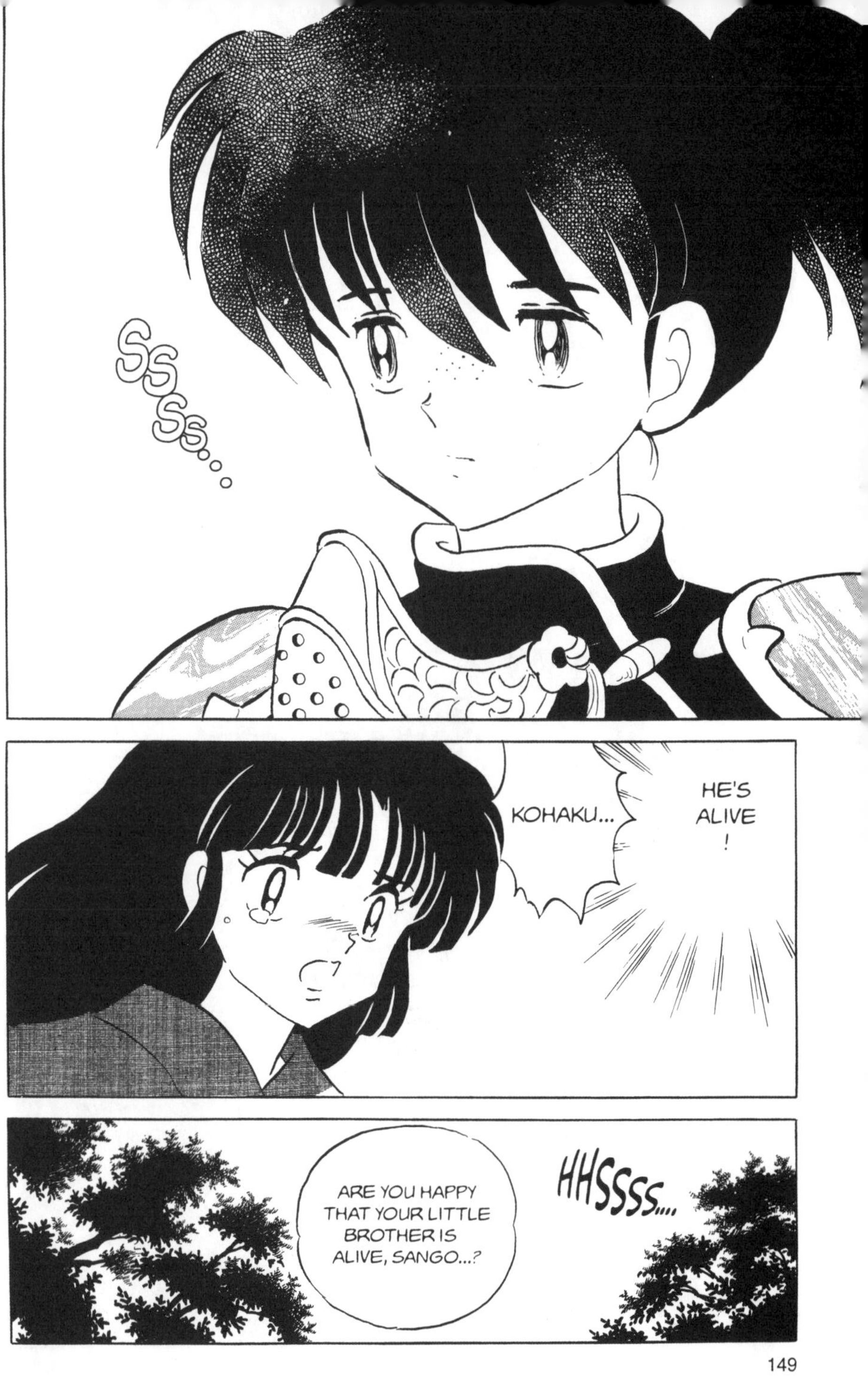
SsSs...
KOHAKU...
HE'S ALIVE !
ARE YOU HAPPY THAT YOUR LITTLE BROTHER IS ALIVE, SANGO...?
HHSSSS....

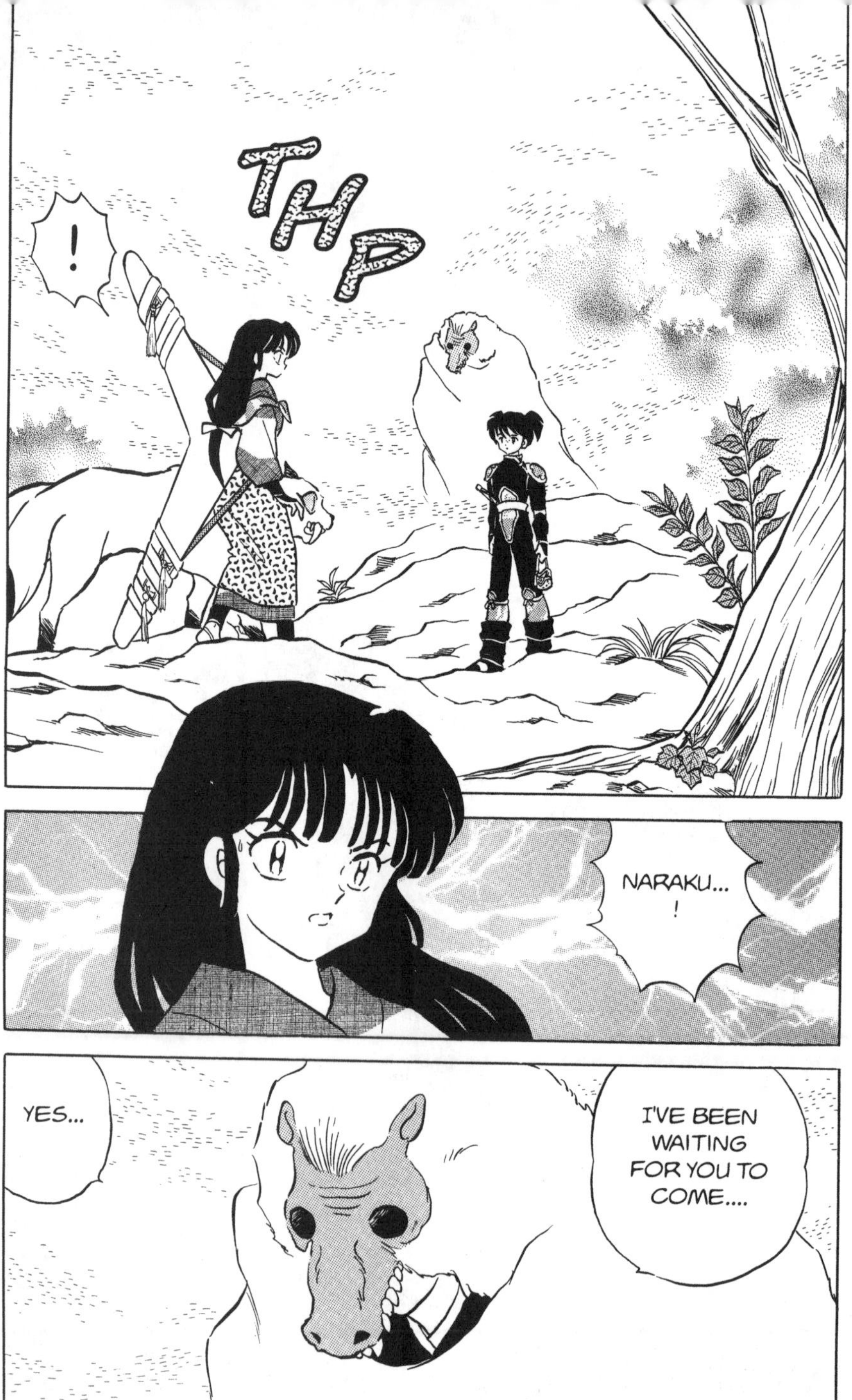
THP
!
NARAKU... !
I'VE BEEN WAITING FOR YOU TO COME....
YES...

SCROLL NINE
NEW LIFE

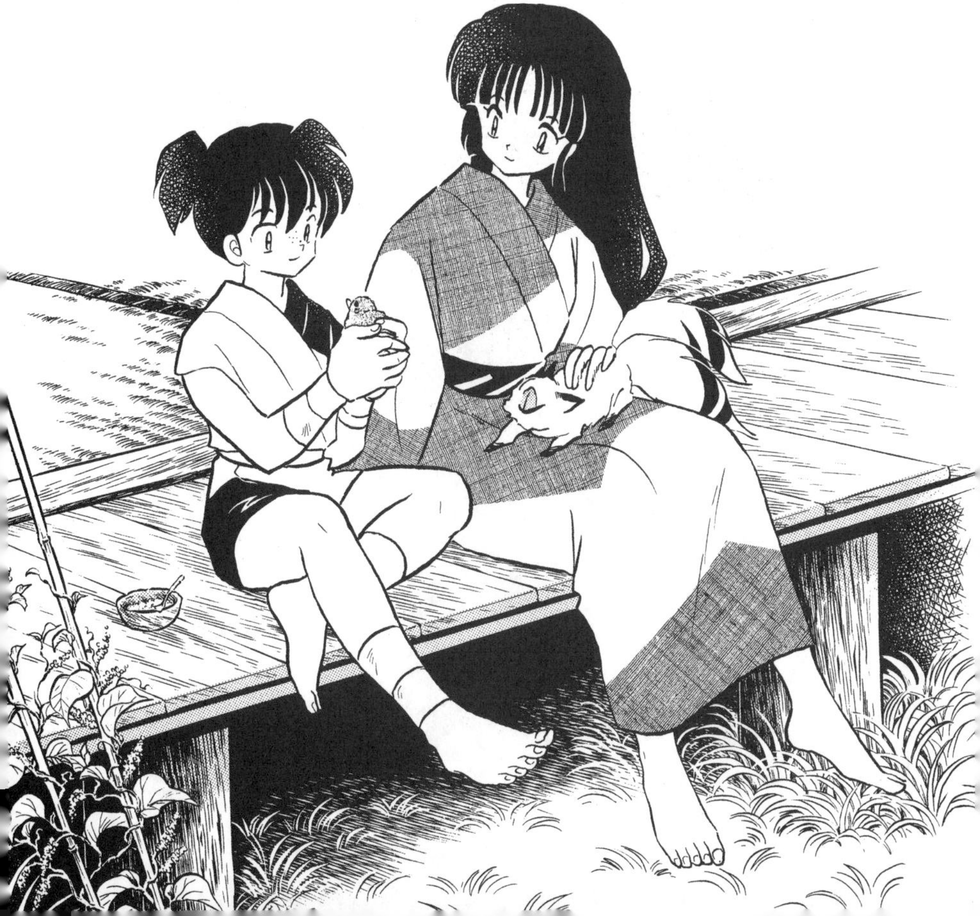

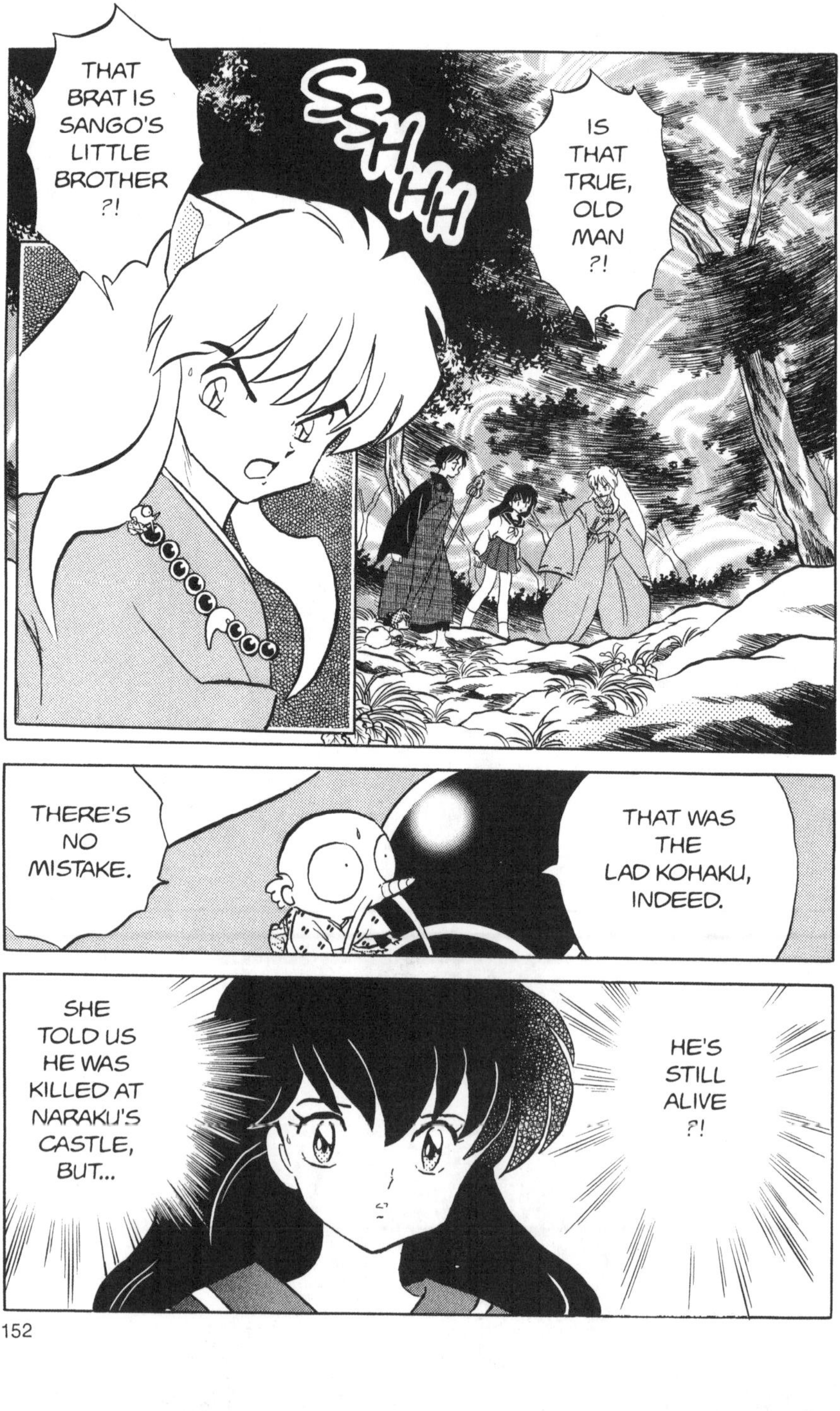
IS THAT TRUE, OLD MAN ?!
SSHHH
THAT BRAT IS SANGO'S LITTLE BROTHER ?!
THAT WAS THE LAD KOHAKU, INDEED.
THERE'S NO MISTAKE.
HE'S STILL ALIVE ?!
SHE TOLD US HE WAS KILLED AT NARAKU'S CASTLE, BUT...

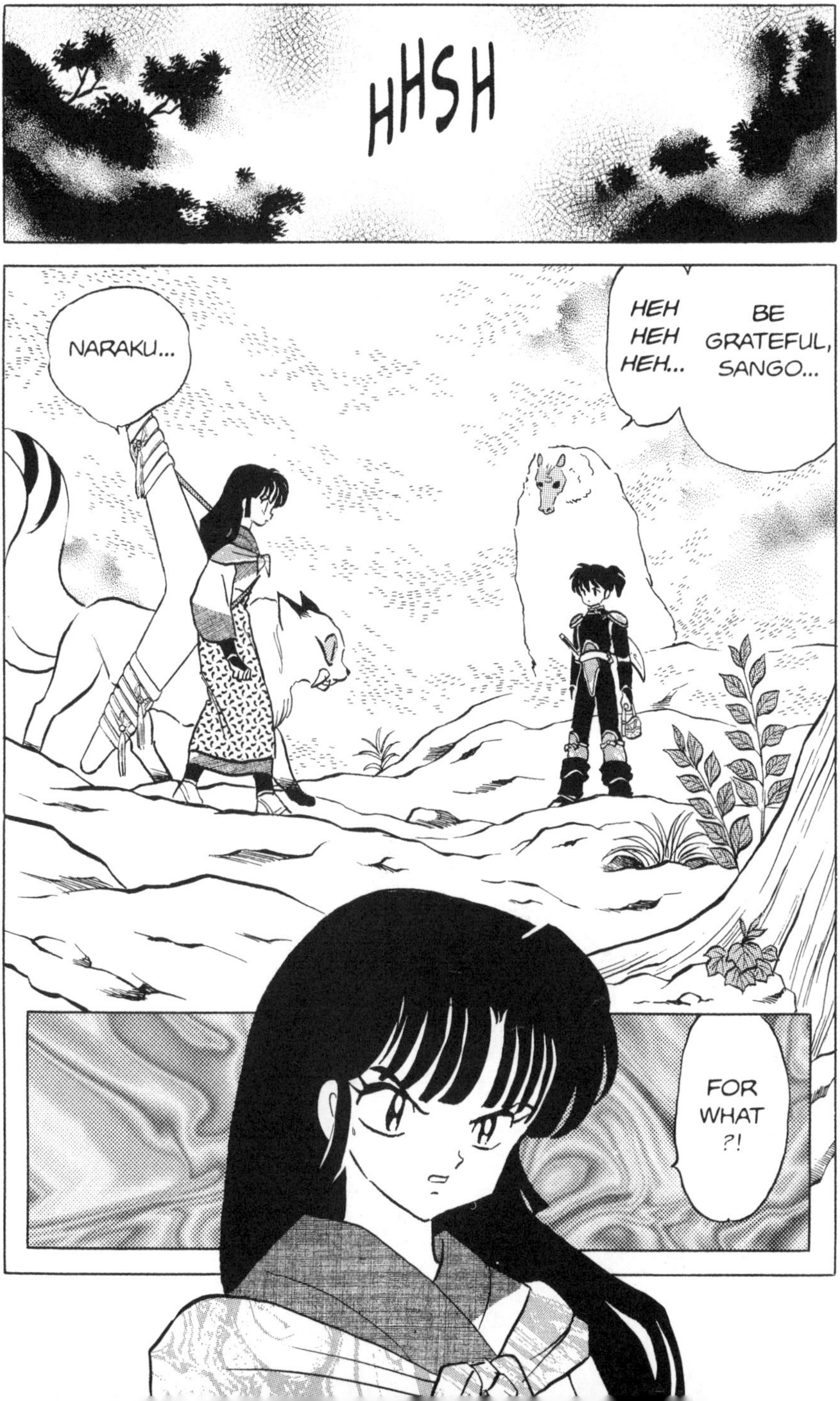
HHSH
HEH HEH HEH... BE GRATEFUL, SANGO...
NARAKU...
FOR WHAT ?!

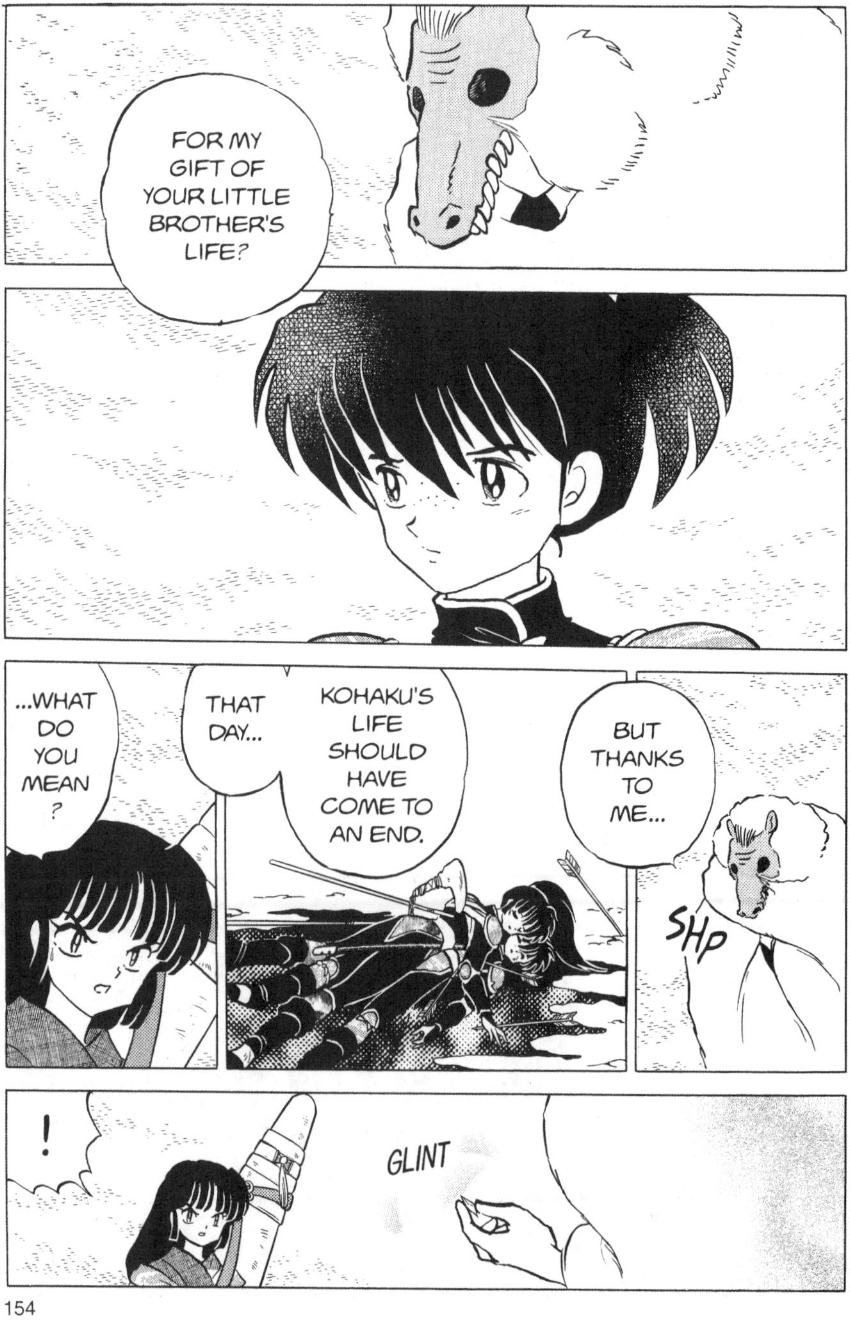
FOR MY GIFT OF YOUR LITTLE BROTHER'S LIFE?
...WHAT DO YOU MEAN ?
THAT DAY...
KOHAKU'S LIFE SHOULD HAVE COME TO AN END.
BUT THANKS TO ME...
SHP
!
GLINT

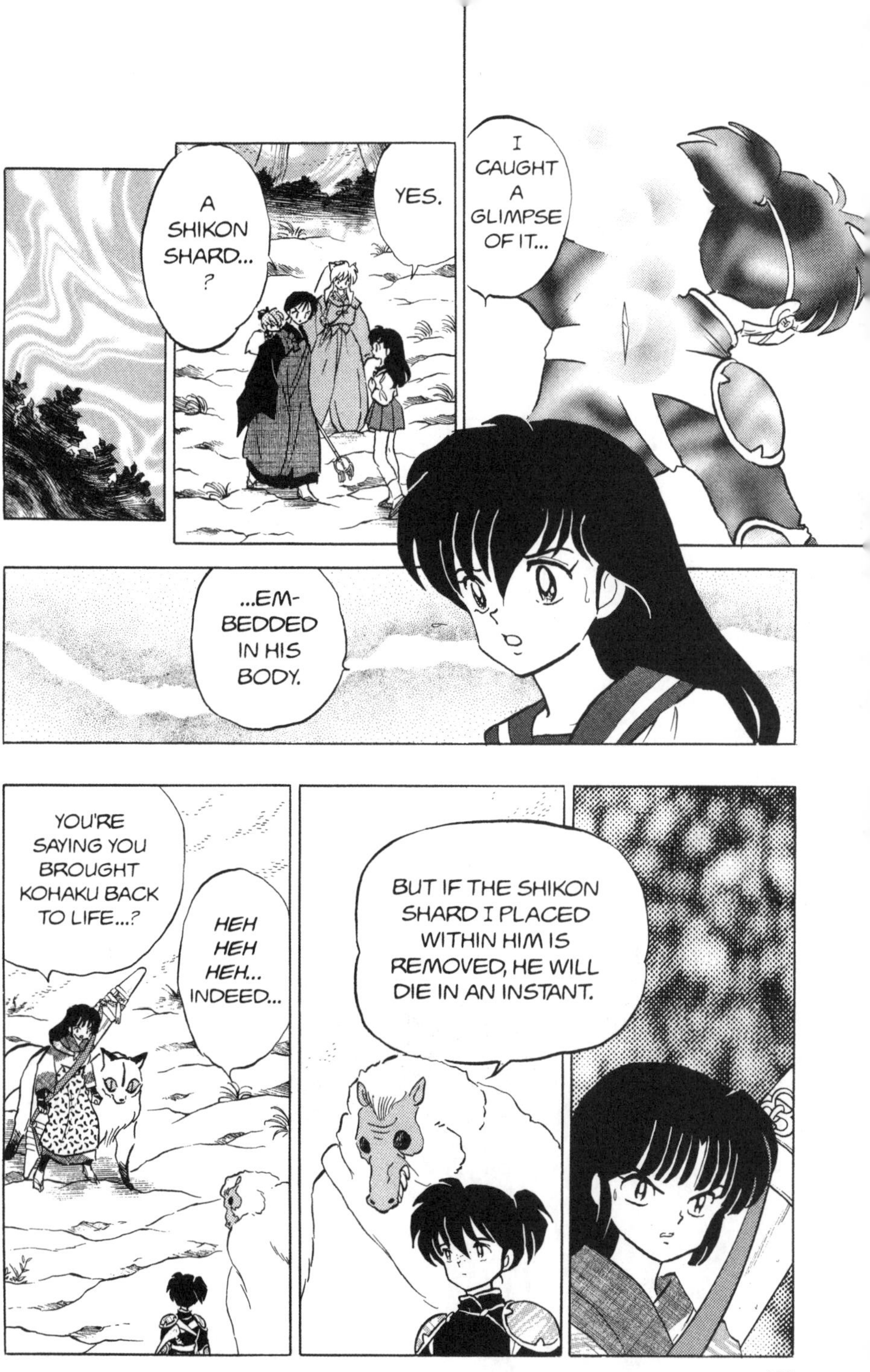
A SHIKON SHARD...?
YES.
I CAUGHT A GLIMPSE OF IT...
...EM-BEDDED IN HIS BODY.
YOU'RE SAYING YOU BROUGHT KOHAKU BACK TO LIFE...?
HEH HEH HEH... INDEED...
BUT IF THE SHIKON SHARD I PLACED WITHIN HIM IS REMOVED, HE WILL DIE IN AN INSTANT.

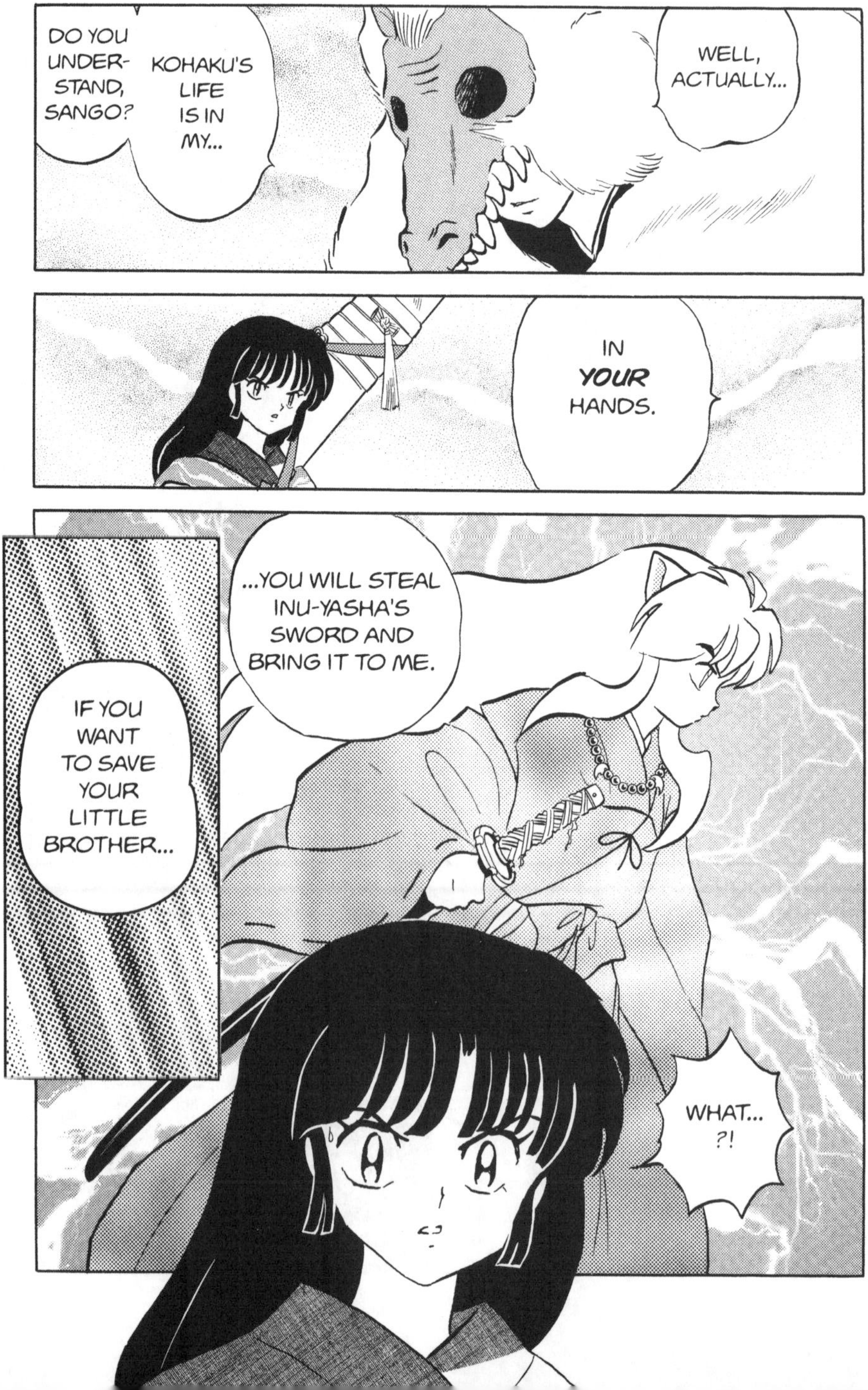
DO YOU UNDER-STAND, SANGO?
KOHAKU'S LIFE IS IN MY...
WELL, ACTUALLY...
IN **YOUR** HANDS.
IF YOU WANT TO SAVE YOUR LITTLE BROTHER...
...YOU WILL STEAL INU-YASHA'S SWORD AND BRING IT TO ME.
WHAT... ?!

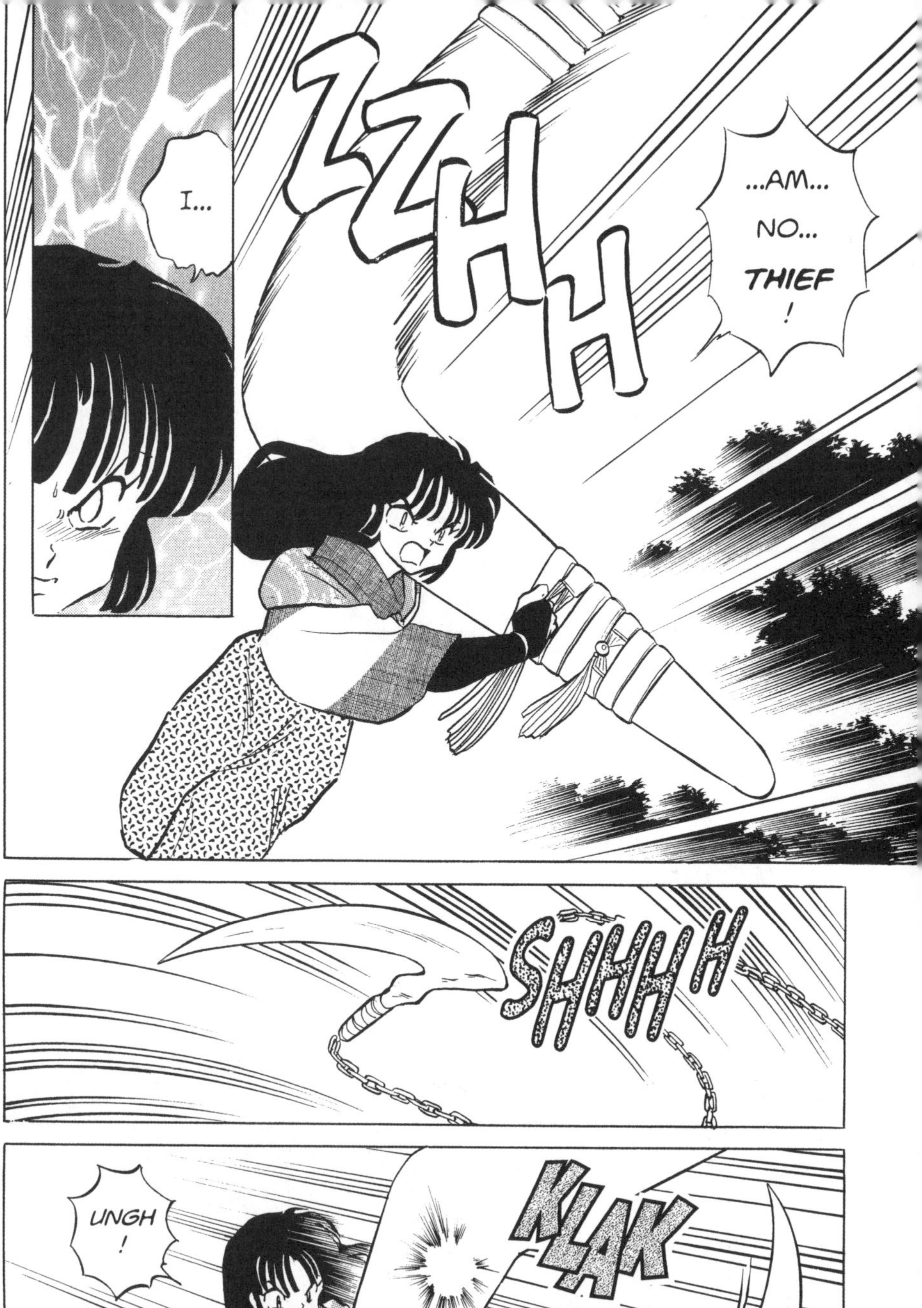
I...
ZZHHH
...AM... NO... THIEF!
SHHHH
UNGH!
KLAK

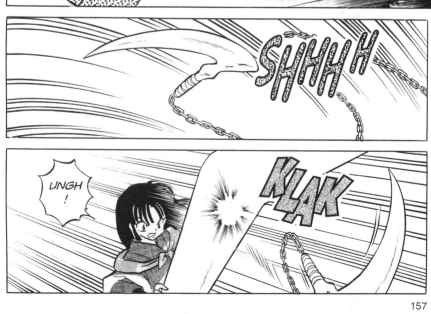

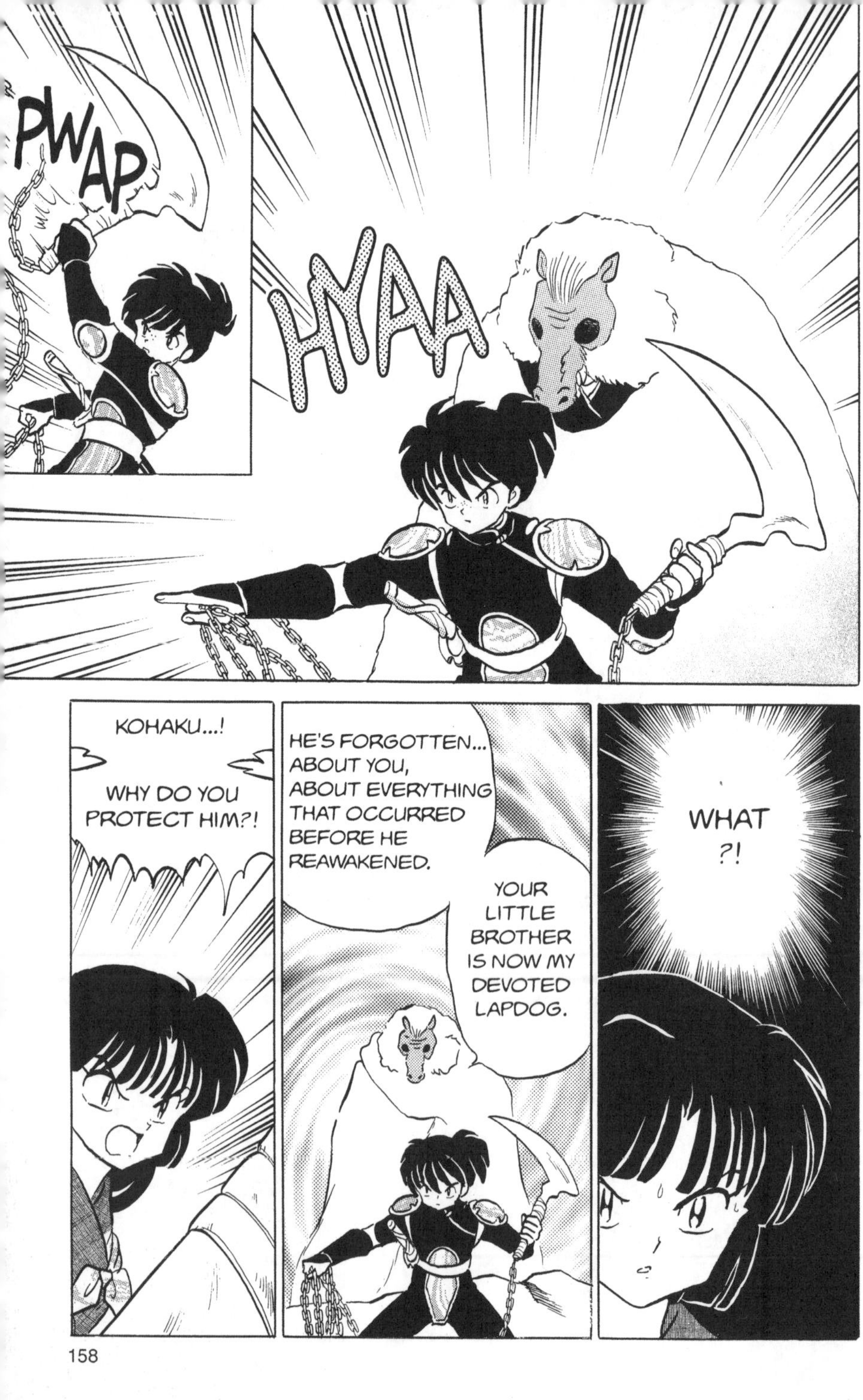
PWAP
HYAA
KOHAKU...!
WHY DO YOU PROTECT HIM?!
HE'S FORGOTTEN... ABOUT YOU, ABOUT EVERYTHING THAT OCCURRED BEFORE HE REAWAKENED.
YOUR LITTLE BROTHER IS NOW MY DEVOTED LAPDOG.
WHAT ?!

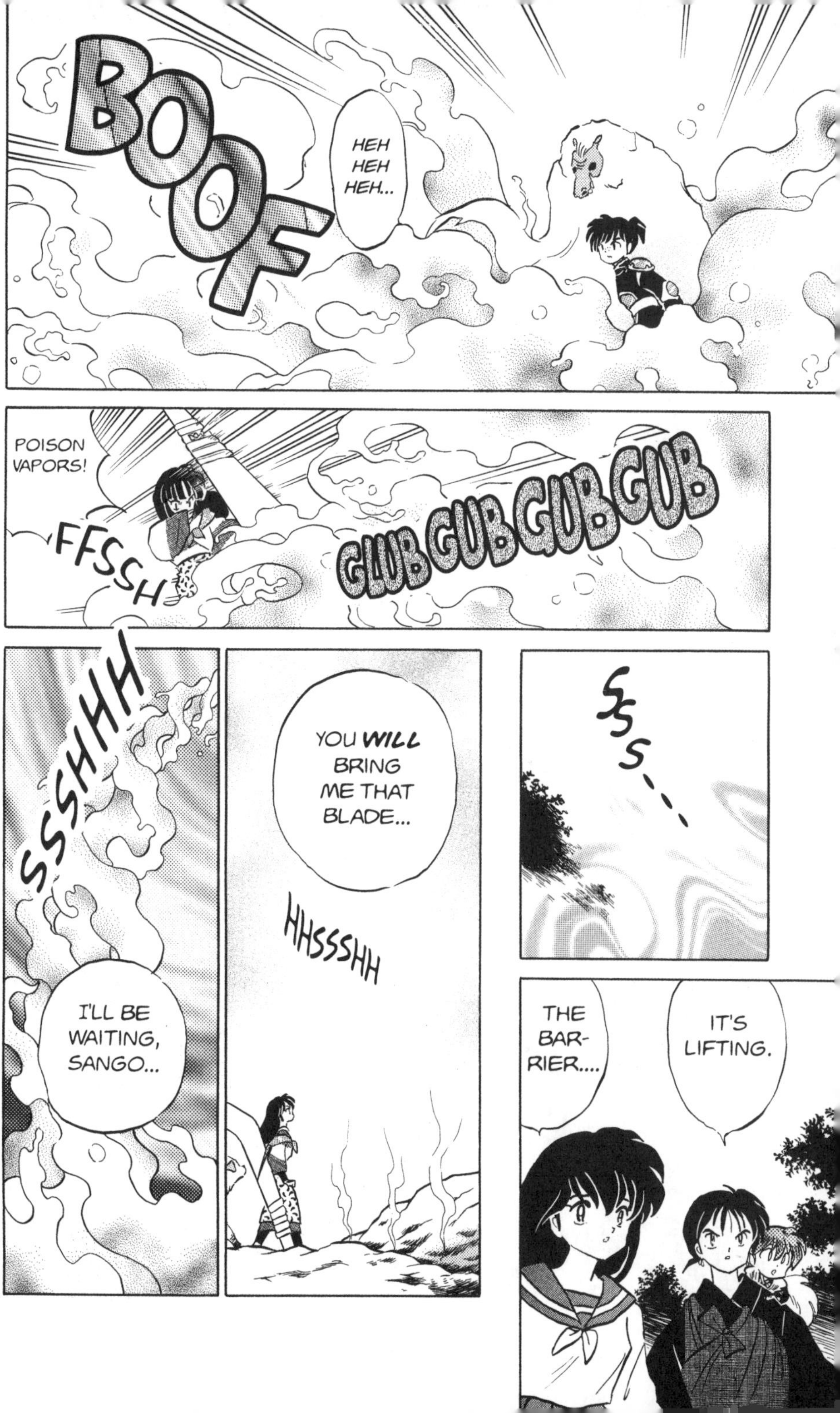
HEH HEH HEH...
BOOF
GLUB GUB GUB GUB
POISON VAPORS!
FFSSH
SSS...
IT'S LIFTING.
THE BAR-RIER....
YOU WILL BRING ME THAT BLADE...
HHSSSHH
SSSHHH
I'LL BE WAITING, SANGO...

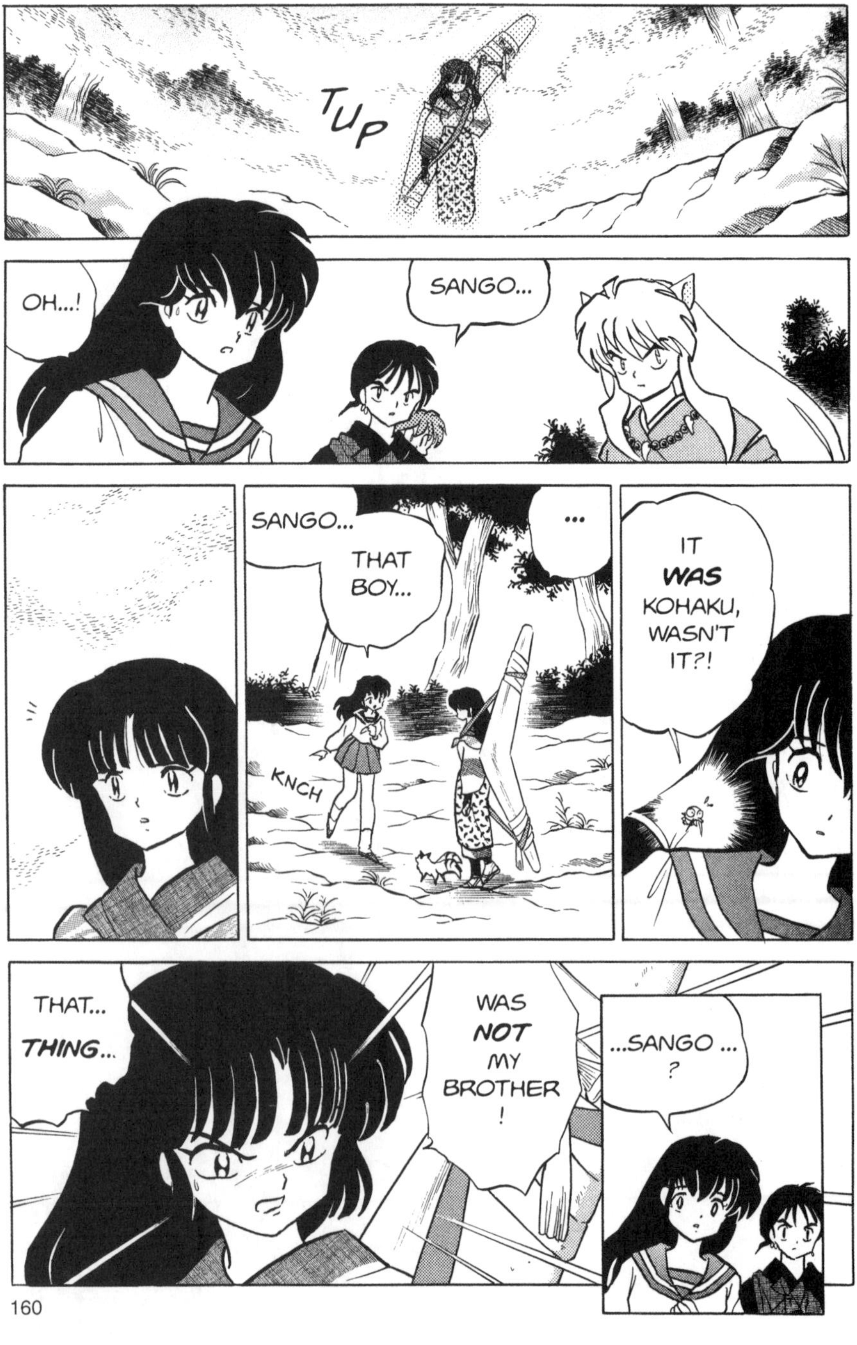
TUP
SANGO...
OH...!
IT WAS KOHAKU, WASN'T IT?!
...
SANGO... THAT BOY...
KNCH
THAT... THING...
WAS NOT MY BROTHER!
...SANGO ...?

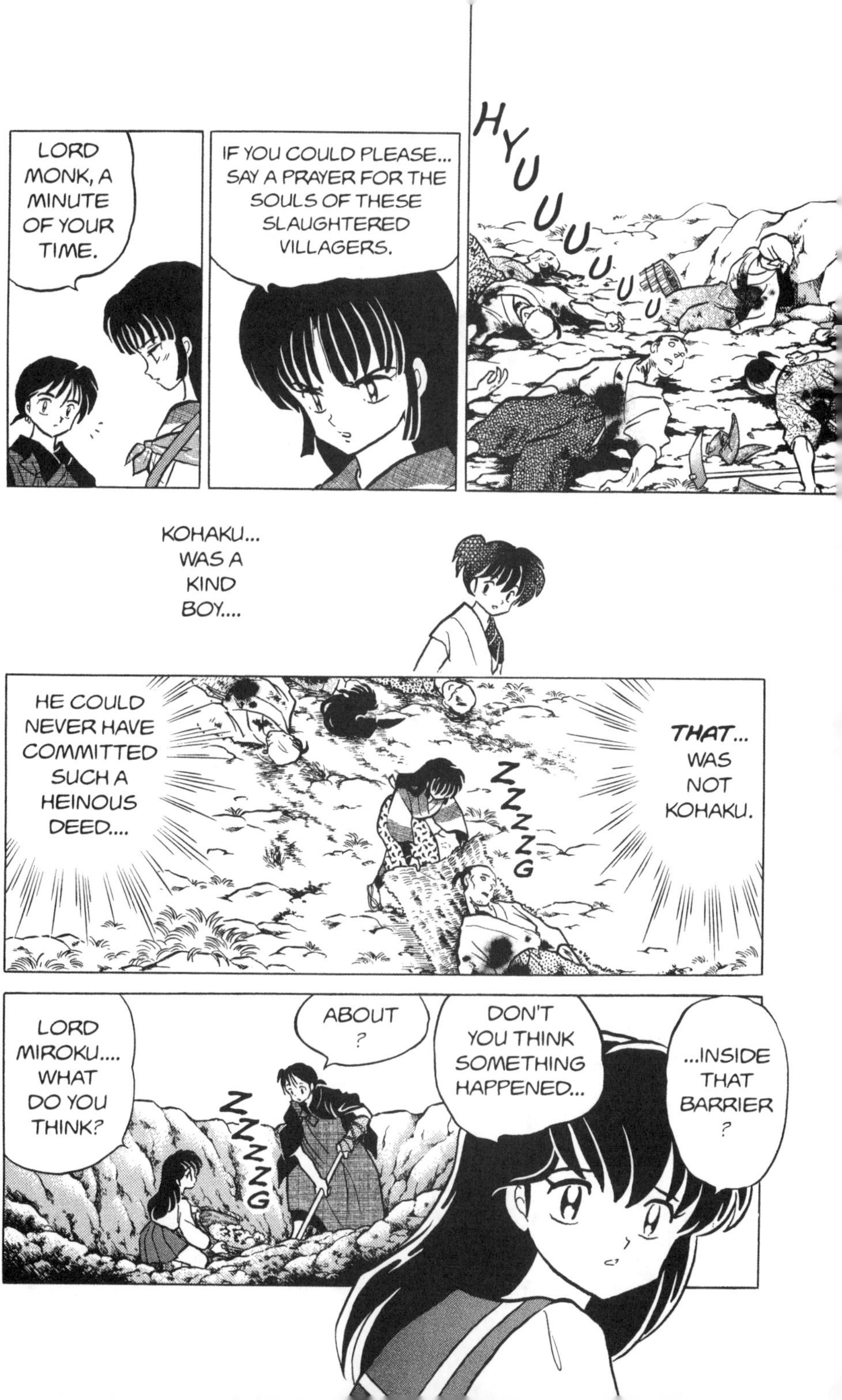
HYUUUUUU
IF YOU COULD PLEASE... SAY A PRAYER FOR THE SOULS OF THESE SLAUGHTERED VILLAGERS.
LORD MONK, A MINUTE OF YOUR TIME.
KOHAKU... WAS A KIND BOY....
HE COULD NEVER HAVE COMMITTED SUCH A HEINOUS DEED....
ZZZZG
THAT... WAS NOT KOHAKU.
LORD MIROKU.... WHAT DO YOU THINK?
ABOUT ?
ZZZZG
DON'T YOU THINK SOMETHING HAPPENED...
...INSIDE THAT BARRIER ?

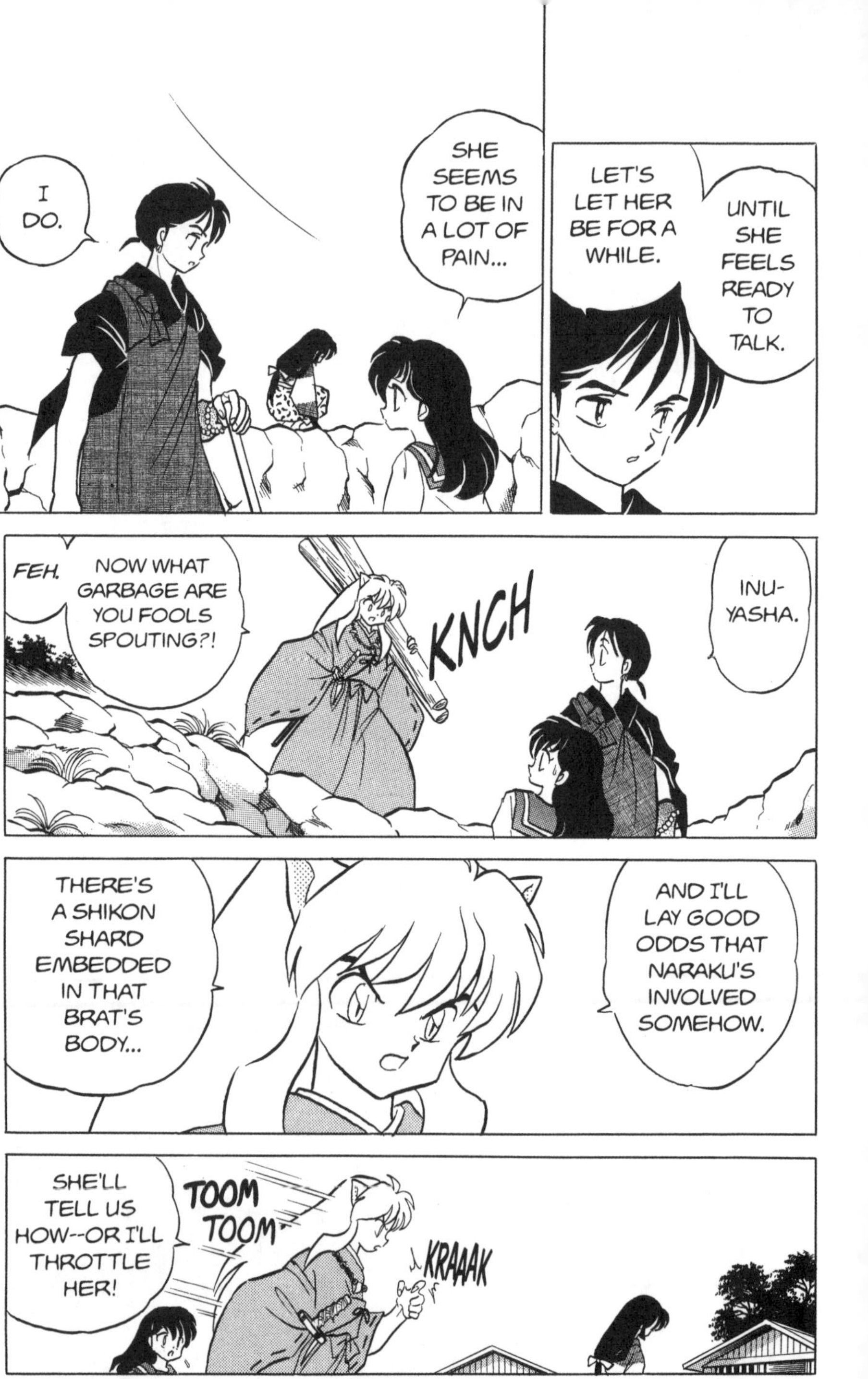
I DO.
SHE SEEMS TO BE IN A LOT OF PAIN...
LET'S LET HER BE FOR A WHILE.
UNTIL SHE FEELS READY TO TALK.
FEH.
NOW WHAT GARBAGE ARE YOU FOOLS SPOUTING?!
KNCH
INU-YASHA.
THERE'S A SHIKON SHARD EMBEDDED IN THAT BRAT'S BODY...
AND I'LL LAY GOOD ODDS THAT NARAKU'S INVOLVED SOMEHOW.
SHE'LL TELL US HOW--OR I'LL THROTTLE HER!
TOOM TOOM
KRAAAK

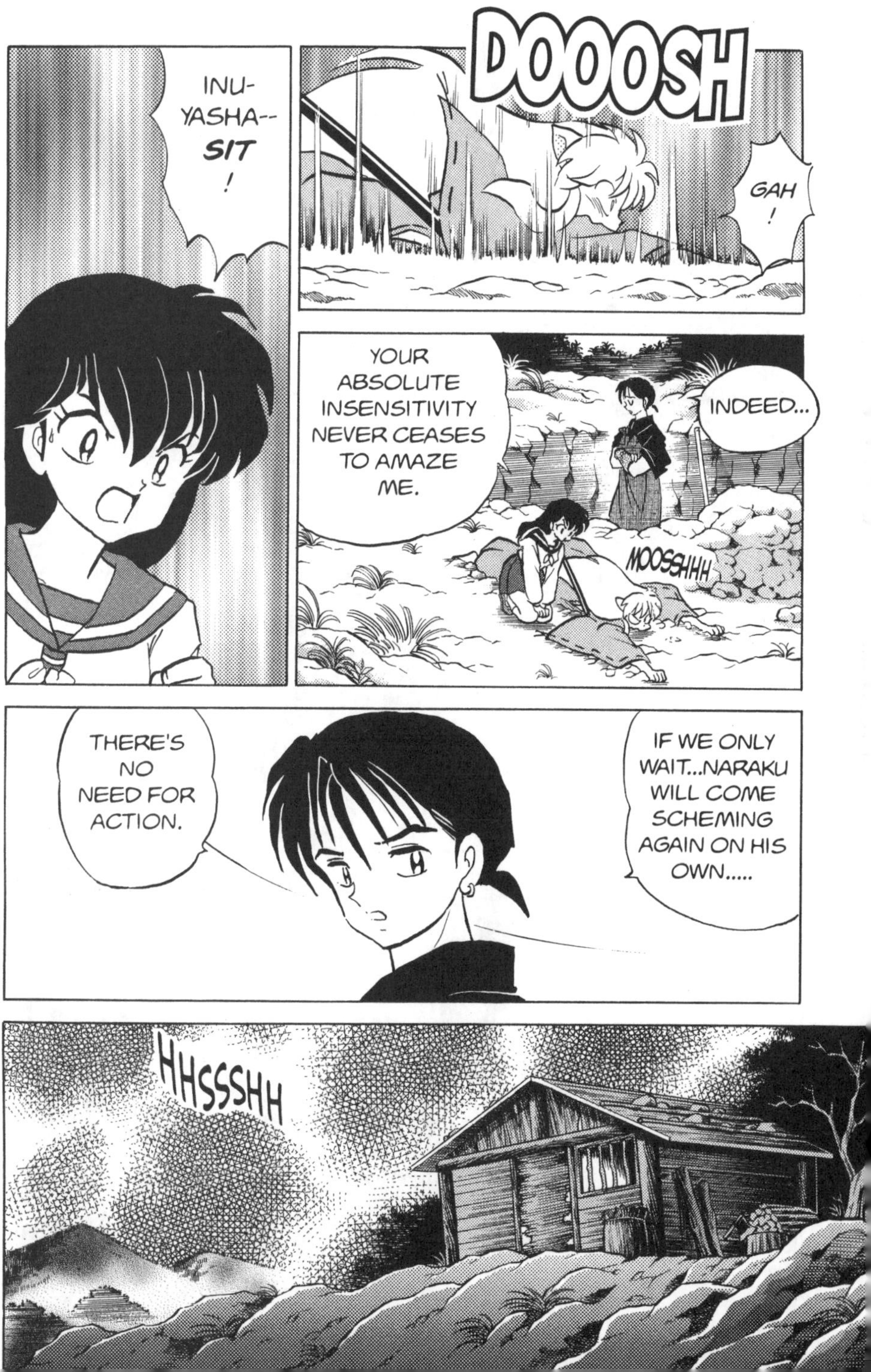
INU-YASHA-- SIT!
DOOOSH
GAH!
YOUR ABSOLUTE INSENSITIVITY NEVER CEASES TO AMAZE ME.
INDEED...
MOOSSHHH
THERE'S NO NEED FOR ACTION.
IF WE ONLY WAIT...NARAKU WILL COME SCHEMING AGAIN ON HIS OWN.....
HHSSSHH

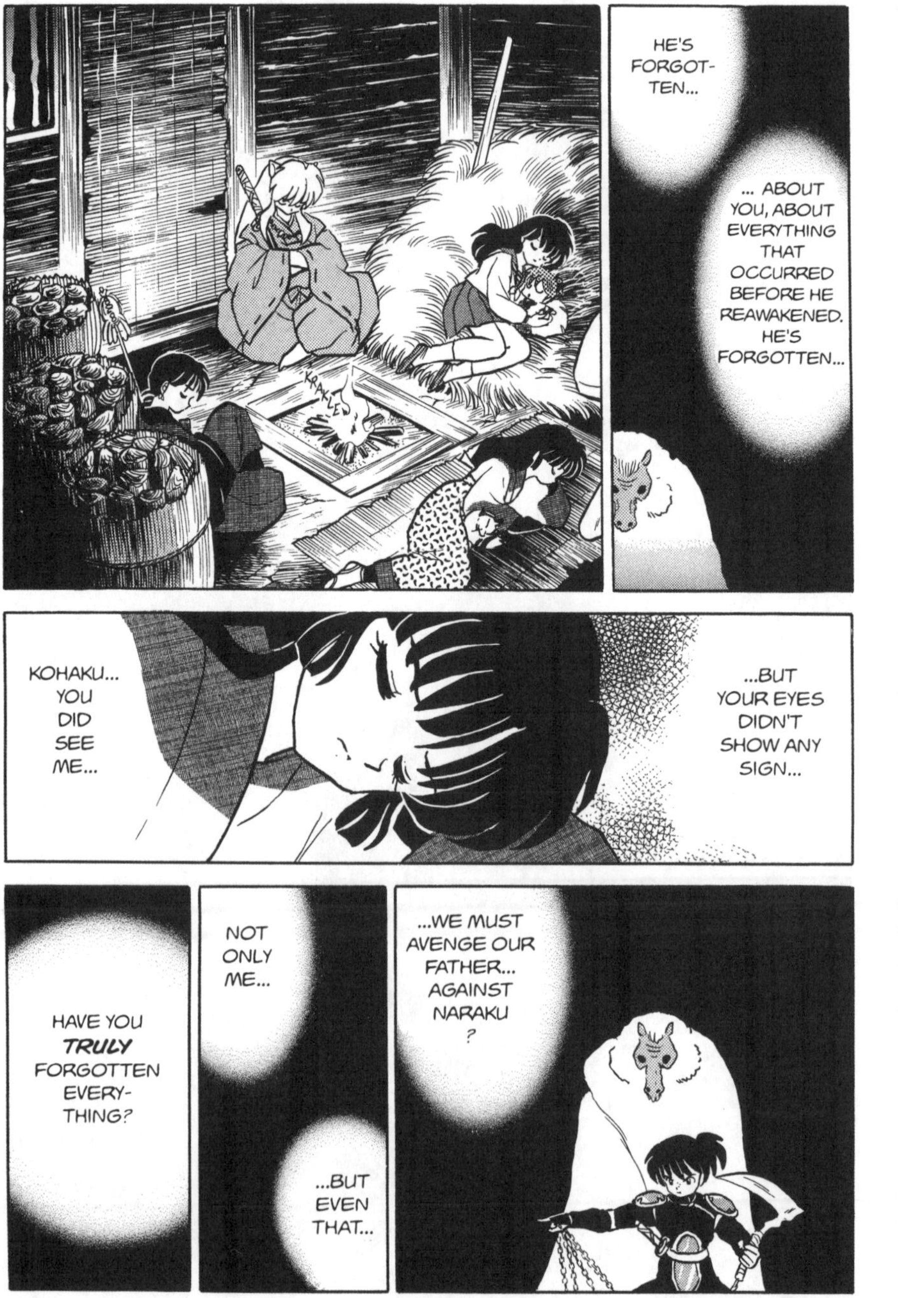
HE'S FORGOT-TEN...
... ABOUT YOU, ABOUT EVERYTHING THAT OCCURRED BEFORE HE REAWAKENED. HE'S FORGOTTEN...
KRAKLE
KOHAKU... YOU DID SEE ME...
...BUT YOUR EYES DIDN'T SHOW ANY SIGN...
...WE MUST AVENGE OUR FATHER... AGAINST NARAKU ?
NOT ONLY ME...
...BUT EVEN THAT...
HAVE YOU *TRULY* FORGOTTEN EVERY-THING?

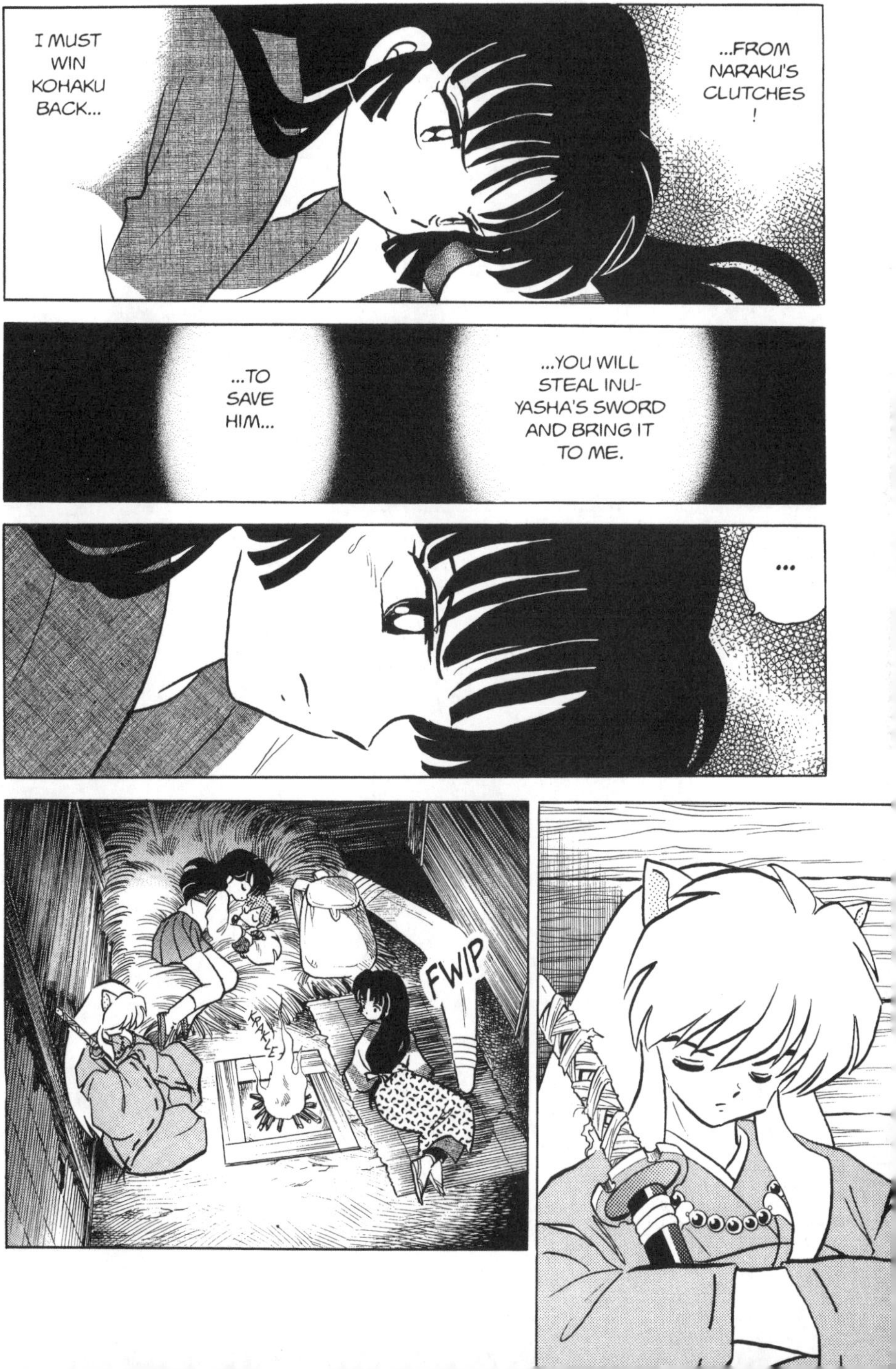
I MUST WIN KOHAKU BACK...
...FROM NARAKU'S CLUTCHES!
...TO SAVE HIM...
...YOU WILL STEAL INU-YASHA'S SWORD AND BRING IT TO ME.
...
FWIP
KRAKLE

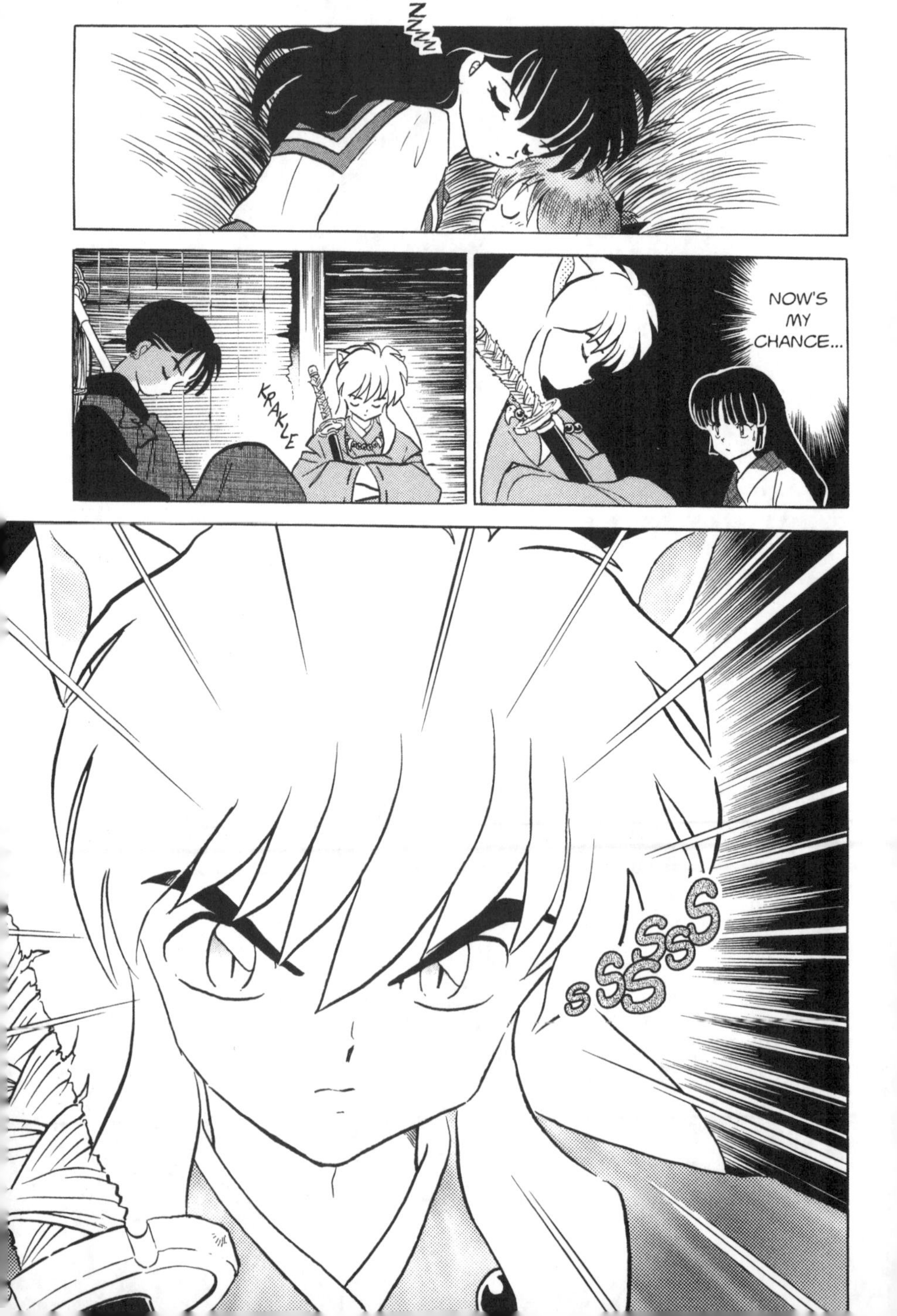
ZZZZ
NOW'S MY CHANCE...
KRAKLE
SSSSSSS

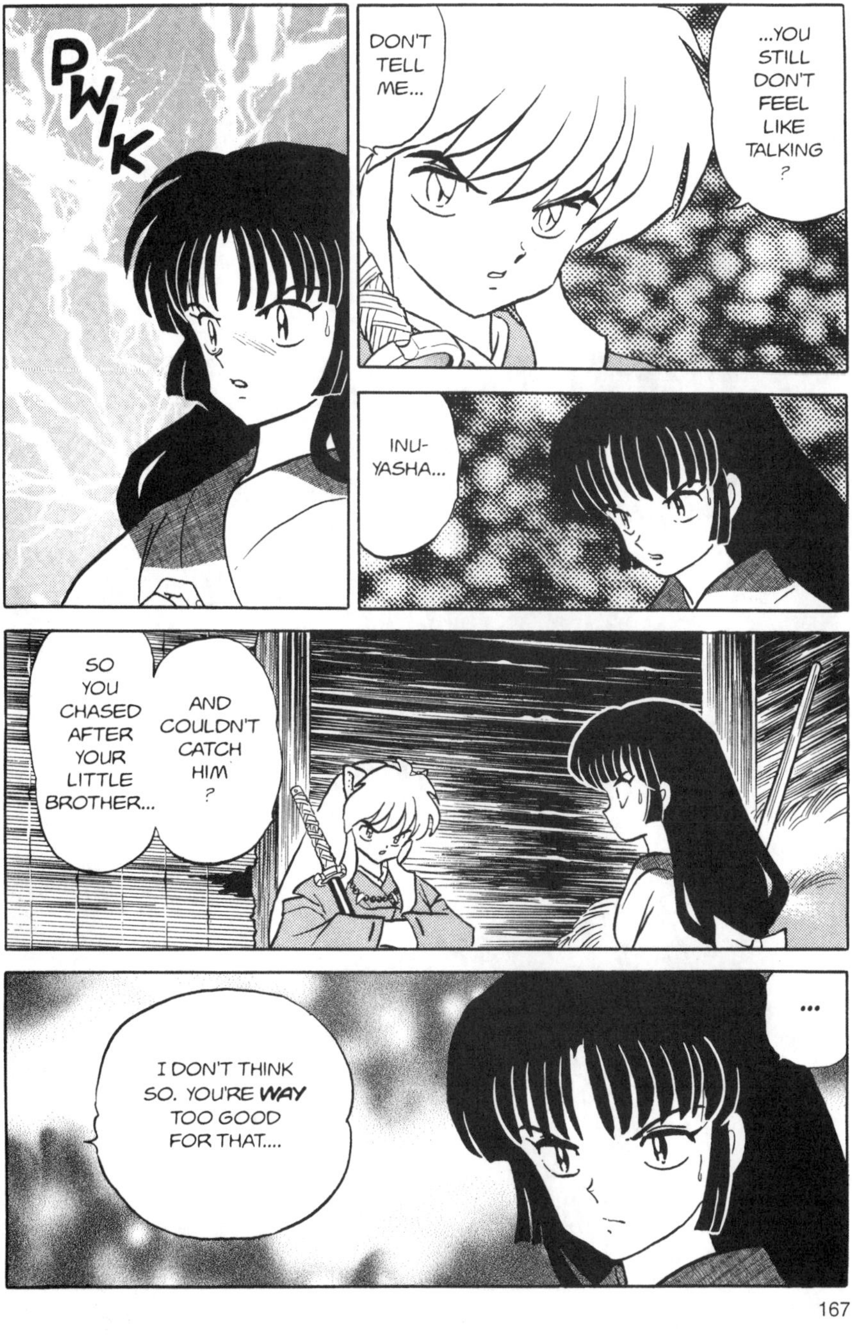
PWIK
DON'T TELL ME...
...YOU STILL DON'T FEEL LIKE TALKING?
INU-YASHA...
SO YOU CHASED AFTER YOUR LITTLE BROTHER...
AND COULDN'T CATCH HIM?
I DON'T THINK SO. YOU'RE **WAY** TOO GOOD FOR THAT....
...

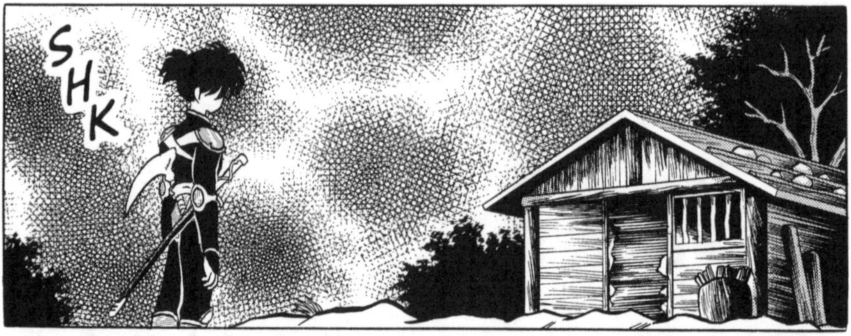
SHK

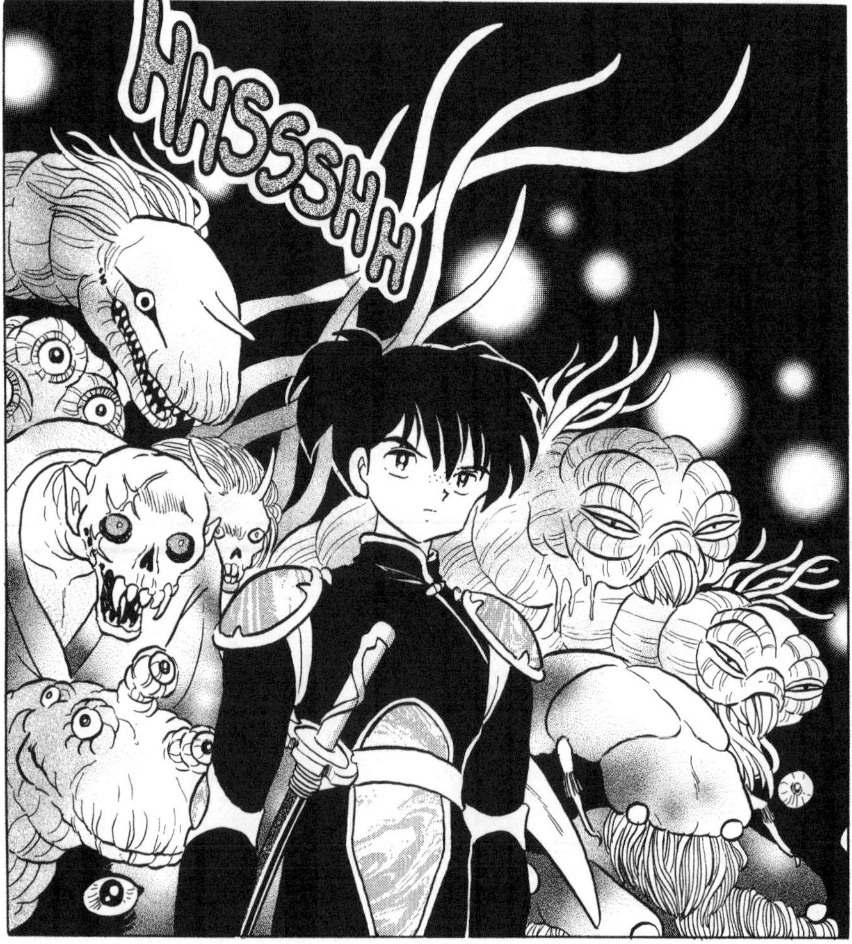
HHSSSSHH

SCROLL TEN

SANGO'S BETRAYAL

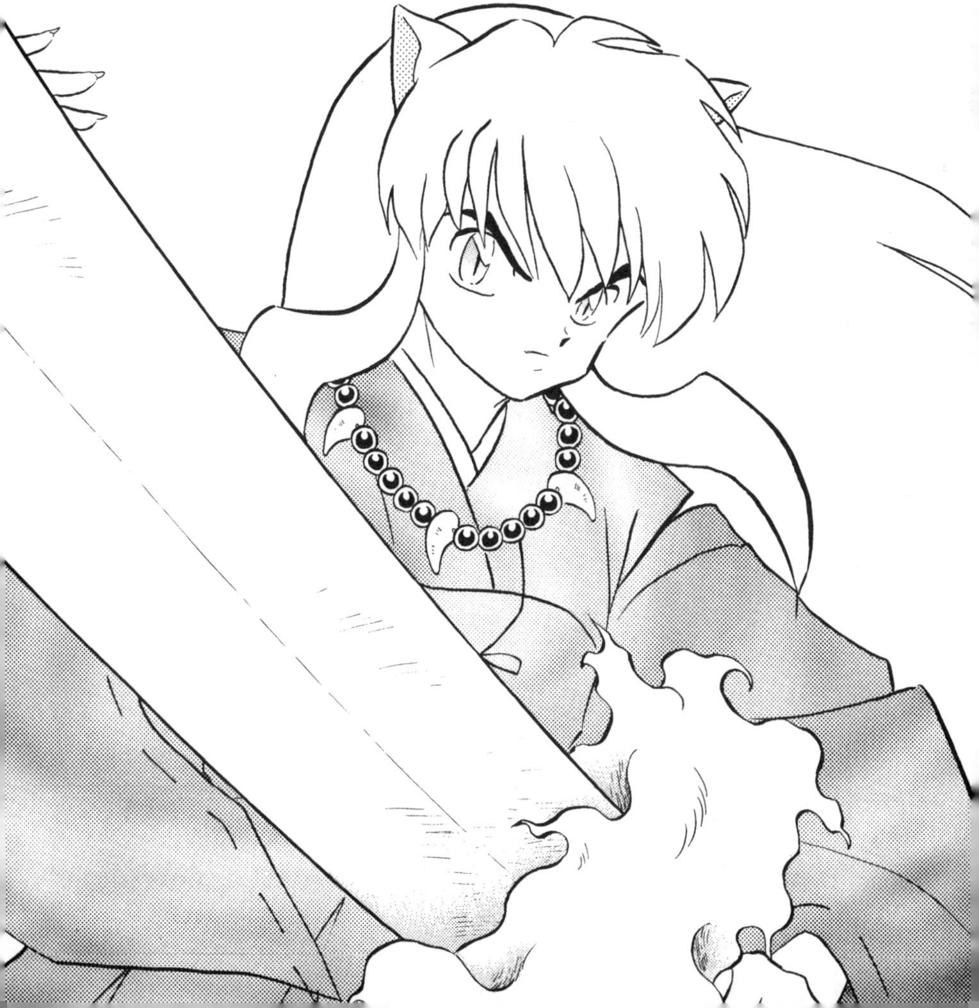

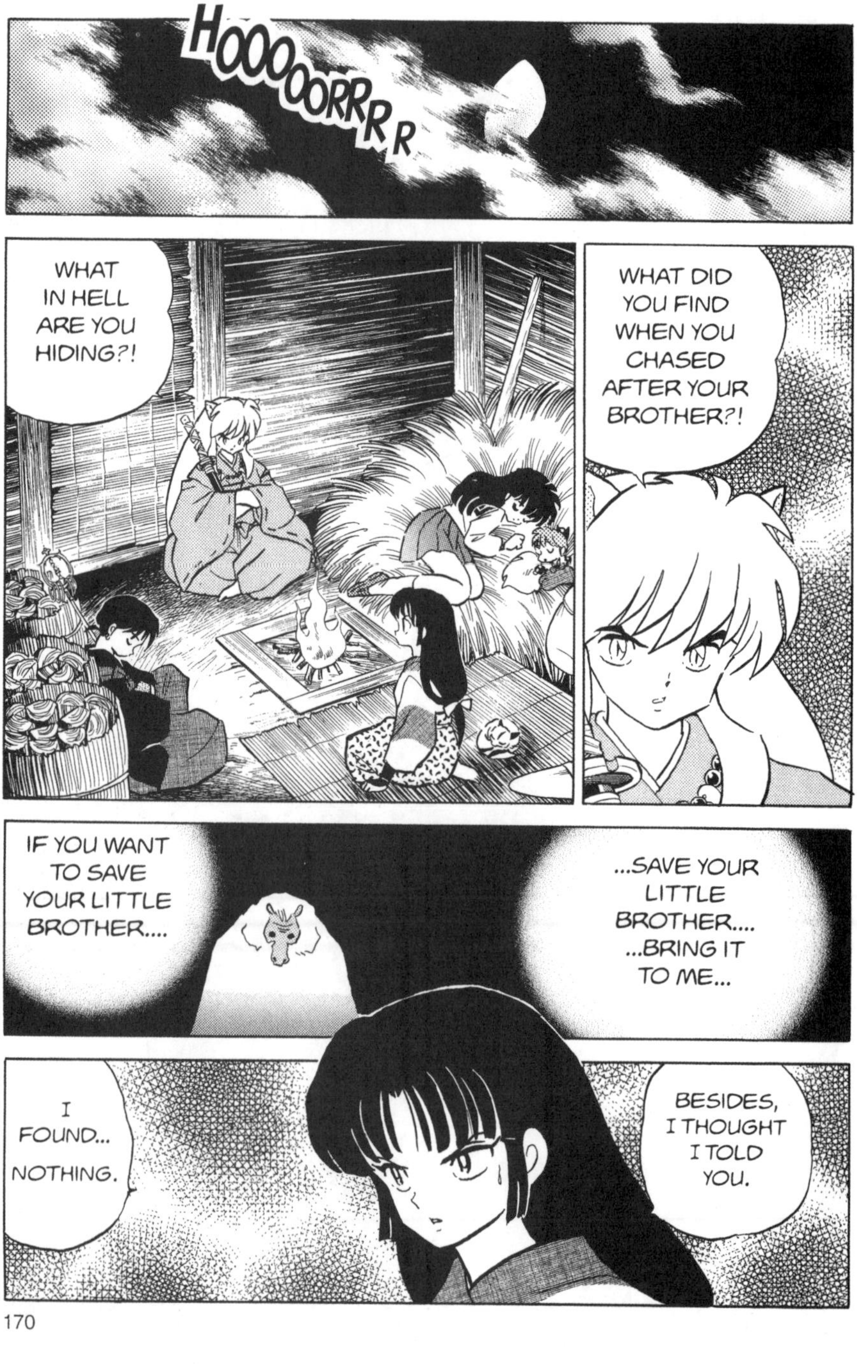
HOOOOORRRRR
WHAT IN HELL ARE YOU HIDING?!
WHAT DID YOU FIND WHEN YOU CHASED AFTER YOUR BROTHER?!
IF YOU WANT TO SAVE YOUR LITTLE BROTHER....
...SAVE YOUR LITTLE BROTHER.... ...BRING IT TO ME...
I FOUND... NOTHING.
BESIDES, I THOUGHT I TOLD YOU.

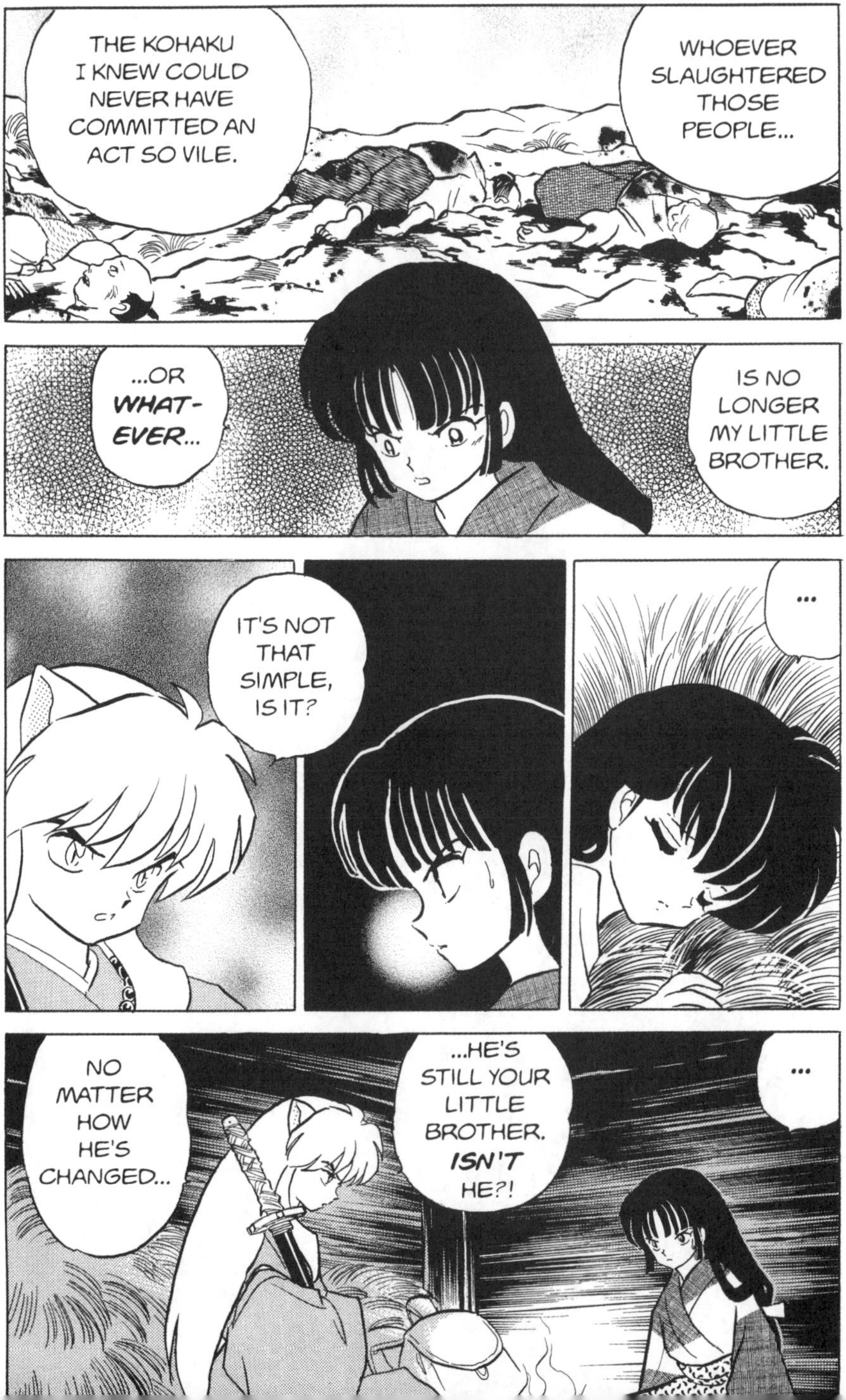
THE KOHAKU I KNEW COULD NEVER HAVE COMMITTED AN ACT SO VILE.
WHOEVER SLAUGHTERED THOSE PEOPLE...
...OR ***WHAT-EVER***...
IS NO LONGER MY LITTLE BROTHER.
IT'S NOT THAT SIMPLE, IS IT?
...
NO MATTER HOW HE'S CHANGED...
...HE'S STILL YOUR LITTLE BROTHER. ***ISN'T*** HE?!
...

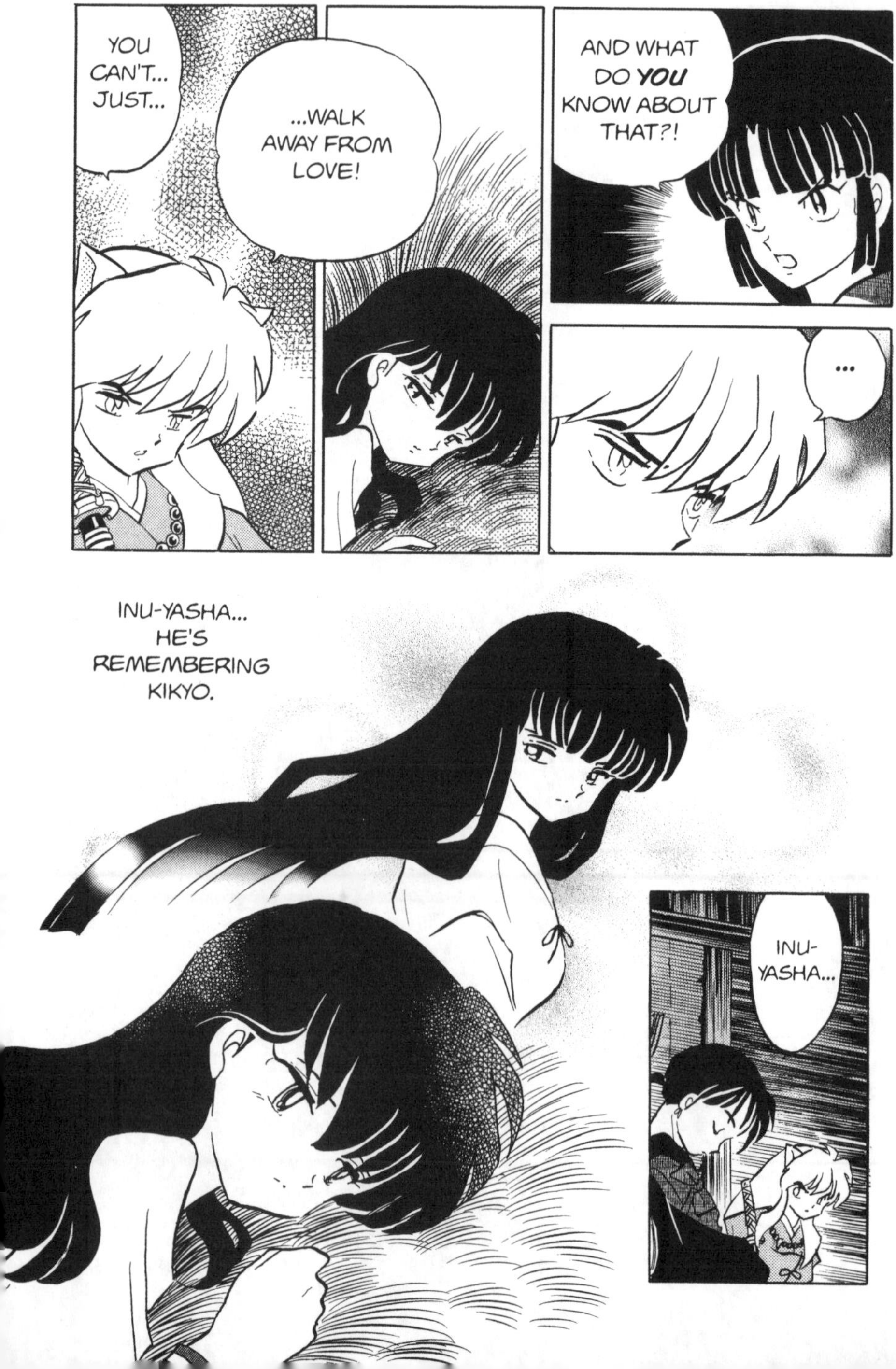
YOU CAN'T... JUST...
...WALK AWAY FROM LOVE!
AND WHAT DO YOU KNOW ABOUT THAT?!
...
INU-YASHA... HE'S REMEMBERING KIKYO.
INU-YASHA...

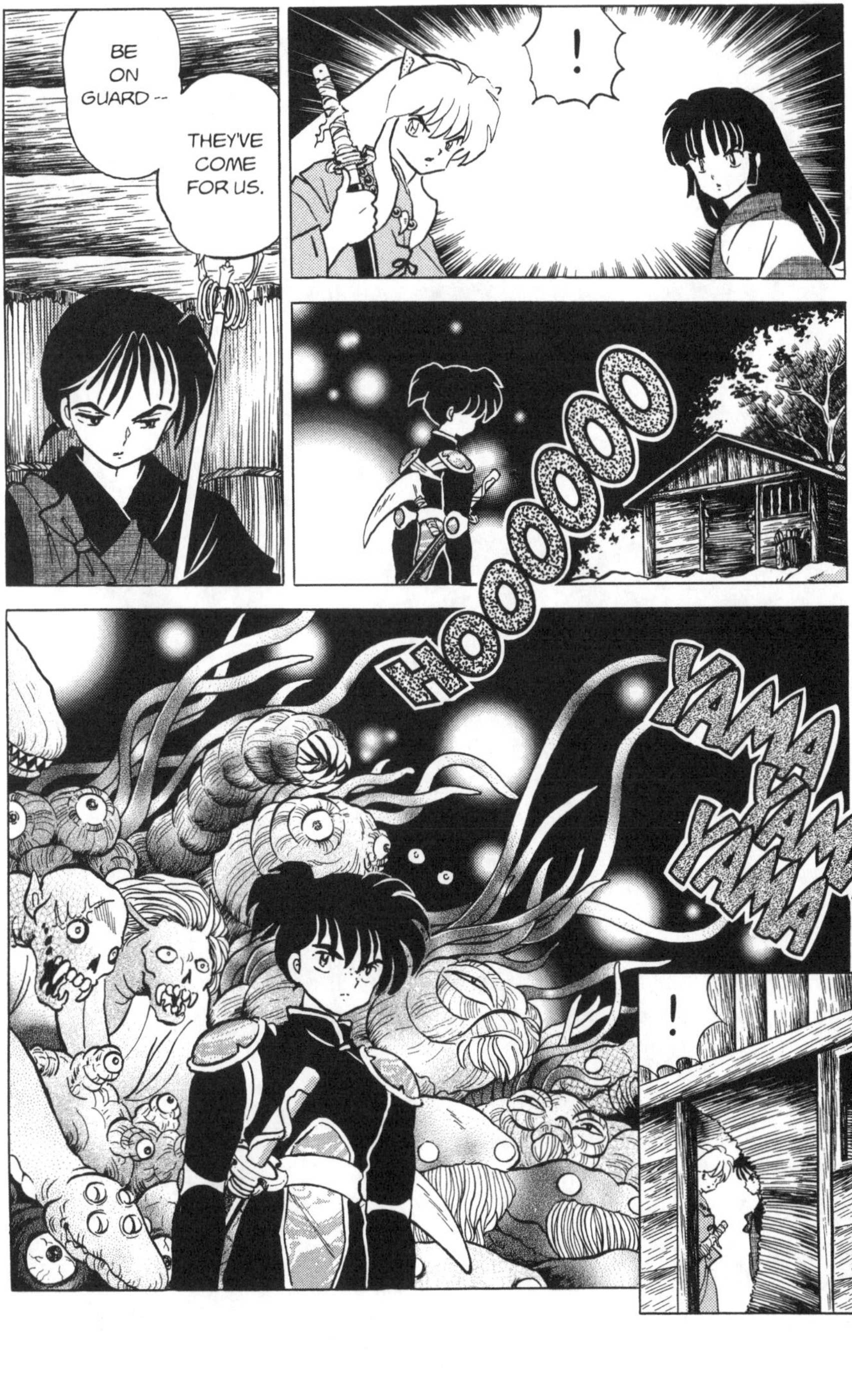
!
HOOOOOOOO
BE ON GUARD --
THEY'VE COME FOR US.
YAMA YAMA YAMA YAMA
!

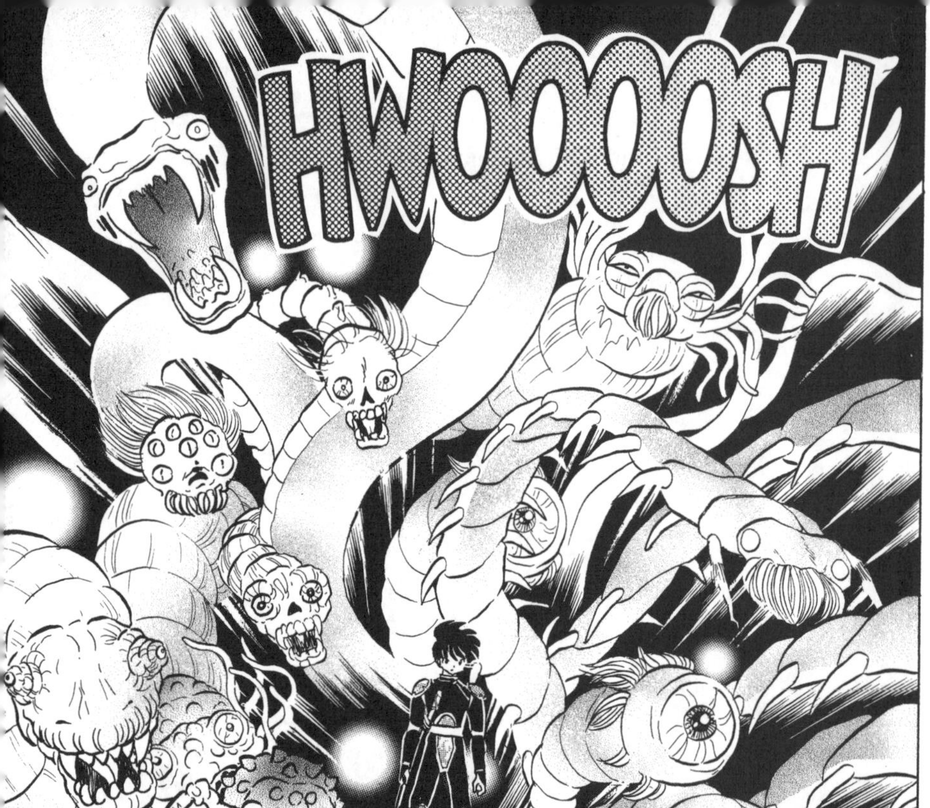
HWOOOOSH
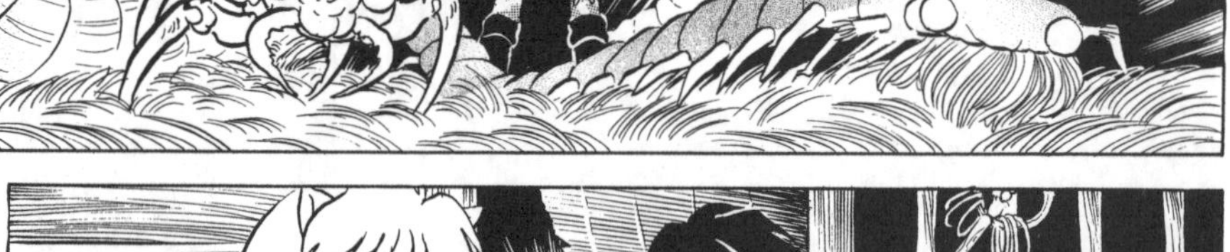
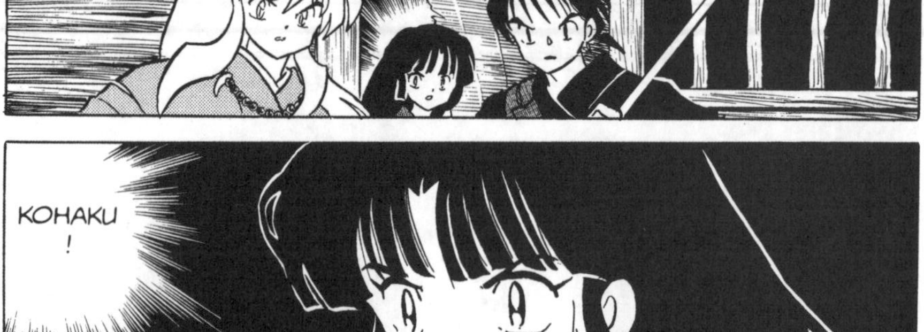
KOHAKU
!

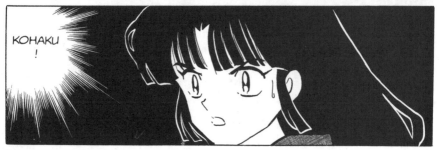

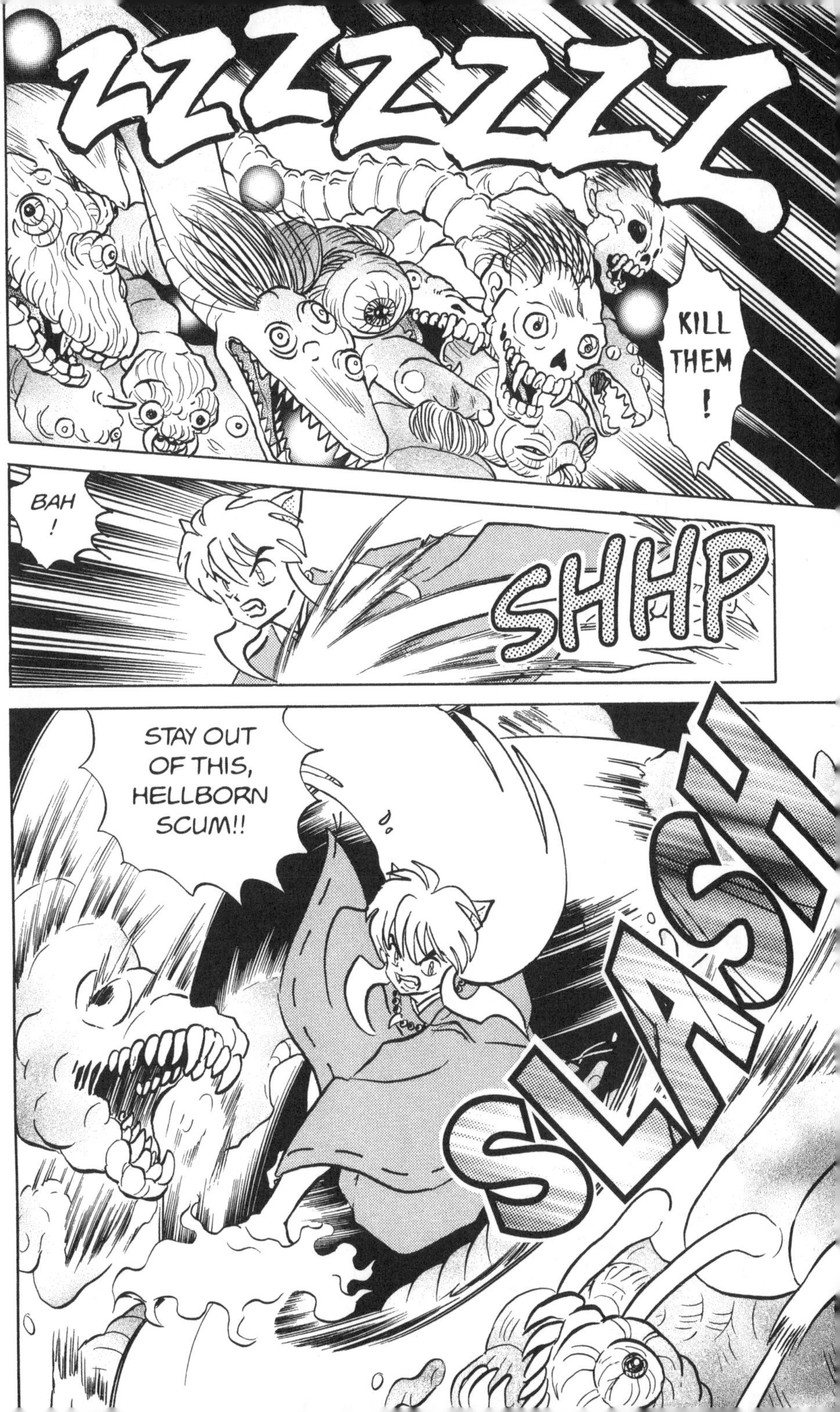
ZZZZZZZ
KILL THEM !
BAH !
SHHP
STAY OUT OF THIS, HELLBORN SCUM!!
SLASH

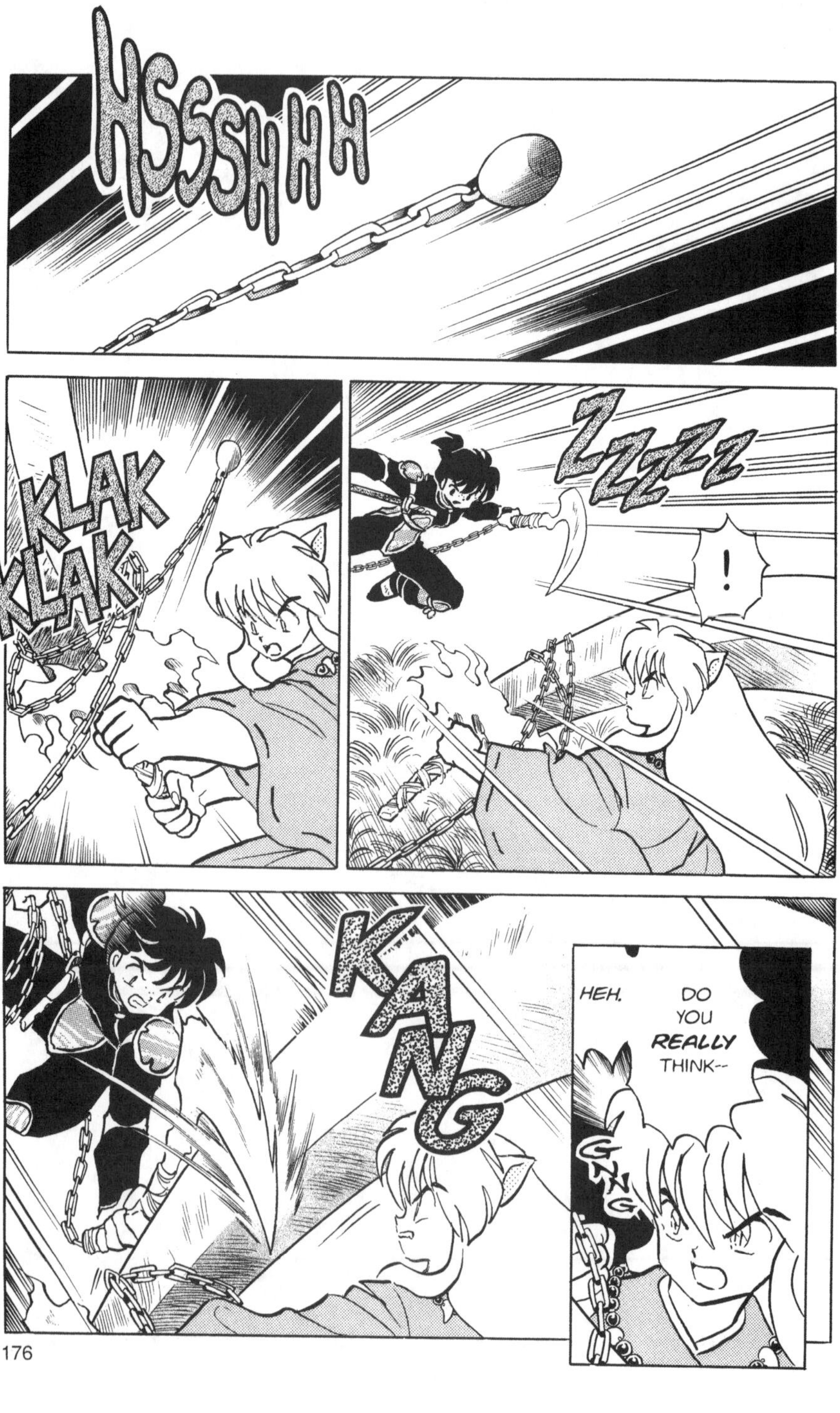
HSSSHHHH
ZZZZZ
!
KLAK KLAK
KANG
HEH.
DO YOU REALLY THINK--
GNNG

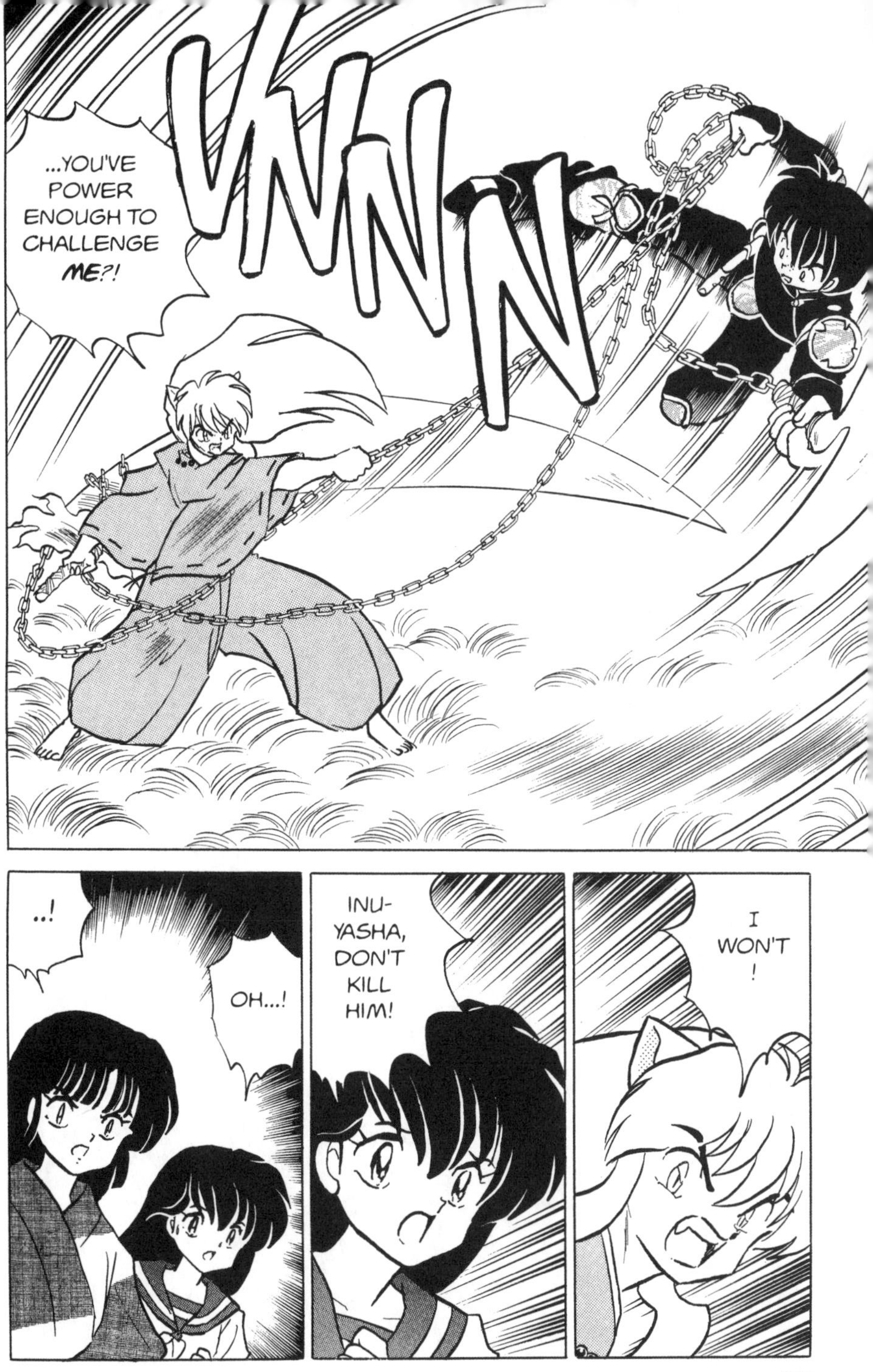
VNNNN
...YOU'VE POWER ENOUGH TO CHALLENGE *ME*?!
I WON'T!
INU-YASHA, DON'T KILL HIM!
OH...!
..!

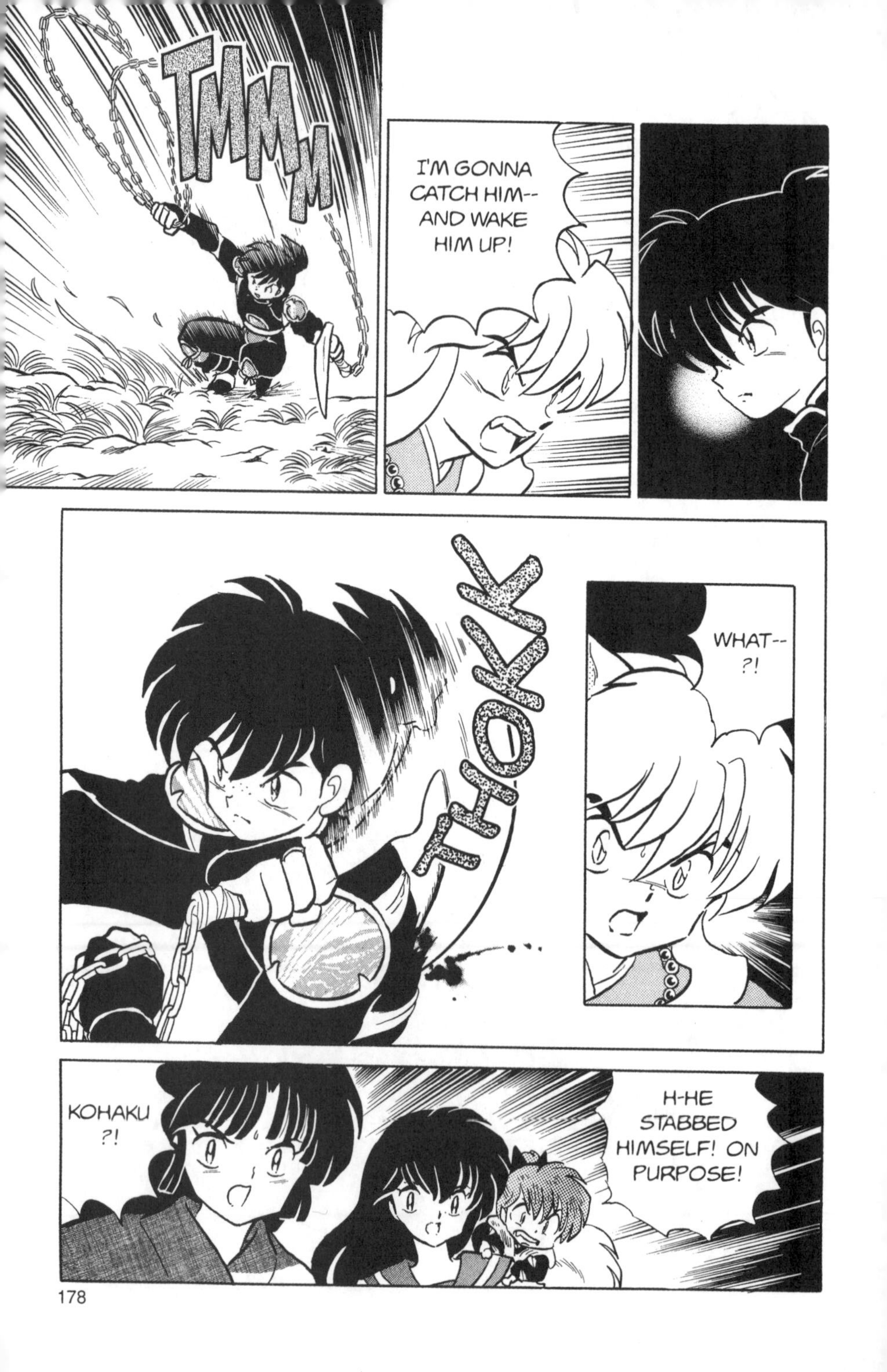
I'M GONNA CATCH HIM-- AND WAKE HIM UP!
TMMMM
WHAT-- ?!
THOKK
H-HE STABBED HIMSELF! ON PURPOSE!
KOHAKU ?!

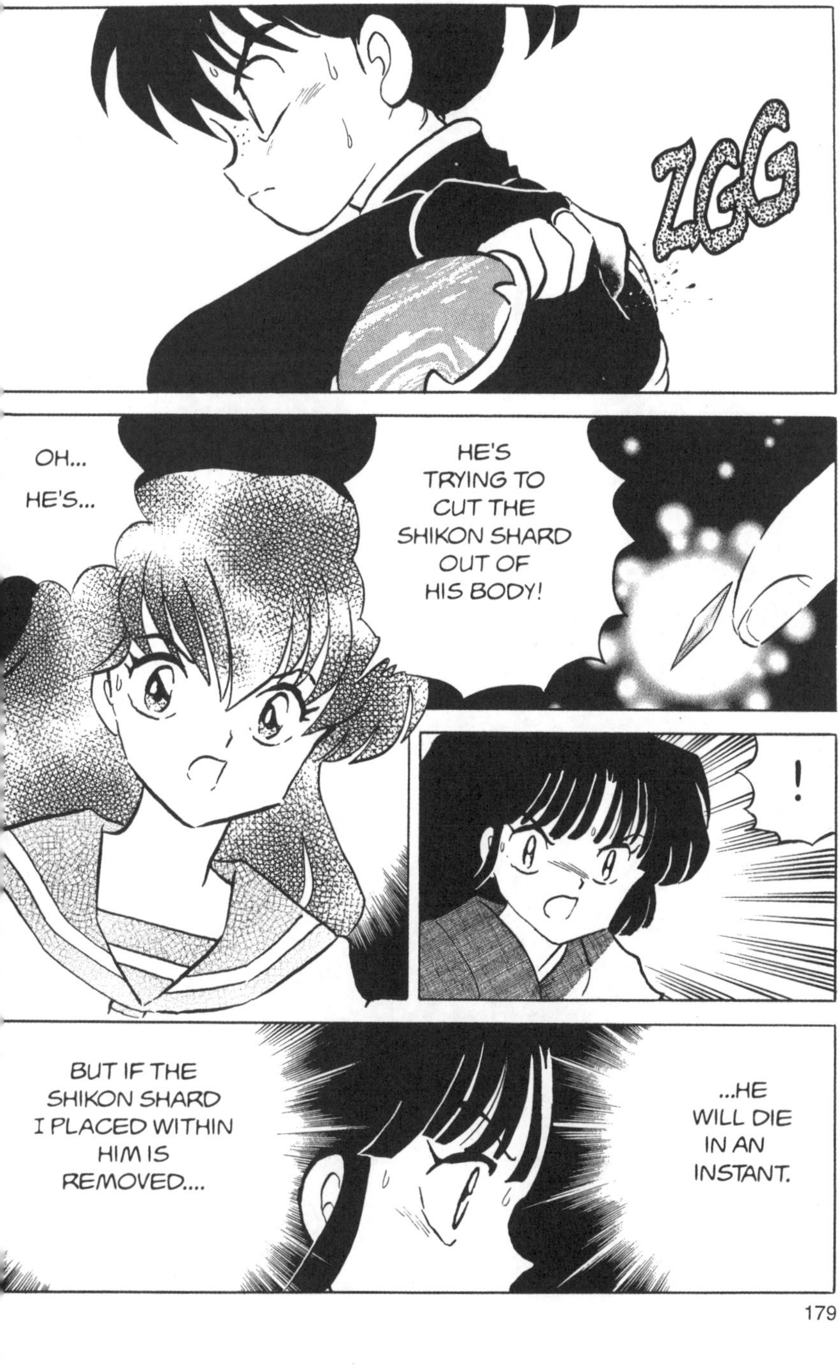
ZGG
HE'S TRYING TO CUT THE SHIKON SHARD OUT OF HIS BODY!
!
OH... HE'S...
...HE WILL DIE IN AN INSTANT.
BUT IF THE SHIKON SHARD I PLACED WITHIN HIM IS REMOVED....

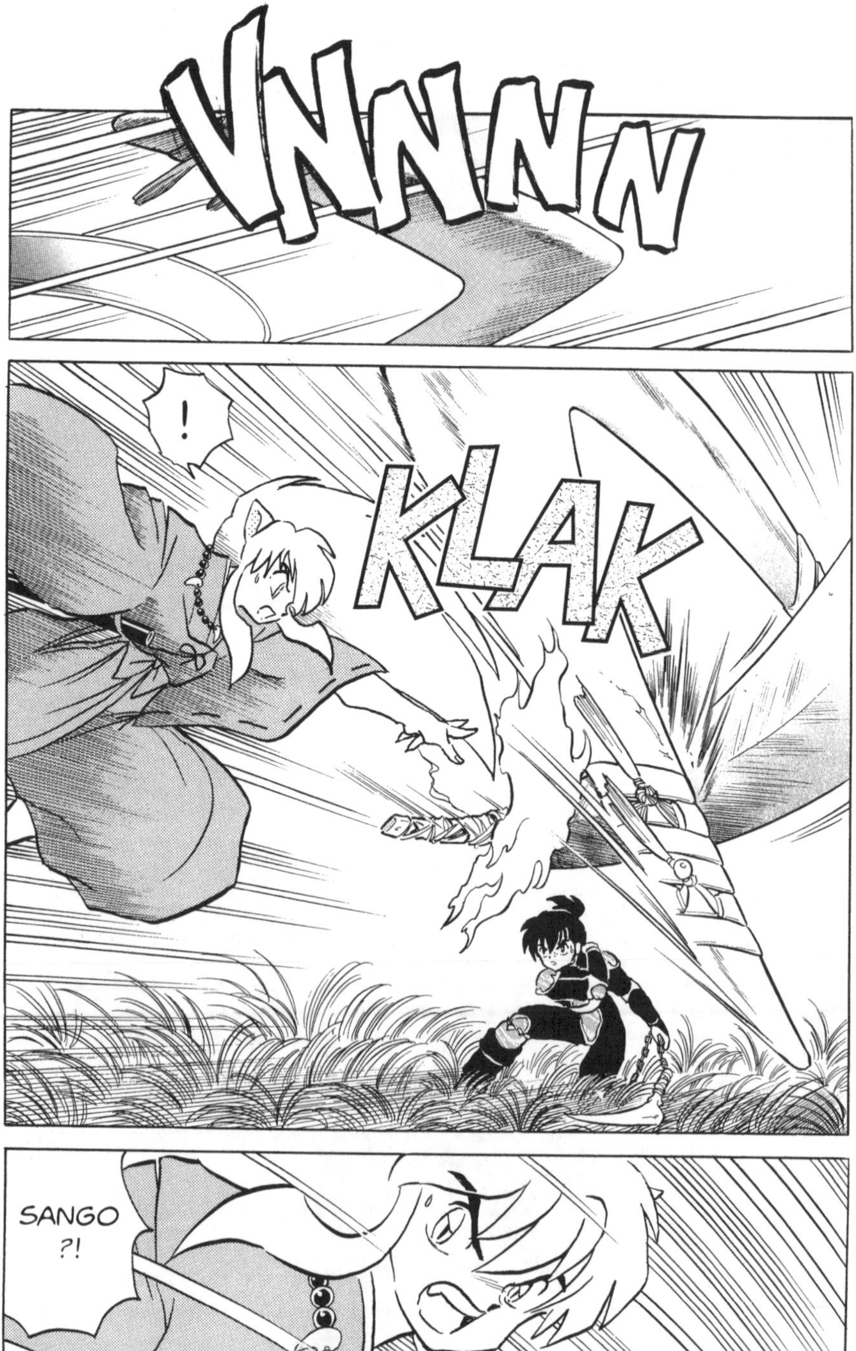
VNNNNN
!
KLAK
SANGO ?!

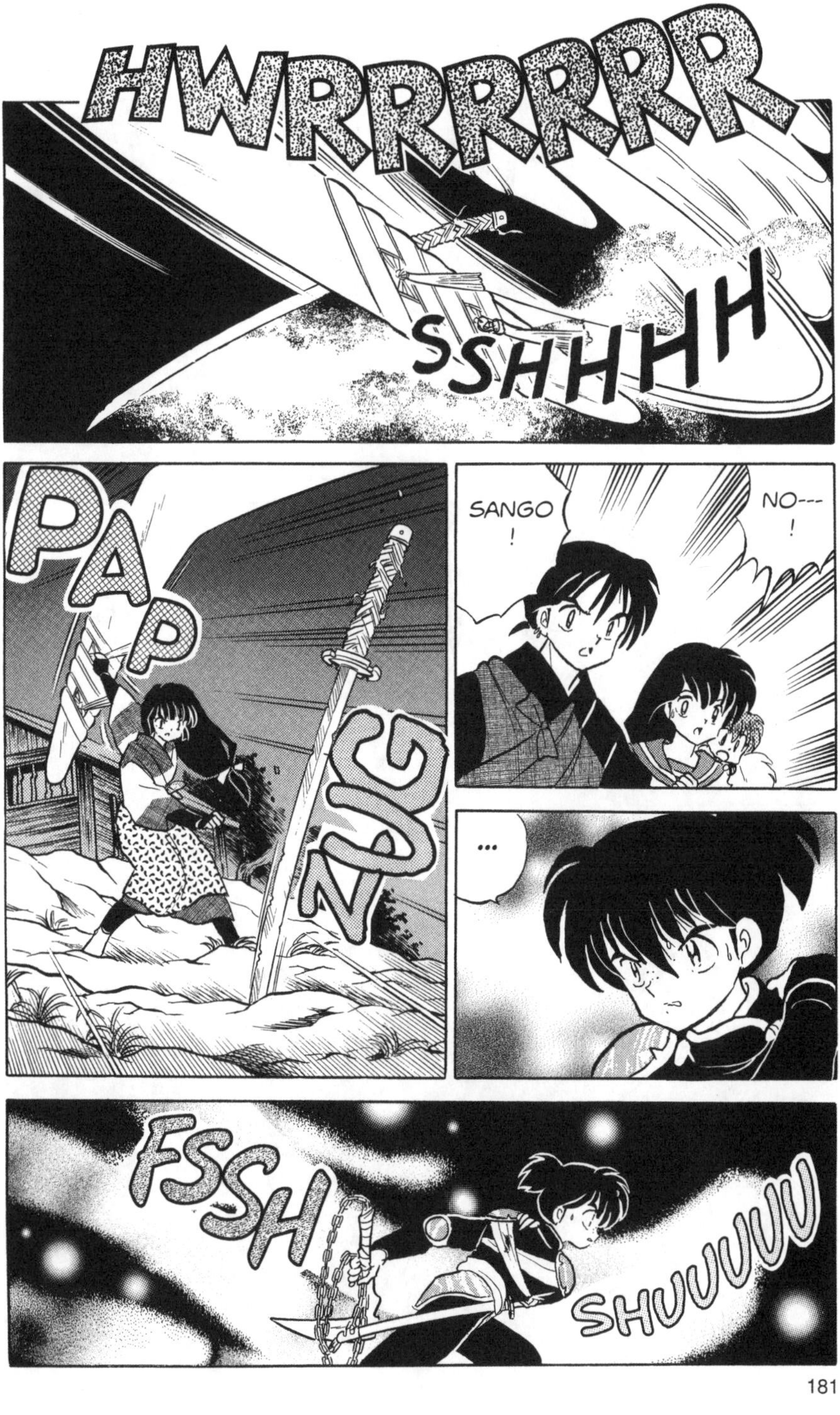
HWRRRRRRR
SSHHHHH
SANGO!
NO---!
...
PAP
ZUNG
FSSH
SHUUUUU

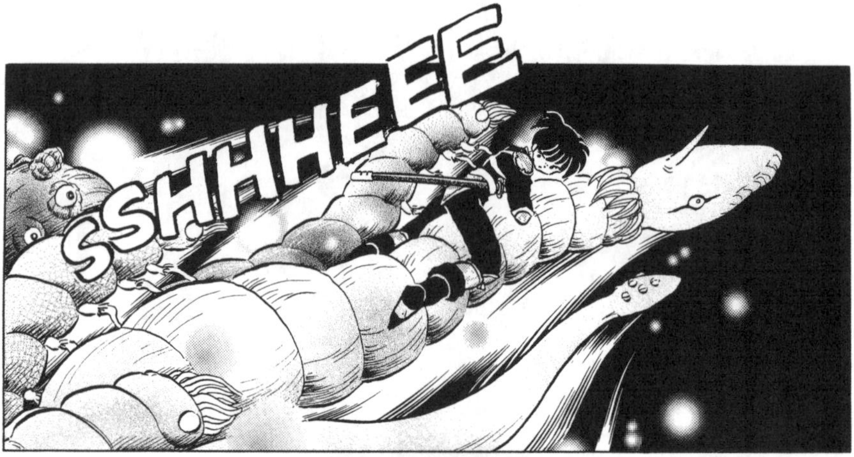
SSHHHEEE
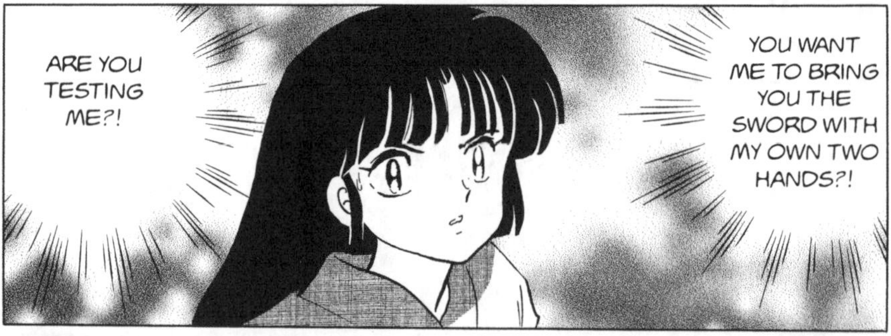
YOU WANT ME TO BRING YOU THE SWORD WITH MY OWN TWO HANDS?!
ARE YOU TESTING ME?!
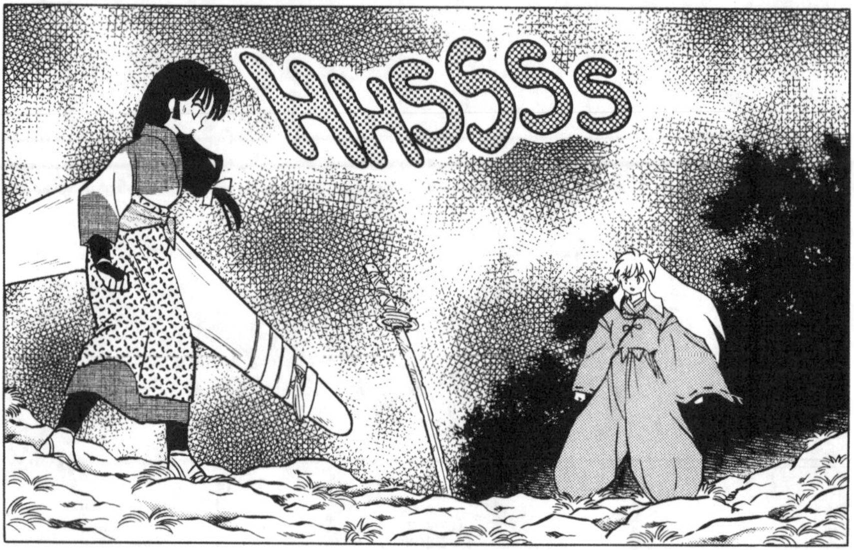
HHSSSSS

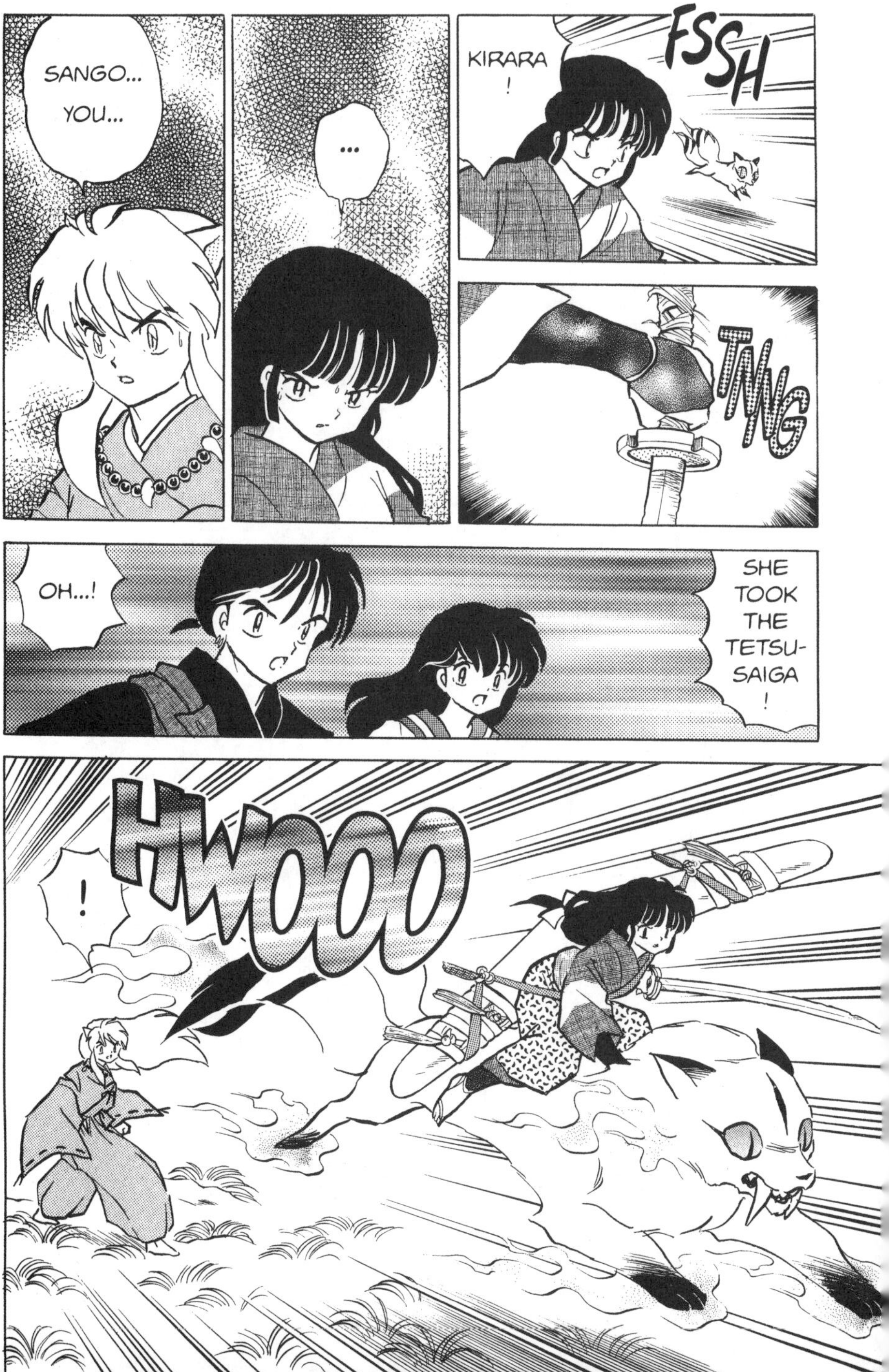
SANGO... YOU...
...
KIRARA!
FSSH
TNNG
OH...!
SHE TOOK THE TETSU-SAIGA!
HWOOO
!

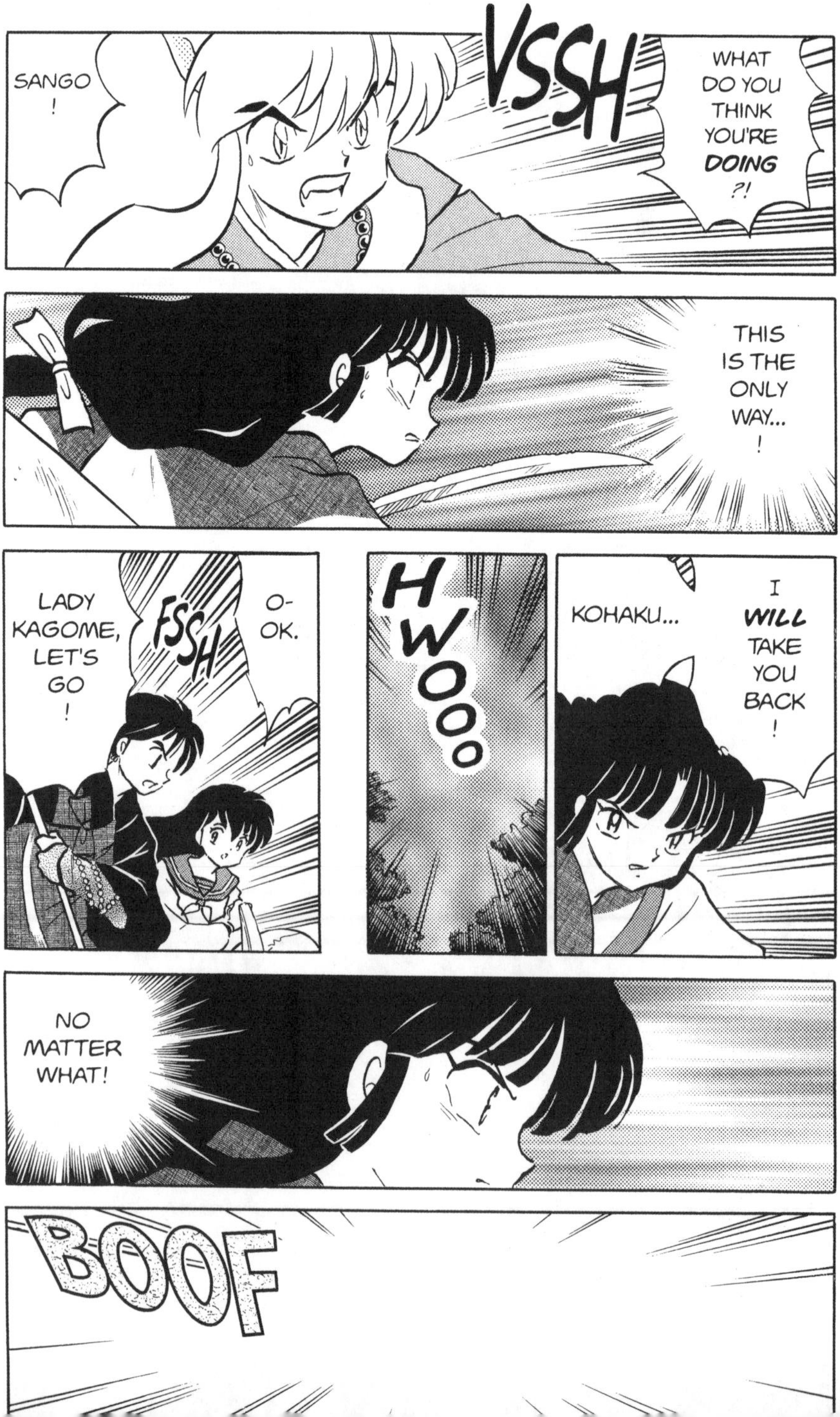
SANGO!
VSSH
WHAT DO YOU THINK YOU'RE **DOING**?!
THIS IS THE ONLY WAY...!
LADY KAGOME, LET'S GO!
FSSH
O-OK.
HWOOOO
KOHAKU...
I **WILL** TAKE YOU BACK!
NO MATTER WHAT!
BOOF

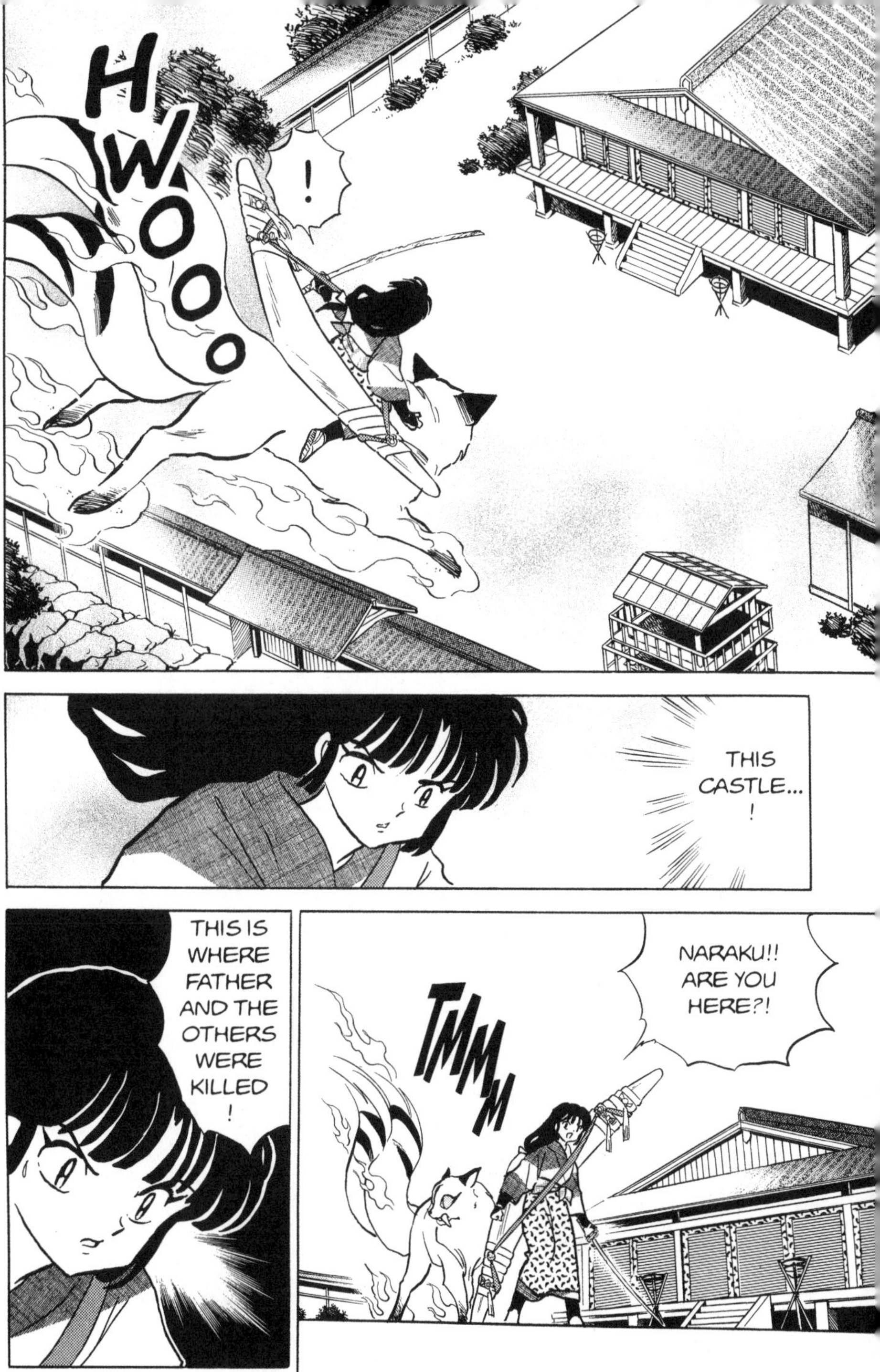
HWOOOO
!
THIS CASTLE... !
NARAKU!! ARE YOU HERE?!
TMMM
THIS IS WHERE FATHER AND THE OTHERS WERE KILLED !

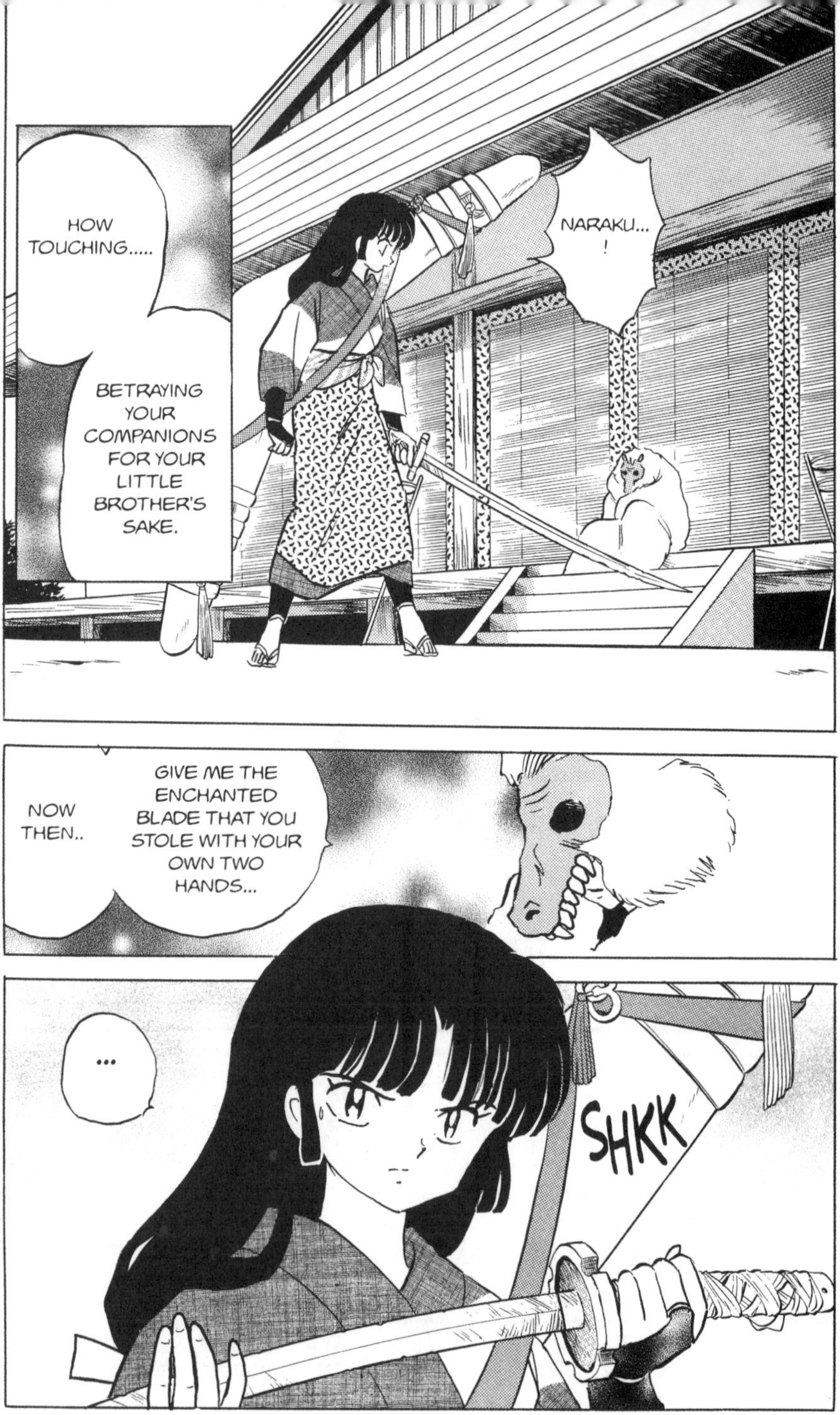
HOW TOUCHING.....
BETRAYING YOUR COMPANIONS FOR YOUR LITTLE BROTHER'S SAKE.
NARAKU... !
NOW THEN..
GIVE ME THE ENCHANTED BLADE THAT YOU STOLE WITH YOUR OWN TWO HANDS...
...
SHKK

TO BE CONTINUED...

Rumiko Takahashi

Rumiko Takahashi was born in 1957 in Niigata, Japan. She attended women's college in Tokyo, where she began studying comics with Kazuo Koike, author of **Crying Freeman**. She later became an assistant to horror-manga artist Kazuo Umezu. In 1978, she won a prize in Shogakukan's annual "New Comic Artist Contest," and in that same year her boy-meets-alien comedy series **Lum*Urusei Yatsura** began appearing in the weekly manga magazine SHŌNEN SUNDAY. This phenomenally successful series ran for nine years and sold over 22 million copies. Takahashi's later **Ranma 1/2** series enjoyed even greater popularity.

Takahashi is considered by many to be one of the world's most popular manga artists. With the publication of Volume 34 of her **Ranma 1/2** series in Japan, Takahashi's total sales passed *one hundred million* copies of her compiled works.

Takahashi's serial titles include **Lum*Urusei Yatsura**, **Ranma 1/2**, **One-Pound Gospel**, **Maison Ikkoku** and **Inu-Yasha**. Additionally, Takahashi has drawn many short stories which have been published in America under the title "Rumic Theater," and several installments of a saga known as her "Mermaid" series. Most of Takahashi's major stories have also been animated, and are widely available in translation worldwide. **Inu-Yasha** is her most recent serial story, first published in SHŌNEN SUNDAY in 1996.

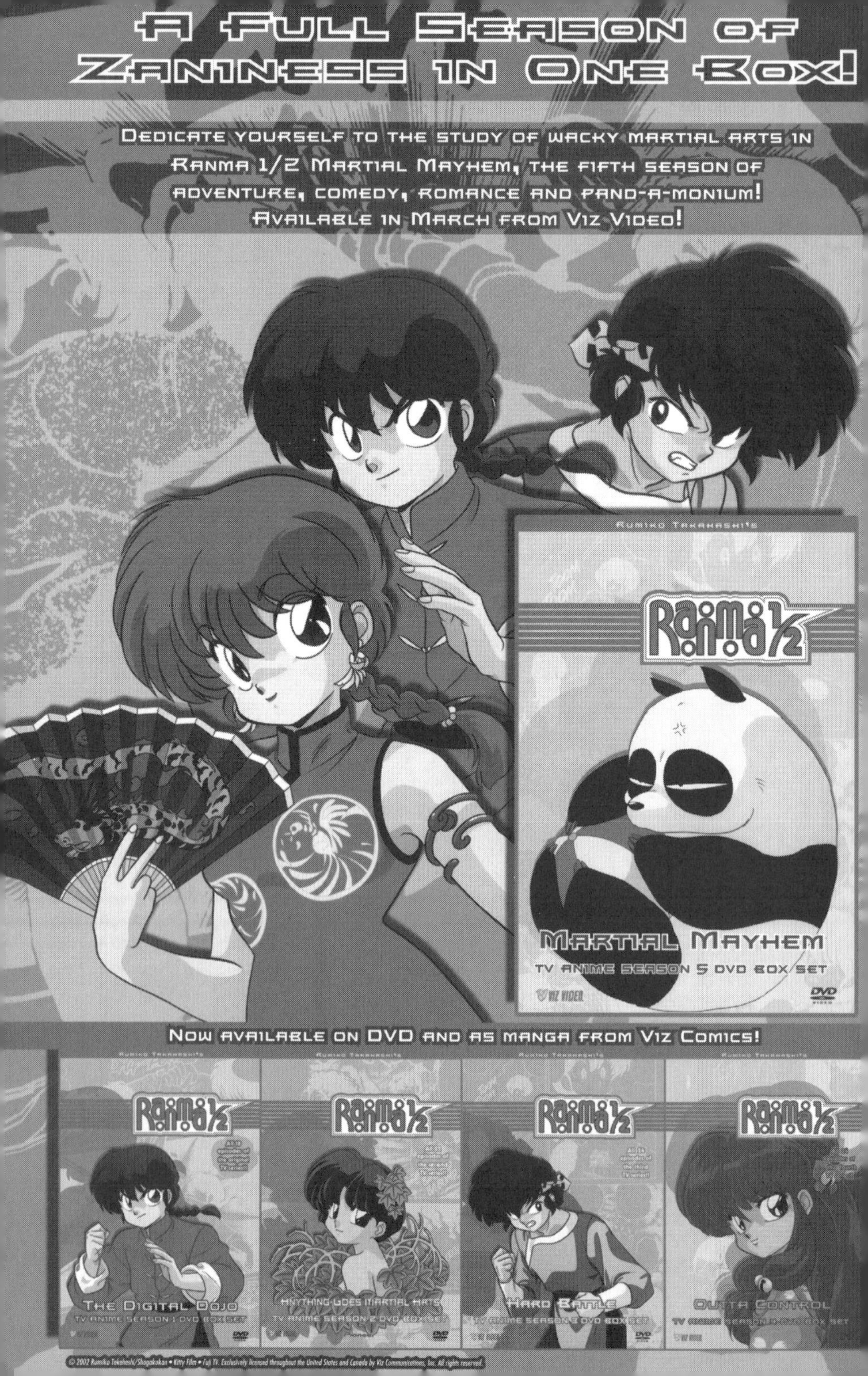
A Full Season of Zaniness in One Box!
Dedicate yourself to the study of wacky martial arts in Ranma 1/2 Martial Mayhem, the fifth season of adventure, comedy, romance and pand-a-monium! Available in March from Viz Video!
Rumiko Takahashi's
Ranma 1/2
Martial Mayhem
TV Anime Season 5 DVD Box Set
Now available on DVD and as manga from Viz Comics!
The Digital Dojo
TV Anime Season 1 DVD Box Set
Anything-Goes Martial Arts
TV Anime Season 2 DVD Box Set
Hard Battle
TV Anime Season 3 DVD Box Set
Outta Control
TV Anime Season 4 DVD Box Set
© 2002 Rumiko Takahashi/Shogakukan • Kitty Film • Fuji TV. Exclusively licensed throughout the United States and Canada by Viz Communications, Inc. All rights reserved.